THE HOUSE BEYOND THE HILL

A Novel of Horror

by

MICHAEL R. COLLINGS

The Borgo Press
An Imprint of Wildside Press

MMVII

SECOND EDITION

CONTENTS

ABOUT THE AUTHOR

MICHAEL R. COLLINGS, a retired Professor of English, is the former director of Creative Writing and Poet-in-Residence for Pepperdine University in Malibu, CA. He has written books and articles on Stephen King, Orson Scott Card, science fiction, fantasy, and horror, as well as volumes of poetry. He currently lives in Meridian, ID—returning to the state of his birth after almost sixty years—where he and his wife, Judi, make jewelry and enjoy watching the seasons change.

PART ONE

CHAPTER ONE

A DECLARATION OF INDEPENDENCE

- 1 -

Dracula stared malevolently over Pac's shoulder.

Without turning his head, Pac could feel the cold intensity of midnight-shadowed eyes peering beneath arched eyebrows, peering over the glossy folds of a death-black cape draped like a negative *maître-d*'s napkin across an upraised forearm. The back of the young man's neck prickled with an icy ripple. He suppressed a shudder.

Pac *knew* Dracula was standing behind him, but he refused to look over his shoulder.

"Fuck off," he murmured, never taking his eyes from the objects arranged carefully on the makeshift table. This was the tricky part; unbroken concentration would mean the difference between success and total failure.

He couldn't stand the thought of failure...not now, not after a lifetime of failure and of coming in second behind Richard. Mr. Do-Good Richard. Mr. Perfect Richard.

This time, Pac thought with self-indulgent malice, things would be different. A crooked smile crept slowly across his lips. He would show Richard and everyone else what *he* could do.

Of course, there was more than mere pride involved now. Failure now meant more to Pac than it might to others; for him, it would mean *death.*

He worked steadily on, though subliminally aware of Dracula peering over his left shoulder—Bela Lugosi in full melodramatic regalia, reproduced on a cheap reprint of the poster that had hung in Pac's bedroom in St. Louis. Over his right shoulder, on the far wall, the Wolfman stared down with evil discontent from the peeling wall, frustrated perhaps by his unwilling proximity to the small porcelain bowl in which globs of silver were melting, bubbling, and steaming on their way toward becoming a projectile for Pac's revolver.

A silver bullet, in fact.

Pac's smile widened until, grotesquely, it almost threatened to split his face.

It was not a pleasant smile, even beyond the questionable aesthetics of neglected, yellowing teeth desperate for the touch of a dentist's drill. The young man's cheeks were too narrow, to hollowed and wasted for that smile. His cheekbones seemed too thin to support the weight of teeth and gums as lips released their hold.

It was a demented Cheshire-cat smile, as if the Cheshire cat had been a carnivore or, worse, a cannibal.

Pac wiped a slick bead of sweat from his forehead and squinted through the living room window into the growing gloom of the California twilight.

He felt a surge of relief as the sun sliced its way beneath the distant ridges.

Soon he would be able to *Drive* again.

He hadn't Driven for almost a month now, not since he had finally realized—suddenly and explosively—what he needed.

During his earliest Drives, he had known intuitively that he needed...protection. But it had taken a long time for him to discover precisely what *kind* of protection, and even then the discovery had come in phases.

The first step, taken nearly three months before, had involved hanging an oversized silver-plated crucifix from the rear-view mirror. He had suspended it from a thin string long enough to allow it to spiral as the car vibrated over the freeway lanes and send it spinning and flashing fragmented light.

The silver light helped. For a while. But soon even that was not sufficient. More and more, Pac felt fear closing in, boxing him in as he sped over nighttime freeways, weaving in and out, changing lanes, eluding the thick shadows that crept nearer every night.

For a few days—a week, no more—the reflections from the crucifix had shattered the darkness, shooting spiny rays into the darkness that crouched on the torn back seat of Pac's VW. For a few days—a week, no more—he had been safe.

Then the silver light failed and the shadows crept closer again.

The last time he had Driven was almost a month ago. He had been speeding down the Golden State, one eye on the freeway, one on the spinning crucifix. He happened to glance in the rear-view mirror.

It crouched in the darkness behind him, formless, nameless. *It* reflected like the single burning eye of Satan, fiery in the polished glass.

Pac screamed. He clawed at the steering wheel, the VW careening toward the edge of the tarmac before he regained control and swerved at the last moment back into the lane of traffic, cutting off a Nova that squealed and shimmied as it veered into the path of an oncoming pickup. For an instant, his attention was diverted from the shadow in the mirror to the potential crash that—frustratingly—never happened.

When he glanced into the mirror again, the shadow was gone.

His thigh muscles trembled with tension. He released his breath in a long, stale sigh of fear.

But Pac wasn't stupid. No, siree. He wasn't stupid. It might be gone, but if it had found him once, it could find him again.

When it did, he would be prepared.

Now, during the early days of July, he was almost ready. He had worked hard, real WASP-ethic type work that even Mr.-Do-Good Richard would have approved of. He had squirreled away his money until he could afford to buy a battered and cracked sterling silver tea set from the antique shop in Simi Valley and the nineteenth-century bullet mold he found in another antique place in Glendale.

He had spent most of the first week studying, then most of the next experimenting, exploring with the molten silver until he found just the right heat, just the right amount of shattered tea-service to give him what he wanted...*needed.*

He learned to heat the silver on the hot plate, checking out his mistakes in the pages of a library book on metallurgy (he had sneaked it out of the Research section of the Tamarind Public Library, carefully slicing the computer-activated tab from the inside binding so there was no record he had ever read it). He learned slowly and carefully, always aware of shadows swirling fluidly behind him as he worked through the long, hot nights. He hadn't read anything but that one book for the whole two weeks. He hadn't rented a single film.

He hadn't even *considered* Driving!

And now the long but necessary wait was almost over. Tonight he could Drive again.

He grinned as he hefted a polished bullet in one hand, tossed it lightly in a low arc and caught it deftly in the other. This would make an even dozen, enough for weeks of Driving.

Over Pac's shoulder, Count Dracula peered in stony immobility. The upper corner of the movie poster curled away from the stained wall. The Wolfman grimaced eternally, his poster fixed to the studs with rusted six-penny nails that stuck out an inch from the wall.

They watched; Pac worked.

Somewhere out there, perhaps already riding the intricate web of the Los Angeles freeway system, the shadow waited.

Pac grinned again.

Tonight, it would die.

- 2 -

This is a *hell* of a way to spend the Fourth of July, Richard Mann thought. Today, his normally pleasant face was as surly as the voice echoing through his head.

Already, before he had even started up the stairs, stale heat from the attic radiated down the staircase, an unwelcome foretaste of what was waiting at the top of the narrow wooden treads. Hot air prickled along his bare legs, feeling as if every wave carried an electrical current that set each hair against all the others. Wearing nothing but sneakers, worn shorts, and a thin, ragged T-shirt with holes gaping under each arm (Bonnie had insisted on that—no use getting good clothes filthy), Richard was already sweating, and he hadn't even begun the job.

Helluva time to get on a cleaning binge, he thought more emphatically, directing his frustration as much at his wife as at his mother. Emma had a right, he supposed, to want the rat's nest of accumulated junk cleared out of the attic. For a couple of months now, she had been making noises about selling the place (*I'll believe that when I see it,* he thought with an inward snort that barely translated into sound), so it seemed natural for her to suggest, in that maternal way that came across an imperative no matter how gently worded, that Richard get busy.

Bonnie had agreed with her mother-in-law.

"It won't take that long," she had argued, pitching her voice into the little-girl-asking-dadums mode that sometimes he found appealing but that today had made the hair on the back of his neck stand on end.

Easy enough for them to say, Richard thought. They're sitting in the kitchen, in the only spot in the old house where a cooling breeze might flicker through on even the hottest summer day. They were probably just sitting there, sipping lemonade and munching freshly baked cookies while they thought up something more for him to do when this chore was over.

No, he decided glumly, that really wasn't fair. The old place *was* getting out of hand. He had promised himself when he and Bonnie moved into their apartment that he would always be around when Mom needed him. He would be the man of the house now that Dad was over a decade dead and Donney was...wherever he was. Mom simply couldn't handle things the way she had. Not that she was getting too old, mind you; she wasn't much more than fifty-seven. But she was...Richard struggled for the right word. She was *slower* now. She moved more deliberately, as if each step were a struggle.

Arthritis? Richard had wondered occasionally, especially over the past few weeks when he caught clear glimpses of pain etched in her face as she stood up too quickly or twisted unexpectedly. He didn't think she knew that he knew...what?

Only that something was not right.

So. Richard was cleaning the attic on the Fourth of July to let her know that she could count on him. He would always be there for her, even when what she asked him to do seemed unnecessary, or dirty, or just plain unfair.

At the head of the stairs, he pushed the thin plywood door open, stepped through, and peered down the shadowed length of the attic. He wiped his forehead. Up here the July heat was even more stifling. He crossed the western end of the attic, stopping only momentarily at the four-foot-high window set like an eye into the blank wall beneath the gable. The window panes were crusted with dirt. The unpainted sill was so thick with undisturbed dust that he could have written his name in it. He almost did. His finger even reached out toward the narrow ledge, but he pulled it back in revulsion when he glanced down.

The bodies of a dozen bluebottles studded the dust like raisins in the rice pudding Emma used to make when Donney was still home—Donney loved it, Richard hated it, so Donney managed to make sure Emma fixed it at least every other night. On the rare evenings that Donney actually *made* dinner, Richard could count on rice pudding with the inevitability of death and taxes. Sometimes, even now, when taxes were more a part of his experience, he still wasn't sure which of the three was the worst.

Raisins in rice pudding. Fat, slug-like, moisture-soaked raisins half covered by boiled rice that looked like gooey maggots.

Richard's stomach twisted.

He shook his head and forced the image back into the shadowy recesses of memory. Without looking, he grabbed a rag from the box near the head of the stairs and swept his hand along the sill, sending dust and flies spiraling. Sunlight misted where it passed through motes suspended in the still, hot air.

He choked and coughed, then his lungs were clear again.

Ahhh. That was better. Flies were flies, and Donney was gone, and Richard was going to clean out this rat's nest one way or another, heat or no heat.

He pulled off his T-shirt, already damp and clinging and grey with air-borne particles, and tossed it to the floor. He ran his fingers once through his tousled hair and—chest gleaming with sweat—set to work.

- 3 -

Pac *lived* for the Drives. He had discovered them almost accidentally. Running an errand for a friend late one night, he got lost in the jumble of streets that webbed the San Fernando Valley. After what seemed like hours of twisting and twining along dimly lit streets bordered with ramshackle old houses and littered with the hulks of abandoned cars, he finally stumbled on a freeway onramp and—for the sheer, frustrated hell of it—swung onto the raised highway. He cranked both windows down, turned the radio up to full, and suddenly found himself Driving into the darkness.

He never could remember exactly where he had Driven that night. He remembered the tinny crackling as the engine cooled in the breaking dawn. He remembered the VW's tread-bare tires stopping inches from the crumbling sandstone edge. He remembered the sun slipping over the ocean, and the VW parked on a cliff above Pacific Coast Highway near Santa Monica. It took him two hours to get home, but he had been Driving for nearly seven.

The next day, he hung the silver cross on the rear-view mirror. It helped keep the shadows at bay.

That was his first time. Since then there had been uncounted others. He had probably traveled over every mile of the freeway systems that wound through the LA basin, from Santa Barbara up north to San Diego in the south, east to Palm Springs and, once, in a fit of nervous energy, he had penetrated the barrenness east of Barstow clear to Las Vegas, clear to the white-hot center of the Dark Man's stronghold.

For a while, the Drives sustained him. They provided an outlet for the need that welled inside him like crude oil gushing from a new bore-hole. Then, when they had begun to pall, when he had dropped to Driving only one night in two or three weeks, spending the others tossing in fitful dreams or watching silver-flecked nightmares on the VCR screen until the sun rose and relieved him of the need to stand sentry, he discovered something new.

He didn't know who started it. No one ever gave a name. One of the TV news programs talked about freeway shootings, then the others mentioned them, then the radio picked it up, and suddenly they were everywhere. A dozen in a week. Forty in a month. People peppering cars with handguns, shotguns, rifles, anything.

Pac thought about it for a long while before he decided to try.

First he stole the gun. It wasn't hard. There'd been two or three holdups at all-night stores in Tamarind Valley over the past six months, punks with guns ramming them into the ribs of scared night attendants and demanding money. There weren't all that many robberies, certainly not compared to the mayhem and the body-count in LA each night, but they were enough to scare Cliff, the manager at the All-Nite-Delite on Tamarind Boulevard right where it cut through the center of town, not a mile from the Ventura Freeway.

Good ol' Cliff bought an unlicensed .38 (illegal as hell but what did he care) and slung it from a hook under the counter, loaded and ready, just in reach but hidden behind a swinging plywood panel. Keeping a loaded weapon on the premises was against company policy, of course, maybe even against the law, but a little thing like that never bothered Cliff. He just swore the others to secrecy, threatening their jobs if word leaked out.

The first night in June, Pac worked the midnight to 8:00 AM shift. He simply lifted the gun (along with forty-seven dollars in bills and spare change, just to make the job look real), hiked out to the VW parked in the employee's slot by the smelly dumpster behind the store, and stuffed the piece into the trunk. Later that night, during a lull in trade, he called the cops to report the hold-up.

"They didn't get much, the damn punks," he told the cops when they finally rolled up in their black-and-white. A few bucks. It was a slow night.

Yes, sir, officer, sir, I gave them the loose cash and showed them the empty register and they ran out. No, sir, officer, sir, I wouldn't recognize either of them. One was tall and black, the other tall and Chicano. Both wore ski masks. Neither spoke. They wore jeans and black T-shirts.

Nothing recognizable, nothing traceable.

Later that night, after the cops left, Pac whispered to Cliff that the black dude had spotted the gun and taken it. *Couldn't say any-*

thing to the pigs about it though, could we, huh? Cliff glowered but nodded.

The .38 slept safely in the trunk of Pac's VW for the rest of his shift.

The next night, he had Driven.

He couldn't believe the difference. He propped the gun between his legs like a hollow erection. It pointed up at his chin and vibrated with the engine as if hungry to expel its deadly semen.

He didn't fire it that night. It was enough to feel the piece there, to know that he *could.*

He Drove for eight hours and arrived home spent, exhausted. There were no dreams, not even when he fell asleep naked on the lumpy couch, beneath the watchful and threatening eyes of his posters. The gun lay on the floor, inches from where his curled fingers hung over the edge of the couch.

The next day, he asked Cliff about extra hours. *Sudden expenses, you know. Operation for poor ol' Ma back home in St. Louis. Pretty Please.*

Cliff grunted, muttered about Pac not giving out the store's profits to the next creeps who tried something funny—glancing pointedly at the counter, where a new handgun hung behind the swinging plywood—and said okay.

Pac hadn't Driven for nearly a month.

Not until the night of the Fourth of July.

- 4 -

At first, the memories Richard disturbed in the attic ran to the mildly pleasant, even faintly nostalgic—*mice creeping along the silent edges of his anger, careful not to disturb the sleeping rats that might rise ravening and consume them.*

Grandma Ottley's old bureau stood sentry in the shadows beneath steep, cobwebby eaves. He remembered its drawers as a treasure-trove of pleasures that a young Richard and a younger Donney had shared during interminable summer afternoons.

He pulled open the top drawer and lifted something out. Bits of bright glass fashioned into strings of multi-colored beads caught and refracted the dim light. He grinned and carefully set Grandma Ottley's old costume necklace back into its place in the drawer.

Other drawers held old-fashioned hand-carved bone and wood buttons that could be infinitely strung and re-strung (*Donney cut the knot of my string that time, damn him, and the beads fell back into the drawer and he snatched the best ones and strung them on* his *string*) until young fingers prickled with heat and, like the stiffening fingers of arthritic old men, refused to bend.

Hidden deep in the corner of the lowest drawer lay the old doll's tea-set that they had surreptitiously played with, blissfully unaware that boys weren't supposed to play with such things. Richard pulled out one of the cups. Where his thumb slipped in to hold the cup tight, the inside surface felt rough and ragged, more like a torn thumbnail than fire-smoothed porcelain. He held the cup up to the light and scratched at the glaze. Something crusted and brown clung to the crazed surface. The stuff was hard, knobby, faintly glistening in the dim light.

Ahhh, he remembered. How many years ago? He and Donney had mixed water and graham crackers and salt, mad chemists in their secret labs, and left it to age in the doll cups. They never went back to clean them up. The hideous-tasting concoction had lain there all these years, hardening and compacting in the bottom of the china cups, mute evidence to a long forgotten moment of irresponsibility.

I wonder if Mom ever saw these, Richard thought sadly as he pulled two more irreparably stained cups from the darkest part of the drawer. *I wonder if she knew that we ruined Grandma's set.*

He sighed and scratched at the caked-on remnant of graham cracker. It was as hard as concrete. Finally, he set the cups back into the drawer, reminding himself to take them downstairs later. Maybe Bonnie could soak them and get the gunk out.

He turned his attention away from the hidden enticements of the bureau drawers to the more overt clutter in the attic.

Just behind the bureau, an old headboard leaned against bare rafters. God only knew whose it was or how ancient it was. Its thin wooden slats were probably oak, iron hard but warped and cracked and blackened. Hand-joined lengths had dried and pulled away from the frame. The weight of Richard's hand was enough to set the whole thing to shimmering.

He made another mental note. *Take this out back and split it up and burn it in the incinerator.*

Lying on top of a smaller dresser were the remains of a sampler framed in a dark oak. No glass protected the worn linen. Richard vaguely remembered it hanging in the hall, years before, when he was still a kid and too short to read it. It had simply disappeared somewhere along the way, maybe the year Mom had the hall repapered and some of the old things just never found their way back onto the wall.

He held it up.

Mice had been at it—no great surprise, considering the condition of the attic. Dust caked it so thickly he could not make out the letters. He tapped it against the edge of the dresser, then coughed and sneezed as the dust flew and mixed with the overheated air and tickled his nostrils and settled like damp potter's clay in his throat.

Sweat inched down his side. His underarms felt sticky and clammy. For a moment, he wished that he had left his T-shirt on. But it was too far away for him to want to get it. Besides, he was so grimy now that he shuddered at the thought of pulling cloth over his head and across his back and shoulders.

Instead, he carried the sampler over to the dirty window at the back of the attic. He smeared off a reasonably clean spot with the rag tucked into his waistband and held the faint embroidery up to the light.

He could almost make out what it said.

"A-l-l. T-h-a-t. I-s."

He took a deep breath, held it, and tapped the frame lightly against the sill, dislodging another layer of accumulated dust.

He squinted and held the stitchery closer. "All that is necessary," he read aloud, his voice echoing hollowly in the empty air, "for the triumph of evil is that good men do nothing."

There was something more at the bottom, in a faded blue that was barely legible. *Mary Ottley.* There was a date, too, but that was almost entirely gone and Richard couldn't even begin to read it.

The sampler had to be ancient. No wonder Mom had finally relegated it to the attic, along with the other non-functional memories that otherwise would have cluttered up their lives. He examined the linen closely. It really was too far gone to be salvaged. Most of the edges were completely eaten away, and some of the letters were almost indecipherable.

He tossed it into a large cardboard box that sat in the middle of the attic waiting for its freight of useless memories. The frame made a dull *thud* when it hit.

He turned toward the far side of the attic. A second peninsula of junk, mostly cardboard boxes, huddled against he eaves opposite the old furniture he had just explored

He didn't recognize the boxes.

Some of the stuff in the attic had the comforting familiarity of old toys. As a child, he had rifled through drawers and shelves and boxes and piles of indefinable things, spending hour upon hour up here—at least until he had married and moved to the apartment.

He thought he knew most everything there.

But that stack of boxes was new. Even the cardboard surfaces, where they showed in the dusky light, seemed newer. They gleamed in a way the decades-old boxes no longer could.

He crossed and looked at the top one.

There was nothing on it to indicate what it might hold. No name, no date scribbled in black magic-marker across the top.

He folded the flaps back. And immediately knew what it was, what they all were.

Emma had stored Donney's things up here. Richard had realized—as much subconsciously as consciously—that Donney's room had gradually changed from the way it had been that last night. His things had disappeared, replaced by things Richard remembered from years before, childish things, things that reminded Emma of her baby, not of the irritating, arrogant little shit he had become.

Funny, but Richard hadn't even wondered what became of the other stuff, the stuff that had disappeared. Emma must have packed it away and carted the boxes up here herself, one by one, and stacked them neatly in the darkness.

Behind him, flies buzzed noisily, slamming themselves against the dusty pane in futile efforts to escape the attic.

He pulled the top box off the stack and set it on the floor and opened it up. It contained mostly clothes—the dead black things Donney had affected during the last year, tattered, worn, slashed with useless zippers or glittering studs along fraying seams. Richard gingerly pulled out a limp, sleeveless sweatshirt. He let it hang limply across his palms; for an instant, he could almost *feel* the heat of Donney's body, the smell of his sweat. Recoiling, Richard dropped the garment back into the box.

Burn it, he reminded himself. *Burn it all.*

The next box seemed to hold nothing but Donney's underwear, as rumpled and unkempt as it might have been if this were a drawer in Donney's bureau. On top lay half a dozen wadded up briefs, tattered along the leg bands and the seat, with rippled waistbands where the elastic had finally given way. Even without touching them, Richard could see that some of the shorts were repellently stained in spite of Emma's obvious attempts to wash them. A couple of once-white T-shirts with stretched-out neckbands and filthy ochre half-circles at the armpits stared up at Richard. There were several pair of socks that had become two-toned: white uppers, indefinably grey-brown lowers.

The essence of Donney.

Richard closed the box in disgust.

The third was long and narrow. Richard poked at it with his toe. It seemed lighter than the others. He flipped it open and saw a stack of rolled-up posters, each cinched tightly at both ends by disintegrating rubber bands. He did not even have to unroll one to know what they were. Movie posters, horror movies mostly, gruesome and gross and disgusting but infinitely enthralling to Donney. He had wasted almost every spare cent he could scrounge on those things, then strung them up along the ceiling moldings in his bedroom. After a while, Richard had become distinctly uncomfortable about entering the room under their unchanging gaze; Emma felt even more strongly about Donney's gallery and finally quit going in there entirely, relying on Donney to change his bedding and to weed the refuse from drawers and under the bed and of the closet floor. He hadn't.

Richard closed that box, folding the flaps over each other and then tossing the box toward the top of the stairs. *Fire-fodder for sure,* he thought.

The fourth box was, in some indefinable way, even worse.

It was larger, sturdier, resting at the bottom of the outermost stack. Richard slid the box into the center of the attic floor. It was too heavy to lift comfortably, and even tugging at it, he felt the cardboard flaps threatening to give way. He wondered briefly how Emma had managed to get it upstairs in the first place. He didn't like imagining her struggling with the unwieldy weight on the narrow stairs.

He knelt beside the box. Grit from the bare planking cut into his knees. He rubbed his hands on his shorts, leaving long dark streaks of dirt and sweat.

He didn't want to touch the box. He wouldn't. He would get up and walk down the stairs and shower and join Bonnie and his mother in the kitchen. He would drink lemonade and wait until dark, when they would walk the half block to Centennial Park and sit on one of Grandma Ottley's ragged old quilts and watch fireworks. He would....

He folded the first flap back. Then the second. The third.

His hand trembled and his back ached. His knees felt as if someone were sandblasting them. Sweat dripped from his forehead and neck and underarms.

He folded back the fourth and lifted up a thin sheet of Styrofoam.

A huge, glassy eye glared at him. Startled, he dropped the Styrofoam sheet. His heart pounded. A headache began somewhere behind his eyes.

18

At both windows, bluebottles buzzed insistently.

He drew a deep breath, hot with fear and with stale air. He lifted the Styrofoam again and looked into the box.

It wasn't an eye. He knew that almost immediately, of course— had surely known it from the first glance—but he was surprised nonetheless to see the portable Sony sitting there. Its screen canted upward and caught the fragmented light. Next to it lay Donney's Atari; and scattered over both were the dozens of video-games he had played possessively, obsessively, hour upon hour upon hour.

Richard stared at them.

Right on top, its faded label mocking him, was Donney's favorite, the Pac-man game.

The heat increased. So did the pounding in his head. The blood beat its tattoo as it throbbed across Richard's temples. His cheeks felt inflamed, rough, mottled and itchy, as if he had stumbled into a patch of poison oak the day before. He was suddenly ill, nauseated.

He licked his lips. They were cracked, and his sweat stung like tiny needles.

He dropped to the floor and sat back, balanced on his toes. His eyes were drawn to the jumble of plastic and glass.

The box crystallized his hatred of Donney. *Mom bought that television for him and told me I couldn't get a bike I needed that bike for my paper route and she bought that damned TV instead and he gloated about it running it night and day playing that idiotic game Christ he knew how much I needed the bike* and now the Sony was sitting in the attic collecting dust. The least she could have done was to set it up in the living room downstairs. Or let Richard use it. God knew Donney wouldn't have minded. If he hadn't written home in over a year, he surely wouldn't have minded if Richard watched the damned television.

He stared at the malevolent eye that stared back at him and matched his hot hatred degree for degree.

Beneath the clutter of video games, the screen winked at him.

Richard's breath caught in a painful gasp. Then he forced himself to breathe again.

No, it was just a trick of the light, a branch rubbing against the window and casting a momentary shadow that looked like....

Except there *were* no branches at that end of the house. The ash had died years before. Richard himself had chopped it into kindling *while Donney farted around with his games and let me do all the work* that had burned brightly, cheerfully, during the long winter nights.

But it wasn't a trick—not of light, not of imagination. The television flickered and hummed, and small circular monsters appeared on the screen chomping and chewing and devouring everything that stood in their way.

Richard watched. Fear nestled in the pit of his stomach like rats in a cellar, unseen but hungry, waiting to gnaw away at him.

He swallowed.

The thing was...*alive.*

Behind him, flies smashed against filthy panes, starring the glass in their suicidal fury. *Escape! Escape! Escape!* sounded like a litany against the throbbing undercurrent of his pounding head.

"This has got to be a dream," he finally muttered, mopping his brow with the rag that was more brown than white, more sodden than dry.

The images changed. The game disappeared. He saw...something too indistinct to be identified.

Slowly he bent forward. His knees popped in the silence, loud and frightening, as if he were an old man.

The screen cleared.

Richard bent closer, his face only inches from the glass screen.

The *something* became a shiver of light.

The shiver became a vague form, distorted and threatening.

The form became...Donney.

Donney reached out for him, Donney skeletal, dying, laughing insanely.

"No!" Richard screamed as he straightened so quickly that he almost overbalanced, knowing that it was a dream—a hallucination induced by heat and dust and darkness—and hating himself for letting himself respond violently, for letting Donney get to him again...as always.

"No!"

His foot lashed out and smashed the screen, shattering glass and tube in an explosion of fragments. The video games scattered. One of them flew out of the box and skittered across the floor.

He kicked the screen again, again. Again.

Glass shards spun through the air, glistening and quivering like motes of dust.

He yelled, incoherent sounds that were at once attack and defense.

He stopped. His throat felt tight and raw.

He stared at his foot, wondering how dream glass could sparkle so brilliantly on the toe of his worn K-Mart sneakers.

And then *there interposed a fly—with blue—uncertain stumbling buzz* the buzzing of the flies died as if someone had switched them off.

The attic was silent. Richard could hear his heart beat, his breath rasp, his sweat as it runneled down his chest.

Emma cleared her throat.

Richard spun around, his heels crunching loudly in the shattered remains of the Sony.

Emma stood at the head of the stairs.

Behind her, sunlight struggled to penetrate the dirt that coated the window. The desiccated bodies of pharaonic bluebottles lay still, embedded—embalmed—in the dust of the sill like raisins in rice pudding.

"I," Richard began uncertainly. "I...the heat. I must have been dreaming."

She smiled—wanly, it seemed to Richard—and glanced at the ruins of the television.

- 5 -

By eight o'clock on the evening of the Fourth of July, the bullets were ready. Pac was ready.

He watched the county-sponsored fireworks from the slippery tile roof of the ruinous old house that huddled behind the pregnant—or perhaps coffin-like—curve of a low hill. He crouched between the crumbling stone fireplace and a blood-red bougainvillea that nearly covered the rest of the roof. From that vantage point, the crest of the hill above the Oaks Mall was barely visible. Right on time, at nine o'clock, the first flame-flower burst over Tamarind. Then another, another. Bang, poof, *oooh, ahhh.*

So much for patriotism.

He watched for almost ten minutes.

Then it was time for the *real* fireworks.

He gassed up the car at the Econo-Serv, paying cash as always, and headed out of Tamarind, south on the Ventura Freeway, long before the fireworks display was over. Half an hour later, he hooked onto the San Diego at Sepulveda, cutting onto the east-bound Santa Monica twenty minutes later, and finally spinning onto the Golden State at the downtown interchange.

It seemed appropriate, he thought, grinning. Silver bullets for the Golden State.

He was careful, that first time. He chose cautiously, a late-model Chrysler, the kind little old ladies with blue hair liked to drive. Of course, by now it was well into nighttime, and little old lady types were all safely enfolded in the arms of Sominex, but there were a few of the right style of cars. He was pretty sure none of the drivers would be alert enough or ballsy enough to chase him, even if they were in any condition to try. With luck, they might not even be able to identify him beyond vague descriptions of a dinged, rusted VW. To be on the safe side, he had smeared his license plates with a thin layer of mud, just enough to plead ignorance if the cops pulled him over. He was careful to splatter some on the bumper and fender as well. *Sorry, muddy driveway, officer, sir. Didn't notice, officer, sir, try to do better next time, officer, sir.*

It was easy. He spotted the dark grey car wallowing along the outside lane at a steady, boring fifty-five. He pulled even with it, paced it for a quarter of a mile until he could see a halo of silver hair and the profile of a sunken hawk nose. Then he raised the pistol, and fired.

Before he sped away, twin stars appeared as if by magic in the rear side windows, driver-side as well as passenger-side. The bullet spun into the darkness.

And he was off into the darkness, too, watching in the rear-view mirror as the Chrysler waffled heavily once or twice, slowed, then pulled to the side of the roadway.

By then, he was out of sight, and a mile later, he made the transition onto the westbound Ventura, from there north on 405 to 118, and from there home.

He hadn't found the shadow yet—he knew it was still out there, crouching, waiting, biding its time.

But he had proven that he could act when the time came. He grinned, that disconcerting Cheshire-cat grin. He had *Driven* tonight, for sure.

- 6 -

They stood for a long time, mother and son, trapped in the whirlwind of Richard's waking nightmare.

Except that he knew in some deep way that defied logic and denied impossibility that he had *not* dreamed.

He hated Donney even more. *Even half a continent away he destroys everything he touches kills my love twists my fears.*

"Don't," Emma said softly. She rested her hand on his arm, as if unaware of the sheen of sweat and dust that coated his body.

"What?"

"Don't think like that."

"I...."

She shook her head, sadly, it seemed.

"I know that look. I know what you were really trying to do there." She glanced at the ruined television, the video games crushed and useless. Richard hadn't been aware of treading on them, but he had. Many of the black plastic protective cases were split and the guts spilled out in glossy black dribbles on the wooden floor.

"I...," he began again. Then stopped. She was right. There was another long moment of silence, while Emma stepped to the window and traced a small arabesque in the dust with one long finger. Richard waited.

When she spoke, still staring outside, away from him, her back rigid and her neck stiff with an emotion that Richard could not identify, he wished that she had remained silent.

"I am going to die."

"Mom!"

"It's true." She turned to face him. She was not smiling, exactly, but something that could almost have been a smile played over her face. "I am going to die. Soon. Maybe six months. Maybe less."

"What...?"

She waved him to silence.

"It really doesn't matter, not now at least. There will be plenty of time for that."

He felt a chill at her words, at her tone, that was worse than the blind rage he had just experienced, worse even than the nightmare—hallucination, dream, vision, whatever—that had welled up through the disemboweled Sony.

This was *real*.

His mother was dying.

Dying!

He started toward her, but she motioned for him to stop. His foot ground bits of television screen into the grain of the attic floor, *cruuunch*. The sound stung like acid eating into his brain.

"Right now, I...I need you."

"Anything I can do...."

"I know that," she said, and now she was smiling. Richard understood the warmth of her love for him. "I know that. But what I need is...difficult. It is more than just clearing away this clutter." She indicated the dust-haunted corners of the attic.

"I need you to clear away a more important...clutter." He swallowed, willing her not to say anything more, afraid that she would speak the one word he could not stand to hear.

Her lips moved soundlessly.

He knew what she was trying to tell him.

"Donney," he said, his voice throbbing with defeat. It was not a question.

She nodded.

"Let him know. I write and write but he doesn't answer. I know that you write, too. Maybe if you...if he knew...maybe he would...."

She turned away. Her shoulders shook. The back of her hand wiped across her cheek.

When she began tracing the same arabesque in the dust a moment later, the tip of her finger was damp. The newly disturbed dust clotted blood-black on the glass.

"Forgive him." Quiet. Simple. Direct.

Impossible.

Richard felt the old anger, the old hatred. He shifted his weight, conscious of the *cruunch* beneath the soles of his shoes.

"I"—*can't*—"I'll try."

He took his mother by the arm and led her to the steps. "I'll try."

This time, he truly believed that he meant it.

- 7 -

The barrel of Cliffy's stolen .38 rode snugly between Pac's thighs, rubbing against the worn denim of his jeans, rubbing against skin that prickled and drew itself into gooseflesh.

Donney was dead; long live Pac!

He was Driving again.

He had his crucifix, still spinning hypnotically from the rearview mirror, fracturing light and sending it in glistening knives through the interior of the battered VW.

He had his bullets.

He had his gun.

For now, the shadow was gone from the back seat.

He was safe.

For now.

- 8 -

Richard slept badly that night, perhaps a carryover from the sick headache that had continued through the rest of the day and kept him from enjoying the fireworks display just visible from the squeaky porch swing. They hadn't walked to the park after all. Neither he nor Emma felt up to that.

He went to bed early, but even after he fell asleep, he was disturbed and restless. Perhaps it was only that he was exhausted from the enervating heat of the attic, from the vicious nightmare he had had that seemed so real but was obviously just imagination.

Perhaps it was because his mother was dying.

He woke at 2:00 panting and reaching wildly into the air for...something.... It dissipated—the dream, the headache, the sense of needing to reach out and hold on and pull back and protect.

"What's wrong?" Bonnie whispered. Whenever they spent the night at Emma's, Bonnie whispered, from the moment they closed the door to Richard's old bedroom, where he had spent all of his lonely childhood nights, until they opened it in the morning. It made Richard feel like they were two horny teenagers fumbling at each other, stealing a few frantic moments on the couch while his parents, or hers, watched Johnny Carson in their bedroom and waited to be interrupted by unwarranted (unwanted) sounds of passion from the darkened living room. It was almost funny.

Almost.

"Nothing," Richard whispered back. "Just a bad dream." He hadn't told Bonnie yet. Emma asked him not to. *No use making her fret before it's time. And the time will be soon enough. Just give me a few weeks, okay.*

Sure, Mom. Anything you say, Mom. Glass of lemonade, Mom?

"I'm sorry," Bonnie said, laying her head against his shoulder and rubbing her fingers across the warm skin of his chest.

He pulled her tighter. Her fingers moved more forcefully, sweeping in larger and larger arcs, clipping against his nipples, running over the contours of his belly, finally dropping and touching and arousing.

Fully awake, drawn completely from the horror of a forgotten dream, he responded.

- 9 -

Emma lay awake. The day's pain was finally beginning in earnest. The earlier tendrils that had curled, vine-like, around her spine and through her arms and legs and that had frightened her so much now seemed insubstantial. Ghost-like. An unpleasant dream almost welcome in memory.

What she was feeling now was the *real* thing. She hadn't slept well for too many long, long nights. She lay in her double bed and let her thoughts range further and further. Sometimes, she almost believed she could reach out far enough to touch him, to feel him and comfort him.

Now *she* needed comfort.

The boards in the ceiling groaned, protested a sudden shifting of weight, a sudden twist and thrust in the room above her.

Emma closed her eyes.

Richard and Bonnie.

Life goes on.

She smiled, and for a moment the pain retreated into the shadows, leaving her a too-brief glimpse of pure, exhilarating light.

CHAPTER TWO

IN THE VALLEY OF THE SHADOW

- 1 -

An unhealthy—and for that reason exciting—glow hung in the sky over Tamarind Valley when Pac cut off the 101 North and onto the Simi Valley Freeway. As he made the sweeping turn eastward onto the overpass, the glow focused over the hill behind the Oaks Mall. Only hours before; the shopping center had hosted thousands of cars filled with more thousands of rubber-neckers out for a glimpse of the fireworks. Now the parking lot was empty, but the hillside roiled with movement as firefighters worked to put out the blaze the celebration had caused.

Pac saw the movement dimly, partially, as he glanced out of his side window. It seemed as if the hill were alive with black bugs that crawled frantically over a layer of bright red foil. Occasionally the foil shimmered and burst into light, just as another spot darkened and died.

Pac smiled.

He turned on the radio.

"...in at least twenty separate sites through the Southland. The worst is still burning out of control in Tamarind Valley, where the finale of the city-sponsored fireworks display was accidentally touched off ten minutes early. In the resulting explosion and blaze, sparks showered the hills. It is feared that...."

Pac twisted the knob, a knot of cold pleasure forming in his stomach.

First the Drive.

Then the shooting.

Now a *fire!*

He fought down a temptation to take the Tamarind Avenue exit and park somewhere nearer the firefighters and watch them beat out the flames. Instead, he pulled into the outside lane, watched that exit pass, then sped off at the next exit.

In the early morning hours, the south-eastern portions of Tamarind Valley were like a graveyard. No one moved. No dogs barked, no birds sang. The roads unrolled like blank strips of silvery duct-tape, occasionally shining in the glare of a crosswalk. Few other lights burned except the vapor-lamps edging streets in the newer developments.

Pac felt like he was the only person alive. Like Charlton Heston in *The Omega Man,* or Vincent Price in the earlier version. Fearless vampire hunters, all!

He laughed and blinked and laughed, his voice rising above the VW's arthritic whine. For an instant, he was the Survivor, careening through ghost-haunted streets, driving frantically to make it back to his lair before the walking undead sniffed out his presence and followed him with their own vicious stock of pointed sticks and mauls and hammers.

He imagined that he could almost see the shuffling mob, zombies from *Night of the Living Dead,* slow and stiff but impossibly keeping up with his VW as it skidded around the corner.

He glanced at the rear-view mirror.

"Shit!"

He *saw* the shadow.

No imagination. *It* was there, wispy and billowy but as real as his own hand where it trembled against the warm plastic of the steering wheel.

"Shit!"

The Drive had not been enough. Not even the silver bullet had been enough to keep the shadow away.

It still hunted him. Haunted him.

He shivered, a wash of cold fingering like graveyard air over his skin. His armpits were damp and clammy.

Without looking directly at the rear-view mirror, he reached out and touched the crucifix, running his thumb along its smoothly polished surface. He tightened his thighs, clamping down on the gun lodged between them. For an instant, it was as if he could feel the fluid heat of molten silver like a current through the steel barrel, through the worn fabric of his jeans, through his flesh It entered him and filled him and warmed him and brought his blood to a fevered boil.

He was *Pac!* And he was *Driving!*

Taking a deep breath, he looked at the crucifix. He studied its simple lines, imagining a broken body twisted and bleeding from the virginal cross-piece. He laughed and raised his eyes to look in the mirror again.

The shadow was gone, most of it. The rest disappeared even as he watched.

He slowed down to the legal limit of thirty-five, slipping past the rows of tract houses that over the past three years had sprung up mushroom-like in the fallow fields that once bordered Tamarind Valley. He turned right, right, left, left again, then passed beneath the deeper ink-spot shadows of centuries-old twin oak trees and drove over the low rise to his house.

It stood dark and empty, as he had left it. The house exuded a cold welcome. Its shadows seemed to open to swallow him as he approached.

The wheels of the VW crunched on the finely crushed gravel of the driveway. It sounded like static on a badly tuned TV set. It sounded familiar, comforting.

He was suddenly tired. His eyes felt red and scratchy from the smog that had hung over the LA basin like a shroud well into the early morning hours. His back and thighs were so knotted and tense that when he killed the engine and opened his door and climbed out, he stumbled and almost fell. His feet felt as if he were walking on raw muscles and tendons, bare of flesh.

His thin face pinched in a deep frown.

He had expected to be tired, but this was not a good tired. This was a bone-gnawing frustrating tiredness that promised only restlessness and bad dreams. He knew what it meant.

In spite of everything, he was not yet finished. He had not really destroyed the shadow, merely forced it to move on temporarily. It would return.

Luckily, there were plenty more nights. More chances to Drive. More silver bullets.

- 2 -

By six o'clock on the morning of July 5, more than a dozen police patrol cars and motorcycles had congregated at half a dozen spots dotting the maze of the LA freeway systems.

Patrolman John Gilmore was the first to respond to a call that came in just before dawn.

A trucker had reported being fired on. *Another* one. Like most of the LAPD, Gilmore had watched the approach of the Fourth of

July with an apprehension that verged on dull black dread. It was bad enough in normal years, what with idiots setting vacant lots, back yards, houses, occasionally even themselves on fire with contraband fireworks.

But *this* year.

There were more crazies than usual out, that was sure. And that, coupled with nervous Nellies that reported every backfire as rifle fire, made the specter of the Fourth of July more a horror-day than a holiday.

The long night had confirmed his fears.

So far, there had been over thirty-five reports of weapons fired on the freeways. Most of them had proven wrong. What with the media attention being focused on the freeway drive-by shootings, a lot of drivers were mistaking Fourth of July celebrations for gunfire.

Unfortunately, Gilmore realized after only a few moments, this was not one of them. The trucker, a husky Latin-looking guy named Trujillo whose speech was crisper, less accented than his name might have suggested, was right.

There had been a sniper. The double windshield of his Mack cab was shattered. Stuffing fluffed out from two bullet holes in the upholstery of the seat, one not six inches from where the man's shoulder must have been resting. Trujillo had already dug one slug out with his pocket knife. He held it like a charm in the callused palm of one hand.

The guy was lucky, Gilmore thought. Some targets died. Gilmore was taking down the man's statement when the second patrol car rolled up. He glanced over, recognized the two officers, nodded, continued.

"Did you see anything, Mr. Trujillo?"

"Nothin'."

"No car, no people?"

"Nothin', I said. I was just toolin' along 'n' somethin' went *smack*. I knew what it was the minute it hit. I was in 'Nam, I've heard the buzz when the lead passes. I was stopped 'n' outta the cab before the second one smashed the other window."

"And you didn't see anything after that shot?"

"No. Lucky for the bastard. If I'd 'a' seen him." The trucker made a quick twisting gesture with his hands. Gilmore had seen its close relative when his wife opened stubborn Mason jars, but something told him that Trujillo was *not* offering to open a sticky jar of home-bottled pears for the sniper.

"Yeah," Gilmore said noncommittally, although privately he agreed with Trujillo. There were plenty of times over the past couple of weeks when he would have loved to wrap his own hands around a few necks. He'd seen the results of other freeway shooters at work. Some of the victims weren't as voluble as Trujillo, or—from their beds in intensive care—as articulate. Two were dead.

"Be right back, Mr. Trujillo," he said, flipping his notebook closed and walking to the other patrol car.

"Gil," the driver said in greeting.

Gilmore nodded. Gilmore particularly didn't like Bruce Jorgenson—wasn't even sure he trusted the man even though he was a fellow officer and had been on the force almost as long as Gilmore. There was just something about him.

"Anything?" Jorgenson asked, his own tone as curt as Gilmore's. There was no love lost from his side, either, Gilmore realized

"No," Gilmore said. "No clues, no suspects, nothing. Just the slugs embedded in the seats. Forensics will have to work them over."

"Well, don't let it get you down," Jorgenson said, more affably than usual. For a moment Gilmore suspected Jorgenson was quietly pleased to see him caught in a case with no suspects, no leads "Maybe you'll get something good. Like that one last night down on the Golden State."

"Huh?" Gilmore hadn't heard about anything odd—at least odd from LA standards.

"Really weird. Some old guy shot at. He's all right, bruised, bumped around, but the bullet missed. They checked over the place where he said his car was when someone fired at him. He figured it out pretty well, too, because someone dug the slug out of a tree trunk alongside the freeway—damn tree must've been three, four feet in diameter and the slug hit dead center, shattered the bark and made a mark easy enough to find at night with a flashlight."

"So?" Gilmore looked over his shoulder, anxious to get back to Trujillo. The big man was starting to look even angrier at being kept waiting than he had at being shot at

"So...the slug was made of silver."

"Silver?" Gilmore turned slowly to face the open window.

"Yeah. We musta had a real nutcase out last night. Hunting vampires."

"Werewolves," Gilmore said automatically.

"Huh?"

"Werewolves," he repeated, feeling suddenly on the far side of foolish. He already got enough razzing at the station for the tattered paperbacks that stuck out of his pockets when he came in for his shift. "Silver bullets for werewolves," he continued. *What the hell they already figure I'm crazy.* "Wooden stakes for vampires. And crucifixes."

"Uh, yeah."

Gilmore grinned hugely. This was too much; he wasn't going to let Jorgenson sucker him into this joke. "What's the matter? Didn't you learn anything at Monster School? Silver bullets kill werewolves. Wooden stakes through the heart take care of vampires. Each monster has its own neat little execution packet. Get the right weapon, kill the right monster."

Jorgenson stared at his hands, where they gripped the steering column.

"Right. But what kills the vampire-killer?" He looked up at Gilmore, suddenly serious. "I'm not kidding. The reports says the damned thing was almost pure silver."

- 3 -

Pac stayed close to the house for over a week; the shadow had almost caught up with him, and he wanted to take no more chances. He burrowed into a new Stephen King novel, a monstrous thing hundreds of pages long. His pen hovered over the words like a vulture on the watch for signs of death. The pages he had already read were mottled and marred by underlinings and marginal notes.

Once or twice, just as twilight stained the window golden, he jerked his head up, staring out at the car, feeling, hearing the call.

Come and find me, Donney. Come and get me.

"Not tonight, fucker," he whispered. The words were brave but his eyes were not as they flickered from page to window and back to page again.

Finally, though, the pressure built too far. He had the gun, he had the silver bullets—only one gone from the neat stack—he had the crucifix. That helped a little.

If he stayed holed up in the house, it would only come for him, find him, destroy him. He had to get it first.

He had to *Drive.*

He started just after sunset, while the western fringes of the valley were still pale with twilight spilling over the ocean and filtering through clefts in the Coast Range.

Not that he saw the beauty of the sky, or would have cared if anyone had pointed it out to him.

No, he was intent on only one thing. He drove for almost twenty minutes without even noticing where he was.

The crucifix swung wildly as he changed lanes on the west-bound Ventura to cut off onto the San Diego over Sepulveda Pass. By itself, he knew, the cross could do little. But as one more link in his armor, as one more weapon against the shadow, however small, it made him feel better. The .38 still rested between his legs, and every now and then he would clench the upper muscles of his legs and feel the hardness of steel between them.

He studied the cars closely.

It was out there. He *knew* it was; he *knew* that he could find it and kill it and be free.

He drove for hours, aimlessly, arcing from ramp to ramp, free-way to freeway.

"Soon. Soon," he murmured, downshifting viciously when he made a sudden transition somewhere in the heart of LA. "Soon."

As it turned out, it was later rather than sooner. It was, in fact, almost one o clock when he spotted the car. He grinned ferociously.

This was no sedate little-old-lady car. No, the shadow wouldn't hide in one of them again for a long time. This time it had chosen something long and lean and fast, much faster than the old VW that was already straining and vibrating at barely sixty-two miles per hour.

He probably wouldn't even have seen it if a truck up ahead had not momentarily slowed in the outside lane and she had zipped by, staring straight ahead, her eyes riveted on the roadway. Luckily, there was a brief moment of traffic, unusually heavy for early morning, and the inside lanes slowed as well. In that instant, he had caught, then passed the sporty red car, close enough to see across the passenger seat and glimpse her silhouette against the uneven light thrown by cars in the inside lanes. *Lips twisted in a smile that carried daggers instead of kisses. Laughter equally sharp. Eyes that penetrated deeper than a woman's eyes had any right and she saw and knew.*

The bitch had followed him out here, had found him somehow and was on her way to gloat and laugh and tell everyone. The gun between his legs reminded him—this time, *he* was in control. This time, *he* would destroy *her*.

The blockage on the freeway up ahead broke loose. The mysterious happening that had slowed traffic just as suddenly dissipated, and cars surged ahead. He jockeyed in front of the red car. In the rear-view mirror, he could see black blankness. It was her windshield, nothing more.

She pulled up close behind him.

He signaled for a left turn and carefully changed lanes, pushing the VW just a little more. She accelerated until her front bumper was even with his rear bumper, then with his side window.

She was directly across from him.

She *turned and grinned at him and it was—*

He raised the gun and fired.

Her head shattered.

He only saw it peripherally as he jammed the pedal to the floor and willed a few more mph from the old car.

Her head shattered and blood sprayed all over and the red sports car slewed to the right, its front right headlight dying in a shower of sparks as the metal and glass scraped against a six-foot-high concrete retaining wall. Without looking back, he could imagine it *see it* scraping along the wall, paint smearing like blood, sparks haloing fenders and door and chrome until the car struck a shallow recess in the concrete and spun and flipped and exploded.

Already a mile down the road, he didn't have to look back to see the fireball hanging over the asphalt.

- 4 -

"Damn you!" Margot Elkins screamed incoherently as the battered Beetle disappeared into the shadows of an overpass. "Damn you! Damn you!"

She finally regained marginal control of the car, just as the front fender scraped against the retaining wall and bounced her back onto the roadway. She struggled with the wheel, yanking it first left, then right, finally releasing just enough to let the tires grab and let the car's momentum help stabilize it.

She skidded to a halt. Through force of habit, she reached around the steering wheel and switched the engine off. She unlocked her door and swiveled her legs around, but instead of climbing out, she dropped her hands into her lap, not noticing the merry jangle of the keys on her ring.

She trembled, almost cried. Then she took a deep breath and stood up. The cool night air helped steady her. Carefully she walked around the car, examining it for damage.

The sniper was long gone. All that was left of his passage was a crumpled front fender on the driver's side and a jagged puncture where the bullet had passed into the engine block from the passenger side. The sound of gunfire and the echoing *thunk* when the bullet struck had frightened her enough to throw her off balance but apparently did little more than superficial damage. The car was still running all right when she turned it off, she vaguely remembered.

"Damn him," she said, this time almost sadly. Behind her, a red light winked on and off as a large sedan sped down the lane toward her. A cop must have already spotted her stalled along the side of the freeway.

She waited patiently for the black and white to roll to a stop.

By the time the officer was out of his car, she was calmer, ready to tell her story.

Too bad she hadn't seen the sniper.

Too bad all she could tell them was that it had been a dark, beat-up Volkswagen.

Too bad she was going to have to tell Murray that the car was wrecked.

Really too bad.

The deductible and inevitable surcharge, on top of the alimony and the child support, should make him mad enough to spit nails.

In spite of what had happened, she felt almost like grinning.

- 5 -

Pac slept badly that night. The Drive should have been one of the best, but there had been no release, none at all. Her face floated through his dreams, glowering, haunting, exploding.

And each time, he screamed and woke, his own blood throbbing at his temples.

She wasn't the one!

It was still out there, growing stronger. Waiting.

For him.

- 6 -

The call came late Monday morning.

Friday the thirteenth came on Monday this month, Richard thought despondently as he watched the lines around his mother's mouth deepen and harden. Not good news.

Bonnie reached over and took his hand as they sat on the old sofa and waited while Emma listened. Occasionally she nodded. Once she shook her head, fractionally, as if the voice at the other end of the line could see the minute movement and interpret it as hesitation or refusal or fear. Suddenly she stood and held the receiver out to Richard. He took it. Emma turned and disappeared down the short hallway that led to her bedroom.

Richard waited with his hand over the receiver until he heard the bedroom door slip closed.

"Dr. Smith?"

"Richard?"

"Yes."

"I'm sorry about all of this. I wish it could have been otherwise. I wanted her to come in to the office, where I could talk to her about it. Face to face. It's better. But you know how she is. After thirty years I still can't get her to do anything she doesn't want to."

"I know," Richard said.

"Well, the upshot of it all is that the tests came back this morning."

Pause.

"Richard?"

"Yeah."

"Sorry, son. It's bad. Worse than I thought originally."

"How long?"

"With unusual care, a lot of luck, immediate hospitalization, and extensive treatment...."

"How long?"

"Three months. Two. Maybe four."

Richard could see Dr. Smith shrugging as he spoke, the action, so superficial-seeming, wholly at odds with the intense pain the man must be feeling. He had been Emma's physician for three decades, had helped bring Richard and Donney into the world, had presided over Roland's painful last months.

Richard grieved for his mother, but at the moment he knew that Dr. Smith's pain was also, in its own way, unfathomable.

"Thanks."

That was all. They needed spare no more words. "Have her call me, Richard. Soon."

What with another doctor might have come across as a callous disregard for a terminally ill patient's well-being was, in Dr. Smith, an acknowledgement of deep respect. Richard understood the ulterior meaning informing the words: *Emma can handle it. Richard can handle it. Together they will face it and grow to it and through it.*

Through death.

"All right. Thanks."

He hung up the phone.

"How bad is it?" Bonnie asked.

"August, September."

Bonnie paled.

"I wish she had let me know sooner," she said. "Maybe I could have...."

"There's nothing you could have done. And until yesterday, you had one less burden. That's what she wanted."

They were speaking in a whisper.

A floorboard creaked. Emma stood at the door to the living room.

"Mother," Bonnie said.

Emma smiled at her daughter-in-law. Emma's eyes were red-rimmed, her cheeks puffy. But she smiled.

"Mom." Richard said. Then stopped as she turned to look at him.

"Find him."

- 7 -

Gilmore wasn't really following the cases that closely. By mid-July there had been over two dozen; some of the pessimists were estimating as many as fifty shootings by the end of summer. The politicians down at City Hall were furious, vocal, worried. They were already making noises about tough new laws.

Some group at USC came up with an idea to sell little blue stickers assuring passers-by that the inhabitants of the car sporting it were courteous drivers—not crazed maniacs toting an unbelievable variety of firepower.

Gilmore laughed sardonically.

As if a little blue sticker could insure security. Or safety.

He shook his head. Every day it grew worse. And it was starting to spread. Dallas. Sacramento. Who knew where else.

He wasn't following the cases closely, but he was aware of general developments. That's why he noted the single word in the print-out summarizing information about the last half-dozen attacks.

This one had happened at the beginning of the weekend, when Gilmore was off duty. If he'd been around then, maybe he would have tried to follow it up. But by now, enough others would have noticed and gotten on the case. It was too weird to be a coincidence. And suddenly the specter of random shootings was deepened by the realization that at least some of them were no longer random. Now there was a pattern. A scary pattern.

He re-read the line, shivering when he came to the word again.

Bullet embedded in the engine block.

Silver bullet.

- 8 -

"No."

It was a gentle denial, full of love and compassion and understanding. But it was a denial nonetheless. Emma stared, as if unable to believe what she had heard.

"No, Mom. I'm not going to leave you. Not right now. You need someone here to be with you.

"But if you went out there, if you *saw* him?"

He took her hand and pressed it. The hand was cool, and the skin felt loose, as if already the envelope of flesh were too large for her bones.

"Listen, Mom. I know you want him back more than anything. More than if I were the one gone and he was here."

"That's not true." Emma's words came out stridently, but her eyes dropped and her pale cheeks flushed.

"Yes, it is," Richard said softly. He pressed her hand again to reassure her. "But it's all right. I've understood for years that there was a special...bond between you and Donney. I haven't liked it sometimes, but I've understood.

"And if I thought that it would help, I would walk to California, I'd *crawl* there and get him and bring him back, even if I had to drag him by the ears."

"Then...." The sudden hope in her voice wrenched at his heart.

"But it wouldn't help. He wouldn't come. I know it, and so do you. And if he did, what would it accomplish?" Richard flashed back to the boxes still hidden in the attic shadows. Black shirts, posters of monsters and demons, ephemera of a troubled and troubling child who had ceased to exist long ago. "He would hate me, hate you. And he would make it worse for us both."

Emma didn't answer.

There *was* no answer.

Richard knew that perhaps he was wrong, of course. There *was* hope. Donney might change. People could always change.

But deep inside, Richard felt that he was right, fundamentally and devastatingly right. There had been two years of adamant silence, except for an occasional tantalizing postcard with little more than a return address—Donney's way of keeping the wound open, scratching at it just as it was almost healed, keeping it bleeding and agonized and tender. *Gangrenous,* Richard might have added if he were more honest with himself.

If Donney had simply disappeared, they might have borne it. They might have accepted absence in the place of death, and an idealized brother/son might have gradually filled the emptiness left by the flight of a frustrating reality.

But he had not let that happen. He had nagged and niggled, torn at the half-healed scab and laughed when the blood and pus oozed out again.

Richard still had the postcards. He had hidden them underneath the red-velvet lined oak jewel-box that had been Roland's and then had come to Richard and now held what little was left to them of Donney captive beneath its weight.

"Mom," Richard said, as gently as he could. "You don't know how long you have. I *can't* leave you. Please don't ask me to." She didn't answer.

"I'll...make some calls, write again. And again. Every day, if you want." He straightened. The muscles along his jaw line tightened. "But I won't leave you now."

Bonnie stood and moved across to touch her husband and the woman who was only her mother-in-law but was as dear as her own mother.

Together, they formed a triangle, a barrier keeping love in and pain and hatred out.

Emma wept. Bonnie embraced the older woman and wept with her.

Richard did not weep. In place of tears, he felt a coldness that he did not understand, a numbness that he did not like.

- 9 -

The shadow was too strong. Too close. He hadn't wanted to kill that woman. *It was a mistake,* he screamed to himself as he replayed the moment that her head had shattered and the blood had gushed out and flooded the interior of the car until it looked like a crimson-filled wading pool.

It had tricked him.

He could not trust the crucifix or the Drive. Or the silver bullets.

For almost a month, except for random hours spent earning enough to keep himself in food and rental videos, he stayed inside the house beyond the hill. Where he was safe.

CHAPTER THREE

A MIDNIGHT SHOOTING ON THE GOLDEN STATE FREEWAY

- 1 -

It was mid-August. The days had been unusually cool for Southern California, the nights short but studded with violence.

At first the incident seemed like just another random shooting on the Southern California freeway—one of over forty since the middle of June and still no end in sight. Not a night had passed during the last week without at least one televised news-report of gunfire: a trucker pointing to a shattered front window; a motorist with punctures in the door of his late-model Toyota; a motorcyclist who followed a too-aggressive driver in order to get a license number, only to become a target himself and barely escape alive.

Many shootings had resulted in injury; a few, too many, in death. This one looked like just one more in the series. But it wasn't.

* * * * * * *

Fred Zimmerman worked the four-to-midnight shift at the Kwik-Time Parcel Service outlet in Eagle Rock, one of the innumerable and virtually indistinguishable suburbs on the western fringes of the Los Angeles basin. Since his transfer from the Griffith Park branch six months ago, he had worked the evening shift, even though it meant a fifteen-minute drive on the Golden State to and from the little house he and Thelma had bought almost twenty-five years ago. Someone with his seniority could have squawked and gotten a more convenient daytime shift, but he didn't mind the late hours. He didn't mind missing Thelma's steady offering of low-cal

TV dinners warmed in the microwave, or the incessant chatter that after forty-three years of marriage had become the background of his home life—like static on an old radio set. No matter how carefully you twisted the knobs, the static still hummed through...sometimes more, sometimes less, but always an irritant and a distraction.

He didn't mind the relative peace he found in his office, usually almost deserted after six or seven o'clock each evening.

He didn't mind driving home late at night, not even now, with crazies driving around shooting people. He was a safe driver, a cautious driver, a courteous driver, never had an accident, not even when he was driving trucks daytime for the company, not even during the Christmas rush, when trucks were pulling in and out of the yard every five minutes, crammed with orders that had to be delivered yesterday.

Through all of that he drove calmly, coolly, and above all safely. So he wasn't unduly worried when he left the office at 11:43 and pulled out along Third Street. It was only three blocks to the on-ramp, then fifteen miles along the Golden State to home and Thelma and sleep. Or, he reminded himself wryly, if he was lucky, just sleep.

He drove slowly along Third, watching for greens ready to change to amber, listening to the quiet *ping-ping-ping* that had developed in his 1973 Volvo over the past three days. Thelma noticed it first, but now even Fred knew something was wrong. He would have to take the heap in to Cal's garage on his first day off and have the engine checked.

He glanced at the bank of dials on the dash, relieved to see unbroken darkness instead of a red warning light flickering balefully up at him.

He sniffed cautiously. No oily smell, nothing burning. Just that confounded *ping-ping-ping.*

At the light at the bottom of the on-ramp, he flicked his turn signal on and swung right, noticing how empty the streets seemed that night. They were even quieter than usual. Good. Nothing to worry about.

He hit the freeway at precisely the prescribed fifty-five M.P.H. It was much hotter up there, a dozen feet or more above the roofs of offices and homes. He rolled the window up, sweat already forming on his lip, and flipped the air conditioner on. He drove in silence. He used to listen to the radio—when he was younger, he had enjoyed Wolfman Jack on late-night trips—but now he preferred silence. It helped him concentrate.

So he was concentrating when the Caddy passed him.

It wasn't going terribly fast, maybe sixty-five or so. Just enough to slip into the night without any problem. He noticed the car, though, because it was an old Caddy, one of those late-sixties jobs with the fins that stuck out to the moon, studded with red lights all along their length.

The car was unusual, being so old, but he didn't give it more than a moment's thought. For an instant, he felt alone and frail and unutterably afraid, staring at the wrong side of retirement in a world that flew by too fast and would soon forget him. Then, as soon as the Caddy's taillights winked by, he laughed to himself and tightened his double-handed grip on the steering wheel—two o'clock and ten o'clock hand positions, just like they taught him in Driver's Ed more years ago than that Caddy had been around.

A couple of other cars passed him as he tooled along at fifty-five in the middle lane. That was his only major form of social comment. If the law said that he could do fifty-five in the middle lane, then he would, by gum, and anyone who wanted to break the law could just go around him.

They did. A semi roared by at well over sixty-five, rocking Fred's little Volvo in its wash. He read the name on the side: Food-World. That figures, he thought, they charge high enough prices—have to pay for all the gas they're wasting. Fred always shopped at Ralphs.

A sedan followed, then a small pickup with a camper shell. Nothing unusual. Just typical late-night traffic on Five. Fred wondered, as he always did, where so many people could be going at this hour.

Then the Volkswagen approached. It was going much more than sixty-five, barreling down directly behind him. It came up so fast out of nowhere that for half a moment Fred felt like he was moving in reverse. The car was an old-style Bug, dark, not black but deep blue or green, a pregnant bulge in the night. And the dome light was on—Fred had time to notice that.

That, and the six-inch silver crucifix glistening from the rear-view mirror. It caught the light from the interior and reflected it as the cross spun and spun, rocked by the vibrations as the VW's engine roared.

"Darned fool," Fred muttered. "Goin' to kill someone, prob'ly himself." For an instant, he unaccountably felt his blood boil and almost wished he could floor the gas pedal and have his sedate Volvo streak ahead and catch that punk and...and then maybe he'd flip him the bird. Show him he couldn't push Fred Zimmerman around.

Still, there had been those shootings. Probably fools like this one. He eased up a touch on his accelerator instead, dropping behind a bit more as the VW racketed by. He almost saw the driver; he did see a silhouette as the bug swerved around him, taking the right-hand lane, the slow lane, since the Datsun pickup was still only a few yards ahead of them in the left-hand fast lane.

An overpass slipped by above them. Another loomed ahead, maybe half a mile distant, the lights along the pedestrian walk looking like dim yellow beads. The semi was about a quarter of the way there; the Caddy only half way or so. The VW spurted ahead, and Fred was still close enough to see that it was nudging alongside the Caddy. From where he sat, it looked like the two cars were fender to fender. The brake lights on the bug flicked a couple of times; the driver was apparently slowing.

Then Fred saw a fleck of light and, an instant later, heard a backfire. The VW spun away.

The Caddy, though...it slewed slowly around, waffling on the pavement before it punched up against the pilings of the overpass, spinning in a half circle until its grill faced toward Fred's Volvo, a toothless, mangled grin. Both of its headlights glared into his eyes.

For a moment, blinded and startled, Fred panicked. He started to jerk at the steering wheel but then his lifelong habits of cautiousness kicked in. Looking away from the Caddy's headlights, he slowed gradually, pumping his brakes to avoid losing his own traction: fifty-five...forty-five...thirty-five.... Finally he slowed enough to pull over toward the shoulder, fifty yards or so from the Caddy.

Right next to a luckily placed emergency phone.

The semi disappeared, along with the Datsun. Either they didn't see what had happened or they didn't want to take any chances on becoming victims themselves. But Fred Zimmerman, cautious though he was, knew his duty as a citizen. He slowed the Volvo and pulled onto the shoulder. He didn't want to approach the Caddy too close, though—sometimes wrecks exploded, he knew that from watching the reruns of *CHiPS*. No, he didn't want to chance getting too near. But he could certainly report it.

As soon as the Volvo was safely stopped, ignition off, parking brakes on, key removed and tucked into his pants pocket, Fred got out. He fully intended to approach at least close enough to look in the Caddy's window and make sure the driver was all right.

He even took four or five steps in that direction before he stopped.

The punk in the VW had made him mad; but something about the way the Caddy just sat there, glaring at him, swallowed any residual anger and cooled him, chilled him. He thought seriously about hopping back into the Volvo and heading out, speeding home and locking the car safely in his neat-as-a-pin garage and slipping into the house and stripping and crawling naked in bed with Thelma and feeling her heat radiating through his old body.

For the first time in years, even Thelma seemed a good alternative.

His hand dropped to his side; he could feel the lump of keys heavy against his leg. He half believed that he could tell which one was the Volvo key, could hear it urging him to take it out, shove it in, get out of there.

He shivered.

But finally his long-ingrained sense of civic responsibility won. He turned back, not to his car but to the call box. His voice shaking and harsh, even to his own ears, he mumbled out his report to the impersonal female voice that answered over the static of the phone line. It didn't take long. Afterward, he stood with his back to the steep hillside that bordered the freeway. He stared over the lanes of traffic, watching cars pass in both directions. He didn't look toward the Caddy. It was enough to feel safe among the light and the noise and the movement.

A few minutes later he heard a siren and, looking back over the glistening top of his Volvo, he saw the red whirling lights approaching.

- 2 -

Jeff would have been embarrassed silly to admit it to anyone, of course, even to his best friend, Brad—but he had been *waiting* for this night. For days. For weeks. For months.

For his whole life, his hormones screamed, whenever he thought about Sara.

He shifted uncomfortably. The thin foil-wrapped square packet in his front pocket pressed against his thigh through the worn material of his jeans. As a favor to Jeff, Brad had spirited the Trojan from his older brother's drawer—*He keeps boxes of 'em under his bikini shorts, buys 'em by the gross, I think,* Brad had said as he chuckled, winked lewdly, and handed over the packet more than a week ago. Jeff knew that Brad was still trying to figure out if Jeff and Sara had done "it" yet or not.

Jeff played it cool. Maybe. Maybe not. A gentleman never tells. Brad laughed out loud at that, making Jeff feel young and naive and stupid. Brad had done 'it' the first time with MaryAnn almost a year ago, and since then hadn't let Jeff forget the single fact that separated them for the first time in their years-long friendship. There were the men, who *had*...and then there were the boys.

Lately, Jeff had felt more and more like a boy whenever he hung around Brad.

He felt like one tonight, sitting here next to Sara with the Trojan in his pocket.

What if she screams or cries or hollers rape?

Or worse *What if she laughs?*

He had thought for days about Brad's brother's bikini briefs, had even stared for half an hour at the men's-wear display in the K-Mart, trying to decide whether a pair of low-cut briefs might make Sara think he was sexy...or just absurd. He had stared and stared at the packages, not quite daring to pick one up, until the old lady holding the key to the men's changing room looked his way for the tenth time, and Jeff decided she probably thought he was gay or something. He saw a smirk twist the old lady's wrinkled lips.

What if Sara laughs! thudded through his mind. The thought—the fear of ridicule as much as of rejection—agonized.

At the last minute, he hadn't bought the briefs. It was probably just as well, he decided, as he felt Sara's hip rub against his. Her touch was electric. Suddenly, his plain white jockeys seemed plenty tight.

He took a deep breath and thought he might raise his arm and rest it on the back of the seat.

- 3 -

Jeff might have been more relaxed if he had been a mind-reader and had known that Sara was looking forward to the night, too—but that *she* would have rather died than say so to *Jeff,* and that her own responses were as frustratingly ambivalent as his.

She knew that he wanted *(hoped? planned?)* to go all the way this time. Not that he had ever right come out and *said* so; he was too much a gentleman to be that gross. But there were plenty of little hints and signs, things even she could interpret easily enough. Those long, hot looks in Home Room. The way he felt against her when he hurriedly kissed her good-night after their dates at the movies or the pizza parlors or the ice cream places.

She could tell, even though knowing made her feel somehow...uncomfortable. Flattered, sure, but also rushed, propelled toward a precipice she was not sure she wanted to approach...just yet.

Sometimes the view was just as nice from a little further back, at least for a little while longer.

Still.... She had decided—well, she still wasn't sure whether she really wanted to, but she was willing for him to at least *try*. She could always call it off if things got too hot and heavy.

She hoped.

The two of them were parked at the end of Miller Avenue, close together in the front seat of Jeff's car. Miller Avenue used to continue on, clear across LA, almost to Santa Monica. But when the freeway came through, decades ago, it was one of the streets that lost out. It didn't merit an overpass, not even a connection with the frontage roads.

Over the years, it had died as businesses moved to more profitable locations. A light or two still glimmered in some buildings, but for the most part Miller was quiet and dark.

Not a traditional Lover's Lane, of course. But it was hard to find any of them in urban LA, and although Jeff and Sara did not have a particularly early curfew (after all, it *was* midnight), they didn't dare drive all the way up into the hills.

Anyway, Miller Avenue wasn't so bad. The cul-de-sac circled around just above Five, topping a small natural hill that the freeway engineers had decided to leave intact. Through the wire diamonds in the rusted chain-link fence, the lights of the basin glittered— romantically, it seemed to Sara.

"It's nice here," she murmured as Jeff reached down and killed the engine. She rolled her window down. Other than the muted roar of traffic on Five, it was quiet outside. She could hear a cricket or two in the bushes that had sprouted along the fence. A bit of breeze fanned through Jeff's old Galaxy, washing away the musty, gassy smell that always hung around it no matter how many little pine trees he strung from the rear-view mirror.

"Yeah," Jeff answered. "I like it too. I've been here lots."

She knew that he hadn't. This was his first time. Her older brother Mike, whose locker was next to Jeff's in sixth period PE, had informed her not long ago that he had checked Jeff out and quietly assured her of Jeff's status—and given her *his* permission to go on seeing Jeff. As if she needed it!

In spite of Mike's occasional intrusions into her private affairs, she usually appreciated his concern. She knew that she was, after all, still pretty naive. Even so, she *had* already learned that boys believed that girls liked experienced men; Mike had heartily agreed with that observation. Probably Jeff did too, and had correspondingly rehearsed his role carefully.

She certainly had.

"This is my first time up here," Sara said coyly.

"Lights are nice." That was Jeff's contribution.

"Pretty."

There was a long, strained silence. She knew—and knew that *he* knew—why they were there. And it wasn't to comment on the scenery.

Jeff shifted a couple of times, as if he couldn't quite get comfortable on the old vinyl upholstery that had split and been patched half a dozen times before he even bought the car. Sara wanted to help him but wasn't sure how.

Finally, to her intense relief and even more intense embarrassment, Jeff hitched himself up, stretched, and dropped his arm along the back of the seat.

"Here it comes," Sara thought, quivering with anticipation. It did. His hand dropped slowly, resting first against her shoulder, then against her arm. His hand was nice—warm with a heat that almost stung her bare arm. His hand was strong and big, but not too big, with wide white nails and tiny hairs along the crest of his knuckles that Sara found unbelievably sexy. She glanced at his hand out of the corner of her eye.

It moved again, lower, just touching the edge of her breast where her bra cup curved outward. The fingers jerked slightly when they felt the rigid nylon binding. For a fleeting moment she hoped (or feared?) that they were about to retreat.

"Darn," Sara thought, "maybe I shouldn't have worn the thing." Then she flushed in the darkness. Maybe she would let Jeff go all the way tonight, but she'd be switched if she would let him think that she *planned* to.

She shivered.

"Cold?" Jeff asked, solicitously, his left hand reaching across the steering wheel toward the heater.

"No," she said quickly.

He dropped his hand. It landed on her knee, where it lay warm and heavy before it began twitching and moving upward. For a brief second, Sara flashed on their beach trip last weekend, and his hand suddenly seemed like a mutant five-legged crab hitching itself up the sand at high tide.

She giggled.

The crab stopped, trembled, almost began retreating back to the safety of the ocean.

She forced herself to relax.

"Comfy?" Jeff asked. The words were too off-handed for Sara to really believe that he was worried over whether she was in a draft or if the broken spring in the seat was digging into her back.

She answered anyway—in kind, she hoped. "Mmmm."

She didn't say anything more.

Apparently that was as good as an invitation. Both Jeff's hands suddenly became more insistent, his fingers flexing, pressing gently into her flesh, the soft unresisting flesh of her thigh and her breast.

And then she was twisting in her seat toward him, steeling herself to touch him *there,* not quite knowing what to expect, forewarned only by the pictures Carol smuggled into class and surreptitiously passed around. Carol hadn't exactly *shown* them to Sara—they weren't in the same circle, after all—but Sara had seen enough to be excited and embarrassed...and a more than a little curious. If it got *that* big, how could guys manage to wear such tight...?

Metal crashed against concrete, the reverberations rocking Jeff's Ford. His hands clutched convulsively and Sara yelped in pain.

"Hey," she said angrily.

Then she realized what had happened.

Not fifty yards from them, just at the edge of the overpass for Sunglade Road, a big black car had crashed.

For a moment, they just sat, stunned, Jeff's hands still perilously close to compromising positions, Sara's suspended open above a crotch that was suddenly nowhere near as full as it had seemed a moment before.

"Shit, a wreck," Jeff whispered, awestruck. "Let's see it."

"No, Jeff," Sara pleaded. The magic moment was ruined, she knew that; but she still had little desire to muck around a wrecked car. Somebody might be hurt...bleeding...*dead!* "Stay here."

But he was already outside the car, straining to see beyond the link fence.

"Come on," he urged. "Maybe we can help or something."

"Oh, all right," she said, unlocking her door and pushing it open.

By that time, Jeff was over the fence, waiting to help her.

Some date, she thought as she caught her jeans on the top spikes of the link. She had expected something romantic, and instead they were going on a hike! Still, Jeff *did* wait for her, and when he grasped her to help her down from the fence, his hands were strong and masculine. In the reflected light from the freeway—and the wrecked car's headlights—he looked so hunky in his tight, sleeveless T-shirt and tighter jeans that she nearly stumbled. Her legs felt like jelly. She started to let her eyes drop, then jerked her gaze back to his face. He grinned sheepishly, a foolish look of innocent passion that endeared him...and made her wish fervently that the dumb driver had totaled his car somewhere else. *Anywhere* else!

Together, they climbed down the embankment toward the pavement.

There seemed to be a lull in traffic. Nothing was coming in any lane, and the only other car in sight was a late-model sedan huddled by the emergency call-phone a few yards away. A mousy little man was already talking into the receiver—probably reporting what had happened. That's what Sara would have done, anyway.

"Come on, let's get closer," Jeff said.

Sara hung back.

She didn't know why. She couldn't explain to herself any better than to say she just didn't want to get near that car. She didn't consciously think about the car exploding and hurting them, or seeing mangled bodies lying in their own blood, or any of the images she might have associated with a bad accident. She saw no images at all. She only knew instinctively that she would rather do *anything* than walk another step toward the impact-starred window staring blindly at her.

Just then, the headlights on the wrecked car flickered out. The embankment plunged into shadows and darkness.

"Jeff," she screamed.

He spun around and ran back toward her. Her heart was thumping wildly, and she could see in the dim light that he was terrified, too. She wanted him to be brave, to risk his life pulling someone from a burning wreck (as long as it wasn't a girl prettier and more vulnerable than Sara) and show her what kind of a man he was, but something in her voice had apparently startled him, and the startlement transmuted inexplicably into fear...terror. He grabbed her arms and held on, tightly. So tightly that it hurt, but even the hurt was desirable at that moment.

They pressed against the warmth of the other, closer than they had ever been before, almost as close as they would have been had the night progressed as planned and hoped. But she felt nothing even remotely akin to sexuality or passion; where Jeff's body pushed against her belly, he seemed as defenseless and empty as a six-year-old.

And suddenly, she was no longer trembling on the edge of womanhood. She was a just-barely-sixteen-year-old, scared of the dark.

- 4 -

The police cars pulled up within five minutes of the alleged shooting, lights flashing, sirens blaring.

Officer Ron Siegel arrived first. He was visibly relieved when he saw the man standing at the emergency call-box, a white-faced little man who seemed as afraid of the police car as shaken by the accident. You never knew any more when calls were real and when they were traps, and a sniper might be hiding along the pedestrian crosswalk of an overpass. This looked okay. Two kids were standing up on the shoulder, midway between the call box and the totaled Caddy.

Officer Siegel approached the little man first. "Your car?" he asked, nodding toward the crumbled fenders of the Cadillac.

"Heavens no," the man answered. "I reported the crash. I'm Fred Zimmerman." He said his name clearly, as if knowing it would make a difference.

By this time the kids had drifted closer. "Theirs, then?" Siegel asked.

"Uh, no, I don't think so," Zimmerman answered. "They came a few minutes later. From up there." He pointed to the embankment. The chain link fence was invisible but Siegel knew it was there. They must have climbed over to get a closer look at the wreck. Later, he would have to talk to them about trespassing onto freeway property.

"Where's the driver?" he asked, pitching his voice to reach the two kids as well.

"Uh...," Zimmerman said.

Inexplicably, the kids looked down at their feet.

"You mean he's still in there?" Siegel yelled. "Did anyone look...oh, hell!"

He raced across the tarmac. The boy followed a few steps behind. The girl hung back, standing a foot or so from Zimmerman, both outlined in the light above the call box.

Siegel cursed himself inwardly for not checking sooner. If there was an injured man in there and he died, there would be hell to pay. Siegel couldn't quite explain why he had not gone directly to the car; usually he would have. But there was something....

The feeling of intense unease deepened as he drew nearer the long black wreck. From this angle, it seemed foreshortened, nowhere long enough to be a car, especially not a hulking luxury model. The play of light and shadow made it look like a elongated, ebony box, decorated on one end with an abstract metal sculpture where the smashed grillwork caught the light.

He slowed, then stopped a couple of yards away.

Fracture-stars crazed across the front window, hiding the interior in a sheen of reflective silver lines. There was no light inside; no light outside, either. Both headlights were intact but dark.

Unconsciously, Officer Siegel fingered his holster. If the boy noticed the action, he said nothing, but he did step closer to the policeman—who in spite of all normal procedure did not order him away. Siegel was as relieved as the boy seemed to be by just having a human presence near. They approached the car.

From the passenger side, now facing the lanes of the Golden State, the damage seemed less serious. The side windows were unmarked, except for a single star surrounding a small hole in the front passenger window. But otherwise the glass was opaquely dark, reflecting the freeway lights. It was impossible to see anything inside.

Officer Siegel noted without realizing it that not a car had passed since he had arrived. The Golden State was deadly quiet, quieter than he could ever remember seeing it. Distantly, he heard a siren. Someone else responding to the original call, probably.

He stepped closer and flashed his light through the window.

The glass *was* blackly opaque. It hadn't been a trick of the light.

Something had coated the inside of the windows, something that absorbed the light.

He swallowed hard and touched the doorknob. It was icy cold. He pushed his thumb on the old-fashioned stud and jerked the door open, bringing the light up as he did so.

"My God," he breathed.

He turned to push the boy away, but the boy had already seen and was stumbling back along the edge of the tarmac. Suddenly he crawled up the embankment a few feet and knelt at the base of some dark bush. Siegel could hear the boy vomiting, again and again. The girl was running up toward him, yelling "Jeff! Jeff!" in a voice that seemed frail and terrified.

Siegel ran back to his patrol car to request backup.

This case was going to be ugly.

By that time, the second car had arrived, pulling in behind Siegel's just as he laid his head on arms braced across the night-cooled top of the patrol car. He breathed deeply, trying to forget the blood pooled everywhere inside the Caddy.

- 5 -

An hour later, most of the work was done. Traffic was back to normal. Witnesses had given preliminary statements, and an officer had escorted the two kids back to their car, then followed them home to assure presumably worried parents that their offspring were safe.

Too bad they had to get involved in something so brutal as this, Siegel thought. He wondered how long it would be before either of them drove out to the point on Miller Avenue at night—alone or together.

Zimmerman had finally gotten into his Volvo and headed home, angling slowly into the lane of traffic, his left-turn indicator blinking fervently, even though there was not a car in sight for the length of the freeway.

Half a dozen other officers had searched every off-ramp and access road for a mile around, had scoured the embankment, climbing up with flashlights to check behind shrubbery and brush.

Their reports were all frustratingly identical.

No one.

Which meant that if Zimmerman and the kids were to be believed—and for some reason, Siegel *did* believe them—no one had driven the black Cadillac.

There was no one in the car.

All three witnesses swore solemnly that no one had left the car; Zimmerman said that he hadn't turned away for a second, not even when he was talking on the call-box. And the boy, Jeff something, said that he had had the car in sight almost from the moment of the crash.

But there was no driver.

No blood on the tarmac around the car. No evidence of anyone climbing up over the embankment—except where the kids had come down, and they obviously hadn't passed anyone.

It was a puzzle.

But there was worse to come.

Griffin, from the coroner's office, finally arrived to take samples of the red stuff that had spattered over the interior of the windows, the seats, and dashboard.

"Not blood," he said, looking up when Siegel asked him what he had found out so far. "This is only tentative, of course. We'll have to check it out at the office. But this isn't blood. Something like it, close. But not blood."

Halterman, from Forensics, found evidence of a single slug, flattened against the Caddy's steel interior frame.

"Looks like it was fired from a moving vehicle pacing the Cadillac," Halterman said quietly in answer to Siegel's question. "But it...."

"What?"

"Nothing. It just doesn't look...right."

He began prying the slug away.

"Hey!" That was one of the other officers, a first-year rookie named Daly. Siegel knew him but not well. Siegel looked up.

"What's that gawdawful smell?" Daly yelled over the top of the Caddy.

It was funny that no one else had smelled it. Maybe the excitement, maybe the oily ozone smell that hung over the freeway like a mist. Maybe....

But once Daly mentioned it, everyone noticed. Siegel pulled the keys from the ignition and walked back to the trunk. There were only two keys on the ring, an anonymous metal ring like those found in every five-and-dime in the country. No evidence there.

As soon as he cracked the trunk lid, he knew that whatever was causing the smell was inside.

Swallowing hard and holding his breath, he raised the heavy lid.

"God!" This time it was Daly's turn to head for the bushes and fall to his knees. Siegel didn't even register the acrid smell of Daly's vomit; the stench from the Caddy overwhelmed everything else.

"What are they?" Siegel murmured, but he already knew, and when Griffin looked over his shoulder, the coroner's words were no surprise.

"Human," Griffin said, dislodging one of the bones with the end of a long, thin pencil. "Femur." He shifted another. "Humerus."

Leaning into the trunk, farther than Siegel's stomach would have allowed, Griffin found half a skull tucked behind the spare tire.

The bones were all gnawed, with rancid bits of human flesh hanging from the tendons.

And that was it.

There were no prints anywhere. No plates on the car. Serial numbers had been filed away, and the Cadillac was, ultimately, untraceable.

None of the witnesses could identify the Volkswagen, or its driver, other than vaguely. It was dark, not black but maybe blue or green or brown. A VW beetle. No idea what year. No idea about the plates, not even if they were from California.

Nothing.

An absolute dead end.

Just as Siegel was sliding into his patrol car, long after most of the others had left, Halterman walked up. He stood there, silent, staring across the freeway lanes.

"Find anything interesting?" Siegel asked. Halterman nodded before turning slowly to face Siegel. He took a small plastic envelope from one flap of his coat.

"This."

"Looks like a .38 slug to me."

"It is. But that's not what makes it interesting. They're not going to like this downtown." The last sentence was spoken almost too softly for Siegel to hear, as if it were a private afterthought Halterman really didn't want to share.

"Why?" Siegel felt bad about this one; Halterman had found something important, and there wasn't a scrap of evidence to point to a suspect.

Again there was an uncomfortable pause, as if Halterman wanted to say something more but didn't quite dare.

"Because," he began. He took a deep breath and shoved the plastic pouch back into his pocket. "Because it's another goddam silver bullet, that's why!"

CHAPTER FOUR

THE END OF THE GAME

- 1 -

It was after two in the morning when the battered Volkswagen rolled up the drive and crunched to a stop in front of the darkened windows of the house beyond the hill. The engine coughed, sputtered, and died before the driver could move to cut the ignition.

It was another hour before the driver's door squeaked open. A figure tumbled out, almost falling to the gravel before grabbing the car frame and forcing himself to stand upright. For a long while the figure leaned against the sagging door. Finally, he staggered toward the front door and disappeared into the waiting darkness.

* * * * * * *

A moon the size of the sun, blood-red, rimmed with silver. An eclipsed moon that stared down vacantly. Then it smiled, a slit like death that split its face with a thin band of blackness against the red and expanded hideously until it grew huge enough to swallow the Dreamer and his World. Still it grew, hunching closer and closer through the night, until the Dreamer could see the crater-blotches on its skin, celestial acne gone wild, miles deep and shadowed with deep maroon and purple.

And still it smiled at the Dreamer, hissing as it settled on his chest and placed its mouth against his and breathed in. It drew his air into its lungs, stripping his World of atmosphere. The Dreamer writhed, panted for breath where there was none.

Then it exhaled, a gentle hurricane of pent-up breath acrid, pungent and burning where it touched the skin and lungs of the Dreamer. He pulled it unwillingly into his lungs, screaming in-

wardly as it burned the tender tissues of his mouth and nose, screaming wordlessly as it seared his lungs, acidic, nauseating....

* * * * * * *

Sunlight touched Pac's face. The first harsh shafts of morning cut through the open window and crawled with a spider's terrifying patience along the doorjamb, down the wall with its peeling ducks-and-rifles wallpaper, and edged to the pillow before perching like a glowing bird of prey on his pallid forehead and cheek.

He groaned and turned, but it was too late, as always. He could pretend sleep, lay without movement for another hour or more, but the desperate fact remained. Suddenly and irrevocably, he was awake.

Pac kicked back the matted sheet. He threw his arm over his eyes as protection against the light and the heat. He lay naked on the bed. His thin, pale chest rose and fell, his flesh tented tautly over the uneven scaffolding of ribs and gut and jutting hipbones, but otherwise there was no movement. Then, as if surrendering to the inevitable, he sighed, a deep, painful release of breath that burned and tasted like sour vomit in the back of his throat. He dropped his arms and raised his head.

Pac surveyed his room, awake but still groggy. His head throbbed and his mouth felt dry and raspy. He blinked several times, as if trying to convince himself of the reality of what he saw, where he was...*who* he was.

That wasn't his real name, of course, *Pac*. God, no. Just what people called him, almost everybody except Ma and Richard Do-Good, *that goddam wimpy buttinski who wouldn't let half a continent keep him from meddling in Pac's life.*

He stood and stretched, long and hard, feeling as well as hearing joints creak and crack as he forced his arms back, back, far beyond the level of his shoulders. Sudden twinges of pain in his shoulders and back felt good, helped him wake up. He brought his arms down to his side and scratched himself. His rough nails left long red welts along his ribcage, startlingly red against the dead-fish pallor of his skin.

His toes pressed into the nubbled, worn woven carpet that hid the cold linoleum along the edge of the bed. He crossed the bedroom and walked into the dark hallway and across to the bathroom. Still scratching his ribs, he stood by the toilet. Its lid was open, its water secret, dark, stained and smelly from the day before...or maybe the day before that, he couldn't remember and didn't much care. Almost unconsciously, he let go, enjoying the warmth of his urine as it spurted out and disappeared into the darkness.

He left the bathroom without flushing. By now the acrid odor of urine and dissolving excrement had permeated the walls, the chipped and groutless tiles, even the torn plastic daffodil shower curtain that hung faded and mildewed by its three remaining rings, crushed against the far wall and not moved once since Pac had arrived six months before. The shower rod was spotted with patches of rust.

He padded back into the front room, a living room/kitchenette combination, with a chipped porcelain sink jutting out from one wall like a crazily angled tooth half-consumed by decay. On the other wall, a rock fireplace shed mortar every time Pac brushed against its loosened stones. In front of the fireplace hunched a broken-down sofa Pac had found outside a house on a secluded street in one of Tamarind's better neighborhoods (for that, read "more boringly predictable tracts"). It had been perched on the low curb, littered with black plastic garbage sacks already surrounded by swarms of fruit flies and assorted other aerial vermin. The sofa had been waiting patiently for the maw of a blue-and-white city garbage truck, until Pac came by early that morning, saw it, and—with more luck than skill—lashed it to the roof of the VW and managed to bring it back to the house. It was still the largest and best piece of furniture in the place.

A wobbly table leaned against one wall. Once perhaps a darkly handsome piece, it was now marred with stains and burns and cuts in its grey wood-grain Formica top. It supported a hot plate that was connected by a fraying extension cord to the single outlet in the kitchenette, half a dozen pieces of stained and bent mismatched tableware, a couple of chipped plates, and a cardboard box that served as Pac's cupboard and pantry.

His TV, VCR, and Atari crouched in one corner. They sat directly on cracked and rippled linoleum so old that even if he had wanted to Pac probably could not have identified its pattern. All three machines were connected to the same outlet with a worn octopus plug.

Above them his books lay helter-skelter on a single plank shelf. Most of the books were paperbacks, well-read, their spines cracked but stiffly black, seeming to absorb rather than reflect the morning sunlight.

The walls were hidden behind his collection of pictures and posters.

It was not a hell of a lot of house, but it was certainly enough for him. And the rent was right. He could work his few hours at the All-Nite-Delite, pay rent, buy a few books at the used bookstore three miles away, rent a couple of films at Bonanza Videos on dollar-days, and still have money left to Drive.

Naked but comfortable in the warmth of a Southern California summer morning, he slid a worn aluminum pot beneath the faucet and dribbled water into it before setting it on the hot plate. Coffee would be ready in a few minutes.

For a long time, he simply stared at the water in the pot, watching as the faint ripples died away and the fluid became so still he could see himself reflected in it. He glanced quickly away, crossed the room, dropped heavily onto the couch, and stared at the wall. He focused on a glint of light in one blood-red eye at the edge of a garishly colored film poster.

He sighed and shivered and tried to remember—or forget, he wasn't sure which—more about the Drive last night.

A mote on a spider's web of silvery sheening silk, sliding up and down the angles, uncontrolled and unrestrained. The fear was gone, the pain. Nothing left but energy and strength and impregnability. Silvery silk against the cruciform darkness.

- 2 -

This time, he had *done* it. He was sure of it. The shadow was finally, definitively *dead*.

The Drive had begun almost as usual. He didn't bother with the mud on the license plate but carefully gassed up the car. Then, as soon as he was on the freeway, he slipped the gun from between the seats and propped it between his legs, enjoying the slippery coolness that soon warmed and became part of his own body, enjoying the vibrations that blended with his own pulse.

He followed a different route than he had followed that last, disastrously terrifying time. Ventura Freeway to Las Virgenes Road, then to Pacific Coast Highway at Malibu (that haven of golden-fleshed surfers and beach-boppers), then south to the Santa Monica Freeway, and from there to the Golden State Interchange. He had left later than he had wanted (good ol' Cliffy needed some boxes moved), and there was a traffic tie-up on PCH and Sunset Boulevard, so it was almost midnight before he hit the Golden State. Later than he liked, but still plenty of time.

Five minutes later he saw it.

An old Caddy waddling along, looking as arthritic as its driver must be. It had to be twenty-five, thirty years old or more, finned and shiny. He could remember such cars from when he was a kid—and even then they had seemed anachronistic and excessive. But there was something more, something unnamable that drew him to the car.

A coffin the size of the moon, blood-black, rimmed with silver. It smiled, a slit like death that split its face with a thin band of light against the black and grew hideously until it could swallow the Driver. It grew, hunching close and closer, until the Driver could see crater-blotches on its skin, acne gone wild, miles deep and shadowed with deep maroon and purple. Paint peeled from fins like marlin spikes; red lights glittered in a necklace row.

He passed two or three other vehicles and pulled in behind the Caddy. With each movement, he felt the essential *rightness* of the choice in spite of the juddering tension that had begun to percolate through his veins. He licked his cracked lips and studied the fins and rear bumper just ahead. The car seemed more a shadow than a thing of steel and chrome and rubber. Pac felt a coldness flowing back from it, striking his face and hands like a winter storm from the Arctic.

The Caddy swerved slightly and sped up just enough to lengthen the distance between itself and the VW on its tail. Pac nudged the accelerator and closed the gap. The closer he got, the more he knew—*knew* in every bone and muscle and drop of blood—that the shadow had chosen that car tonight with the express intent that Pac search it out, find it, destroy it. It was as if the car had been made for him, built three decades before, maybe more, for the single purpose of serving as a target for his silver bullets.

Carefully, he drew alongside, flipping on the dome light—for no good reason other than that it seemed the right thing to do. He wanted the old duffer in the other car to *see* who was getting him

The crucifix shimmered.

He glanced over. At first the Caddy's windows seemed opaque, reflecting the light from his own car. Dimly, he heard the music blaring from his radio, something hard and fast and primitively, atavistically rhythmic that he did not recognize. It hurt his ears, and the hurt kept the shadows away. He heard wind whipping through his open passenger window, felt it hot and humid and laden with the oily smell of the freeway. He heard his heart thumping and the roar of the two cars as they sped in tandem along the nearly deserted lanes of the Golden State.

He reached between his legs, pulled up the gun and pointed it. And gently, oh so gently, squeezed. Like making love.

At the last instant, he glanced across the open space between the two cars. In the moment that the gun belched its smoke and fire and silver, the driver of the Caddy turned to glare at Pac.

Pac screamed. Once. Long and loud, the sound echoing through the VW and drowning the reverberations from the gun's single sharp report. His foot jammed down on the accelerator and the VW leaped forward, more like a grasshopper than a beetle, screeching along the concrete roadway.

* * * * * * *

When he came to his senses, he had already passed the 134 Freeway transition at the base of Griffith Park and the LA Zoo. To his right, the huge cross on top of the mausoleum at Forest Lawn glowed futilely against the encroaching stars.

The wind whipping through his open window was cooler now. It smelled of moisture from the water-rich grass of the zoo grounds, with faint suggestions of things wild and rank.

For a long while, until he was well past the interchange and following the Golden State into the Burbank/Glendale area, he drove numbly, as if on auto-pilot, changing lanes without noticing, staring straight ahead.

When he finally shuddered, blinked, and once more became aware of his surroundings, he was almost to the 118 cutoff just south of the mountains that separated the San Fernando Valley from the deserts surrounding the basin.

He signaled for a right-hand transition and slowed for the high looping overpass that brought him heading westward on the Simi Valley Freeway.

He was only thirty minutes from home, more or less. He tried not to think about what he had seen—the eyes glowing in the darkness of the Caddy's interior as the bullet shattered the window and grazed something that exploded in a flood of red that washed against the crazed glass.

And the blackened slit of the smile.

- 3 -

In the harsh light of morning, with the water for his instant coffee spitting and sputtering in the open pot across the room, the episode seemed less frightening.

In fact, he could not understand why he had reacted so badly.

He had killed the Shadow, hadn't he?

Wasn't that the point?

He heaved himself out of the sofa and crossed to the table that served as stove, work-counter, and eating surface. Caught up in his thoughts, he reached for the metal pot handle. Heat scorched his fingertips. He dropped the pot back onto the hot plate, cursing loudly and volubly as a few drops spattered against the unprotected skin of his thigh. Sucking on his burned fingertips, he wrapped the metal handle in a bit of filthy cloth that served as wash rag whenever he decided to clean his few dishes. He poured hot water into a marginally clean mug, then ladled in the crystals, stirring the liquid with the same spoon. The smell percolated through the room, but Pac drank it without savor, almost without noticing. It was hot and caffeinated. It would get him going. That was all he needed.

He left the rest of the water in the pan on the cooling hot plate. He absently switched the plate off. White rings inside the pot marked tide lines for other heated water on other mornings. He didn't care. He turned on the cold water tap and caught a handful of water and splashed it on the reddened places on his thigh. The water was icy enough to numb the sharp pain.

He was about to sit down and finish drinking his coffee when a sound reached him. The crunch of tires on the gravel driveway. A car.

He went to the window and pulled back the tattered curtain. A single car, not new, not old. Comfortably and anonymously nondescript. Someone coming to see him.

He stared, his mind not yet working well enough to accept that datum. The pain in his fingertips and his leg settled to a dull throb.

No one—*no one*—ever came to see him. Not since he left St. Louis two years before and began his wanderings. Richard wrote once a month. He used to call, but since the last move, Pac had carefully neglected to install a telephone, so the creep had to depend on the U.S. mails. Sometimes, just for the hell of it, Pac wrote an answer, off the wall, jarring, to shake the old boy up. But good ol' dependable Richard Do-Good took it all in stride, and the next letter would be full of boring news from the home front (*Mom's not at all well. The doctors only give her two or three months. She wants to see you*) and irritating questions about Pac's life in Wyoming or New Mexico or California.

Maybe next time, he decided, there wouldn't be a forwarding address. Wouldn't that floor old Mr. Big-Nose. Help keep death away. But in the meantime, he shook his head to clear his thoughts.

He stared out the window again. This was real. There was a car outside.

He watched for a few seconds before dropping the edge of the curtain and scurrying into his bedroom to pull on a pair of nylon gym shorts, once yellow but now faded and stained to a dirty brown. He slid his feet into vinyl thongs.

He emerged into the living room just in time to hear the knock on the door.

Once. Twice. Three times.

A pause.

Once. Twice. Three times.

There was something familiar about the rhythm. He had heard it before.

Without stopping to think when or where, he hurried to the door and flung it open.

"Hey, man, how's it goin'?"

Pac stared.

"That's it? Just an idiot stare? After all this time?"

Pac stepped back and motioned awkwardly for the figure to enter.

"Hammer?" he asked tentatively as the other man crossed into the living room.

"Who else? How's it hangin', man?"

"Hammer!" Pac yelped, his face suddenly animated and alive. For an instant, an objective observer might have seen some faint traces of a pretty baby, a cute child, a handsome youth, submerged beneath self-constructed, self-imposed alienation and isolation. Then Pac was moving, as if to grab the stranger and hug him and spin him wildly in the center of the room. But the other man stepped back slightly, and Pac's face betrayed an instant of doubt flecked by deeper, darker emotions. Hammer flashed a smile that lit the room, and Pac himself stood back a step or two. The flash of darkness disappeared almost as quickly as it had appeared as, with a broad, silly grin that seemed too vital for the squalid room he had lived in for so long, Pac studied his friend.

Hammer hadn't changed a bit. That was God's own truth. Not a bit in two years. Still the same off-brown hair cut exactly the same length as the last time Pac had seen him, striding off toward the St. Louis central bus depot. Wide-set eyes that saw right through you, sometimes cutting as they did so. Angular jaw that slipped in an instant from smile to scowl that could chill at fifty feet—not that he had ever used it on Pac, at least not much. Not unless Pac deserved it. Still the same lanky frame, all legs and arms, wide shoulders, narrow waist.

"Hammer!" Pac repeated, pleased when the other man responded with a ready smile. "Whatcha doin' here?"

Hammer laughed. "Wearing my feet out waiting for you to ask me to sit down."

"Hey, man, this is home. Help yourself. You know that"

Hammer walked once around the small room, slowly, taking in the details. For the first time since he had moved in, Pac allowed the tawdriness to sink into his consciousness. He sniffed as Hammer sniffed, aware all at once of the fetid odor from the bathroom.

"Minute," he mumbled lamely as he hurried into the hallway and reached inside the bathroom and flushed the toilet. The water gurgled, as it always did, its normal preliminary to three or four minutes of growling before it finally quieted down.

"Wasn't expecting anyone," Pac said as if in apology as he re-entered the living room. He was suddenly equally aware of his own shaggy, oily hair, shoulder-length and matted from sleep...of his bare chest and filthy shorts and five-day growth of beard. For the briefest instant, he found himself wishing that Hammer hadn't come...at least not right now.

"No?" Hammer answered. He lifted his eyebrows and cocked his head in the way Pac remembered so well. Everything about his body said that he was surprised by Pac's comment, but Pac knew him well enough to understand the cynicism that might lay just beneath such appearances. He shook his head.

"Naw. You know how it is. Out here alone."

"All alone. Yes," Hammer said slowly. "I do."

"Uh, whaddya think?" Pac gestured helplessly toward the room. He suddenly felt like a little kid again, trying to impress a favorite teacher, or an older boy whose good graces seemed especially important at the time.

"Interesting." Hammer crossed to the interior wall, the one covered from baseboard to ceiling with posters, reproductions of stills from *Dracula, Wolfman, An American Werewolf in London,* Carpenter's *The Thing, Tremors,* half a dozen Stephen King flicks, and more.

"Still into creature-features, I see."

"Sure," Pac said simply. "Why not?"

Hammer didn't answer. He walked to the far corner and stood over the VCR, TV, and Atari. His shoulder was next to Pac's shelf of books—black-spined paperbacks, mostly, with imprints from TOR, Signet, Bantam, Zebra, houses that carried horror lines.

Hammer knelt by the electronics equipment.

"No games?" he asked after a short silence.

"A few. In the closet." Pac gestured toward the hall with a quick jerk of his head. "Don't play much anymore. Now I like to Dri.... I got other things now," Pac finished lamely.

Unaccountably, he realized that he didn't want to talk about Driving with Hammer—with his closest buddy from back home, the stud that he used to be able to tell anything to, even about the time he had tried to lay Tiffany Anne and she was willing as hell but he couldn't get it up and Hammer hadn't laughed or nothin', just said "Happens to the best of us sometimes" and made Pac feel like he was a man anyway. He could tell Hammer *anything.*

But he didn't want to now. Not this time.

"Not even Pac-Man?" Hammer said, breaking the silence. Pac stared at him for a moment, trying to break from his memories back to the present, to what Hammer had just asked.

For a moment, image and memory overlapped, then things snapped back into place.

Pac grinned again, that same silly grin that so seemed out of place on his pale, angular face—the face of a man who hadn't eaten well in weeks, or slept well in months. The face of a man who knew fear intimately.

"Haven't played that one in a long time. Not since St. Louis. Prob'ly no good at it anymore." He flexed his fingers. "Gettin' old."

Hammer nodded, straightened, and trailed his finger over Pac's books.

"Good collection."

He studied the titles spidering up each spine. King was there, of course: *Salem's Lot, The Stand* (both versions in hardcover), *Christine, Pet Sematary, It, The Dark Half, Insomnia.* Koontz's *Twilight Eyes, The Bad Place, Lightning.* Straub's *Ghost Story, If You Could See Me Now*, and a tattered copy of the Corgi *Full Circle.* Wilson's *The Keep.* Strieber's best stuff, *The Hunger* and *The Wolfen,* but none of the later things, the disappointing ones where he got monsters mixed up with reality, not even *Communion.* Maybe four, five dozen others, all dealing with vampires, werewolves, horror creatures in every shape and form.

Hammer ran his fingertips along the spines. He paused at one, Simmons' *Carrion Comfort.* For a moment it looked like he would take it off the shelf, but he let it drop back. With an odd smile, he muttered, "Close, but no cigar." Pac started to ask Hammer what he meant by that, but at the last instant felt his jaws snap shut on the words.

Hammer reached to the shelf again and pulled *It* out with one finger. He hefted the thick paperback in his hand, as if weighing its mass.

"King's pretty good. Beautiful transmutations of classic horror motifs."

"Yeah. I got some of his other stuff in the bedroom. In the closet." Suddenly Pac felt ill-at-ease. Something was...well, if not downright wrong, then certainly not exactly right. Hammer never talked like that. Hammer probably didn't even know what a book was for, except to keep the door open on a hot evening so the breeze could swirl around his apartment while they sat around in ragged cutoffs and nothing else and rapped and killed one cold beer after another.

"Pretty good," Hammer repeated approvingly. "He almost got it right in this one. The monster taking the shape of the thing each kid fears the most. Scary stuff."

"Yeah." Again, Pac felt the wrongness. He shivered even though the room was hotter now than it had been before. The sun was full up and beating down on the unprotected tile roof and the air inside was growing thicker and staler and more stifling....

Hammer continued as if Pac had not interrupted.

"Almost right, but not quite. That spider bit, the monster-spider-from-outer-space, that was too much. Too bad he didn't leave well enough alone, just let the Fear work instead of importing all that *Tulpa* garbage, the *Loup-Garou* stuff. That was too much. Laughable, really, if you look at it from the right perspective."

Pac backed away slowly until he felt the splintered edge of the table digging into his legs. Remnant heat from the water on the hot plate steamed through his cutoffs.

"Who...who are you?"

Hammer turned at the question. The novel hung limply from one hand. He opened his fingers, and the black-bound book dropped. heavily to the floor. *Thud.* It lay there, open, one page fluttering back and forth in the slight breeze that came through the open windows. Back and forth, back and forth, a ghostly whisper.

Pac heard the muted gurgle of the toilet as it still struggled to swallow his refuse.

Hammer smiled.

"I'm you," he said simply, shrugging and holding his hands out as if to embrace Pac even though the width of the room separated them.

"What the hell! Who are you? What do you want? Get out of here!" Pac spat the phrases out pell-mell, heedless of any logic or illogic. He started to sweat. Beads formed across his upper lip and down the small of his back. Salty drops angled coldly down his sides from armpits suddenly damp and musty and spicy with his own effluvia.

Hammer did not answer, but turned his attention back to the book shelf. He twisted his head as if to read the remaining titles more clearly. Sunlight outlined his forehead and the high ridge of his cheekbone. From that angle, Pac realized that Hammer *had* changed. There was something...odd...about the shape of his head, the color of his hair, too dark, too ashen-black for Hammer, bleached-blond Hammer who spent every waking hour during the summer stretched out in the sun on a mat behind the splintered wooden porch, as if staid, dry old St. Louis were the tan-heaven of the universe.

Behind him, in the bathroom, he could still hear the gurgling of the toilet bowl as it washed away two day's accumulation of his wastes.

"You heard me," he said, startled at the anxious quaver in his own voice. "Get the hell out of here!"

Hammer turned.

Only it wasn't Hammer.

It wasn't anyone Pac knew. The general shape of the face was the same as Hammer's, the wide-set eyes, the heavy jaw. But now there was more, an amalgam of faces he had seen...in nightmares, on black-inked horror dust-jackets, in creature-comics, on reflective silver screens hung in front of terror-rapt audiences of teenyboppers, himself included.

Dracula's eyes, with the absurd reverse-raccoon shadows that might have worked for a 1930s' theater audience but that came across as silly when Pac watched the film on his VCR.

Hints of Frankenstein's monster's neck-bolts that might just have been a trick of the light and shadow through Hammer's long black hair...or something else.

His knuckles were knotted, swollen, darkly and thickly pelted. The nails were long and sharp and frightening.

"Hey," Pac began, then faltered as Hammer—or whoever, *whatever* he was—moved nearer, almost gliding. He...*it*...stopped midway across the room.

"I'm...an old friend, Pac. You've known me for years, since you were a kid watching to those old films on television late at night, sneaking into the horror movies when your mother thought you were with Richard watching *Star Wars* or *ET* or re-runs of Disney's mindless pap.

"Back then, of course, you didn't know me as well as you do now. You didn't keep me hanging on your walls, on the shelves, swirling into and around and through the expanse of your existence like a perennial mist. I existed only in a tiny part of your brain, where you could open and close the door, shut me out at will.

"Then you moved away. To be on your own. And you surrounded yourself with my icons. With me."

He gestured toward the poster-studded wall. He walked back to the bookshelf and kicked negligently at the VCR on the floor. Pac winced when a dent winked in the aluminum casing.

"Bet you watch them here, too. Images of fear and terror and pain and death. Huh?"

"Yeah," Pac answered, in spite of himself. "Look, who...?"

"Shut up."

This time the voice was not Hammer's. It was Lugosi's, heavy with exotic terror. Vincent Price's, hissing threats. Langella's, erotic and husky. Goldblum's, enervated by ironic comedy and despair. "I would have left you alone. I would have ignored you. *But you came after me.*" The hideous voice enunciated each word, cutting at consonants, lingering on the final vowel until the sound was less than a hiss, more than a whisper.

Pac's jaw dropped. Blood thudded through his temples.

"I...what...when....," Pac began.

Then he knew.

He knew when the Hammer-thing turned its head to face him, the cheekbones highlighted by the sunlight through the windows. Knew when it smiled.

"I was just passing through, as it were," it said quietly. "Minding my own business, really. Working my way west. 'Go west, young man, go west.' New England has been frighteningly overused recently, picked over, as it were." It smiled mockingly. "And there is so much, uh, fresh blood, so to speak, out here. I knew you were here, just as I know where each of them is, each of my followers, devotees of fear.

"But last night, you took the initiative. You followed me, you chased me, you fired...."

"I didn't!" Pac screamed. "I don't know what the hell you're talking about but I...."

"You killed me!" the Hammer-thing roared, its face flickering from one visage to another so quickly, so abruptly that Pac felt dizzy and nauseated. The small room seemed to quiver with the intensity of his rage. *"You shot me and you* killed *me!"*

It stopped, breathed deeply, recovering control. The face settled again into Hammer's. Then the voice—Hammer's also—continued.

"That is, to be precise, you killed the form I had chosen to take, my *incorporation.* There is so much fear out here, disguised beneath a superficial layering of laid-back mellowness, but it's here, simmering beneath the surface. It takes so little to bring it to a boil. It is so easy to enflesh myself here."

Enflesh.

Pac memory caught on the word and, in spite of his suddenly frantic efforts *not* to remember, flickered back to the last night at Hammer's place. Part of him struggled to listen to the Hammer-thing; part of him struggled even harder to close his eyes and his ears and shut himself off from what was happening. *It's a bad dream I'll wake up any minute now in my own bed and ma'll be knocking at my door to rouse me for breakfast and....*

"A harmless old man," it continued abstractedly, as if Pac were not even in the room. "What more innocent a cover could you imagine? And driving an old car that nobody could possibly want to steal. Even in East LA."

It stepped forward, smiling more broadly. "You see, Pac—Donney—my old friend, I am Fear. I am what you make of me. What each person makes of me. Most shudder and writhe and turn away. Most know me only occasionally, marginally.

"But you chose to focus on me. You diverted me into your life."

In the bathroom, the gurgling sound changed, deepened. Pac tore his attention away from the Hammer-thing long enough to risk a glance over his shoulder toward the closed doorway. He was not surprised to see liquid, dark and turgid and rank, seeping through the crack.

He smelled it, too, the overpoweringly cloying fetidness of decaying waste.

"I," he began, then stopped, not knowing what to say.

"You see," the thing continued undisturbed. "I don't really need a spider-from-space, or shape-shifters, or werewolves—although each of them has proved helpful in the past. I can simply form myself on what you want most to see.

"On what you fear most.

"On what you *want* most.

"On what will scare you to death."

Hot evening breeze barely moving through a hot humid summer night made only marginally bearable by cold beer and the darkness, the darkness. Sweaty flesh, pounding drunken blood, a voice that sounded slurred and whining and childish, even to himself, as he murmured forbidden words and remembered—hot, searing pain of admission that scarred his cheeks with red and choked his voice—*as he revealed his embarrassment, his humiliation with, his impotence with her. Then Hammer's voice, soothing, calming, reassuring, seductive. A hand on his shoulder, a hand on his thigh, higher, higher, touching him, touching him, touching him! Hammer whispering. Hammer assuring. Hammer touching again. Again. Hammer!*—

Hammer lunging forward.

Pac screamed. In that final moment, Hammer shifted through a thousand shapes, a special-effects encyclopedia gone berserk.

Pac stumbled backward, then threw himself sideways with such force that he shattered his collarbone when he slipped on something fetid and cold and spun out of control and struck the protruding edge of the sink. For an instant there was a welcome darkness, then the red wash of pain, the blur of vision returning...and Hammer.

It was Hammer again, lean and smooth and smiling. He bent at the waist and extended his hand to Pac, offering comfort and warmth and love.

Pac reached out with his good hand. The movement shifted his body weight. Broken bone scraped against broken bone and torn tissue and agonized nerve endings. He nearly passed out, but did not. Hammer smiled.

Pac's fingers trembled. There was something he should know, something he was forgetting, but the pain, the pain....

"Let me help you," Hammer whispered, bending lower and bringing his hand closer to Pac's.

Yes—no—yes!

Pac gritted his teeth against pain and the hovering shadow of unconsciousness and the brittle awareness of death, and stretched his fingertips until they brushed against Hammer's.

Nothing!

His hand passed through Hammer's as if flesh had suddenly become dusky air.

And Hammer disappeared, finally and irrevocably. Kaleidoscopic and horrifying, he surrounded Pac in a shadow-darkness that was neither tactile nor material but that stifled and crushed and destroyed..

Pac screamed, knowing as he heard the sounds and felt the rush of air ripping at the inside of his throat that the house was too far away, cut off from the main part of Tamarind. No one could hear him, just as he had heard no one during all the months he had lived there.

The darkness coalesced around him, a second womb.

In his last seconds of his life, he felt coldness against his toes and smelled the stench of his own bowels regurgitated from the toilet.

Warmth on his legs, trickling down. Like meeting like. And then Pac knew a deeper darkness.

Where there was no more fear.

CHAPTER FIVE

THE JILTING

- 1 -

She was not that old—barely past her mid-fifties. But with her cheekbones jutting through gaunt flesh, her hair coarse and roughly white, the skin around her mouth drawn taut with pain, she looked closer to eighty.

Richard looked down at her. *This isn't my mother,* part of him whispered silently, sullenly. *She isn't here any more.* He didn't like such thoughts, but in spite of himself, he was forced to regard Emma through an increasingly frightening mixture of love and distaste and regret and guilt that had been building in him for weeks. His nose wrinkled in spite of his determination not to notice the stale odor of urine and talc and medications and inexpensive perfume.

He hated being with her, especially here in this room, hated it more than anything he had ever experienced in his life; but he hated worse the thought of trying to stay away.

He leaned over the side of the bed and held his mouth close to her ear . He rested his hand lightly, as gently as possible, on the husk that had once been her arm. The skin seemed several sizes too large for the brittle bones it encompassed. There was no sense of muscle or of tissue between his fingers and her fragile core. He could feel blood moving sluggishly through blood vessels now far too close to the surface of her skin—just as she herself was far too close to the surface of her life. With each breath, she approached the interface where life broke through into...something else.

"How's it today, Mom?" His voice was pitched low, but he tried to keep it as near normal as possible. Emma had always disliked people who resorted to a quasi-religious pseudo-sincere tone in the presence of near-death. Now that she was the patient, she appreciated her visitors' honesty more than their self-pity. Not that there were that many visitors.

"Fine." He had to strain to hear the single syllable; he could only guess at how much it cost her to speak. Her skin paled even more, but she took a deep breath and struggled to continue. "Really. Much better."

He had to bend closer to understand her. Her breath was frightful, rancid-smelling, like a pat of butter after a month in a too-warm refrigerator.

That was her. Spoiled. Rotting from the inside out. Gone bad before her time, he thought, then cursed himself for the innate frivolity.

"I'm glad," was all that he could manage to say.

- 2 -

She had never been a beauty, not even as a young woman. Her strength lay in forceful character and firm resolve rather than in the simpering superficial loveliness men of her generation seemed to find most attractive in young women. Emma had decided simply not to change or to compete. She took life on its own terms and had reconciled herself to it long before most of her school friends were wed and mothers. Yet in spite her parents' dire warnings and constant haranguing, Emma had managed to find and love and marry a comfortable and companionable soul—Richard's father. Roland Mann had loved her—and she, him—with a quiet, passionate intensity that lingered still in the looks she cast at the framed picture propped on the end table next to her bed. In the picture, Emma and Roland stood next to each other beneath the elms that stood sentinel at the front gate of the old farm house where she was raised. Their arms were linked, their faces creased by unfeigned smile. They were happy. They had been happy for five years, before cancer took him.

Now it was eating away at her. Two years ago she had had much to look forward to. Even a year ago, there was still something—Richard and Bonnie and their hopes for her first grandchild.

Now, nothing.

She shifted her head marginally, so that she could no longer see the photograph. The movement cost her dearly, depleting her dwindling stores of energy. But she could not bear to look and think and remember.

Her hands lay crossed on her lap, the skin jaundiced looking against the crisp, newly washed pastel sheets. With her head propped up on several pillows she could see her hands, withered remnants that seemed more like artifacts from a pharaoh's desiccated mummy than living hands. They were not hers, couldn't be hers. Not even if they were connected to the rail-thin arms that protruded from her dressing jacket. She closed her eyes against an unwanted tear. *They were not her hands.*

Taking a deep breath, she forced herself to open her eyes again and look.

This is death, and it will come. You can't hide from it.

She began her daily inventory again.

Her nails—her best feature, really, since they had always been long and smooth and well-cared for, even during the interminable years of rinsing diapers in cracked toilet bowls and washing dishes three times a day—her nails were still long, but now they were yellowed and brittle, ridged and curling at the ends. With her bony hands clasped over each other, her fingers and nails suggested an animal's claws and talons.

Her skin was stretched taut over bones that seemed too large for her body. She could see the long bones in her hands, the knots of bone at her wrists, impossibly large and looming. But in reality, or course, her body had shrunk to fit them, then shrunk further, like someone on a diet that has gone out of control, like that man in that book Donney told her about that time, just before he left.

Donney.

Again, she closed her eyes against tears. She preferred to think about the cancer. That pain was at least bearable.

Day by day, she became less, her cancer became more, until now there was more cancer than Emma.

She knew it.

Richard knew it.

Mercifully, they had passed beyond the stage of pretending with each other.

Now he was standing by her bed. She wondered vaguely how he had managed to enter the room so quietly; she had not noticed him come in at all. But there he was. She reached out one claw and rested it lightly on his wrist, letting the fingers curl around the muscle and bone of his arm almost of their own volition. The warmth beneath his flesh burned her palm.

He said something. She didn't understand the words, but she easily understood their meaning.

"Yes," she managed to say. "Much better." It was a lie.

Both of them knew that, too.

Bonnie knew as well. Emma could not see her but knew that she would be sitting stiffly in the armchair beneath the dormer window

73

in the front room, her fingers running nervously over the hand-embroidered antimacassars that had come to Emma on her wedding day from Grandma Ottley. Round and round they would run, following the curves of the multi-colored peacocks perched gaily on the arms of the worn maroon chair, round and round, as if in doing so they could deny the stillness in the next room. Bonnie always did that when she was nervous. Emma thought she might giggle at the memory, then decided that the giggle would probably come out wrong and Richard would worry. Instead, she lay motionless.

Bonnie was all right, Emma supposed. At first, Emma had hoped Richard would find a girl with more spunk, more life, someone to prod him into becoming the man he might be. But, after all was said, Bonnie was all right. More than all right. And she'd been there when Emma needed her most, helping out in the kitchen after Doc Smith had broken the bad news. Then she had begun to help Emma dress and go to the bathroom when such common chores became too much for her. Even now, she faithfully changed the sheets and bedding every second day and emptied the bedpan when it needed it.

Yes, Bonnie was all right. More than all right.

In her imagination, Emma saw Bonnie's thin, graceful fingers following patterns around and around and around the crocheted figures. Standing next to Emma, his hand on hers, Richard was making a faint hissing noise. Soon, now Bonnie could relax. It would be over soon. Emma smiled to herself.

And closed her eyes.

- 3 -

Watching her, Richard felt the bitterness of fear backing up against his throat. It was a hot, vile bitterness like vomit that he wished desperately he could void but that merely lay there, turgid water rasping against a concrete dam.

Donney.

Dad had died. Emma was dying. And Richard was helpless. She wanted only one thing, and he was helpless to get it for her.

He stood beside her bed for a full five minutes, watching her chest rise and fall so faintly that the quilt barely moved. Once she had been a full-bosomed woman; now she was as flat as the drug addicts whose obsessions had denied their bodies of nutriments until the flesh began to consume itself—*consumed by that which it was nourished by.* He had read that somewhere, sometime, back when life was bright and clean.

He stared at his mother. Her outline could have been that of an adolescent boy, or a young girl before she began to bloom. But it was no longer Emma.

When he was sure she was asleep, he left the room. He swung the door almost closed, leaving an inch-wide crack, just in case. He left the light on, the sweetly pink light that fell from a twenty-five-watt bulb inside the mock-crystal and brass wall lamp he and Donney had pooled their money to buy for her fiftieth birthday party. It did little to push back the shadows that crowded in the corners of the room, but Emma had always liked the way the light brought out the roses in the wallpaper.

Bonnie was sitting in the overstuffed chair when he entered the living room. She was staring blankly out the window at the bleak mid-afternoon August sun.

"How is she?" she asked, already knowing from the look on his face that the question was worse than useless.

He shrugged. What could he say? *She'll be dead in a week, a day, an hour. She's fine, just dying.*

Maybe he should cry and get it over with. But he couldn't cry.

He slumped into the sofa and put his feet up on the coffee table. Not too long ago, if he had done that, a soft voice would have echoed from whatever room Mom was in: "Dickie, watch the furniture." He would have sworn in a court of law on a stack of Bibles head high that she didn't even need to see him do it; with infallible maternal radar, she just *knew* when the feet swung up and onto the polished mahogany that was at least a generation older than he was. And it didn't even matter if he was wearing sneakers or thongs or thick white athletic socks stained with dirt around the ankles and on the heels.

Dickie, watch the furniture.

Dickie.

Donney.

Silly names.

He missed them.

The realization hit him like a hot poker, somewhere below his heart. It was almost a physical pain that caught his breath and held it and threatened to choke him.

He straightened, swinging his feet back down to the floor. He hunched over the table, searching with one outstretched finger for the faint line that marked the place he had so carefully filled in with stain and varnish while Mom was out visiting one hot July afternoon years before. The place where Donney scratched it with the penknife that had been Dad's before Mom gave it to Richard and that, up until that moment (Richard had believed), had rested carefully nestled beneath the crisply folded clean handkerchiefs in Richard's middle drawer.

The scratch had worn so much over the intervening years that Richard could only find it from memory, not from sight or feel.

Bonnie was watching him intently, he knew, trying to judge his mood, trying to tell how best to help. But her parents were still alive; for that matter, so were all four of her grandparents. There hadn't been a death in her family for...it had to be nearly twenty-five years now, more years than she had been alive.

She was looking vacantly around the room. For an instant, he envied her for her parents' sake.

Richard's father was dead. He had died so long ago that his memory was only a fragile, evanescent ghost, bit it still tainted every breath Richard took. And now his mother, dying. And his brother, as good as dead. Better off dead than living the kind of life he was heading for. Out of the corner of his eye, he watched Bonnie. The house probably *reeked* of death to her.

"That's not fair," Richard said suddenly, first standing, then pacing along the border of faded roses along the long edge of the carpet.

"What?" Bonnie looked at him, startled.

"What you were thinking."

"What I was...I was...." She flushed and looked at the floor.

"You were thinking about Donney, weren't you." He forced his voice into a gentleness he didn't, couldn't feel.

"Yes."

Simple, honest. Richard knew that they had always been honest with each other. He treasured that knowledge. In part, that had given them the strength to weather this new crisis. Donney had simply walked out one night, only weeks into their marriage.

"I could tell," he said. "You get a look. Like something's rotten in the refrigerator but you just can't place what."

"That's not fair, Richard. I try, I really do. But if he had any decency, if he had any love or compassion for that woman dying in there, he'd...."

"He'd what? Crawl home? Play the loving son? The prodigal? Shit, I don't even know for sure where he is or that he knows she's dying. Or that he would care if he did. It's been months since he wrote last, more than just a nasty line or two on a cheap postcard, and two years since anyone has seen him. If it weren't for those postcards Ma made me tuck in the mirror frame in there, I wouldn't even want to bet that he was still alive."

"Okay, so he had to go off and be his own man. But that doesn't excuse...."

"I know it doesn't," Richard said, his voice crumpling. He sat next to her on the edge of the armchair, almost crying with relief at the solid touch of her shoulder against his chest. He held her tight. "I know it doesn't, but it helps."

They sat together, quietly, holding each other, waiting for her to wake up and call out to them.

- 4 -

—ants crawling up her arm stinging her sugar ants grease ants what uncle john used to call pissants but only when gramma wasn't in the room or she'd whack him with the side of her hand no cursing in this kitchen john ottley i won't listen to such language and you know it—

Vaguely, something told her that it wasn't ants. The ants, they came from something she had read, some story out of that long-ago time before Dickie and Donney, even before Roland, when she taught high school English, trying to instill a love of books and words and language into boys whose primary concern was getting into some girl's pants, and girls whose concerns were primarily reciprocal.

What was it? Ants. Sugar ants. Stinging.

She sighed, a sound so faint that even had Richard or Bonnie been standing in the room, leaning over her bedside, they would not have heard it.

That missing piece of her past would come to her eventually. No need to worry about it now.

Maybe she should rouse a bit, though, call out, let the children know that she was still there.

Maybe not.

She drifted again.

—ants crawling up her arm stinging her sugar ants grease ants what uncle john used to say before he died that Donney was the best of them all the time he would say that even in front of Richard and she told the old man to shut up or he would breed trouble but he wouldn't

best of them all Donney was—

She startled awake to a sudden tightness in her throat, a burning in her breast. She desperately needed to cry, but there were no tears left. Most of them had wasted away, along with her arms and legs and breasts. All she could afford now was the faintest hint of moisture at the corner of her eye.

Now that she was awake, she wanted to close her eyes and go back to sleep, but the skin felt tight and tingly where it pulled across her cheeks. Closing her eyes would take more effort than she could afford.

There wasn't much of her left, but now she focused everything there was.

Donney. Donney! I need you!

She waited. If stilling her heartbeat would have made her cry more audible, she would have willed it to stop that instant.

Nothing happened.

She tried again.

- 5 -

Half a continent away, it stirred. Someone called.
It would answer.

- 6 -

Anyone watching from the crack at the doorway would have thought—wondered? hoped?—that the old woman was finally gone, finally released. Her breathing, for hours now marginal at best, had virtually ceased. Only a thin fluttering around the half-open eyes, the dilation of dark irises as the room seemed to fade, would have assured watchers that she was still alive.

She waited.

Nothing.

She tried a third time.

Donney!

It was an ancient, anguished, soundless cry—mother-love calling to the prodigal.

And he came.

She almost choked when she saw the door slanting open. She couldn't turn her head, not even far enough to see the photograph of Roland on the nightstand, so she had to wait for him to enter the room. But it was him! She knew it was him! She could *feel* him coming through her cancer-rotted bones, through nerves strained until they emitted a constant hiss of pain. Even through all of that, she knew it was him.

Donney!

Ma.

I knew you would come.

Hey, how could I miss? My best girl, you know. Heard you were cooking stew tonight. Never could get enough of that stew.

He laughed.

She laughed.

He crossed to the foot of her bed and stood there, six feet and miles away. She wanted him closer, next to her, where he could touch her arm, her shoulder, her cheek the way he would when he was little and frightened of the dark or of a too-close thunder storm.

She tried to tell him to come nearer, but the words wouldn't come out. Her lips were dry and her mouth could not move enough to form sounds.

He stood there and smiled.

My, he looked good. But then she had known that he would. He had been too thin when he left, rail thin, sickly thin and pale, with a bony chest that made those hideous black T-shirts look like death-canvas hung over the spars of old-time sailing ships, like the one in the picture still hanging over the head of his bed. Those friends of his—she snorted contemptuously and shook her head, unaware that she had made neither sound nor movement that would have been noticeable to any observers—those *friends* of his, all the time drinking and smoking and snatching a greasy hamburger every now and again. And him, never coming home for meals any more. It worried her. She was afraid, back then, that he would never get his true man's growth.

But he had filled out, just the way she hoped he would. He stood taller than Richard by half a head. Broader of shoulder and arm. Muscular, even. More like his father than her. Like Roland. Even stronger than Roland.

She smiled.

He smiled.

Where....

But she didn't have to finish. He knew. He always knew how to answer her questions. When he chose to.

Here and there. Wyoming. New Mexico. California last.

She smiled. In her mind she nodded, but on the bed, her neck refused to move.

Did you like it there?

It was okay. He shrugged noncommittally. *Not like home, though. Not like here.*

That was right, too, just what he would have said.

- 7 -

A disturbance roiled against it, making it shimmer in the light and twisting it cruelly out of focus. It retreated...but only temporarily, only for a moment, to re-group its strength.

- 8 -

He touched his index finger to his lips and slid into the shadows.

Don't say anything.

As if she would.

The door that had been flung wide an instant before now opened to let in a crack of yellow-white light, just enough for Richard to put his head through and watch her.

"Mom?" he whispered, as if afraid to speak too loudly in case she was resting. But he was not afraid to check on her.

There was a small catch in her breathing. The hand-pieced quilt that covered her—her favorite, the indigo and emerald Drunkard's Path that the pink-toned light bulb unfortunately made bilious and sickly—trembled. Richard straightened and disappeared, swinging the door gently shut again.

He came out of the shadows.

That was good, Ma. Ya done dam' good.

Donney. You know I don't like it when you talk like that.

He laughed. The sound echoed from the walls of her small room, the room that had been sanctuary and prison for so long now.

Yeah. I know. It usta drive ya crazy.

She wanted to shake her head. She didn't want him to talk about then. She only wanted to talk about *now*. What was he doing? How was he doing?

And when was he coming home?

Never.

She stared.

You heard me. Never.

She strained. The light was dimming—that had to be it. He couldn't be changing, not her Donney, not the golden-haired little boy who was born after his father had already died and had come from heaven to comfort her, to make life—*death*—bearable. Richard tried, yes, God bless him, but it had always been Donney, Donney, Donney for her.

He smiled.

She winced.

It was not a pleasant smile; a trick of the light, a cast of shadow that made the teeth seem dark and uneven and broken. He had beautiful, straight teeth, she had seen to that even though visiting the dentist had made him nervous and fretful and once almost hysterical. But he had had straight, strong teeth when he grew up.

He leaned over the foot of the bed frame, close, closer, as if either he were stretching or she were diminishing.

I'm outta here, man. For good!

No!

Those had been the last words, flung back in anger through the open screen door as he stalked away following a flair-up that neither she nor Richard had ever fully understood. He had gone to see that friend of his, that unbearable lazy good-for-nothing....

Hammer, he supplied.

Hammer, she repeated.

He smiled.

- 9 -

"Are you sure she's all right?" Bonnie asked tensely. "I thought I heard something in there. Is she choking?"

Richard listened. The house was silent except for the muted ticking of Grandma Ottley's pendulum clock on the mantle, the fragmentary cracking of an old wood-frame house still settling after half a century, his own breathing, and Bonnie's. He could hear nothing from the bedroom.

"I swear, I can hear something." She started to get up.

Richard held her arm and stopped her.

"It's okay. I'll check again."

He crossed the room.

Sometimes he admired his mother's decision not to treat the cancer with chemotherapy, to stay in her own home, to die in her own bed instead of in some sterile stiffly white-sheeted hospital bed. It showed real guts.

Especially now, when it was so close. Doc said it could be any time now. Bonnie always had the telephone by her hand, either here or at home, the number memorized in case....

He looked through the door again.

She was still breathing, still sleeping. Her eyes flickered fitfully behind the thin lids, but she was asleep.

He want back to Bonnie. And to waiting.

- 10 -

This time it surged. It knew the way, the had prepared the ground for the seed, it had drawn on all the reserves it dared to span the distances. But the exertion would make the feast that much more pleasant, the feeding that much more savory.

- 11 -

This time, Emma knew that there was no mistake.

He was different.

His eyes were deeper, clouded, turbulently hot, not the quiet clear blue ones she knew. The lips curled insolently around blackened teeth, decaying teeth that formed a ragged portcullis for a tongue and throat that spat out lies and cheated and promised things they knew they would never do.

His arms were shrunken now, with long lines of festering sores along the insides of the wasted flesh, clustering around the places where veins rose blue-black close to the surface of his pale skin.

Donney?

Yeah, Ma. It's me. Really me. Pretty, huh?

He smiled.

She shuddered.

No, this wasn't the way he was. She *knew* better than that. She knew what kind of boy he was, in spite of the stories....

What stories, Ma, what stories?

The voice taunted, dared her to dredge up the pain and the fear and the hidden terror that had built over nearly two decades.

But she didn't want to think about that. She concentrated on something else instead, something wonderful. Eighth birthday picnic, happy laughter fun smiling *ants crawling stinging*

Yeah, that one. That's a good one. That's when I killed the kittens. Drowned 'em 'n' listened to 'em screaming 'n' tearing at the canvas bag. I held 'em down, felt their scrawny spines bulging against my hands.

Richard saw me and threatened to tell you and I told him I'd get him if he said a word. Some time late at night when he was asleep I'd cut his thing off with scissors and watch the blood gush down the insides of his legs and I'd laugh—but not loud enough to wake you up, not until after he was dead. He was too young to know what his thing was for then—hell, so was I—but the threat worked. Great picnic. Fun.

No, she screamed, but there was no sound.

Hey, Ma. What about the ring? Your wedding ring, the one that got lost in the drains that time, just before I cut out?

She strained to move, to shake her head, but her muscles were locked against her will. The blackness of her cancer was invading the rest of her cells, burning and destroying and—God!—winning.

I sold it. Yea, ma, sold it to Hammer for some first-class shit....

ants crawling up her arm stinging her sugar ants grease ants what uncle john used to call shitants but only when gramma wasn't in the room or she'd whack him with the side of her hand no cursing in this kitchen john ottley none of that and you know it—

Drugs. Cocaine. It was great stuff, kept us high for days. Too bad about Daddy's ring. The voice minced.

No no no no no.

She struggled, battled the growing darkness, the locked muscles, the numbness spreading from her feet and hands toward her center.

He laughed.

And changed.

The flesh shredded away, putrid, cancerous beyond anything in her as he leered over the bed. She felt it dripping onto her, staining the hand-pieced Drunkard's Path. It spread its putrescence onto the quilt, urging it toward her.

Hey, Ma. Look at me—in a grotesque parody of the voice Donney had used when he was a kid and zipped by no-hands on his new Schwinn, the year before Uncle John died and things got really rough for them and she had to work and left him alone more and more.

She wanted to close her eyes—*God, let me close my eyes!*—but the skin was stretching tighter, cutting down over her nostrils until drawing each breath was agony but an agony minimal compared to that coursing through her as Donney decayed in front of her.

She struggled more, pushing back the weakness where she could, holding it from advancing in other places, keeping it from winning before...before what?

The Donney-thing laughed, reached toward her with a hand that shifted beneath the flesh, shivering like aging lime Jell-O.

Hey, Ma. Come on in, the water's fine.

She summoned every ounce of will and energy and focused it through her withered throat and *screamed.*

"No."

- 12 -

It wailed. Nooooo! This isn't the way it was supposed to be. The boy had been so easy, so gullible—and he was young and strong in spite of the abuse he had subjected himself to. This old woman, this shell, this...this pitiable nothing! How could it be!

- 13 -

Richard must have been nearly napping, his head nodding as he sat beside Bonnie.

"Richard!"

He jerked awake and looked around.

"What is it?" Bonnie asked.

"Did you say something? "

"No."

"*Richard!*" This time he recognized his mother's voice coming dimly, as if from a great distance. *"I love you. I'll be back."*

He sat upright. Bonnie felt his body stiffen.

"Richard?" It was both statement and question. Suddenly Bonnie knew.

They looked toward the bedroom but did not stand up to cross the aging wood floor hidden beneath the carpet.

This time there was no mistaking it. Neither had heard anything, but they both knew. They walked toward her bedroom, not hurrying. Somehow, they understood that the time for hurrying was past.

- 14 -

"No." It was a sound so soft that it barely escaped her lips, thin lips dry and caked from the struggle.

It was a sound softer than the goose-feather pillow that cradled her head motionless, softer than the flesh of her two innocent babies when she held each of them for the first time and stroked them and loved them. It was a sound that echoed silently.

And it forced the darkness back.

- 15 -

Half a continent away, the thing that called itself Hammer thrust its mouth to the sky and screamed, furious at having missed out on half of the banquet it had promised itself.

- 16 -

"No." The rest of the words remained unspoken, but they echoed through Emma.

That's not Donney. It's a lie and I reject it. I refuse it.
He made mistakes. I know. I don't deny it. I don't hide it.
He rejected me. He abandoned me. I know that.
But I love him and THIS IS NOT HIM!

Of all of this, only one small syllable escaped to negate the coils of fear that had looped endlessly around her in her last moments.

"No."

The Donney-thing writhed and twisted—it should have been screaming but it wasn't, or if it was, she couldn't hear anything.

In the smallest fragment of a second she had left, she let pictures flood through her mind, Donney smiling; Donney laughing; Donney touching her; Donney kissing her cheek as she stood at the sink washing dishes; Donney, silvered by the light of the television as he knelt at her feet, absorbed in his Pac-man games; Donney as he should have been, growing and loving and marrying and fathering and, in the fullness of his years, dying.

The darkness withdrew. The soft pink of the mock-crystal and brass lamp Richard and Donney had scrimped to buy her for her fiftieth glowed quietly on closed eyes, still breasts. The light caught in the beginnings of two tears stillborn.

Emma gratefully entered the darkness and only found a greater light.

- 17 -

The partial defeat stung.
For an instant, it nearly lost its tenuous hold on corporeality.
But only for an instant, because the defeat was only partial.
A wizened, withered old bitch whose life was over long ago, who had just been sitting around waiting for her body to notice that she had died. Too burned out to feed its vast appetite.
But there had been the boy.
And there would be others.

Chapter Six

Gifts of the Spirit

- 1 -

The two young men were walking briskly, trying to work off the abnormally moisture-choked chill of mid-August twilight.

In spite of the fact that Tamarind Valley belonged to the vast area in Southern California that is technically classified as desert, and that August is not traditionally a wet month, it had rained that morning. The precipitation was not just a dewy sprinkle, either, but an out-and-out gully-washing storm. Water was pouring from the drainpipes just outside their window and pooling on the sun-crazed asphalt below when they woke up to the alarm's *buzzzzz* at 6:00.

Both felt an unseasonable chill, and even though neither was native to the area, both realized at once that rain like that was almost unheard of in Southern California in August.

All day, it continued to rain fitfully. Clouds had glowered over Tamarind Valley. Dingy grey clouds caped the Coast Ranges, looking like rotting mushrooms collapsing from the weight of their own decay. The normal cooling breeze over the Camarillo Grade—southeastern sea breezes ripe with subtle hints of melon and grape wafting from acres of fertile soil cradled between the mountains and the sea—had been replaced by a stormy coldness.

The ground, cracked and dusty and dry the day before, was moist and spongy, though both of the young men knew that that would soon pass. Yesterday they had been sweltering and sweaty in their short-sleeved white dress shirts; tomorrow they would swelter again. But today, especially as the wind picked up at sunset, they buttoned their suit jackets gratefully.

All day long they had trudged through the dampness and the chill, stopping only long enough for a quick burger at the McDonald's in the center of town. For most of the afternoon, they had met no one, talked with no one. Their feet were tired, their skin tender from the unaccustomed cold, and their hearts heavy.

As twilight began to threaten, they had just finished tracting out the long up-grade of Whitechapel Place where it curved into the scrub-topped hills surrounding the southern end of Tamarind Valley. Most of the houses were new, less than a year old. That meant few trees, few lawns, few moments to spare from the busy lives of the husbands and wives who had to pay for their newly found upper-middle-class luxury.

Now they stood at the end of Whitechapel, approaching an area new to both of them. To the right, down slope, the houses continued and—even though there was no specific corner to mark the end of Whitechapel—the street twisted once and suddenly became Chancery Place as it wound back toward the heart of Tamarind.

To the left, up-slope, the roadway narrowed to pebbly asphalt decomposing along the edges where tenacious Bermuda grass sent out runners to pry the black composition away from the crumbling bedrock.

The two young men had a decision to make. Thomas Snow and Brian Patterson—missionaries from their church to the heathen in Southern California.

"Okay, which? You choose," Patterson said. His voice revealed touches of fatigue mixed with momentary impatience as Snow stared down Chancery, then up what a tilting street sign identified as Old Conejo Road.

"Come on," Patterson said after a few moments. He pulled his arms tight against his body for what little protection it would give against the increasing cold.

"Get with it. Which way?"

"*Conejo,*" Snow said finally. His voice was more resigned than enthusiastic. "That means 'rabbit' in Spanish, doesn't it?"

"Yeah."

Snow nodded as if knowing the word helped him decide.

"Rabbit Road. Why not?" Snow shrugged and started toward the up-grade. A second later, shaking his head as if wondering why his companion didn't show more joy in the Work, Patterson followed.

- 2 -

They approached the first house. It was a dilapidated clapboard, a ramshackle two-story place probably forty or fifty years old, maybe one of the original farm houses in the valley. It was clearly divorced in time and spirit—and economics—from the brand-new, earth-tone stucco $450,000 jobs half a mile away.

"Your door," Snow said under his breath as they crunched along the twig-strewn walkway. He nearly stumbled on the first of several pressure fractures where ash roots thrust the concrete upward every couple of yards.

Patterson nodded. The muscles of his throat worked tightly as he rehearsed again what he would say.

Door approaches were supposed to get easier, the young man thought disconsolately. Everybody said they would—his older brothers, his friends who had gone on their missions and wrote back glowing letters about their spiritual growth and how easy the work became. But it hadn't yet, not for Brian Patterson. Whenever it was his turn to introduce the two of them at a door, sweat welled under his arms, his throat constricted, and his mouth dried out until English emerged as a foreign language interpretable only to someone blessed with the Gift of Tongues.

Still, fair was fair.

It *was* his turn.

Swallowing hard, he stepped up to the tattered screen door. The paint was peeling from the lintel, and a thick pile of crushed dead leaves had blown up against the base of the door. Neither was usually a good sign.

But one never knew who would be receptive to the Message.

Patterson took a deep breath and knocked.

- 3 -

The hardwood door slammed with a resounding thud before Patterson had managed half of his opening lines. He stepped back and let go of the screen. It whacked against the doorjamb as if answering the rude comment of its larger, sturdier, inside brother.

From his place at the bottom of the narrow porch, Snow looked up two steps at his companion and shrugged. "It's like that sometimes." He said the same thing every time.

Patterson nodded numbly. His ears were still ringing from the explosion of rhythmical and highly original profanity they had just been subjected to for daring to interrupt the live-telecast of the Raiders game. He had heard most of the words before, he even knew what they meant; but he didn't think he had ever heard them strung together so...so artistically before.

"Another door?" Snow asked, his voice more calm than Patterson felt. It was the same thing he asked every evening.

"Okay." Patterson really wanted to say *no,* but he knew that Snow respected the rule requiring the missionaries to continue working until nine o'clock. That meant there was time enough for a couple more doors before finally turning around and heading home.

Patterson shivered. It was getting close to dark, and the air was still heavy with the day's rain. He followed Snow up the sidewalk.

The next house was newer than the first one. It was probably built five years or so before, when this end of Old Conejo Road was still miles from the bustle of downtown Tamarind. Now it was not half a mile away from subdivisions clotted with new houses and new cars and new lawns.

"Yours," Patterson said as they approached. Without answering, Snow took the two short steps in one stride, knocked smartly on the gleaming aluminum screen, waited twenty or thirty seconds, then opened the screen and rapped sharply on the front door.

His large knuckles knocked with authority. Again. Again.

That's enough, Patterson said to himself, as he did at every door. *Three strikes and you're out,* although he knew he shouldn't be thinking in those terms. But Snow always went the extra mile.

He knocked again.

"No one home," Patterson said.

"Yeah. Guess not. One more, then," Snow said.

He pointed to single mailbox stationed like a lonely sentinel beside a gravel drive at the bottom of a small rise a hundred yards or so further on. "Looks like there's probably one more house beyond that hill. That will finish this area. Let's do it."

"Sure," Patterson said, but his voice was slow and quiet. They walked from the empty house back to the road, at this point little more than large hunks of isolated asphalt floating like smoke-choked islands in a rough sea of county-strewn gravel. They walked in silence to the end of the lane.

Up close, the mail box looked unused. It had been battered and shot at with B-B's until it hung precariously by a single nail from a splintered post.

"There's probably nothing back here," Patterson said, relieved—disconcertingly more relieved than he had ever been before.

He shivered, pulled the lapels of his suit jacket closer. The wind was no stronger where it rippled the leaves of the scrub oaks on each side of the driveway, but the air seemed demonstrably colder. Patterson wouldn't have been surprised to see his breath outlined against the night sky. "Ghost-breath," someone had once called it in a book he had read. Good description.

Then he wished heartily that he hadn't said that word, even to himself. *Ghost.*

He shivered again.

"Cold?" Snow asked, then shivered himself, as if the power of suggestion were working overtime.

"Yeah, I...," Patterson started to say, then stopped. That wasn't it.

Sure, it was chilly, but he'd been lots colder lots of times up in Wyoming. It was a damper chill down here, what with the sea breeze and all, and he wasn't really dressed for the nighttime—but that wasn't the problem.

This cold was deeper, bone-deep, coming from the inside and working its way out, like some great white slug burrowing through his flesh and freezing his blood. His skin rippled tight in gooseflesh.

"No," he amended. "I...hey, let's head on in, okay?"

Snow paused and stared up the rise. Patterson followed the direction of his companion's gaze. Between two of the scrub oaks, the gravel drive disappeared over the hill. Patterson swallowed hard. A driveway. A house. A door.

A challenge.

Snow wouldn't let the chance of a house pass. In fact, he was already halfway up the rise, rapidly disappearing into the shadows beneath the oaks.

Patterson watched him, trying to catch the breath that had suddenly drained from his lungs at the thought of walking up that gravel driveway. The shattered pebbles glinted whitely in the moonlight, in a way that scared Snow in spite of his being nineteen and a half and very grown up and out on his own in the real world for the first time.

Don't go up there Snow don't go.

The rocks gleamed like the bones of an old cow that had stumbled over a cliff during the dead of winter and hadn't been found until well into the next spring. Patterson—just plain Brian, way back then, *Bri* to his friends—had spotted the heap of white in the moonlight on a tenting-trip with his cousin. They had climbed down the face of the cliff by moonlight to see what it was. The skull had stared eerily up at them, the jackstraws of ribs and spine jumbled crazily. It was only a cow, Brian had understood, but it spooked him anyway.

Like that gravel spooked him.

- 4 -

The driveway wound over the crest of the low hill. It was bordered by spindly weeds broken beneath the heat of August, then battered by the morning's unseasonable rain. One or two pools of dampness glistened along the edge of the gravel, dark under the moonlight, black, impenetrable, no longer recognizably water.

Patterson didn't want to go any further, and it had nothing to do with knocking on doors.

The skin on his arms crawled.

He wished Snow would turn around and head back for home. He opened his mouth to call out, then stopped. *The creep wouldn't listen, anyway,* he thought. *He'd just go on, if only to show me up.*

He walked faster until he caught up with Snow. Together, they crested the hill.

The house crouched in the bottom of a shallow valley. There was no light showing.

"Nobody home," Patterson whispered quickly. As if answering the faint disturbance of his voice amid the silence, a single light suddenly glowed in the one window visible from the front.

"Nope," Snow said, his voice edged with satisfaction. "They're home. Maybe just waiting for us to come."

"Don't be stupid," Patterson said. "There's...."

But Snow had already started down the driveway. Patterson wanted to cry out something, a warning perhaps...was *about* to cry out, he told himself...but instead he started down the drive as well. His long legs covered the distance between himself and Snow in only a few seconds. They walked side by side, unspeaking. In all their months together, he had never been so angry, so frustrated. Usually Snow was a great guy, supportive and encouraging, even when Patterson didn't really feel like going out and knocking on doors again.

But tonight...tonight Patterson was half tempted to beat Snow up, knock him down, take him apart—anything to stop the other man's progress toward that house.

"Let's...not," he said, struggling to find the words to tell Snow how important it was that they not get any closer to that house. Already Patterson could see the dull sheen of the door knob and the flat black surface of the door itself. "Please...."

Snow stopped.

The door on which Patterson would have knocked in only a few seconds, the door he would have had to touch with the skin of knuckles that suddenly burned with precognitive cold—that newly terrifying door silently swung open.

A knife of light fell from inside the house and cut across the gravel.

Someone stepped between them and the light.

Snow's breath hissed faintly.

- 5 -

At first, Patterson saw only a man, young and thin from the looks of the silhouette, standing with most of his weight hitched onto his right leg. His arms were spread wide, with one hand on each side of the doorjamb. He seemed relaxed, as if he were waiting for them.

But suddenly, to Patterson, the shadowy figure looked like nothing so much as the crucifix he had seen through the window of the big Catholic Church on Stone Avenue just a block from their apartment back in Tamarind Valley.

The figure leaning against the doorjamb looked dead. Its weight was not supported by the canted right leg or the left leg angling back into the room, but by huge iron spikes that tore through bone and muscle and ligament of palm and wrist, pinioning the body to the splintered oak doorjambs.

Patterson shivered at the thought of the pain...the agony of slashed nerves.

Black blood dripped to the floor, lying like molten gold in the light.

And *he was back a decade or more ago, whisked through time and space to the first night after his oldest brother came home, returned in glory from his mission in Colombia, South America—a place that had no identity, no position in space for young Brian, except as a pinkish splotch on the world globe on Dad's desk. It was a special Family Night, with grandma and grandpa, aunts and uncles, cousins there to celebrate Fred's return. Later, after a bigger dinner than even Brian could easily handle, Fred showed everyone some of his slides from Colombia.*

Most of them were fun: carnivals and parades (but why did the policemen carry Browning semi-automatics? Brian had asked. Fred had glanced quickly at his mother and father, then smiled at Brian but didn't answer the question), *outings with other missionaries, landmarks, and native scenes, and jungle countryside greener than anything Brian had imagined.*

And a Church.

The largest brick church in Colombia.

The Crucifix hung inside that church. The gilded figure was twice as large as life, a stricken Christ with his head sunk to his chest in despair, his blood dripping in monstrous gouts on the gleaming gold inlay of his flesh. Legs like bones, arms like bones. Eyes deep and hurting enough, enough to lose your soul in them if you dared to look.

It was more than grotesque, it was abominable, especially to an unusually impressionable eight-year old just beginning to understand who and what Christ was, and whose only image of Him to that point had been a sepia-tinted painting in the Sunday School room—a wide-browed Christ, with gentle-brown eyes and long hair flowing like a liquid halo.

Brian had shivered when he saw slide of the Crucifix, six feet high, shining back at him from the sheet tacked up as a temporary screen on the far wall of the dining room.

The boy had had nightmares for weeks afterward, but he was afraid to tell his father or his mother—or even Fred, whom he adored with all the passion of an eight-year-old for a twenty-one-year-old, strong, grown-up brother. What could he say?

That he was afraid of God?

Instead, he stifled his screams with his pillow and lay awake, night after night, until sunlight broke through his window and released him from his terror.

This time, like then, the scream started low in Brian Patterson's gut, swirling upward, spinning through his intestines and stomach, screeching up his gullet and hammering at the back of his throat.

- 6 -

Thomas Snow felt no incipient scream, just the cold, deathly silence of exposure.

The figure at the door was a woman, her arms arced seductively from doorjamb to doorjamb, her legs slightly apart and the light tantalizingly, hauntingly glimmering between them.

Even seeing her in silhouette, he knew she was naked. Her breasts would be small and pointed, her stomach flat, her thighs smooth and inviting. He knew all of that, even though he could see nothing except a black cut-out, a lewd paper doll propped against the dim golden backdrop of a low wattage bulb.

It was her.

He trembled, but this time not because of the cold. He no longer felt the air, the breeze, the chill.

It was her, Sue Ann. It couldn't be, of course, not after over a year, not here in California. But it was.

They had driven out to the pond together that last night before he decided to go on his mission, to talk things over, to decide whether what they had between them was strong enough to last two years. He knew it was. She said she knew it was. They exchanged promises, kisses.

And then, because it was July and hot and they were wearing swimming suits and T-shirts, suddenly they were kissing and whispering, his hands in her hair, her hands on his back, tighter and compelling. And then she was naked, and then he was naked, and they were touching...and more....

And he had hidden it, not told anyone, lied when they asked him if he was chaste.

And gone out on his mission to live that lie.

Now she was here to punish him for his lie.

She reached out to him, twisting her fingers as if she had him on a long string and, like a master puppeteer, could manipulate him, make him run and dance. He felt the pull and wanted to rush toward her.

He moaned, low and painful and grating, as he felt the strings pull taut around his gut. He stepped into the tension on the strings, relieving it for an instant, only to have it return, renewed and more insistent. Then, more intuitively than consciously, something pulled him back and forced him to ignore the tug of pain that the movement caused. *No,* he cried voicelessly, *let me go let me confess let me die. I can't live the lie.*

But a deeper something choked off the child in him and held him back.

For a moment, he had a flickering vision of darkness and emptiness that terrified him. The vision faded, leaving behind only a fragmented sense of dread. There was a *wrongness* here, he suddenly understood, a deeper wrong than his having touched a naked woman—touched her, that was all he did, that was all!—deeper than having lied about it.

He struggled, praying silently for strength to penetrate to the wrongness.

Snow became dimly aware of Patterson standing beside him, sobbing, tensing muscles as if struggling to pull away from the hideously writhing figure in the golden doorway. Snow reached out and touched Patterson's hand. He knew that Patterson was seeing *something*...perhaps not the same thing he was, but something that terrified the young man. Patterson's face was white in the dim light, glowing with sweat and tension. He felt Patterson's fingers grasping at his own and closing tightly.

Something snapped in each of them.

- 7 -

Thomas Snow leaned against the concrete lamppost halfway down Whitechapel, on a corner overlooking the lights of Tamarind Valley. His eyes were hidden in shadow as he stared at his feet.

Brian Patterson stood close by, almost close enough for the stiff cloth of their suit jackets to touch. But he did not touch Snow. His breathing was still ragged and painful.

Neither moved. Neither spoke.

Along Whitechapel, parents were herding unwilling kids indoors. It was, after all, not yet nine o'clock on an August night that was, in spite of the chill, still summer. The cloud cover had finally dissipated, and the sunlight had only just faded into recognizable night. Televisions flickered through open windows, spreading their full-range color and high-fidelity sound through rooms where mothers and fathers and children watched and talked and read and snacked on Orville Redenbacher's gourmet popcorn. One six year old wheeled up on his bicycle and dropped it onto the newly laid sod that still showed cuts every foot where it was unrolled. He would catch it for that the next morning.

But all of that was like a dream. A welcome dream, to be sure, but evanescent, transitory, not to be trusted.

Because back there, over the hill, around two curves and through a shadowed entryway guarded by druidic oaks—back there lay....

Reality?

No, neither of them could believe that. Everything they knew from their own lives, everything they had been taught about life and love and faith by their parents and grandparents, everything they stood for and believed and taught to the people here—everything they trusted whispered that what they had seen might have been real, but was not *reality*.

Patterson tried to re-create the image of the dying Christ that had haunted him from the doorway, but failed. That was not the Christ he believed in, not the Christ he loved and whose Word he had come here to preach. Maybe He belonged in that Catholic Cathedral in Colombia, but that tortured Christ had no place in Brian Patterson's mind or heart or prayers. His was a God of love, not of....

Of fear.

And with that recognition, the moment passed. He straightened.

Thomas Snow straightened at the same moment. He had struggled with memory in the same way that Brian Patterson had. He and Sue Ann *had* gone to the pond that last night, that he knew was truth. They *had* spoken long and seriously about their future, about his mission, about their love. They had kissed and held hands, and he had run his fingers through her hair and spoken quietly to her, and she had held him tightly, as if more afraid of time and distance than he was.

But they had done nothing more than that.

What he had seen, the images that had formed as he had stared at the golden doorway—they had no substance beyond his own imagination. He loved Sue Ann passionately; in any other circumstances, they might have gone all the way that night, might have fumbled at each other's nakedness. *But they had not.*

He loved his God and his mission. And she was still waiting for him, writing once a week, supporting him and encouraging him. There would be a time when he would see her naked, her arms open to him, her body inviting him; and he would respond with love and passion, and through that meeting would come spirits to be clothed in flesh as their children forever.

What he had seen tonight shared nothing of that purity, that devotion.

It was a lie. It spoke of the darkness that was within him, to be sure, but a darkness that he had never allowed to surface and—God willing—never would. It had spoken the essence of his fear.

He laughed—a hollow, echoing laugh that gradually built in resonance. It was infectious.

Patterson joined in with a curiously high-pitched giggle that had never failed to break up his friends at home. That made Snow laugh even harder, and by the time they turned at the stoplight on Whitechapel and Tamarind Avenue, they were deep in their plans for the next day. There was that family over on Luther Way that wanted them to come back; and maybe they could open up a new tracting area in the development across the freeway.

Working together, as they had always done, they could accomplish anything.

They slept that night without dreaming.

- 8 -

It had tried to take too much, to hold two minds at one time. And they had broken away at the last moment.

Next time, it would be more cautious.

Chapter Seven

Special Edition

- 1 -

First prize was a brand-new bike, an honest-to-God racer specially designed for newspaper deliveries. It even had the *Tamarind Times* logo engraved on a silver plaque that was welded to the frame.

The prize didn't mean that much to Kenny, of course. He already had a good bike and wasn't delivering for the *Times* anymore.

But for Spence, it would be the answer to a prayer. Being the youngest of six children, two already going to Tamarind Community College and looking forward to even more expenses when they transferred to Pearce or Cal State Northridge, Spence always came in last, got the hand-me-downs in everything from clothes to the rattle-trap old bike that had probably last seen a paint job just after the Revolutionary War. And Kenny was pretty sure that Spence's old man couldn't—or wouldn't—shell out the bucks to buy a new bike. Certainly not one that must have run $250 or more.

So the contest was Spence's only chance. Maybe that was why Kenny agreed to help. Or maybe he offered just because Spence was his best buddy.

They had known each other since kindergarten. Two shy little boys, immature even among five-year-olds, they were immediately attracted to each other. They had shared a scratchy red wool blanket during nap-time the first day, crumbled graham crackers into their milk in tandem, and had been largely inseparable since. Even though they lived far enough from each other to make visiting a conscious effort, they managed to spend at least a few minutes of every day together. Some days, especially the long hot days of summer, they were together most of the hours.

Kenny felt about Spence the way he imagined he would have felt about his younger brother if Matthew had lived more than four years before leukemia got him.

Kenny knew that he and Spence would remain best friends as long as they both lived.

Which would be just under twenty-four hours more.

- 2 -

After the freak August rainstorm the day before, Kenny wasn't quite sure what to expect, so he was pleased to wake up to clear skies and a warm but not yet hot wind. The desert winds—the devastatingly dry Santa Anas—that sometimes scorched Tamarind in August and made the valley a potential firetrap hadn't yet struck, so the weather was about as pleasant as possible when Kenny biked over to Spence's place just after nine.

As they had agreed the night before, Spence was waiting for him by the front gate. Kenny didn't like to have to go inside Spence's house that much. Spense's sisters sometimes wandered around in just their slips or their bras and panties, even when they *knew t*hat Kenny was there, and in spite of the boys' not-quite adolescent jokes about boobs and asses, he had let Spence know often enough how much their behavior embarrassed Kenny. So lately, whenever possible, the two boys met outside and headed out from there on their various errands and adventures.

"Ready, Freddy?" Spence yelled as soon as Kenny rode up the last grade and angled in toward the worn picket fence that bounded an equally worn patch of tired looking Bermuda grass.

"On the way," Kenny yelled back, not even slowing as he skimmed once around the half-circle drive that arced past Spence's front door before coasting back down the hill.

Spence hopped onto his old bike and pumped away, struggling to catch up with Kenny, who had the advantage of a head-start, a down-hill slope, and a bike that didn't shrill metal-on-metal with every crank of the pedal.

Kenny grinned as he sped along street. He could hear Spence coming up behind him, so he tapped his brakes—not enough for Spence to see, just enough to let him catch up. Kenny knew that, given the quality of the two bikes, he had an unbeatable advantage, but that would change, he vowed. Today the two of them would get enough signatures on the subscription list to shoot Spence up to first place in the contest and win that bike.

Spence pulled even with Kenny and caught the other boy's eye. He grinned broadly and Kenny returned the grin.

Today!

Between the two of them, nothing could stand in their way.

They sped to the work. They had to be finished by six o'clock, both because that was the deadline for handing in the subscription lists and because of the overnight campout scheduled to begin that evening at Jenkin's field. It would be just Spence and Kenny and the rest of the Panthers. No grown-ups this time.

The overnighter would be fun, but before then he and Spence had to dig up a lot of subscriptions...and win that bike.

That meant that every minute counted.

They biked up to the new houses in the Oakdale development. The five blocks were studded with oversized pseudo-Mediterranean stucco houses. The people there obviously had money, many of them had just moved in, and Spence's route addresses showed that there were still a lot of families in the subdivision who didn't take the *Times*. Oakdale seemed the best place to start.

They divided up each street. They would park their bikes at one end of the block, then Kenny would canvas one side while Spence hit the other, both trying every approach they could think of to get new customers, from putting on a shameless "oh what a poor little thing" face for the occasional grandmother-type, to assuming the "young man aware of his responsibilities in the world" look for the few executive types still at home on a Friday afternoon, even descending occasionally to a "please, Ma'am" for their wives.

Most of the time it worked. At the least, it garnered them a couple of glasses of lemonade ("It's *so* hot out there, today") and three or four handfuls of cookies ("Why, you must be *starving!*").

By 1:00, they had collected twenty-six new subscriptions between them. A pretty good haul, and, added to what Spence already had, just about enough to insure him the bike.

They had lunch at the Carl's Jr., hamburgers and fries and shakes, with dessert of a Penguin's frozen yogurt sundae. It was expensive, but worth it. Kenny treated for the yogurt. He had received twenty-five bucks from his grandparents for his birthday last week and still had two fives and a couple of ones wadded in his pocket. He didn't begrudge Spence the treat, either. Spence would have paid if he could, but his allowance of a buck a week was laughably small. A buck a week! And even that was only when his Dad actually remembered to pay him, which was maybe every other week or so. Poor kid.

By 1:45, they were hard at work again, pedaling up and down the streets, talking to anything on two legs that looked old enough to read and subscribe to a newspaper. Once they passed two guys in white shirts and ties who were knocking on the doors in the neighborhood. They didn't look like they were selling subscriptions to the *Times,* so Kenny didn't worry too much about competition. The boys waved at the two guys—who looked to be six or seven years older than they were—as they wheeled by. The two guys waved back. They looked so happy that Kenny found himself grinning ferociously as he and Spence pedaled four or five streets further into the development, figuring that it would still be best not to follow too closely on someone else's heels, even if the other guys weren't selling newspapers.

- 3 -

That was the only time that those four particular individuals crossed each other's paths. Of the four, two had already escaped but were unaware, except on the lowest levels where fear hides in the deepest shadows of the mind and imagination and bides its time for the next assault, how close they had been to death. One would soon die. And one would live on to try to avenge his friend, knowing that to do so would terrify him more than anything he could ever imagine.

- 4 -

Kenny and Spence finished with the Oakdale development by 4:45.

"That's probably enough, anyway," Kenny said, pointing to the additional names on Spence's list. "That makes over a hundred, and you told me that the only guy close to you was the Sanderson kid, and he only had eighty-two."

"Yeah, but that was Wednesday. I don't know what he's done since then, and I don't want to take any chances."

"You're the boss," Kenny said, straddling his bike and bracing one foot on the raised pedal. "Where to now?"

Spence thought for a moment. There were other large, expensive developments like Oakdale in the valley, but most of them were at least fifteen or twenty minutes away by bike. And, as Spence knew from studying the subscription routes, most of them were pretty well picked over by the other carriers. He glanced around.

"Let's try up there," he said, pointing to a stretch of homes that crested the ridge of a low hill. "Look's pretty good to me, and we still have at least an hour before we have to get these back to the office. Okay?"

"Sure. Beat you there," Kenny yelled, already speeding away.

As usual, he did.

"Damned bike," Spence muttered as they stopped at the foot of the first street—the sign read *Whitechapel*—and started working. Kenny took the right-hand side, Spence the left.

Within half an hour, they were neck and neck, walking up the sidewalks of houses exactly opposite each other.

"How many?" Spence called across the narrow street.

"Five. You?"

Spence grinned. "Seven. Beat you!"

"Still a block to go," Kenny answered, running up a sidewalk toward a lady weeding newly planted bare-root roses. He glanced across the street at Spence's next house. It was apparently empty, with blank windows that looked like the dead eye sockets of a modishly sand-colored stuccoed skull. The front yard was bare dirt, and a "For Sale—Millikan Realty" sign was planted halfway between the street and the porch. Spence ran on past, turning in at the next walkway.

They met at the top of Whitechapel. The subscription tally was fifteen for the street—not bad, considering there were at most forty houses in all.

"Good choice," Spence said, nodding, congratulated himself on selecting this street. It had proven the most successful of any they had tried since the competition began.

"D'you think we have enough?" Kenny asked.

Spence shook his head. "Let's do those," he said, pointing to two houses further along one of the branchings where Whitechapel curved downward again. "Just to make sure."

"Got it," Kenny said. They took off running. On foot, Kenny and Spence were almost an even match. They would have arrived at the first sidewalk at exactly the same moment if Kenny hadn't stumbled on a rough spot in the pavement and broken stride. As it was, Spence was halfway to the front door by the time Kenny caught up, so Kenny continued on. He glanced at the house, taking in its broken shutters, peeling paint, crumbling concrete sidewalks, and neglected lawn. He felt inwardly pleased that the house would be Spence's, not his. Whoever lived there didn't look like the type to keep abreast of community happenings.

The next house was a ways down the road, but the closer Kenny came to it, the likelier a prospect it seemed. The place was much newer than Spence's house and radiated an openness that appealed to Kenny. After a week of working with Spence, he had gotten so that he could almost tell, just by the looks of the houses, who might be interested in the *Times* and who would tell him to get lost.

And this looked like a possibility.

Full of confidence and energy, he knocked.

A woman answered. She was an older lady, maybe thirty or so. She had a neat, quiet smile and pretty eyes that crinkled along the edges but fluttered oddly when she spoke to him, kind of like Kenny's Aunt Madeleine when she was gearing up to give him a good-bye kiss after a week-long visit.

Part of Kenny's confidence drained away, inexplicably, as he looked at the woman. Suddenly, the smile didn't seem so neat, and the way her eyes shifted up and down when she looked at him, as if analyzing him head to toe, bothered him. He felt strangely like an *it*, rather than a person.

"We're taking subscriptions for the *Tamarind Times*," he said quickly. He gesture with a small nod toward the house down the street to explain the *we*. He paused, half hoping that she would turn him down and shut the door. Instead, her eyes traveled across him once more...up and down, then up again, stopping at his eyes.

She stood away from the door, her posture clearly inviting him in.

"It's hot out there, today," she said as she led him through a darkened living room that showed no signs of having ever been lived in. They ended up in the kitchen at the rear of the house, with large windows opening out onto a hillside studded with chaparral and sage. The view was beautiful, but Kenny barely noticed it.

"Ice water?" she asked as soon as he was seated at a narrow table in a windowed alcove. He felt surrounded by the light and the hillside and the brush.

While she opened and shut doors on the cupboard and the refrigerator, then ran water over a couple of ice cubes in a tall, clear glass, he told her more about the *Times* and the subscription competition.

"So you see, ma'am"—the word seemed excessively formal, and he almost choked in saying it, but something forced him to spit it out—"So you see, ma'am, I'm really trying to help out my friend, Spence. He needs that bicycle more than anything. But you'll enjoy the *Times,* too," he added quickly.

"We've just moved in," she said, "my husband and I, and we *do* enjoy reading local papers, and it was so nice of the paper to send such a handsome young man out to talk to us about it."

Kenny figured that he had a sale. Now all he wanted to do was get her signature on the subscription agreement and get out of there. But she wasn't ready for that.

She kept talking. Twice she got up and, without asking him if he wanted more, refilled his glass. He drank the water, although he was beginning to feel uncomfortably full.

If she doesn't quit watering me, he thought morosely, I may have to ask if I can use her bathroom. And he distinctly *didn't* want to ask that.

But she was already talking about something else. She was a coupon-clipper, she said. She showed him neatly labeled envelopes stuffed full of cents-off coupons for everything from Mayonnaise to Maisie's All-Breed Dog Food.

Kenny surreptitiously looked around the kitchen, but he couldn't see any sign of a dog.

She handed him a stack of coupons to look at. Her fingers were warm, almost sticky with sweat where they brushed against his.

"Uh-huh," he said. His tongue could not find any words that seemed right. He shoved the stack back toward her as quickly as he felt would be polite. He curled his fingers into his palms and thrust them against his jeans legs, hands hidden beneath the oak table top.

As he sat in a stiff-backed kitchen chair, uncomfortable but unwilling to jeopardize a potential subscriber, he glanced through the darkened living room toward the front door, still open, promising him freedom if he could just get her signature and get away. As he was looking, Spence raced past, heading for the next house, probably just beyond the hill.

It took fifteen minutes more—and yet another glass of ice water almost forced onto him, along with a rather stale oatmeal cookie from a paper bag marked "Vons," but he finally signed Mrs. Coupon-clipper up for a year's subscription.

She scribbled her name on the form as he stood by the edge of the table. He leaned over her shoulder, trying to figure out what her name was. All he could see was an illegible scrawl. Her penmanship was worse than his, even worse than Spence's, and Kenny had always figure Spence to be the world's worst writer.

Just then she turned to hand him the form. Seated, she looked up at him, then pulled her eyes down again, then up. She smiled.

"Uh, thanks, Mrs....uh, thanks a lot." He almost ran to the front door, but she was right behind him, leaning against the screen and waving a tiny little wave with her two middle fingers.

Kenny took the two porch steps in a single leap and headed down the walk.

Just then, a man—Mr. Coupon-Clipper, Kenny assumed—pulled into the drive. He stopped his year-old Z-car, stepped out, waved briefly at the woman on the porch, asked what he could do for Kenny, and listened pensively as Kenny repeated his sales pitch and showed the man the woman's signature on the subscription form. The man nodded approvingly, and Kenny had to listen to another discourse, this time on youth and responsibility and how a paper route could eventually lead to great things. The whole time, the lady stared pointedly at Kenny instead of at Mr. Coupon-Clipper—and the guy was rubbing his hand sensuously along the chromework of the Z-car as if he were married to it instead of to Mrs. Coupon-Clipper. That made Kenny almost more nervous than Mrs. Coupon-Clipper's long looks had.

Maybe the guy wished he *was* married to the car, Kenny decided. But it didn't bother him any more. He had a subscription, and now it was time to get out of there and deliver the list to the *Times* office and wait for the final count.

"Thank you, sir," he said, interrupting when the man paused to take a breath. The man's hand hovered over the Z's front fender. "I really appreciate this, thanks a lot. I gotta get going now. Thanks." The last *thanks* was tossed over Kenny's shoulder as he ran down the sidewalk toward Whitechapel.

Given the time he spent with the Coupon-Clippers, Spence should be finished and waiting for him.

And even if he wasn't, standing alone in the middle of the street would be preferable to getting trapped between those two back there.

He kept running.

He knew somehow—he *knew*—that Spence would make it. Maybe the Coupon-Clippers would be the one name on the list to put him over Sanderson's total, and then Kenny would feel just great about having helped his buddy out. The whole weird scene back there would have been worth it.

He ran down the sidewalk. Spence wasn't there. Kenny looked downhill, toward Whitechapel, in case Spence had finished up ahead and was waiting for him by the intersection.

No Spence.

That meant that he was still up the street. Probably got a live one, too, and was reeling him in, Kenny thought.

He headed back up the road, half jogging, humming a nonsense tune that he had known for years but could no longer remember the words to. He sped up when he passed the Coupon-Clippers' house, but the Z was no longer in the drive—probably put to bed for the night in the garage—and no one was in sight.

He came to the end of the road.

No Spence.

There was a long driveway that disappeared over a small hill, and a mailbox standing lopsidedly by the driveway, so there must be a house over the hill. Spence was probably signing someone up right now.

Still grinning, Kenny ran along the driveway, grateful for the momentary coolness beneath the shade of two trees. Then he ran out into the sun again and follow the gravel drive to where it disappeared over the crest of the hill.

At the top, he stopped. There was a house there, all right, but it was pretty small and dilapidated. There wasn't any garage, and the only car in sight was a dusty VW with dented fenders and a bent radio antenna. No Z-car here, no kitchen with picture windows and a hundred-thousand-dollar view. There was not even a garage or a driveway. The gravel road just stopped suddenly in front of the door. There was no lawn, no grass, no trees, just a bush with bright red flowers growing up the side of the place and spilling over onto the roof.

It didn't look like a good place, Kenny decided instantly. Spence *couldn't* have made a sale here.

But if not, then where was he?

Kenny turned around and stared back the way he had come. From the top of the hill, he could see most of the houses, at least as far as Whitechapel. Spence was nowhere to be seen.

Which meant that either he had ditched Kenny—something that Spence would never do—or he was inside that house, pitching the *Tamarind Times* to the old hermit type, or maybe the young hippie type, that probably lived there.

Kenny waited uncertainly at the top of the hill for a couple of minutes, then sighed and started down the gravel driveway toward the house.

Each step was harder than the last, though. The closer he got, the less he liked the place. The single window looked even more like an eye than the empty windows in the vacant house on Whitechapel—only this eye wasn't empty. Something glinted in it, something bad, like in the *Halloween* movies, or the *Nightmare on Em Street* movies.

"Nightmare on Old Conejo Road," he said out loud, purposely mispronouncing the name as "Cone-joe," though he knew that it was really "Ko-nay-ho." His voice echoed hollowly in the stillness.

The words were a joke, an in-joke that he and Spence shared, mispronouncing all the Spanish names in the area and giggling as they ordered "tortil-las" at the Del Taco on Tamarind Avenue. Once they worked over a map of California and burst into hysterical laughter at such places as Vallejo.

But this time the joke didn't make him feel better. If anything, it increased his discomfort. He wanted to turn around and run back over the hill.

By now he was only a few yards from the house and feeling decidedly worse once he saw the place up close. The wood clapboard was broken and splintery, its paint flaked and shredded. The windows were so dust-caked that he could see nothing through them; it was as if a black sheet were hung behind them for curtains. There was no sign of life, except the VW that looked more battered and abused the closer he got to it.

Hey, he thought, almost speaking aloud but choking off the words at the last minute. *I can always just ask if my friend is here. No reason I have to try and sell them the* Times *if they don't seem friendly.*

He reached the door.

He glanced behind him, hoping that Spence would materialize somewhere between here and the top of the hill, that he could race back up the gravel and feel the coarse rocks scrunching beneath his sneakers, and then two of them could whoop their way down the hill and retrieve their bikes and race to the newspaper office.

No Spence.

He turned back and raised his hand to knock on the door.

It opened.

The inside of the house was pitch black, so Kenny couldn't see anything except Spence's head, then the rest of his thin body as he slipped though the narrow opening between door and jamb.

For an instant, what with the shadows and all, Spence's face seemed to flicker, then he was in the sunlight and grinning widely, his crooked front teeth catching the light and looking bigger than ever.

"Got one more," he said triumphantly, waving his list.

Relief flooded through Kenny, although he would have been hard pressed to say exactly what he was relieved about. All he knew was that Spence was standing next to him, and the door was closed, and they could leave this house and walk on over the hill and get their bikes and take off.

"Great," he said finally, letting that one word carry the weight of his emotions.

"We're outta here!" Spence yelled gleefully as he ran up the driveway, his sneakers spraying fine gravel behind him. One small piece almost hit Kenny in the cheek before he took off, too, determined this time to beat Spence to the top of the hill.

He didn't, but that was all right. Just being there, then over the edge and out of sight of the house, seemed to make the day brighter.

Kenny checked his wristwatch.

"5:20," he said, winded.

"Let's get going, then," Spence answered, jogging down the hill.

They stopped for a breath in the shade of the two hills where the driveway opened onto Old Conejo Road.

"Hard?" Kenny panted.

Spence looked at him blankly.

"Selling the paper," Kenny explained, nodding toward the rise behind them. "Back there."

Spence's blank expression held for a couple of heartbeats, then his eyes flickered and he tossed Kenny a quick grin.

"Naw." he said. "An old lady. Musta been a hundred. Or more. White hair like this. Like an Afro, only snarled and tangled." He held his hands out from his head six inches or so. "A real bag. Wrinkled and ugly. Breath stank, too." He shook his head.

She must have been scary, or something, though, Kenny thought, *because you're nervous, Spence. I can tell. Frightened. That's the way you talk when you're nervous and frightened, you let yourself babble on and on without taking a breath. And you don't usually talk about people like that, especially old people, not after your Gramma died last spring and you spent the night with us and cried all night long because you loved her and she suffered so much and you were glad she was dead and you were afraid for anyone to find out.* But out loud he only said, "And she wanted to subscribe to the *newspaper?*"

"Not really. But you know the old super-salesman?" Spence flashed the grin again. He flipped out his notebook and showed Kenny the signature on the bottom line.

It was a scrawl, so loopy and snaky that Kenny could not even come close to guessing the name. It made him cold just to see it. *Glad you took that one.*

"How'd you do?" Spence asked as he slipped the notebook back into his pocket.

Kenny pointed to the Coupon-Clippers' house as they passed it. The doors were still closed and the blinds were shut against the afternoon sun, so the boys couldn't see any signs of life. "Got one."

Kenny paused, breaking stride just a moment, and glanced over his shoulder at the house. "You know, I think she...I think the lady was flirting with me or something. She kept lookin' at me, like she...."

"Like she was hot for your rod?"

"What?" Kenny stumbled to a halt.

"Like she was hot for your bod," Spence said, walking on as if he hadn't noticed Kenny's behavior.

"Hot for your bod"—that was their standard line whenever they talked about girls and the incipient sexuality they were both curious about and half afraid of but nonetheless beginning to feel.

"Yeah," Kenny said, embarrassed. *Hot for your* rod, *not bod, that's what you said and it didnt sound right it didnt sound like you spence* Blood pulsed at Kenny's neck and temples, *boom, boom, boom.*

Spence dug his elbow into Kenny's ribs and took off running. "Come on, stud, beat you to the bikes."

Kenny followed, and this time he really did almost beat Spence.

- 5 -

They were on their bikes by 5:40, and pumping away for all they were worth. Kenny was worried that they wouldn't have enough time to make it back to the office before the deadline.

"Hurry up," he yelled across to Spence as they coasted down Whitechapel toward the stoplight at Tamarind Avenue.

Spence shrugged. "Who cares?"

For a second Kenny was stunned, before he realized that Spence was just covering up. Spence was counting on that bike. It would mean a lot to him, not only in making it easier for him to handle his route, but in making him more a part of the gang. Not everyone was as understanding as Kenny, and some of the guys razzed him about his faded clothes and tattered toys and broken-down bike. It would mean a lot to him to win it, but just in case he didn't, Spence was getting ready for the disappointment. Kenny understood.

They slowed at the intersection, then sped up as they caught the green and whipped around the corner and onto Tamarind. The *Times* offices were still three long blocks away, and they only had twelve minutes.

At 5:59, Spence handed over his list to Mr. Gresham, the subscription manager whose brain-child the competition had been. He and Kenny were standing in the large foyer of the *Times* building, one of the few times they had ever been there, since usually the delivery boys (and girls) picked up their stock out back. The place was nice, classy almost, with metal and glass furniture and thick rugs and real plants sitting in all of the corners.

But none of the guys waiting in the foyer gave a whooping hang about the furniture or the rugs or the plants.

They only had eyes for two things.

Mr. Gresham, hunched over a computer terminal punching in numbers and names and nodding and hmmming now and then.

And the bike, propped along the wall opposite the glass double doors that opened onto the parking lot.

The bike.

It was long and lean and mean. Red as fire, with silver glinting on the frame.

As soon as they entered the foyer, Kenny saw how intently Spence stared at it. It glittered and reflected in Spense's eyes. For that matter, it reflected in dozens of pairs of eyes as everyone waited for Mr. Gresham to finish the tabulations.

He had promised them the results by 6:30—unofficial, of course, and the bike wouldn't be awarded until noontime next Monday, at a special ceremony with the Mayor and the owner of the *Times* there to congratulate the winner.

But 6:30 would be time enough. They would get to Bill's by 7:30, easy, and ride with him out to Jenkin's Field for the Overnighter.

Kenny and Spence stood along the outside of the crowd, where they had a little more room, but also where they could sight along the edge of the wall and see the bike gleaming there, waiting.

Sanderson sauntered over.

"Hey."

"Hey," Kenny said.

Spence didn't say anything. In fact, he looked the other way, as if Sanderson didn't even exist. Kenny wrinkled his brow. Maybe Spence didn't want to jinx his chances.

"Do okay today?" Sanderson tried again. He knew his tally; he wanted to know Spence's.

Again, Spence didn't answer. Finally Kenny broke the silence and said, "Okay."

"Look," Sanderson said, not angrily but irritated, speaking at first to Kenny. "Everyone knows you were helping Spence get names. It's okay, I guess. Nothing in the rules says you can't." He stepped in front of Spence, directly in the other boy's line of vision. "But the least you can do is talk to me. It's not like we're enemies or anything."

Spence stared at the bike, still not speaking.

"Look, Wilcox," Sanderson said, his face flushing and his voice rising above the low din that filled the foyer. "I don't give a damn about...."

Half a dozen faces turned to stare at him, but Sanderson didn't notice.

Kenny did, though. He grabbed Sanderson's arm and spun him around, away from Spence.

"Hey, let him alone."

Sanderson started to say something. His cheeks tingled with scarlet that was probably less embarrassment than anger.

He backed up a step, colliding with Francine Adamson, the first girl carrier the *Times* ever hired, and knocking her into someone else. Kenny couldn't see who.

"You better watch it, too, Robinson," Sanderson said, his voice low and threatening. "You better not get in my way or...."

But just then Mr. Gresham stood away from the computer and cleared his throat.

Kenny and Sanderson shifted their attention to the front of the foyer, dropping the issue for the moment. Spence stared ahead, as if nothing had happened. He was smiling.

"Boys," Mr. Gresham said, then added, embarrassed, "and girls." Three of the girl carriers tittered; he never could remember to include them, maybe because he was so old and set in his ways and girls had only been delivering for the *Times f*or a couple of years now.

He coughed and continued. "We've got a winner."

They all leaned forward. Suddenly, the crowded foyer was dead silent.

"It was close. The final tally shows only two subscriptions dif-ference between first and second place. And you all understand"— he took in the assembled youth with a gimlet eye and as stern a countenance as he could muster (although it probably didn't scare any of them; like Kenny, everyone else knew him for pretty much an okay guy)—"that the final award is subject to verification Monday morning.

"The award luncheon will be at noon. I expect all of you to be there. It was a good competition, and everyone did much better than we hoped. In fact, I've just received word that the *Times* will publish a special edition insert for the Monday evening paper, with lists of every one of you who signed new subscribers. And *pictures* of the top ten."

A couple of the guys grinned and threw ridiculous poses. Gresham glanced over the top rim of his glasses and the carriers settled down again.

He continued.

"Now, as far as I can tell, here it is.

"Second place." He paused, letting the kids edge forward, ears pricked up and eyes pinned to him. "Jeff Sanderson."

Second place wasn't shabby. It would get Jeff a Walkman cassette and a certificate for $15.00 at Music-Plus. A couple of guys slapped him on the back and congratulated him.

Yeah, second place wasn't shabby.

But it wasn't the bike.

Sanderson threw a killing glance at Kenny and Spence.

"And first place," Mr. Gresham continued. Everyone turned to look at Spence. It was no secret that he and Sanderson had been running close. If Sanderson got second, then Spence had to have gotten first.

Spence still stared straight ahead, not even at the bike but at some mysterious spot on the wall a yard to the right of the gleaming handlebars.

"Spenser Wilcox," Mr. Gresham finally said, confirming what everyone believed they already knew.

The guys surged around Spence, slapping his shoulders, tugging his cap over his eyes, generally indulging in the foolishness that young teens found inescapable in moments of excitement.

Only Kenny noticed that Spence seemed unmoved by the announcement. Oh, he smiled, he even grinned that silly grin that reminded Kenny of the Cheshire-cat in the Disney movie his folks rented once in a while, even though he tried to convince them that he was really too old for it and would rather see *Commando* or *Predator* or *Total Recall*.

Spence even stumbled toward the bike and put his hand on the seat and patted it possessively.

But there was an emptiness in the movement. As if it really *didn't* mean that much.

And there was an odd smile playing around Spence's lips, like he knew something that no one else there knew, not even Kenny.

CHAPTER EIGHT

OVERNIGHTER

- 1 -

There were seven charter members of the Panther patrol: Billy Holmes, the patrol leader; Teddy Weiss, his assistant; Chuck Bowder; Brian Lowe; Jerry Philips; and Spence and Kenny.

The Overnighter was supposed to be mostly a shake-down for the week-long Summer Camp Troop 1089 was going to take two weeks later—six days at Camp Muir along the edges of Florence Lake, up in the mountains an hour's drive north-east of Fresno. Billy figured that if the Panthers got together this one more time to check out their equipment, run through camping skills, and polish up their ability to work together as a unit, they could get that much more out of the $125 per-scout camp.

It seemed like a good idea at the time.

Six of the seven charter members were able to meet at Jenkin's field late that Friday afternoon in mid-August. Jerry Philips was out of town, stoically enduring an interminable family reunion held on the desiccated and neglected grounds of a long abandoned church in a forgotten farming town somewhere in the middle of Nevada. Everyone there except his mom and dad seemed at least a hundred years old, and they all seemed to get their kicks by sitting around in the shade of a huge rented canvas dining fly and mumbling about who had died since the last reunion two years before. At the very moment that Billy's father dropped him, his kid brother Timmy, and Spence and Kenny off at the intersection of Sabra and Willowwood, just on the edge of Jenkins' field, Jerry Philips was sweltering beneath a dusty awning several hundred miles to the north and east, prickly and uncomfortable in the desert heat, angry at his folks for dragging him out to the reunion in the first place, and generally just bored out of his mind.

Three days later, when his folks angled their Buick into their driveway back home, and Jerry jumped out before it came to a complete stop—earning him a sharp, warning "Jerry!" from his mother—and ran next door to swap tales with Teddy Weiss, he learned how lucky he was.

Being bored out of your mind can be tiresome. But at least it's not deadly.

- 2 -

By 8:00, the Panthers had all assembled in the graveled clearing that was the unofficial parking lot for Jenkin's Field. For the purposes of this campout, *all* including little Timmy Holmes, who wasn't even a scout yet, and who would normally have stayed at home. But Mr. and Mrs. Holmes had to attend a business dinner in Century City that night and wouldn't be home until early the next morning, so it seemed the best thing to just send Timmy with Bill. Bill was embarrassed that he had to bring him along, but in actuality, none of the Panthers really minded. Timmy was almost eleven, he would be a member of the troop in a month or so anyway, and Bill's dad had insisted. After all, everyone knew that Jenkin's Field was as safe as your own backyard. Besides, it was only a mile from Chuck Bowder's place, and the Bowders would be home all weekend if the boys needed anything. And, Bill's father concluded, smiling to confirm his decision, Timmy needed to spend some 'quality' time with his older brother.

Fat lot Dads knew, Bill thought.

Bill knew that later, after the campout, when Timmy wasn't around to hear, the other Panthers would tease him about having to baby-sit, but for now he covered his embarrassment by playing the role of patrol leader to the hilt.

"Line up, PANTHERS!" he barked, using his best imitation of a television drill sergeant. The Panthers straggled into line, packs ready, canteens slapping moistly at narrow kid-hips (they all knew that there was no water in Jenkin's Field, so, like good scouts, they came prepared), sleeping bags curled beneath packs like tawny cocoons ready to hatch out at any moment, bundles of firewood swinging from the ends of leather or nylon tethers.

They marched the half mile through the center of Jenkin's Field to the stand of oaks that marked their overnighter camping ground.

Most of them knew that the field was doomed. In spite of its use for years by local troops for just such occasions, and the general assumption that the land would always be available for camping and hiking, it was not actually public land. A month ago, the owners had announced the sale of the field to a church group in Tamarind Valley. Within the year, they were going to break ground for a big two-story building that would become one of the landmarks of the community. The new owners had already agreed to preserve the circle of oaks—there was, after all, a $5,000 fine for cutting down even one of the centuries-old oaks that dotted Tamarind Valley—but there would obviously not be any place for camping among the low hanging branches.

Chuck was of two minds about the project. He belonged to the church in question, and he was already excited about the new building. In addition to a chapel and classrooms, it was going to have basketball courts and an outside field with baseball diamonds, and a parking lot big enough to hold a dozen bike-derbies at the same time. On the other hand, he would miss camping in Jenkin's Field. He had struggled with his priorities since the announcement in church a couple of Sundays ago. He had nearly decided that, since in a few years he would probably be too old for overnighters but basketball was for life, he was kind of looking forward to those new courts. He could imagine how they would look and smell and feel the first time he stepped on them, the varnish glossy, the lines crisp and new.

He thought about that even as he swung his pack onto his back and marched across the stand of jimson weed that grew under where the backstop would be.

He thought about it all the way across Jenkin's Field, because he knew it was essentially their valedictory campout here.

He did not know that long before the groundbreaking ceremonies for the new church took place, he would be dead.

- 3 -

They crossed the dry grass, descending into the slight hollow that cut out most of the sounds of Tamarind and hedged back the night lights from the freeways and the shopping district. Even though they were not half a mile from Sabra Street, the boys felt as if they were in the middle of the wilderness. The air smelled different here, drier than in the city, laden with the smell of chaparral and the occasional scrub pines on the hill behind Jenkin's Field. The heat from the sun warmed their necks and arms differently here. They could pretend, without much effort, that there wasn't another living soul for miles around, that they were the surviving members of an expedition into darkest Africa and were surrounded by ravening beasts and cannibalistic natives.

Sometimes, they played at being wild-west mountaineers outrunning renegade Redskins and hunting buffalo.

Once, one of the patrols from another troop had carried things a bit too far and used Jenkin's Field for a survival camp-out. It would have worked okay, too, since there was a stand of wild currants that bore fruit in the right time of the year, and occasionally you could find patches of lousewort and curly dock that were edible—nasty, but they got you past the edible-plants requirement.

But this patrol went all out and got so involved in survival that a couple of the guys went charging around wearing only loincloths made of neckerchiefs, slaughtering every snake and ground squirrel and lizard they could find, screaming like savages and swinging from the branches of the oaks until after midnight. Finally one of the families across Sabra got worried and called the cops. When the cops got there, they found a dozen filthy, nearly naked boys whooping around a campfire, their faces smudged with ochre and green—dirt mixed with water from their canteens, and crushed leaves rubbed onto their cheeks.

"Like somethin' outta that film, ya know, *Lord of the Flies*," an older cop mumbled when asked later about the ruckus. He clearly disapproved of both the film and the boys' inappropriate exuberance.

Half a dozen parents got late-night calls to come down to the Sheriff's station on Olson Road and identify their fractious offspring, and since then the Scoutmasters had drilled their Patrol Leaders on the proper etiquette for Jenkin's Field.

Bill Holmes was unusually responsible as a leader, otherwise his Dad would never have okayed the unchaperoned overnighter. Mr. Mills, the Scoutmaster, would probably have simply said *No way,* but he was out of town on business, and what he didn't know wouldn't hurt him. Bill had three years' experience in the troop; he was a Life Scout with one more badge for Eagle; and he was clearly mature for his age. And, in spite of his complaints, Bill loved his little brother and wanted to be sure he got a good start in the Scouting program. He would have protected Timmy with his life, and everyone around him knew it.

The other Panthers knew they were lucky to have Bill as their leader. He was old enough to have earned their respect, but at the same time, he was young enough to be one of them.

And so, until Bill's leadership, with the tacit approval of the parents involved, the overnighter at Jenkin's Field got off the ground.

When the patrol reached the center of the circle of oaks, they found everything much as they had expected it to be. The hard-packed dirt was already worn smooth, pocked here and there by the remains of innumerable earlier campouts—ragged holes marking the locations of phantom tent pegs and shallow depressions that were once carefully constructed fire pits.

Pitching camp was a matter of minutes, literally. Each Panther performed his assigned task. Kenny and Spence helped Teddy and Chuck put up the three tents. Bill and Timmy unpacked the bundles of firewood each of the boys brought in, since cutting the oak trees was strictly forbidden, both by law and by tradition among the scouts who camped there. Brian Lowe started the campfire, even though the boys had eaten already and their planned menu for the evening consisted of nothing more than hot chocolate and toasted marshmallows. Tomorrow they would work on cooking dehydrated foods—Teddy Weiss was new to the troop and hadn't had much experience with camping, and Bill wanted to give him as much training as possible before they hit Camp Muir.

Camp was up and ready before dark. Bill had intended to work on merit badges during the interim before the evening campfire, but the rest of the patrol was so full of energy that he finally gave up in despair. The boys raced like wild men around the thick oak boles, playing impromptu games of hide-and-seek, screeching and laughing as they ran. After a few minutes of trying to impose order on chaos, Bill threw up his hands and joined in, chasing little Timmy in and out through the low shrubbery, growling and pretending to be a monster. Timmy wasn't scared, of course, but he screamed and giggled with the rest of them.

By dusk, though, the Panthers were ready to settle down. The fire had burned down, the hot chocolate was steaming in plastic mess-kit cups, and plump, sweet marshmallows were browning on thin, crooked twigs from one of the ash trees that clustered on the low hill just behind the circle of oaks.

For a long while, no one spoke. It was quiet, peaceful, still.

"It's getting late," Bill said finally, glancing at the hands of his watch. "Past nine."

"Sure, Ma," someone quipped.

"Shuddup, Chuck," another voice responded, and everyone laughed quietly. Chuck, after all, was known for his weird sense of humor.

The fire had burned down enough that the boys felt its calming touch as flames died into embers that glowed stolidly against the dark backdrop of charred wood.

Bill grinned. "Yeah, but we got a lot planned for tomorrow and I don't want a bunch of guys who can't keep their eyes open when we work with the axes. No need to practice applying tourniquets this trip. Let's give it another half hour, then hit the hay."

No one spoke, which meant that the boys were almost willing to go along with Bill's suggestion.

After a moment or so, though, Teddy Weiss looked at the neat row of three pup tents and said, "Has anyone noticed? We're going to have a problem."

"What?" Kenny asked.

Teddy ostentatiously counted around the ring—one, two, three, on to seven, pointing at each boy in turn. Then he pointed at the three two-man tents. "Seven scouts. Six places."

Timmy looked at the ground and muttered, "Sorry," as if he personally had been responsible for the situation.

"No problem," Bill said. "Timmy and I can bunk outside. Just like in the back yard, huh kid."

"No...."

"Wait...."

"How about...."

"I don't mind...."

Everyone had an opinion about how to divide the spaces in the tent and everyone voiced his opinion loudly, until finally Bill laughed and held up his hand and said, "Let's hold on that decision for a while. We got this great fire and it's going to waste."

"Sure," Kenny said, pushing another marshmallow onto his stick and holding it over a particularly appealing glow. "No need to worry now."

- 4 -

The last marshmallow disappeared, and the embers burned down until they cast eerie red glows on the circle of faces. No one had spoken for a long while, but when Bill tilted the face of his watch toward the fire to check on the time again, Brian said quietly, as if to forestall Bill's telling them that it was time for sleep, "What about a story?"

"Yeah," five voices echoed as one.

"A ghost story," someone said. Kenny thought it was Spence, but the voice was not quite right for Spence, softer, almost...malicious. Kenny shook his head. *Getting tired already. Imagining things.* Actually, it was probably Chuck, he decided. Chuck was known to haunt the horror section of the VCR rental stores and could talk his big brother into taking him to see anything from *Aliens* to *Slaughter Serenade.*

He glanced around to spot Spence, but the fire was so low that all of the boys were little more than red shadows against a deeper blackness.

"Yeah, man," Brian answered, after a long pause.

"A ghost story."

"A real gooshy one." A murmur of approval met the suggestion.

"How 'bout the Poobah?" Teddy asked. He tossed another chunk of firewood into the circle. Sparks circles upward like fireflies, then the log caught, and the fire flickered higher.

Bill shook his head. His face was sliced into sharp angles by the firelight, red-tinted flesh and black shadow, until he looked more like a mask than a person. "Can't," he said. "I promised when I was at Muir last year. That story goes with the camp. You'll just have to wait a week to hear it."

"The Bloody Hook, then," Brian said, his eyes bright embers. "I love it when the guy goes around to his girl's car door and finds the hook sticking in the handle. It makes me...."

Chuck, sitting next to Brian, nudged him with his elbow. "Stupid, now you gave it away!"

Bill laughed. "Yeah, so why do we need to tell it. You've already told the best part?"

Brian looked sufficiently chastened, so much so that the other boys voices rippled in quiet laughter. Brian hunched over and scowled for a moment, then joined in. "Yeah," he said, "pretty stupid."

At the head of the circle, Bill thought for a moment.

Then he leaned into the fire, bringing his face closer to the dying flames, letting the embers underlight his cheeks and brow ridges even more dramatically. The light threw weird dancing shadows across his face.

Kenny saw Timmy and Teddy shiver in anticipation. Bill really *looked* scary. This had to be a great story!

"How many of you," Bill intoned in a low, conspiratorial voice, turning to stare at each of the boys in the circle, "have ever heard of...Sven the Red-Handed?"

Three or four of them had already, including Kenny and Spence, but they weren't about to let that stop Bill. He really *knew* this story, and he always told it well. Already, Kenny could tell that the others felt tendrils of fear creeping up their spines, up their shadowy spines that curved vulnerably away from the welcome if fading light of the fire and into the creeping darkness. The thin nylon tents would seem darker after this story, the sleeping bags flimsier, the oak trees more gnarled and threatening, the night stars more distant and dim.

It was a *perfect* story.

"Yeah," someone breathed. "Tell that one."

Bill grinned, an evil, toothy grin that promised death and blood and murder and mayhem. After all, even the dimmest Scout could figure out why Sven would be called the "Red-handed"—certainly not because he was caught red-handed stealing from his Mommy's cookie jar!

"It all started years ago," Bill began, lowering his voice even more. The other boys leaned in toward the fire, concentrating on his words, on his glowing face. "Back then, this whole valley was covered with trees, so thick that even a squirrel couldn't run through without hitting his head on the trunks."

That was a lie, of course; Tamarind Valley could at best boast a tenuous history as a chaparral area. But this was a campfire story, and for the moment the tale invited them all to imagine immense, dense stands of dark oaks, eerie and frightening, with dead limbs hanging down like skeletal arms waiting to grasp at anyone who dared enter the secret confines.

Timmy closed his eyes and saw the forest scene from the scary parts of *Snow White*. His folks had taken him to see the film on its most recent re-release. They must have figured that a G-rated animated Disney film would be okay for a kid his age, certainly better than the popular and ubiquitous shoot-'em-up cop stories or *Die Hard*-style terrorist films. But Timmy had had nightmares about the forest scene for weeks afterward. He didn't tell anyone but Bill, who understood and didn't laugh or anything. More than anything, he loved Bill for that. Bill understood and didn't laugh or anything.

Timmy jerked his eyes open and glanced quickly around the circle, as if reassuring himself that Bill was still there.

Bill continued, allowing himself to be carried away by the rhythms of the story: "The first people to enter the area were the lumbermen. They were giants among men, seven feet tall and strong enough that they could shiver a trunk with a single blow from their huge steel axes. But the biggest, and the strongest, and the ugliest, and the meanest of them all was Sven the Red-Handed.

"They didn't call him that at first, of course. He was just plain Sven...until the night he went crazy and fifteen men were never seen again and Sven the Red-Handed showed up in camp with his axe all bloody and his huge hands all bloody and there was a trail of blood that led back from the camp into a circle of trees." Bill glanced around him, as if realizing for the first where he was. "In fact," he whispered, "It was *this* circle of trees.

"Sven the Red-Handed walked into the camp down along the Santa Clara River, not two miles from this very spot. Everyone was sitting around the campfire, smoking their pipes and drinking homemade whiskey, and suddenly there he was, seven feet tall and ugly and mean, his axe slung over his shoulder."

One of the boys snickered at the image, but Bill pinioned him with a glance that cut the laughter off. Bill started again: "Sven was covered with blood. He looked around the campfire"—and here, of course, Bill paused long enough to stare at each of the shadowy fig-ures in turn—"and then he said he'd killed the others, all fifteen, and if anyone wanted to find them they could follow the trail of blood back through the trees.

"Then, before anyone could move, he disappeared into the darkness like an evil ghost, and was never seen again.

"The other lumberjacks grabbed their lanterns and followed the trail of blood, even though the blood was so dark that sometimes they couldn't even find it. But finally they came to the circle of trees—to *this* circle of trees."

Bill paused and looked from face to face. Even the boys who knew the story, who knew that Bill would now describe the carnage in as much and as gruesome detail as he could improvise, glanced nervously at each other. The story would end with Bill saying some-thing like, "And Sven the Red-Handed was never seen again—UNTIL NOW!" And he would lunge at one of the faces circling the nearly dead fire, both his hands outstretched as if he were going to throttle his chosen victim. It was a point of pride for the older Scouts that they were never going to let it startle them—but it always did. Timmy was more transparent. He didn't know the story would end, but he had already edged closer to Bill, as if proximity to the story-teller would protect him from the story.

"Well," Bill went on, his voice less whispery, more like normal speech, "when they got to the circle of trees, they held their lamps up and looked around." He pointed to a low-hanging branch that jut-ted out toward their fire. "Over there they found bloody intestines draped in the trees like Christmas Tree lights."

"Sausages, anyone?" Chuck whispered.

"Ugh. Gross," Brian whispered back.

Bill ignored the interruption. He pointed in the opposite direction, toward a thick stump that twisted weirdly before splitting into three large branches about six feet from the ground. "And over there, they found one of the men hanging from his own suspenders...everything but his *head*."

There was a sharp intake of breath, probably from Timmy, Kenny thought, since most of the others had heard this part before and Bill hadn't even gotten to the really good stuff yet.

"And the head," Bill paused again, melodramatically, scanning his audience until every eye was glued to him, every body waiting for him to point. Then he waited an extra breath, gauging his timing perfectly.

"And the head...was...over...*there!*"

He thrust his hand straight out, his finger pointing across the circle like a cry of sin, and every head spun to follow its trajectory. From the darkness beyond the fire pit, two eyes embrous gleamed redly in the decaying light.

"Sven the Red-Handed!" Timmy screamed. He burrowed his face into Bill's jacket and hid his eyes.

Bill could feel Timmy's body quivering, could hear the raspy *huh-huh-huh* of a whimpering that went beyond mere fear. He really did love Timmy, and he would have been ashamed of scaring his kid-brother like that, except that he didn't have time to be ashamed.

- 5 -

There was a head out there.

A disembodied head, floating as if caught in the fork of a twisted branch. The only things visible were its two glowing eyes and its matted filthy hair hanging over its forehead like a fringe of night. The hair reflected the firelight dully.

"What the h...." Frightened, and furious at being frightened, Bill jumped to his feet. "Who's that?"

He scanned the small groups still crouched around the campfire. Everyone was here, Kenny, Teddy, Chuck, Brian. Timmy had let go of Bill's jacket when Bill pushed himself up, but was now clutching Bill's pants legs, his arms wrapped around Bill's knees. Timmy jerked spasmodically, almost throwing the older boy off balance.

Bill stared around the circle again.

"Who did that?" he started to ask, then choked off the words.

Wait. Someone was missing.

Spence was missing!

"Spence!" Bill yelled, jerking his head around so that his voice penetrated the darkness on all sides of them. "This isn't funny."

He glared angrily at Kenny. "Were you in on this, Robinson?" Bill's voice was unaccountably harsh and ugly, and Kenny cringed at the sound of it. "You and Wilcox always do everything together. Did you rig this up to scare Timmy?"

"Hey," Kenny began. "I didn't even know you were going to tell this stupid story...."

Timmy screamed again, a long piercing scream that riveted every boy's attention on him as he crouched, a small packet of shadow at Bill's feet.

"Sven the Red-Handed! He's out there!" The screams dropped off to become incoherent moans.

Bill squatted down and tried to calm his brother. "Hey, kid. Come on. It's only a dumb story."

The others looked around nervously. Spence *was* gone. No mistake about that.

And the gruesome head still hung there in the darkness, like some displaced, grotesque Halloween decoration.

Kenny stepped out of the ring of light. He moved a foot or two toward the head. "Hey, Spence, that's not funny. Don't scare the kid. Come on out...."

Teddy Weiss screamed this time. Then Timmy screamed again. And then Kenny.

Because what stepped from the shadows behind the oak was *not* Spencer Wilcox.

It was Sven the Red-Handed, seven feet tall, mean and ugly, swinging an axe that glinted in the firelight and dripped dark gouts of blood. His hands—so big that his curled fists looked the size of volleyballs—were stained black, but each of the horror-stricken boys knew that the blackness was really red, deep red, blood red, altered to something even more terrifying by the night. The miasmal, coppery stench of fresh blood preceded him.

The figure stepped forward and in two strides halved the distance between it and the fire pit. Timmy's scream had decayed to a whimpering hiccup, as if he could not force his lungs to take in enough oxygen to sustain anything louder. Bill was still half-kneeling, his arms on Timmy's shoulders. He was paralyzed by what he saw, his eyes riveted on the apparition that stood before them, his story come to life.

In that instant of insensate terror, he knew he was going to die.

They were *all* going to die.

Sven the Red-Handed tightened his grip on the long ash handle of his axe and swung it back. The blade disappeared into the night, as if it were a magician's prop and with an "abracadabra" it would disappear and another "abracadabra" it would reappear.

When it did reappear, it swooshed like a thing animate and possessed. It hissed downward like a venomous serpent momentarily transmuted to cold steel. It swooshed through the night, cleaving air, and silence, and darkness, and peace, and Teddy Weiss.

His legs and part of his abdomen stood stock still for what seemed like hours but may only have been seconds. Blood pumped up from severed blood vessels; his intestines slid over his glistening belt and dripped onto his pants. One loop of tissue swung softly against a scorched patch on his knee.

By the time Teddy's legs discovered that they were dead, Sven the Red-Handed had reversed the swing of the double-bladed axe, letting it slide again into the anonymity of darkness.

Bill was stunned, but part of him understood that to stand still was to invite death. He yelled, a karate yell that was as much to kick his heart in gear again as anything, and grabbed the small hand axe they had used to break their firewood and leaped over the circle of logs they had been sitting on and swung at the thing before him.

Sven the Red-Handed grinned.

Kenny felt cold and sick when he saw that grin. But he didn't have time to think about it. Already the axe was sluicing through the air again and this time it was heading for Bill. Without thinking, Kenny flung out his arm as Bill shot by, pushing the bigger boy sideways, amazed that he was able to deflect Bill, not yet knowing of the power of adrenaline in crises. Bill stumbled, fell, and the descending axe head hit him, not edge first and cutting, but sideways and stunning. It crashed into his shoulder and knocked him backward, back through the ring of boys and on top of the embers. His shirt flared and suddenly his screams rang like alarm bells as he rolled on the ground, trying to extinguish the external fire, feeling a matching internal fire when his weight grated against shattered bones in his arm and shoulder.

In the meantime, Sven the Red-Handed stepped closer. Brian Lowe, who had been standing next to Teddy Weiss and whose white T-shirt was now mottled with sticky red, made a muffled cry that might have been a desperate attempt to vomit his fear, and fell backwards, saving his life as the axe swung through the air where he had been standing. He didn't try to regain his footing. Scuffling crab-wise in the dust, he scrabbled out of the circle on the far side of the fire and disappeared into the darkness. He didn't stop to worry whether there might be another...*thing* waiting for him.

Blinded by terror, sickened by horror, he just ran.

Chuck Bowder tried to back up. He raised his arms in a protective gesture that was worse than useless, but it was the only thing he could think to do. The movement was almost instinctive; it was the gesture he had seen innumerable times in the horror films.

It usually didn't work in the films, either, but he was beyond rational analysis. He felt the swelling of mind-numbing fear. He acted.

He didn't die from falling backward over the log. In fact, the fall didn't hurt him at all, other than bruising the large muscles of his buttocks. Had he survived the night, he wouldn't have noticed the tenderness the next morning.

But when he fell, his feet were on the ground on one side of the log and his back against the ground on the other side.

Sven the Red-Handed only needed a single strike to sever both of Chuck's legs at the knees, using the log as a chopping block. For a second, Chuck felt nothing except the ragged pain of a rock digging into his hip; the axe blade was so sharp that he never did *feel* where it had cut through bone and muscle and tendon below his knees. He noticed an odd loss of balance as he tumbled backward, wondered for an instant why he couldn't feel where his feet were scrabbling for purchase on the rough ground. Then his body swung the rest of the way off the log, and he saw the twin jets of blood spurting from his knees, spraying the log, and someone huge and shadowy hunched a few feet away from him, and then he saw Sven the Red-Handed up close and personal as the monster leaned over the log and brought the axe down once more, this time aiming unerringly for Chuck Bowder's face.

Chuck felt that pain for an instant, like a flowering of scorching agony and blood, then felt nothing more.

Perhaps only thirty seconds had passed, certainly not more than a minute...or a century. Kenny was crouching on the outskirts of the fire, reaching for the pitifully small hand axe that lay somewhere in the darkness. Bill was still screaming. The stench of his burning flesh mixed with the coppery smell of blood and the acrid smell of urine and feces and sweaty fear. Chuck was dead. Teddy was dead. Spence had disappeared, presumably dying as the first victim of Sven the Red-Handed even before the horror had burst into the camp. Brian Lowe was gone; Kenny didn't know where.

Timmy was alone, hunched in a tiny heap just beyond the fire, on the opposite side of the fire ring from where his brother still writhed in pain.

Timmy no longer screamed; he no longer even made that awful whooping, hiccoughing sound. He crouched deathly silent and white. His eyes glowed, round and dark and brimming with terror as images stepped out of his nightmares, off the theater screens, down from the television, and intruded into his world. He looked small, alone, pitiable to any but the hardest, cruelest, most despicably evil of hearts.

Surely, Kenny thought madly in an instant that seemed to stretch into hours, *surely he can't...won't....*

The axe flashed, faster than Kenny could imagine anything moving.

For an insane moment, he thought that Sven the Red-Handed must be playing golf, like Kenny's dad did every Saturday morning, swinging the axe like a club, side on rather than over the shoulder.

Whick!

The ball flew from the tee into the darkness *hole in one!*...only it wasn't a ball, it was Timmy's head, and it struck somewhere nearby, and Kenny heard it scraping against twigs and leaves as if fell and rolled and then there was silence.

- 6 -

Sven the Red-Handed looked at his handiwork.

One escaped, but that is all right. There is sufficient here to feed me.

It had already absorbed the terror as each of the boys had died, different terrors, different qualities of agonized fear -tastes, as it were. The uncomprehending horror of the first boy as the blade sheared through him. The knowing, and therefore deeper terror of the second as he pitched over the log and waited for death.

And the best of all. The youngest. The first to see and recognize, the first to pull the terror and the image from within and, screaming and sobbing, pitch it like vomit into the air. And at the end, still the most delightful as he waited there, curled and mindless and watching, his eyes following the backward sweep of the blade, almost comically crossing at the last moment when the blade swept within his focal point. They were still crossed, like an animated elf's, when the head disappeared into the intertwined branches.

Sven the Red-Handed laughed at the image. There was a moan at his feet.

The big boy, the first to attack, twisted on the ground. Sven the Red-Handed took a single step, towering over the boy, a Sequoia overshadowing a dandelion.

126

He reached down and, with a gentleness that was infinitely more frightening than his violence, the monster turned Bill onto his back.

Bill stared up. He saw the thing's eyes. The pain in his shoulder was forgotten. The pain of his burned arm and back and neck and face was banked like embers saved for another day's fire. He felt nothing but numbness, still seeing Timmy's headless body toppling almost onto his chest.

He stared upward into those bitter, cold eyes. He waited for death to bite. He *wanted* it.

Ah, now you invite death, storyteller. Now the pain is too great, not physical pain, no, not that, but the guilt and the fear for the little one.

Sven the Red-Handed raised the axe, studying Bill's eyes as the blade hovered yards above his head.

Sven the Red-Handed saw in them what he wanted, what he needed most to see.

The axe blade dropped, hissing through the air...to stop half an inch from Bill's throat.

You will live. You will love and remember and fear and sometime, perhaps not for years to come but sometime, I will return to you and feast on a festering sweetness that will only grow richer with time.

There were no words. Bill heard nothing. But Sven the Red-Handed saw the fear steeping into the boy's eyes as the axe blade withdrew, stretched upward until it disappeared, and Sven the Red-Handed stepped over Bill's body as if it were nothing but a clump of useless rags, and then pain flooded through Bill's shattered limbs and the anguish through his mind.

On the other side of the fire pit, Kenny had finally found the axe. He hefted it in his hand and brought himself into a ready stance, all while forced to watch as Sven the Red-Handed destroyed Timmy and toyed so cruelly with Bill.

Kenny was crying silently. Tears blurred what little he could see in the fading light from the scattered embers of their campfire.

Not a yard away, the hot chocolate pot had been kicked and spilled during the horror, and its sticky contents were seeping into the hard earth. Kenny smelled the rich sweetness and felt his stomach clench.

He gripped the hand axe so tightly that his fingers went cold. Even in the darkness, his knuckles glowed whitely.

He would die, with the rest of them, but he would die fighting!

He stood, waiting, while Sven the Red-Handed stepped over Bill and callously kicked Timmy's body out of his way and then turned and confronted Kenny over the remains of the fire.

Sven the Red-Handed smiled and held out his hand. The huge figure flickered and wavered. For an instant, Kenny half believed that the whole thing was a nightmare, a horrible dream, a hallucination.

Then Sven was back, solid and huge.

Filled with a horror more devastatingly debilitating than any pain he would ever know, Kenny dropped the axe.

Sven the Red-Handed flickered in the light, his body now solid, now translucent, now as wispy as the November fog that blanketed Tamarind Valley.

Now seven feet tall and stained in blood.

And now barely Kenny's height, wearing a face and form as familiar as his own. This form stepped up to Kenny, held out its hand again.

As in a dream, Kenny reached out to touch the hand.

Time flickered like tree leaves tossed in a storm. A second, and a lifetime. The transmuting form leaned nearer and nearer as it spiraled through its changes, its eyes the only constant as they burned in feverish, gloating triumph.

Kenny's hand closed on nothingness.

Somewhere, far away, in a world of sanity and peace, a siren rose and fell against the backdrop of night sounds.

Kenny screamed and dropped into utter blackness.

- 7 -

When he came to, lights and people and frightening sounds surrounded him. There were people groaning and crying and cursing, and someone was throwing up in a clump of dried grass. Kenny couldn't see anything, but he smelled the stomach-knotting stench of vomit.

He tried to sit up, but a hand held him down . A voice, itself tense and verging on hysteria, stuttered through his confusion.

"Wait till the doc sees you...make sure you're okay...my God, who...how...why...."

He started to speak. "Spence."

But the voice cut him off and then something stung him in the arm, and he dropped into darkness again, but this time the darkness was cool and moist and restful.

- 8 -

The next time he roused to painful consciousness, sunlight hurt his eyes. He closed them tightly and took a few deep breaths before he dared open them again. It was morning. He lay in his own bed, and bright, cheerful sunlight sliced through the window overlooking his backyard. Mom and Dad were sitting next to him on straight-backed chairs, one on each side of the bed. Their faces were etched with worry and fear and exhaustion...and love and relief.

"Kenny?" Mom whispered.

"Mom. Dad." He looked from one to the other. Then the flood of images burst, and he remembered. He wanted to scream but didn't.

"I dreamed...."

They looked across at each other before they dared look at him. In that action he understood that he hadn't dreamed at all. The whole nightmare was real.

He sat up. He felt stiff, as if he had strained every muscle in his body. His neck was sore and his throat rasped when he tried to talk. He felt the ravages of screams ripping across moist tissue. But otherwise—especially compared to his memories of the blood and the pain—he was miraculously unhurt.

"Who...did any of the guys...?" He couldn't finish.

"Later, dear," Mom said soothingly, but he could see the play of muscles at her throat, the spot of fervid color at her cheekbones. Blood throbbed at her temples.

"No, I gotta know. Please tell me. *Please!*"

He looked wildly from one parent to the other.

His father laid a restraining hand on Kenny's shoulder and nodded slowly, as if to say, *I don't want to do this to you son, not now, not while you're still so young, but this is real life and even for children life can be harsh.*

"Bill's alive," Mr. Robinson said carefully. "He'll be intensive care in the burn center for...for a long time. And he's pretty busted up, his arm and shoulder, some ribs. Brian somehow made it to Sabra Road and got some folks to call the police. He's okay."

Mr. Robinson fell silent.

"The others?" Kenny already knew, but somehow he needed to hear someone he loved speak the words. Confirmation would be assuaging; at least the visions that floated behind his eyes would not have come from his own vicious imagination. If the dead were dead....

"Timmy Holmes is...dead. And Chuck and Teddy."

His father didn't say any more, and Kenny didn't want him to. He didn't want...need...to hear any details.

"Spence?" Kenny asked, his mouth hurting and dry. His heart pounded out a violent tattoo, rattling his ribcage. *Let him be dead,* he cried, *please god let him be dead with his body scattered in little pieces all over Jenkin's Field. Let him be dead like his grandmother because even that would be better than the other thing, the thing that I can't won't even put words to. Just let him be dead. God, please.*

His father shook his head. Kenny knew that his own attachment to Spence was mirrored in his father. Both shared a love for the Wilcox boy, loved Spence like the other son and brother that they enjoyed for such a short time.

"We don't know. He's...they haven't found his...."

Body, Kenny completed. *They haven't found his* body. *And they won't. Not ever.*

- 9 -

Later that afternoon, Kenny got out of bed. He felt shaky and his skin was unnaturally white underneath his layers of late-summer tan, but essentially he was all right. He sat in the sunlight by the pool, but even in the heat he had wrapped himself in a thick robe against the coldness that had grown huge inside him.

He watched the sunlight reflecting in bright bits from the water—like silver firelight from a massive flat blade.

He sat, and thought, and remembered, and decided.

Spence was gone. If not dead, at least *gone.* Kenny knew when and where it had happened. Not last night. Not in the circle of oaks. Not anywhere near Jenkin's Field.

No whatever had happened, it had taken place earlier, much earlier yesterday.

It had taken place when Spence had gotten his last subscription, when someone signed his subscription book with a loopy, snaky signature that had chilled Kenny when he first saw it and that now formed and re-formed in his imagination to become a dictionary of obscene words, an encyclopedia of horror.

It had happened when Spence went alone into the house beyond the hill.

- 10 -

It was so easy. They had all shared the same fear. They had all seen the same thing. There had been no pulling away at the last instant. It had been gloriously easy and so fulfilling.

So filling.

For the moment it was sated.

PART TWO

CARRYING THE BATTLE TO THE ENEMY

CHAPTER NINE

THE UPROOTING

- 1 -

For the third night in a row, Richard Mann woke suddenly. The dream disappeared like a vapor.

His body was clammy and damp with sweat. His breathing sounded harsh in the night silence. He still felt the moist imprint of someone's hand on his cheek. He raised his own hand and laid it across the tingling spot, as unerringly as if it were a magnet attracted to a lode of iron.

Mom.

The thought echoed, even though this time—as each time before—he could not remember dreaming, certainly not dreaming about Emma.

He lay awake. His back was beginning to ache, and his legs were stiff, but lay motionless. He was afraid to move for fear that the slightest shift would communicate itself to Bonnie, who had been sleeping unusually lightly for some weeks now. In the mornings, her eyes were heavy and circled with dark rings, as if she had been awake most of the night. Richard did not want to disturb her in what seemed a rare moment of rest for her.

Instead, he stared at the blankness where the ceiling must be, even though the room was so dark that he could not distinguish the spots on the yellowing acoustical tile.

He was restless, worried. His sleep was disturbed by unremembered dreams that flitted back and forth in his imagination, too tenuous to be grasped and identified, too solid to be ignored. He wished that he could remember even one; he was unaccountably certain that the same dream had awakened him each night.

135

He risked a glance at the luminous dial of the alarm clock humming on the night stand. Two o'clock. The same time as each night before.

He sighed and, feeling another twinge in his back, rolled onto his side. Even as he moved, he winced as if struck. He had forgotten Bonnie already. He held his breath.

"It's okay," she said softly.

He twisted back, rolling toward her until his arm rested lightly on the sheet covering her. He could feel the soft swell of her breasts nudging along his forearm and wrist. His fingers closed slowly.

"I didn't mean to wake you."

"I wasn't asleep."

"Oh."

They lay without speaking for a long while. The room was hot and stuffy, even with the two small windows open on each side of the bed. It was as if, inexplicably deciding to be miserly with evening breezes, the St. Louis night had decided to keep its coolness to itself. The thin white curtains pulled against the window sills barely fluttered; outside, the leaves on the black walnut tree were as still as death where they arced across the window.

This was Richard's old room. It had served as his room when he was a boy. He and Bonnie were sleeping on the single bed that he had slept on for so many years before he married and moved out. The bed was small, but not so small that they would have preferred one of the other beds in the house.

Donney's bed, just down the hall, was the same size as Richard's but by unspoken mutual consent neither Richard nor Bonnie even entered the room, to say nothing of sleeping there. They had no desire to disturb the museum-like atmosphere that Emma had given it in the two years since Donney walked out. At first, she seemed content simply to strip the walls of his posters—"those hellish things," Emma had called them in a rare fit of anger as she crumpled a still of Count Dracula and thrust it into the incinerator out back and viciously jabbed a burning match head at the evil Count. She stared at the twisted paper until the flames licked the edge, caught, and flared in a glare of red. Only then did she seem satisfied.

Later, gradually, Richard noticed things re-appearing in the room, mostly things that Donney himself had removed during his last few years at home. String-art from the fifth grade. Mother's Day cards with trite sentiments crudely and laboriously inscribed in crumbling crayon. The lithograph of a sailing vessel that Uncle John had given Donney for his seventh birthday. That sort of thing.

Emma's systematic re-creation of Donney's past struck Richard as unhealthy, but by the time he had screwed up enough courage to confront his mother with the visible evidence of her obsession, she was dying. He had decided not to mention anything.

But as far as guest quarters went, Donney's room was definitely out.

As was Emma's.

It had a double bed, of course, the same bed where Emma and Roland had spent their wedding night and, for all of their married years, every night of their lives together. It was where Richard had been conceived in a night of passion that Emma had alluded to, cryptically and intriguingly, once or twice when Richard was in his teens. It was the bed where Donney had been conceived in a night of cooler, calmer lovemaking...quieter because of two-year-old Richard sleeping in the room upstairs.

But again, as with Donney's room, neither Richard nor Bonnie had even considered sleeping there. The room was full of ghosts—real or imagined—that whispered in Richard's ears whenever he entered to search the bureau drawers or the closet for a necessary document, or to bring out a box of faded and worn family photographs to sort through, or to do any of the hundred things that had to be taken care of...that *he* had to take care of...now that Emma was dead.

That was why they were still in the old house at all. Their cramped apartment was only half a dozen blocks away, in an area of St. Louis slightly newer, slightly more affluent, but more congested. The first night after Emma's death, after the ambulance had taken the body away and the paramedics and the fire truck that accompanied them were long gone, after the officious little man from the coroner's office had taken down the needed data and left them with a pamphlet that explained what they would have to do to get the body released for the funeral—after everything was over and everyone had left, Richard and Bonnie walked silently through the house, switching off lights, locking the screen door in the kitchen, shutting the door to Emma's bedroom. At the front door, Richard had stopped and looked around.

"I can't leave here. Not yet. Not like this." Bonnie had nodded in agreement.

They had spent the night there, in the living room, curled together like spoons on the old maroon sofa with its embroidered and crocheted peacock antimacassars. When the night grew cool, Richard pulled Emma's crocheted afghan down from the back of the sofa and tucked it around them.

Neither could explain exactly why they stayed there. It just seemed right.

The next day they found excuses not to go back to their own place.

There were papers to sign, property to transfer, insurance forms to fill out for the burial plot, the funeral. They found all of the documents they needed, neatly filed and stored in Emma's top dresser drawer, in envelopes carefully inscribed with contents and names and addresses. She had even made out envelopes for mailing, including postage stamps. The Purple Cross burial insurance envelope contained forms completely filled out except for one space: date of decease.

Or there were people to talk with. Neighbors who had known Emma for twenty years filed in one by one during the next morning to pay respects, to grasp Richard's hand and wring it gently or lay commiserating hands on Bonnie's arm and say kind words. Relatives—cousins and second-cousins—began the traditional pilgrimage. Uncle John's kids and their broods drove in from scattered parts of Missouri and fully intended to stay at Aunt Emma's until the funeral. Most of them ended up in nearby motels. Uncle John's oldest was bedded down in Richard and Bonnie's apartment, as a matter of fact. His three kids camped out in sleeping bags on the living room floor.

For whatever reasons, Richard and Bonnie had barely left the house since Emma died. The funeral had been Saturday afternoon. Sunday noon the last of the relatives left, satisfied that Emma had been seen off with proper dignity and respect. And now it was Sunday night—early Monday morning, in fact—and Richard and Bonnie were still at the old place, sharing the narrow twin bed that had been Richard's as a boy. The clock was his old clock. The handmade quilt that lay folded across the foot of the bed had been his when he was sixteen and anxious to be out on his own and free.

Now he was glad for its weight across his feet and legs, even though his chest was hot beneath the weight of the single sheet.

They lay unmoving for a long time, until Richard thought for sure that Bonnie had dropped back to sleep. He started to lift his arm but, without speaking, she held tight to his wrist and pulled it back onto her breast, so he knew that she was still awake.

"Anything wrong?" he asked. There was an unusual urgency about her movement.

"I...I was just thinking. About...the baby." *The miscarriage,* he amended, understanding at once what she meant. Only six months into their marriage, two months into her first pregnancy, it had happened. There had been cramps, spotting, a sudden gush of blood and fluid. Then the frantic, midnight, pell-mell trip to the hospital, and the grim expression on the emergency-room attendant's face when he came out to bring Richard back to Bonnie's cubicle.

"Oh." He couldn't think of anything else to say. She patted his arm, a mother-comforting-little-boy species of pat, and he felt both better and worse.

For a second it seemed as if Bonnie were about to say something. Richard found himself holding his breath, waiting for her words. But then, silently, she rolled against him. Her skin was warm...hot almost, even compared to the heat of the August night. She burrowed against him, as if intent on welding as many points of contact between them as physically possible.

He responded, pulling her tighter, kicking back the sheet and quilt where they had bunched between two sets of legs intertwining with the steady progress of a vine twisting through the trellis against the front wall of Emma's house.

Their movements quickened. The heat increased until it seemed that their bodies must glow with an incandescence that put the lie to shadows hunching in the corners of Richard boyhood room. The twin bed was narrow and cramped, but soon there was more than enough room, and the shadows crept back further, as if aghast at what they were witnessing, here beneath the plastic model airplanes preserved on dust-free shelves and the garish high-school pennants and the line of Hardy Boy mysteries and the complete set of paperback Walter Farley Black Stallion novels that had been Roland's and that Emma had given the boy Richard the year he turned fourteen.

Shame, shame, the shadows might have muttered, as if the couple on the bed were nothing but animated figures from one of the *Playboy* magazines Richard had occasionally smuggled upstairs and hidden between the mattress and springs...and that Emma had found and glanced through and scowled at and carefully replaced in its hiding place. There had been six issues. She kept count. Then they had stopped, as she had hoped they would. That was just after Richard met Bonnie and a couple of months before their marriage.

Shame, shame, the shadows might have muttered, but there was nothing prurient or shameful happening in the small room.

The only sounds were whispers of endearment and love, cries and hoarse breathing. And then a deep and solemn silence until the hands of the clock crossed themselves like a virgin hiding her nakedness and it was well past three.

Exhausted but tingling with sated pleasure, Richard rolled onto his side of the narrow mattress, Bonnie still touching him at shoulder and hip and leg.

In spite of his wish to stay awake and feel her closeness, he slept.

And dreamed he dreamed and woke.

- 2 -

Creeaak. Creeaak. Creeeaaak.

The noise gradually infiltrated the silence. He folded back the damp sheet and was on his feet beside the bed before he became aware of making any movements. He stood for a long moment in the shifting shadows of his room.

He was naked. His toes curled lightly into the texture of the hand-braided rag rug that circled the island of his bed like a soft, multicolored coral reef. The feeling was pleasurable. It reminded him of a thousand midnight awakenings over a young lifetime. Sometimes they were followed by raids on the refrigerator and the lingering aftertaste of chocolate-chip cookies and ice-cold milk; sometimes by sleepy, half-remembered (or not remembered at all) trips along the unlit hallway to the bathroom and the aching pleasure of almost automatically voiding a bladder full beyond the point of comfort; sometimes, mercifully few, by shuffling steps into Mom's room to find release from the grips of a nightmare.

Creeaak. Creeaak. Creeeaaak.

The sound moved inward, touching the fringes of his mind. He searched for an explanation but found none.

He slipped out the bedroom door and into the darker hallway.

Creeaak. Creeaak. Creeeaaak.

The sound was definitely louder, closer.

He stopped outside Donney's closed door. He rested his ear against the cool, smooth wood and, closing his eyes to concentrate, listened. He heard no sound.

No, that was not quite true.

There was a rustling coming from inside the room, a whispered shifting as if Donney were sleeping restlessly and his body were rolling and twisting in crisp sheets. Richard stepped back from the door and raised his hand to turn the knob and check on his brother.

Before his hand could touch the knob, he glanced down at the floor. A thin flicker of light brushed against his naked toes where they rested only inches from the crack between door and polished hardwood floor.

The light seemed like darkness. He swallowed hard.

Creeaak. Creeaak. Creeeaaak.

He dropped his hand and stepped even further away from the door. Now he could not hear the rustling any more. The hall was a silent as death.

He moved on down the hall, enjoying the play of air on his skin as he descended the stairs into the cooler downstairs rooms.

The living room was silent.

Then: *Creeaak. Creeaak. Creeeaaak.*

The sound was louder now, but seemed to be coming from another part of the house.

He turned into the niche that led to the short passageway connecting the downstairs bathroom with Mom and Dad's room *why did I think* Dad *its been years since I though of it as his room too.*

Creeaak. Pause. *Creeaak.* Pause. *Creeeaaak.*

The sound was spaced now, more deliberate. He had heard it before. He entered the darkness of the hallway and padded silently to stand outside his parents' bedroom door.

Emma's door was closed.

Almost instinctively he glanced at the floor. Here the hardwood was covered by worn carpeting that had aged to dusky grey with faded flowers twining in twilight colors in a border six inches out from the enameled baseboards.

Darkness flickered through the crack between door and carpet, brushing against his naked toes where they rested only inches away.

The darkness seemed like light.

He pushed the door open, steeled for the low-pitched squeak that Roland had tried to get rid of with innumerable cans of 3-in-One oil but that had nevertheless persisted, muted but present, until it suddenly disappeared sometime during the year Richard turned nineteen.

The room was dark but Richard could see every stick of furniture, every photograph on the dresser top, the finest details of every picture hung along the flowered walls.

She sat directly opposite, in the small alcove of the dormer window, rocking.

Creeaak. Pause. *Creeaak.* Pause. *Creeeaaak.* Pause.

Bonnie wore only a loose white taffeta robe that shimmered like frost in the moonlight. She held something that curled close to her breast. She did not look up as Richard entered the room.

He took a step. He fully intended to ask her what she was doing, how she got down from the bedroom before he did, why she was sitting alone in the darkness of his mother's room, rocking in a chair that had splintered a decade before, why she was wearing his mother's worn chenille robe with the twining roses in puffs of faded pink thread. He and Donney had pulled so many puffs from the robe that it finally became threadbare and Emma threw it into the incinerator.

But he couldn't speak. His throat was stopped, his breath pent inside his lungs.

He stopped moving.

She was nursing a baby. He could see its tiny mouth where it embraced Bonnie's nipple, and the sight was unendurably erotic. He knew he was aroused and was unaccountably embarrassed by it.

He took another step toward her. A floorboard creaked beneath his naked foot.

The woman turned to stare at him.

"Shhhhhh, Dickey." Emma smiled. She laid one finger against her lips and looked down at where three-year-old Richard stood expectantly just inside the door.

Richard could see the arrow-straight part in her dark hair. He felt uncomfortable that she was looking at his legs rather than up into his face.

"See baby," he muttered in a voice too high-pitched to be coming from him.

"You must be quiet, though," Emma said. "Donney just fell asleep, and I don't want him to wake up."

She lowered her cradled arm, and the bundle in the shadowy blanket lay quietly in her lap. Richard saw her breast, exposed to the night air. The nipple was still taut, engorged with remnant milk. The flesh of his mother's breast was white, whiter than the moonlight itself, and veined with thick blue vines.

He was embarrassed.

But he stumbled closer anyway. "See baby?"

Emma nodded, repeating her "quiet" signal with one hand and, when Richard was close enough to see the baby, folding back the flap of flannel baby blanket with the other.

He knelt and leaned forward so that he could see the tiny figure enclosed by shadows.

"Shhh," Emma warned. Richard looked up into her eyes and smiled, as if to assure her that he understood, that baby was sleeping and that he would have to be very, very quiet. His mother smiled back and, without taking her eyes from his, pulled the flannel blanket down further.

Richard's smile died. His hands trembled where they rested against his mother's knees. Shivers played along his naked spine. He ached to look away from the emptiness that echoed through her eyes to his and entered him and chilled him to the bone. He ached to look up at the water stained ceiling, or sideways at the antique wallpaper, or even surge to his feet and stride across the room and hit the light switch with the palm of his hand and flood the room with light.

He wanted to do anything...*anything*...except look down.

His neck bent.

Tendons and muscles cracked as he struggled to keep his head from moving but something unnamable forced him to bend.

He shut his eyes, but the lids opened against his will. He blinked away tears that blurred his vision and stared directly down at the infant.

He bit his lip until blood gushed salty and warm between his teeth and dribbled down his throat, threatening to choke him.

The baby was a mummy. Its fragile, child's flesh was tight and drawn across the partially formed bones of its skull. Its parchment-grey skin outlined every tiny bone, every desiccated line of withered tendon or muscle.

It was as if all softness had dried away, leaving only the husk, the shell, the carapace of a dead roach arching over stinking nothingness.

He jerked back, pulling away with a convulsive shiver.

Emma's hand snaked out and grabbed his, forcing him to come closer and closer even as he fought desperately to break away.

"Fireman! Save my child!" she screamed almost in his ear. The sound was deafening, but he knew immediately what to do.

Already he smelled smoke, smoke billowing from the kitchen, twisting through the living room and writhing up the stairs to meet its companion cloud, fresh from the tour of the upper floor.

He jerked his hand free and ran from the room, pounding up the stairs two at a time, feeling the impact thud from his naked feet to the bones in his skull. His teeth clacked together, and once he bit down on his tongue hard enough to draw blood. He could barely breathe.

You are the oldest. You are responsible for Donney. In case of a fire in the middle of the night you must make sure that Donney is awake and downstairs. Or if the stairs are on fire, you must make sure he climbs out your window with you, and you must follow the ridgeline of the porch to the trellis and down from there onto the front lawn. You must make sure that he follows you. I will try to help you, but if I can't get to you, Richard, you are....

Responsible.

Donney's door was closed, but he could see the flickering of light that seemed like darkness and he could hear the crackling of burning wood. He smelled heat and ash and something acrid that made his nostrils tingle and coated his throat with a wash of pain.

He touched the knob and jerked his fingers away with a cry of surprise and pain. It was burning hot. He looked frantically for something to protect his hand, something to wrap around his scorched fingers, but there was nothing in the empty hall that now stretched for miles into the darkness.

He gritted his teeth against the pain and with a single motion twisted the knob to the right.

The door swung open.

The room was already in flames. Fire licked the boldly striped wallpaper that Donney had demanded even though Emma had argued that it would make the small room seem half its real size. Fire tore through the monster posters curling from white-hot nubs that marked where Donney had pounded six-penny nails into the studs. Fire swallowed the narrow twin bed that was identical to Richard's, down to the handmade quilt laying in three folds across the foot of the mattress. Fire danced on the stitching of the braided rag rug that surrounded the bed like an island.

And in the center of the room, encompassed by the light and heat and unbreathably hot air, stood a swirling darkness that was Emma and that screamed and screamed and screamed at him. *"Save him,"* she screamed, and thrust the baby into his face.

It was no longer a mummy.

It was worse.

Bare bones grimaced at him. The skull was already fragmenting as the connective tissue—cartilage, not yet bone—parted and the skull portions fell away, leaving emptiness and a rancid smell.

She grabbed his arm. He felt the bones of *her* skeleton as they pinched his flesh and raised red welts and bruises on skin already abused by the superheated air of the conflagration in Donney's room.

For a fleeting instant she pulled him close to her, and he saw into the empty mouth and the empty eyes that were not empty but flared with muted energy.

"Save him!" It was a harsh command, croaked through teeth already breaking from their decaying sockets.

"Save him." It was an urgent plea that rocked him with its fervor.

"save him" It was a whisper, gentle as the sea swells on a distant beach, inexorable as the hiss of sand blowing across desert dunes.

"savehim" It was a breath that touched his heart, and her hand touched his cheek and

- 3 -

Richard woke panting and sweating. His mouth was dry. His skin tingled as if it had been burned. The cotton sheet felt scratchy and irritating where it lay across his chest. It felt like sheets had always felt the night after his first sunburn each summer, and everywhere the sheets touched they grated roughly, as if the worn, soft cotton had been impregnated with coarse, cutting sand. For an instant, he wanted to get up and slip down the hall to Mom's room and ask her to rub cream into the tender, red-angry skin of his shoulders and back and legs.

Then he remembered that he was naked.

And Emma was dead.

He lay for a moment, not yet aware of what was different this time. He had awakened, as he had before. And he was terrified, as he had been before. But this time something was different.

He stiffened.

This time, *he remembered the dream.*

He lay silently for a long time, replaying the images. Then, without his even being aware of it, the details of the dream dissipated, leaving him contemplating emptiness. But the force of the dream remained, compelling and definite.

The night seemed to grow hotter.

Finally, the heat radiating from his skin made the weight of the sheet insufferable. He gently tossed it to one side, trying to let most of the damp material fall between him and Bonnie.

She shifted in the bed and rolled toward him.

"Bonnie?" Richard asked, his voice thin, strange-sounding in the darkness.

"Uhmm."

"Bonnie." He sat up and rest his back against the familiar knotty pine headboard. It felt cool next to his skin. Bonnie roused as well and shifted until she was nearer to him. She leaned against his chest.

"Yes." She waited. Perhaps she already knew what was to come. Perhaps she was hoping that the next words would remain unsaid.

"How long would it take...I mean, how soon could we...."

"Go to California?"

"Yes."

"A day, maybe two. I would need to take care of a few things at the shop. Dolores could probably fill in for me, though. She owes me a favor."

He waited for the count of four or five indrawn breaths before speaking.

"Okay?"

Now it was her time to pause before answering. "I don't want to. But I think we have to."

"Yeah. Ma would have wanted us to try and see him, to let him know...."

His voice fumbled to a stop.

She waited. There would be more.

"I've been having...dreams, and I think that Donney's in trouble, somehow. I don't know for sure. It's more than just Ma, more than her...death. Although there's that, too. I...I just have to try and find him. Give me a week, ten days. We can afford that much time away from...."

She put her finger across his lips.

"I'm not arguing," she said. "I think you're right. It feels right. As if Mom were standing here, listening and nodding and hoping that we can help him out."

Something in the image her words suggested broke through the seriousness that had lingered from his dream.

A flurry of small contractions rippled across Richard's chest, radiating from his stomach.

"What's wrong?" Bonnie asked.

Richard's laugh became a snort as he tried to muffle the sound, even though they were alone in the old house.

"I j-j-j-just hope," he stuttered, only to break off with another round of laughter. Bonnie was laughing with him, even though she had no idea why.

"I j-j-j-just hope she wasn't h-h-here an hour or so ago," he finally managed to say.

For a moment, Bonnie didn't understand.

"Richard!" she whispered, elbowing him in the soft place just beneath his ribs.

Then: "But I *still* feel like she's with us. And just in case she missed it the first time...."

She rolled on top of him and, laughing, they began all over.

CHAPTER TEN

FACING THE FEAR

- 1 -

The funeral was held the next Monday, at the exact hour when, under other circumstances, Spence would have stood, stiff and uncomfortable, at the dark pine podium in the Tamarind *Times* lunchroom and taken possession of the brand-new racer, and then posed proudly with the Mayor of Tamarind Valley, and the owner of the *Times,* and Mr. Gresham while the staff photographer snapped stills for the Wednesday special edition insert.

At the exact hour when, under other circumstances, Kenny would have sat in the audience and grinned and whistled and clapped until his hands burned red, happy for his best friend's success, happy that he had played a part in making it happen.

Afterward, they would have hit the roads together, wheel to wheel. Kenny would ride his year-old bike, but Spence would be on his brand new, first prize racer. They would have chased the wind down the steep slope of Norwegian Grade where Tamarind Avenue curls around the hillsides and dips into the green valley that opens northward onto Santa Rosa Road and the orchards and strawberry fields and pine-tree nurseries where the white pines were gradually reaching up to the right heights to be sold for Christmas trees come November 28.

They would have raced the wind past grey-green clumps of knotty prickly pears that hunched over the edge of the roadway, just enough to make Norwegian Grade an even greater challenge for bike riders—how to avoid the cars that careened around blind curves at twenty miles an hour over the speed limit, and at the same time stay close enough to the pavement to avoid cactus needles so sharp that they would slice right through a tire tube.

They would have raced the wind...and they might have won. They might have wound back across Santa Rosa Road and into Tamarind Valley from the north. They might have stopped at the Baskin-Robbins 31 Flavors. The ice cream would have been Kenny's treat: *Congratulations, Spence, old buddy.*

They might have done all those things.

But instead, it was Kenny who squirmed uncomfortably on the pale wood pew of the Congregational Church on Strawberry Hill. The hard seat hurt his back. His legs felt as heavy as wood and threatened to go to sleep. He squirmed, twisted, and tried not to stare too long at the knife of sunlight glinting off the polished top of Teddy Weiss's massive bronze coffin.

Chuck Bowder's coffin was less flamboyant and obviously less expensive. It was a simple, muted pine-tone box with small handles of brushed copper. Perhaps that was because the Bowders had seven children still living, and Mr. Bowder wasn't what anyone would call rich.

Timmy Holmes's coffin was small and white and lonely, even under the blanket of flowers that rested on top of it. Kenny thought that it looked more like a child's toy than any real coffin he had ever seen before. But then he had never been to a funeral for a kid before. He glanced at the box again. The handles where the pallbearers would curl their fingers before they lifted Timmy's body were silver, as tiny and frail as Timmy now seemed in Kenny's memory.

At first, Kenny had been surprised to hear that there would be a joint funeral. Chuck was a Mormon boy, and Teddy didn't belong to any church at all. Only the Holmses regularly attended the Strawberry Hill Congregational Church that squatted atop the highest point in Tamarind Valley, looking like some drunk architect's nightmare of a huge straw hat. Its windows overlooked banks of plumbago that bloomed faintly blue and white in the sterile August heat. With the sun beating down on the blossoms, the faded blossoms looked almost like snow. Cold. Still.

But now, as Kenny looked around the unfamiliar church, he understood why the families had agreed to hold a joint service. Every face looked stricken, every body tense, every set of shoulders slumped. Every pew held hard, silent fathers, weeping mothers, and fearful brothers or sisters, even when those families had barely known the victims or perhaps had not known them at all.

As a man's voice spoke in low, somber tones from the pulpit, reciting words of comfort that Kenny did not want to hear, an odd and unsettling thought flashed through his mind. He studied the faces nearest him.

The people of Tamarind Valley had not come to the Strawberry Hill Congregational Church that afternoon to pay their last respects to three local boys who had died suddenly and violently and horrifyingly.

No, he realized in an unconsciously adult moment of insight, they had not come to mourn or to comfort the families of the slain. They had come to reach out to each other, even in their silence and their rigid immobility as the Mormon Bishop, and the Congregational Minister, and Teddy Weiss's seventh-grade homeroom teacher spoke in muted tones about life and death, about youth and life and energy.

The people of Tamarind Valley had gathered together from the same impulse for survival that once forced pioneer families to circle their wagons, women and children in the center, men perched behind home goods hauled from wooden wagon beds or prone beneath the wagons where they could sight more accurately along the long barrels of their rifles...at the enemy.

Tamarind was circled for protection. Its families were crouching behind the public face of the funeral, confronting the enemy and drawing together for each other's support.

Kenny sighed and blinked his eyes rapidly to clear them. That thought hurt. The image of wagons circling was too apt—he and the other boys, too many of them now lying dead in satin-lined boxes, had played Cowboys and Indians too often for the image not to hurt.

It had risen unbidden from his imagination, but he knew that it was a true image.

He had never studied symbolism. In fact, he had barely gotten to like reading, let alone progressed far enough in school to understand the finer points of literary figures and devices.

But he knew instinctively that this image was true.

On the surface, the mourners probably thought that they were all there to demonstrate their solidarity in support of the grieving families and friends. They had come in defiance of the madman who had slaughtered almost half the Panther Patrol. After all, the Los Angeles news broadcasts had been full of accounts of the madman, the maniac, the crazed killer loose up there in Ventura County. Channel Five had even played a full-color, live-action spot from the circle of oaks in Jenkin's Field. In the few moments Kenny saw of it before his mother rushed into the room and shut off the television so violently that she snapped the power knob right off and it skittered across the floor like a broken tooth—in those few moments, he had seen behind the meticulously clothed reports to the wide, dark splotches on the dried earth. Spots of dried blood that marked where Chuck and Timmy and Teddy had died.

The reporter's sugary voice had oozed sympathy and regret and frustration: *No leads...Ventura County Sheriff's Office spokesman urges calm...surely the work of a madman...transient...no one from Tamarind Valley could do such a thing...entire community joined together in mourning....*

But looking around at the faces assembled in the Strawberry Hill Congregational Church that bright Monday morning, Kenny wasn't so sure that the reporter had been right.

Oh, not that some unknown aberration from Tamarind Valley had killed Chuck and Teddy and Timmy. That part was true enough. And, Kenny thought glumly and nervously, he knew who had done it.

But that wasn't the problem—at least not yet.

No, the part he wasn't sure about was whether the congregation was joined together in mourning and in grief...or in fear.

The pulsating voice stopped. Kenny looked up. The Mormon Bishop had just finished. Before the Congregational Minister would stand up to talk, staring most of the time at the top of Timmy's little white casket, the congregation rose and sang a hymn.

An organ accompanied the hymn. Usually Kenny enjoyed organ music, but this time he didn't listen to the somber tones that reverberated harshly through the silent, bare chapel. Instead he listened to the words as they were fumbled out by three-piece-suit-clad businessmen obviously unused to singing, as they were mouthed sweetly by old ladies who had seen the deaths of everyone in their families and who now lived on interminably alone in their little clapboard houses with their cats or dogs or fish or birds. As they were mouthed by hard, silent fathers, and weeping mothers, and brothers and sisters:

Rock of ages, cleft for me,
Let me hide myself in thee.
Hide. Fear. *Terror.*

Yeah, that was what Kenny saw as he stared around at rapt faces tilted up at the minister, tilted at just the right angle so that they missed the sunlight, and the flowers, and the polished handles, and the reflective tops of three coffins lines across the front of the church.

The music stopped and the mourners settled onto the pews.

Kenny felt their need to hide. Mothers surreptitiously put protective arms around little boys (and not-so-little boys) who, under other circumstances, would have squirmed away but today huddled closer to the warmth and comfort. Fathers surrounded daughters with strong, lanky arms, their stubble-dark jaws clenching tightly as the Congregational Minister droned on.

Not my child, they all said in a language that perhaps only Kenny Robinson could fully understand that day. *Not my child, please God, not while I am still alive.*

There should have been anger and resolve and strength; but all Kenny could see was frailty. And fear.

The Minister finished. In the moment of strained silence that followed, Kenny suddenly shivered. His heart thudded and his blood pulsed and for an instant he felt as if he were strangling. He wanted to raise his head and look around but did not dare.

If he did, he would see...*something.*

Red-rimmed devil's eyes staring at him behind a rigid, pain-filled smile that promised fear and terror and horror and death and....

He thrust his fists into the pockets of his jacket and stared at a small swirl of dark grain on the pew in front of him. The silence dragged on, as if time itself had stopped to give everyone present the change to feel the full power of the fear that tugged at Kenny. He tried to stop his ears, to block out even the subtle sounds of his parents' breathing on each side of him and people shifting positions on the other pews.

Finally, when the pressure of his fear mounted until Kenny felt like he would either have to jump to his feet and scream, or explode, someone moved. Mr. Halloran, Teddy Weiss's teacher, stood. Clearly uncomfortable at having to speak to so large an assembly, he mumbled a few words about how Teddy was a good boy, a real good student, a hard worker, a real good friend, and we will miss him. His voice sounded ragged.

He swallowed, made as if he was going to say something else, then sat down so abruptly that Kenny thought for a second that someone had pulled on the tails of his dark-blue coat and overbalanced him.

That was it. The funeral was over.

Except for the worst part of all.

The minister nodded. The organ whispered something soft and fragile and solemn.

Eighteen boys came forward. Friends. Hiking buddies. Fellow Scouts in full uniform, scouts from Troop 1089 and from troops all over Tamarind Valley. Brothers. Cousins.

Kenny stumbled forward, too.

For a while, he wasn't sure that his folks would let him. He was the only survivor of that night at Jenkins' Field who was allowed to attend the funeral. Billy Holmes lay wrapped and sedated in the burn center at Los Robles Hospital. Brian Lowe hadn't stepped foot out of his house (some people said he hadn't even left his room) since the police had taken him home in the early hours of Saturday morning.

And Spence was still missing.

So Kenny's folks weren't too keen on the idea of even letting him attend the funeral. His father put their fear into words.

"...look, son," he said, sitting next to Kenny on the boy's bed and holding onto his shoulder as if the boy might suddenly disappear. Kenny's dark suit hung from the back of the chair by his desk. His Sunday shoes were polished and waiting by the side of his dresser. Kenny's father glanced at the suit, the shoes, and frowned. "There's a...there's a crazy person out there. He tried to...to kill you the other night. He might want to...."

"...to try again." Kenny finished his father's thought.

His father nodded. "I think it would be best if you stayed home. No one will blame you. No one will think that you're...."

"...afraid."

His father dropped his hand and looked away. Kenny saw a flash of weakness in the gesture, and turned to face his mother. She was sitting on the chair by his bookcase, staring at him as if trying to memorize every plane and angle of his face.

"Mom," he had argued, softly but determinedly. "I gotta be there. I *gotta*. I gotta say good-bye." His eyes had misted, and, obviously much against their better judgment, Mom and Dad had relented.

Then, when Mr. Halloran had called to ask about Kenny serving as a pall-bearer, they had the same argument again.

They were adamant about his serving as a pallbearer. "No," his mother had said. He was too weak, she said. He hurt too much. He couldn't bear it, knowing that....

"But Mom...."

And now he was stepping forward with seventeen others and slipping his hand around the slim bar of cold brass and lifting Chuck from the bier and walking slowly with him out of the Strawberry Hill Congregational Church, following Timmy's casket, and then Teddy's. Slowly, slowly, somberly, suddenly adults for the moment, the eighteen boys carried the three slim caskets to waiting hearses parked in the shadow of the church where the winds didn't pick up as much and the pall-bearers could walk in quiet dignity without the wind ruffling their hair and teasing and saying, *Come on, the weather's perfect, this stuff is too serious, let's laugh and run and play and fly a kite.*

He moved in step with the others toward the hearse and helped slide Chuck into the back, thinking as he did so of the darkness inside the big black car, of the long, deep darkness that waited there for Chuck.

But not for Spence. There was no darkness waiting to enfold him with gentle quietness or to wrap him in eternal sleep.

Not yet.

For the first time since he awoke last Saturday morning, safe in his own room and—for an instant—half hoping that he had only been having a hideous nightmare, Kenny allowed himself the luxury of release. Standing on the hill above the Valley, with banks of blue and white plumbago rippling at his feet, Kenny finally cried.

- 2 -

After the flowers had been arranged along the ends of the caskets, one of the funeral assistants swung the double doors of the hearses closed. The locks caught with half-heard *snicks* of metal on metal.

The mourners were urged with quiet intensity by the funeral director into the cars that would form corteges to three separate destinations. There had been no unanimity among the families as to final resting places. Chuck was not even going to be buried in Tamarind Valley, as a matter of fact. He would travel by train up to a little farming town in southern Idaho where his Mom and Dad had been born and where almost all of his relatives lived...and most had died. Where his family had always talked about going back to. Kenny could almost hear Chuck's dad talking about moving back—*Back where things are simpler and life is safer.*

Well, Chuck was going now. Alone. Maybe the rest would go back later.

In the meantime, the funeral director was going about his business of separating the mourners into three large groups.

"This way, please, Mrs. Holmes," the man said, his voice as soft and formless as butter on a hot summer day. Kenny shuddered at the sound and turned away before he could see his friend's mother disappear into the gaping darkness of another long, black car. All around him, people were milling around, trying to work their ways to cars that would they have to separate into three solemn processionals as they wove their way down the hillside and away from the Congregational Church.

Kenny moved away from the crowd. He had already decided not to be in any of the three groups. He couldn't watch one of his friends put into the earth and not the others. And he wasn't sure he wanted to see even one. They were dead, gone, finished.

But he had things to do.

He started to walk around the edge of the church. His folks had parked their car there, a few yards away from the press of the crowd. They were waiting for him, like he had asked them to. He could see their heads outlined against the bright light pouring through the front window. He took a step back, then cut around a low hedge toward the side of the church grounds that fell away steeply into a tangle of low shrubs, and then the edge of Old Meadows Park, and then the Valley itself. For a moment—for the first moment since the horrors of the Overnighter, in fact—he was alone.

He stopped in the shadows of the eaves, and closed his eyes, and listened. Somewhere in the distance, birds were singing. He had planned on doing the Bird Study merit badge with Spence that summer, but somehow they had never gotten around to it. He didn't recognize the songs.

He swallowed, trying to dislodge the lump that had suddenly appeared in his throat.

The wind freshened, sweeping around the corner of the church and spilling across his hair. The wind smelled fresh and sweet, dry, but pleasant with the heavy scent of flowers and pine trees. For a moment, it reminded him of Camp Muir.

Distantly, he heard the muted roar of cars on the freeways as they cut through Tamarind Valley, carrying people rushing to and from the important moments in their own lives, people who did not know that other lives were over.

The tears started again.

He brushed them away and walked back across the patch of lawn that separated the church and the parking lot. Across the valley, brushing up against the dry hills like jagged teeth, hunched the houses of Whitechapel Place. Even though he shaded his eyes with his hand, and stepped up onto a low wall near the edge of the lawn, he could not see the house beyond the hill.

Shrugging, he started back to his parents' car.

He was almost to the sidewalk surrounding the parking lot when someone called his name.

"Hey, Kenny. Kenny Robinson."

154

He turned, expecting to see someone he would recognize. It was a man, an adult. The voice was deep and strong, masculine. But he did not recognize the figure loping across the lawn. For an instant, all he could see was a black silhouette against the cutting blue sky. Behind the first man came a second, balancing something on his shoulder.

Kenny started to back up. He didn't want to talk to anyone right now.

"Kenny," the man said abruptly, "please wait just a minute."

Kenny stopped.

In their car, his folks looked up through the half-closed windows of the car and squinted against the light. He could see his Dad started fumbling with the door.

"Yeah?"

"Look, kid, uh, Kenny, we're from Channel 15 News—'Fifteen At Five'. Can we talk to you for a minute?"

"Sure," Kenny said, but his voice belied the word. He was not sure. He knew the kind of questions he would be asked; he had been asked them all weekend, by the Tamarind Valley police, by the Ventura County Sheriff, by reporters from the LA stations, by reporters from the papers—even by someone from the Tamarind *Times* that Kenny didn't even know.

He felt his throat constrict, but he stood and waited for the man to come closer. The alternative was to run like a frightened kid toward the car, and Kenny knew that if he once started running he would never have the strength or the courage to....

"...like in there?"

He drew himself back to the present, dimly understanding that he had been asked a question. He had no idea what it had been.

The second man was closing in on him, hunched over and leaning forward. A video camera perched on the man's shoulder stared like an unblinking, glassy eye at Kenny. He felt an unreasonable desire to throw his hands up and hide his face, like some crook caught by the cameras outside a courtroom or a jail. He tried to turn away, but the man with the camera followed.

"What?" he asked when the first man thrust something—a microphone, he realized belatedly—out toward him.

"What did it feel like, just now, burying your friends?"

Kenny stared. Whatever fear or nervousness or hesitation he had felt an instant before died, replaced by a low, burning anger. His hands clenched into fists.

Is this guy for real? Chuck is dead, and this asshole asks me how I feel!

Something of his fury must have flickered across his face, because the man shifted his feet started over.

"Is it true, what the other boy says, that the murderer was a monster, huge, seven-feet tall?"

The question startled him back into the defensive mode he had been practicing for two days.

"I...," he began. He was going to say he didn't remember. That had worked pretty well so far. *I don't remember. It was awful. My friends were dying. Someone killed them. But I don't remember what he looked like. I'm just a little kid, after all. I don't remember. Leave me alone, please.*

No one had pressed him beyond that, not even his own folks. So he hadn't had to tell anyone what he *really* saw.

Brian hadn't been as careful. He said something about Sven the Red-Handed, about a bloody axe a foot across, a seven-foot-tall lumberjack with glowing red eyes.

They gave Brian medicine and made him sleep. And when he woke up, he probably believed whatever line they decided to string him—it was an escapee from Camarillo State Mental Hospital, or a desperate fugitive from some LA prison just happening on a bunch of kids and slicing them up. Anything that would fit into the world the way the adults preferred to believe it worked.

But Kenny had seen Sven the Red-Handed in the last seconds, after Brian had bolted, when Billy was already out of his head with grief and pain. Kenny had seen the flickering and the fluid melting of face into face and had understood—with a flash of lightning intuition that had burned and hurt even as it had illuminated—more than these nosey reporters ever could.

"I...," he began, but that was as far as he got.

The man asking the questions suddenly lurched toward Kenny, microphone outstretched like a cold metal fist. The man swiveled on one foot, almost slashing Kenny across the cheek with the microphone, before he lost his balance and fell. The man skidded across the smooth concrete. The microphone fell with a metallic *thunk,* and rolled into the bushes, trailing its cord behind it like a swirling black serpent's tail.

In the spot where the man had stood, Kenny saw a black figure, outlined against the sky, seeming huge as it thrust against the cameraman who was just beginning to straighten up turn around. The figure caught the cameraman on the shoulder. The camera started to slip. The cameraman swore, grabbed at the equipment and, overbalancing as well, fell to his knees. Kenny heard a sharp crack as the man fell, but noticed—through a fog of fear and terror—that the camera was still in the man's hand. The man sank back and let out a low moan. The first man started to get up.

But Kenny barely noticed them. He was staring, uncomprehending, at the silhouetted figure that approached him, hugely black and for a horrible moment unrecognized.

Kenny screamed, loud and piercing and shrill. Back in the parking lot, heads jerked up and startled faces stared toward the hedge at the side of the church. No one moved.

Then the black figure stretched out a hand, grabbed Kenny's arm, and pulled the boy away.

"Get out of here," his father roared at the two men on the sidewalk. Kenny could feel the suppressed rage in his father, transmitted as an invisible but violent shuddering that seemed to start in his father's heart and vibrate through his whole body, into his hands and from there into Kenny as well. "Leave him alone. Get away. If I ever see you around my son again, I'll kill you!"

He spun Kenny around and propelled him toward the car where Mom already had the back door open and waiting for him. Dad pushed him into the dark, stuffy interior and was seated and had the engine going before Kenny had time to look out the window.

The reporter was up on his feet, approaching the parking lot. The cameraman a couple of feet behind him, limping and obviously in pain, but still cranking away. At any rate, a small red light glowed like a baleful eye at the top of the camera.

Dad shifted into reverse and squealed out of the parking lot. The reporter skidded to a stop, backed up precipitously as the car whipped by him, and in the process knocked the cameraman over. Kenny held onto the door knob as the car cut around the slowly moving processional of cars behind the hearse carrying Chuck's body.

At the bottom of the grade, where the driveway leading up to the Congregational Church opened onto the main road, Kenny's father pulled over to the sidewalk, stopped, put the car in neutral, and covered his face with his hands. He didn't kill the engine, but even so, Kenny could hear his father sobbing.

- 3 -

Later that evening, Kenny slipped out of his room and walked down the long corridor between his bedroom and the living room.

Mom was busy in the kitchen; he could hear the clatter of pans and cupboard doors. She would probably call for him in a few minutes; she had been doing that ever since Saturday, just calling his name, almost absently, as she did whatever household task needed her attention. Just calling his name.

"Kenny?"

"Yeah, Mom."

Silence. Pause.

Then, again: "Kenny?"

"Yeah, Mom."

Silence. Pause.

"Nothing, dear."

And everything. *Are you still alive, dear? Have you been sliced into tiny pieces by a monster in human form, with the mind of a maniac and the hands of a Cuisinart? Are your arms and legs scattered over the back yard like jackstraws after a tornado? Is your head floating in the Bronson's pool next door?*

Nothing.

At first it had irritated him. By about the fifth time, though, he hadn't bothered to answer. He just sat on the edge of his unmade bed, swinging his legs and letting his bare feet skim across the pile of soiled underwear and socks and shirts and swimming trunks that crept from the darkness underneath. He had just sat, and stared, and remembered.

The door flew open so hard that it bounced off the far wall. The knob punched a three inch hole in the plaster, and Kenny remembered thinking wildly, *Mom's gonna kill me for that,* and then he realized that she wouldn't because *Mom* had done it! Kenny had stared up at her, as frightened and as startled as she was. Her eyes were huge, her face drawn and white.

"Kenny." Her voice was strained. She seemed to have trouble keeping it pitched low, beneath the level of hysteria.

"Yeah?" His voice shook, too.

"Why didn't you answer me?" She was using that voice that always told him she was relieved that he was all right and at the same time mad as hell that he had done...whatever it was that he had done.

"I...uh...I didn't hear you," he said, wincing inwardly at the lie. He understood now what the trouble was, and he was ashamed. He couldn't look into her fear-filled eyes, so he dropped his head and stared at his hands and mumbled, "I...I was thinking."

She rushed across the room and dropped to her knees—she didn't even say anything about the pile of dirty laundry, which had to be a first in his entire life—and hugged him and cried.

Kenny had cried, too. And after a few minutes, she had stood and looked down at him and wiped her hand across her face. "This room is a mess," she said quietly. "Don't you think you had better do something about those dirty clothes?"

Kenny had nodded feebly and started picking up socks. Mom left the room, but he noticed that she was careful not to let the door close behind her.

Since then, whenever she called, Kenny answered. Saturday, Sunday, all day Monday. Every fifteen minutes, it seemed, from the moment he woke up until the moment he went to sleep. And probably even after that. She probably didn't sleep at all, but spent the nights walking down the dimly lit hallway from their room and looking into his room, reassuring herself that he was all right. That he was still alive.

Dad had handled things differently. He got gruff. Not unkind, nothing like that, just super-masculine. *That's the way things are, kid. Friends kick off. Everybody kicks off. I'm gonna kick off someday myself, and your mom, and then you'll have to put us into the ground and live on without us. Life's tough.*

Not that he ever said that, of course. No, he just roughed Kenny's hair every time he passed, squeezed his shoulder once or twice, then went on out to mow the lawn and trim the hibiscus. Life goes on.

Everything's normal.

Except, of course, that nothing really was.

Kenny sighed as he silently opened the front door and slipped onto the front porch. He kept his hand on the aluminum screen door so it wouldn't squeak or bang.

Dad was working somewhere in back, pretending that he wasn't hurting so badly inside that he could nearly scream. Mom was making cookies or washing dishes or arranging flowers or some other *Leave-It-To-Beaver*-ish thing.

Kenny walked to the edge of the lawn and squatted down. He really wanted to go biking. He wanted to let the wind rush through his hair, press against his eyes so hard that he had to squint and throw the whole world out of focus. A memorial ride—*Here's to You, Spence. This one's for you.*

But he knew that if he left the yard, his folks would be so frantic that they would probably beat him half to death when he got back, then smother him with hugs and kisses, then restrict him to his room until he turned ninety-nine or his first great-grandchild was born, whichever came first.

So he settled for sitting on the cool grass and watching.

It was early evening. Not yet seven, not yet late enough for the sunlight to take on that peculiar clarity that heralds night. He looked up and down the length of Sheffield, as far as he could see, from the hill on the west to the T-intersection on the east.

Usually there were kids in the yards and on the street, riding and running and playing tag.

Tonight, it was like a ghost town. Deserted. Nothing. He leaned back, his thin shoulders digging into the thick grass that Dad worked so hard on every weekend.

Tamarind Valley was different. It was more than just that the guys had been killed. After all, that happened almost every day, somewhere in LA, somewhere in California, somewhere in the world.

Sure, it hurt to lose friends, it hurt a lot. But it must hurt other friends and brothers and sisters and mothers and fathers when other children were found cut up on garbage heaps or stuffed into trash dumpsters or molested (he had only vague, half-completed ideas about what that actually *was*, but he had heard the word often enough) and left like sodden, limp rags in the shallow water trickling from sewers along the concrete banks of the Los Angeles River.

God, that had to hurt.

And it happened every day. It was trumpeted every night on the five o'clock news, emblazoned in headlines in every copy of the LA papers that Dad picked up at his office.

SIX DIE IN HEAD-ON CRASH

MISSING GIRL FOUND DEAD

FOURTH VICTIM OF FREEWAY SHOOTING DIES

NEW EVIDENCE IN CHILD
MOLESTATION TRIALS

GANG VIOLENCE ESCALATES: THREE DIE

And on and on and on and on.

Kenny shuddered. When he was a kid, like eight or so, his folks subscribed to the Disney channel for him as a Christmas present. He had enjoyed it, still enjoyed it, in fact, everything but the really stupid stuff like *Dumbo's Circus*.

But all of a sudden, he realized that *Ozzie and Harriet* had never had to deal with child molestation. The kids in *The Shaggy Dog* could run all over town—even turn into great hairy beasties, for Cripes sake—and no one ever worried about them. No one died, like happened so often in this world that kids like himself didn't even bother to notice any more.

In Disney's world, no one got sliced to pieces by things that looked like nightmares one minute and the next minute smiled at you and winked just like....

"Kenny!"

Mom screamed so loudly that Kenny heard doors and windows slamming open all along Sheffield.

He leaped to his feet and run back to the house, brushing dead grass from his hands as he ran.

Dad appeared around the side of the house, his face flushed. He brandished the hoe like he was some medieval knight out to avenge the fair maiden...or the murdered kid.

"Kenny!"

By this time Mom was at the door, pushing it open. Kenny realized with a shock of guilt that stunned him in its intensity that she must have been calling for a long time. He had been so wrapped up in his thoughts, probably hidden from sight through the front window by the hedge. She must have thought....

"Mom, it's okay. I'm here." He rushed up to her just as Dad got there.

"Kenny!" This time, the sound was a rush of relief, frosted over with icy fear. She knelt and swept him into her arms and squeezed until it felt like his ribs would break.

"Young man," Dad began, using his cold, iron-discipline voice. But it was crusted over with fear, too, and Kenny could feel the fear radiating all along Sheffield as people breathed with relief and turned to make sure that their own children were still playing in back yards or watching television in safe, comfortable pine-paneled dens.

"I know, Dad," he said quietly. "I'm really sorry."

His father glanced over at his mother, and something unspoken passed between them. They linked arms with Kenny—almost but not quite an embrace—and walked back into the house. The screen door swung noisily closed behind them.

From the middle of the living room window, aware of Mom's eyes on his back as he stood there, Kenny watched the sunset, staring even when the fading light glinted into his eyes and made them smart and water.

He could feel his parents staring at him. He could sense that they wanted to speak, that they wanted to reassure him that everything was well. That everything would be all right.

But they couldn't speak.

Perhaps they felt—on some lower frequency, beneath the level of understanding—what Kenny knew as he watched the sun slipping behind the hills and throwing the valley into darkness.

There was something out there. It had changed Spence, maybe even destroyed him in ways that made Kenny shudder. It had killed Chuck and Timmy and Teddy. It had as good as killed Billy, and maybe if it had had any compassion or human feeling at all, it *would* have killed him.

It was hurting his mother and his father so bad that Kenny couldn't stand to even think about their pain.

It was there, and it was invisible, and it was fear that had settled over Tamarind Valley like the vampire settling into the Marsten House, except there was no such thing as a vampire.

But the fear was there, nonetheless. It was a palpable presence that Kenny could sense as he watched the last sliver of sun disappear. It had crippled Tamarind Valley, and the Bowder family, and the Weiss family, and Billy Holmes lying in the hospital, and Kenny's mother, with her piteous repetitions of "Kenny, Kenny, Kenny."

Tonight, he would let it rest out there.

But tomorrow!

He clenched his jaw, not in fear but in anger and determination. Tomorrow he would take the battle to the enemy.

CHAPTER ELEVEN

THE EXTRA MILE

- 1 -

The first death that Monday night occurred just after seven-thirty.

Mrs. Fern Baker, age eighty seven last Easter Sunday, had been living for the past six months in a mother-in-law apartment jutting from the rear of her daughter's home on the outskirts of Tamarind Valley. A block lower down the hillside the newer, fancier, more expensive homes on upper Whitechapel, the Abendroth home was substantial nonetheless: two-stories, stucco, patio and spa, three-car garage even though George Abendroth would never consider owning more than one vehicle at a time.

Fern was reasonably happy. Her arthritis kicked up most days, some worse than others, but she could still hobble around and take care of herself. Her cataracts were progressing nicely and any day now that young doctor over to the hospital would agree that they were ready for surgery. Until then, the world remained a pleasant blur, just distorted enough that Fern felt no compulsion to get up and do, as she might have five, ten years ago.

She was content to sit in her soft chair in the middle of the tiny living room George had added to his place and watch the soft wash of color on the television and listen to the voices that came through her ears as musical static.

She was largely cut off from most of humanity. She was barely able to see or hear, rarely speaking, not even to Martha on the frequent but frustratingly short visits her daughter paid to the tiny apartment. Not a day went by but that Martha wasn't out there, puttering around and making sure Mother was comfortable, but in all of the asking after and checking into and running for, Martha consistently forgot just to sit and talk...or to listen, which would have been an even greater enjoyment for Fern.

As it was, Martha would breeze in, treat her like a bed-ridden child, then breeze out on her way to some civic function or another. Since George had retired, Martha had become the busy one in the family, constantly flitting from one group to another.

Mondays, it was volunteer work at the gift shop at Los Robles Hospital. Martha worked the late afternoon shift, so George had to fend for himself for dinner.

George never came out to the small apartment, which suited Fern just fine. The rancor of their run-ins early in his marriage to her only child had never quite died; he spoke to Fern only when necessary and only when Martha was present. Fern, on the other hand, spoke to George volubly whenever the occasion arose. Over the years, Fern discovered, he had learned not to let such occasions arise.

George Abendroth, for his part, was happily working in his study, gluing infinitesimal parts onto a plastic clipper ship—a fifty-dollar model of the *Cutty Sark*—when his mother-in-law died.

Fern was sitting, as usual, in her overstuffed chair, the one that had molded itself to her increasingly frail form over the years, until now she barely had to shift or move. She could sit for hours, comfortably. The worn material enveloped her and held her secure.

She enjoyed sitting in the chair.

The television was humming away, playing some silly thing or another. She didn't care what. She neither watched nor listened, but she liked the feeling that someone was in the room with her.

At quarter past seven, Fern was deep in a conversation with her sister Iris, the one who had died in 1974 after thirty-nine years of old-maidenhood. Iris was the one who stayed home with Mother and Dad after the other children left. Iris was the one who grew wizened and grey with bitterness as she saw life pass her by. Iris was the one who envied her brothers and sisters *their* families and never passed up a chance to bemoan the fact that her sacrifice had left her bereft of comfort in her declining years.

But Iris was also the one Fern loved most, and the one who understood Fern better than any of the others.

So on that Monday night, Fern was talking things over with her dead sister, to the accompaniment of a rerun of *Bewitched!*

"That's not fair, Iris," she mumbled, her voice barely reaching the growing shadows in the corners of her tiny room.

Iris answered.

"Well, I know. But that was *your* choice. No one forced you to...."

Iris interrupted.

"I didn't either," Fern said, her lower lip trembling and a tear welling in the corner of one eye. "I never did and I never would. You know that."

Iris knew that.

"Besides"—the tremble became an outright quiver—"You don't know how lonely it is. Ever since Reuben died...when you've lived for sixty-three years with the same man...."

Iris hadn't. She had never lived with any man.

"I know. But I do understand how you feel. Please try to understand how *I* feel. It's so lonely. Martha hardly ever says anything to me."

Iris asked a question.

"*Martha.* Yes, little Martha. Only now she's...dear me, she's almost sixty. Can you believe it?"

Iris could.

"Of course, I'm not complaining. It's nice here."

Iris didn't like it where she was.

Fern was amazed at the revelation, and more than a little concerned. "You've never said anything like that before, dear. Why didn't you say something if it bothered you?"

Iris didn't want to worry Fern.

"Worry me? Worry me about what?"

Iris wanted to know more about Martha.

But Fern was intrigued. In all the time she had talked with her dead brothers and sisters, none of them had ever mentioned *being* dead. Oh, she knew well enough that they were. She knew that her conversations were one-sided fantasies, imagination impinging on desire. No one else—especially not George or Martha—knew that she had them. After all, she was old, but she was not yet willing to be considered senile. Her talks were, she knew, nothing more than pleasant diversions that helped pass the time.

But now Iris was talking about things that, at eighty-seven and the last of her parents' family still alive, Fern was more than interested in.

"Come on, dear. You've never kept any secrets from me. And I've never kept any from you. Didn't I tell you first about Reuben and me, even before I told Mother and Dad? The first kiss? Remember."

Iris remembered. It did not make her happy to remember what Fern had known and Iris had never experienced.

Fern winced at Iris's pain.

"Then tell me. Iris. What is it like? Where are you? How do you feel?"

Iris dissimulated.

"Tell me, please." Fern's voice took on a cracked whine that could drive Martha crazy in a minute.

Iris considered it.

"Pleeease." The whine intensified.

Across the room, on the small portable color television that Martha had bought for Fern's birthday three years before, *Bewitched!* was almost ready to shift to *I Dream of Jeannie.*

Iris agreed.

"Wonderful," Fern said, her voice less than a breath.

Iris told her what to do.

"All right. I'm sitting back in the chair. Yes, I'm relaxed," Fern said rather more sharply than she intended. She had always hated it when Iris tried to mother *her.* After all, she was a good twelve years older than Iris. "Yes, I've got my eyes closed. Now show me. You promised."

Iris kept her promise.

The hand reached into Fern's breast and found her heart and wrenched it once—like Uncle Ed wringing the neck of a plump chicken for Sunday dinner. Her heart fluttered for a moment, also like the already-dead chicken.

In that instant, Fern discovered the depth of her commitment to living; and the fear that welled up and flooded through her was more bitter than any she had ever known, even when she had almost died giving birth to Martha. She would have screamed, except that she could no longer open her mouth.

The fear doubled and redoubled until it *was* Fern Baker and it consumed her.

Then her heart stopped.

Iris faded and the room lay empty.

When Martha peeked through the door into her mother's apartment not five minutes later, the television was murmuring its static. The lights were still off so most of the room was in shadows, except where the television cast its flickering light. And Mother was resting so peacefully that Martha almost ducked her head out the door, intending to come back later.

But there was something else—a smell, a feel, a taste to the air. Even as she was backing through the doorway into the short, dark hall that connected the apartment with the rest of the house, Martha felt her skin quiver. Tears came to her eyes, without her knowing why, and she had to resist the sudden urge to slam the door shut be-hind her and run back to the main part of the house.

Instead, Martha paused, took a deep breath, crossed the room, and lifted her mother's frail hand. She felt the knotted knuckles swollen with four decades of painful arthritis.

As she touched her mother's skin, she knew—*knew*—that Fern was gone.

She cried out once, sharply and loudly. George was at her side before she even had time to lower her mother's hand to the worn upholstery of the chair that enclosed and surrounded her.

- 2 -

Emmett Hobson did not know Kenny Robinson or Fern Baker. Except for reading an account of the tragedy at Jenkin's Field in the Tamarind *Times* on Saturday and Sunday, and a longer account of the funeral of three boys in Monday's evening issue, Emmett Hobson's life had never intersected Kenny Robinson's or Fern Baker's. If pressed, he probably would not have even been able to remember the name of the single member of the Panther Patrol who had attended the funeral.

But soon, he and Kenny Robinson and an old arthritic woman would have more in common than Emmett Hobson would have imagined in his worst nightmare.

He was forty-five years old, and two pounds overweight for every candle Caryn had stuck into the thick, gooey frosting of the double-Dutch chocolate cake she had served up on his birthday less than a month before. Always a big man, once thickly muscled with slabs of solid flesh, he had become...well, somewhat unstable physi-cally over the last few years, until now his extra-large T-shirts (that once would have hung tent-like from his shoulders) tugged tightly under the arms and rode up along his back when he wore them with his shorts to do yard work.

Worse than that, he had been having trouble lately: shortness of breath, dizziness, increasingly severe muscle spasms in his back and shoulders. Finally, the day after his forty-fifth birthday, with the odor of the double-Dutch chocolate cake still on his breath, a stale remembrance like the aftershock of an earthquake, he had checked in with Dr. Pahrami.

The guy was an Indian or something, foreign at any rate, but with Kaiser Medical you get who you get, and in the three years that Pahrami had acted as the Hobson's family-group doctor, Emmett had developed a grudging respect for the dark-skinned little man who stood a foot shorter than Emmett, weighed in at some hundred-plus pounds less than Emmett, but who could still scare the shit out of Emmett when it was necessary.

It had been necessary.

"You're overweight."

Emmett nodded. He'd heard that before.

"You're not getting enough exercise."

Emmett nodded.

"Your cholesterol count is sky-high." Dr. Pahrami checked off another item on the small clipboard he held in front of him like it was a bullet-proof vest against Emmett Hobson's rage at the news.

Emmett nodded again, this time more circumspectly.

Cholesterol. He wasn't sure what that was or what it did, but the TV commercials made it sound bad.

"You're ripe for heart disease."

Emmett didn't nod. This was new, and he didn't like it at all.

"And...." Dr. Pahrami ducked his head and stared at the printing on his chart, as if he did not understand the words he saw there. Emmett knew that for a bad sign, a real bad sign. Usually Dr. Pahrami could outstare a cobra.

"And there is marginal diabetes."

Emmett went cold. The next thing he knew he was laying down on the crinkling paper-sheet on the examination table, the stiff white stuff sticking to his bare back in a way that he hated. Dr. Pahrami was standing nearby, looking with concern down at Emmett.

Emmett sat up.

"Sorry," he said. "That one was a shocker."

Dr. Pahrami nodded. They two had discussed diabetes often enough before, and each time Emmett had let slip a little more of his fear of the disease. His grandmother had died of complications of diabetes; two of her sisters went blind from it, long before the doctors really understood what it was and how it worked. His own father had contracted his some twenty years before and had died less than half a year before. The doctors said it was a heart attack, but Emmett knew that the old man's heart had been weakened by his continuing struggles against Parkinson's and diabetes. Deep inside, Emmett blamed the diabetes more than anything else.

He hated it.

And he feared it. He had seen what it did to his old man.

"So. Insulin?"

Dr. Pahrami shook his head. "Please understand, Mr. Hobson, that your tests show only marginal diabetes. Not enough to consider pills, certainly not serious enough for Tolinaze or insulin."

He stared at the patient. The doctor's small, round-framed glasses reflected back to Emmett his own mass of flesh, the rolls of fat around the stomach, the double chins and round face that could get a job easily if the full moon ever decided to take a vacation.

"What you've got to do," Dr. Pahrami continued, "and the only thing you *can* do right now, is lose weight."

"How much?"

Dr. Pahrami did not answer directly. "The charts say you should weigh between 150 and 160. I see nothing wrong with those numbers."

Emmett Hobson swallowed. That would be tough.

Then he caught an instant image of his father just before he went into the hospital for the last time, slow, frail, shuffling down the hallway at the old place. He had asked Emmett to cut his toe nails, because the old man couldn't reach that far anymore, and Emmett had. The sight of the old man's feet and toes, the curling yellow horns that had once been toenails—that had sickened Emmett and frightened him.

It would be tough, but he would do it.

"Easy, though," Dr. Pahrami had warned. "No crash diets. No fads. Eat sensibly but carefully. No milk products, no red meat, no cheeses, no candy or cakes."

At that, Emmett had swallowed hard, still tasting the spoor of the chocolate cake.

Dr. Pahrami had continued with his list of restrictions, which boiled down to the simple fact that Emmett could eat chicken and fish and broccoli and cauliflower and that was about it.

"And exercise. You must exercise," Dr. Pahrami warned. "Take it slow at first. No running, no marathons, that sort of thing. I would suggest walking. Start with ten minutes, then work up to twenty, thirty, finally at least half an hour of brisk walking each day."

For twenty days, Emmett Hobson had been following Dr. Pahrami's advice.

And it had worked.

He had already lost nearly twenty-five pounds. His clothing fit better—and he had already given some of the biggest stuff to Goodwill because it was *too* big!

The eating was sometimes a problem, but he had developed a passion for walking. It was good for him, of course, but it also became his refuge. An hour, then an hour and a half, working toward two hours a night, alone, working muscles that tautened and solidified more each day. He was putting on the miles as well. Just last Saturday, he had followed the hiking path through Wildwood

Mesa Park, a good seven miles, in just under two hours. He had averaged almost a mile every fifteen minutes.

Tonight, he was working on eight miles. One more mile, to set a personal record.

He was already well beyond the usual limits of his walks, striding along steadily even though more than an hour had passed since he had put on his black nylon Puma pants and his LA Dodgers T-shirt and waved good-bye to Caryn. He had avoided the whole section of Tamarind Valley within five miles of Jenkins Field—that sicko pervert who killed those kids was probably in Colorado by now, but no use taking chances. Instead, he had followed half a dozen streets through one of the newer developments, looking out for a few new ideas for landscaping his own place, and then had cut off the road to follow one of the innumerable motorcycle trails that laced the hills around Tamarind. He had just now passed a low hill that hid the last housing development, and for a few minutes—in those wonderful golden minutes between sunset and dark—he walked through the silence of a deserted countryside. Not even the roar of the freeway penetrated this far into the hills.

For a few minutes, he just walked, not thinking of anything in particular except his rhythm and his timing.

Then his mind began wandering, as it usually did during the walks. Sometimes that was the best part of all, the directions his thinking took while his body was plugging mindlessly away, step, step, step, step.

He had watched the evening news just before leaving. They had more about those kids, showed some picture of the funeral, in fact, with three coffins and one of the kids from the scout troop standing there by the hearse. The one who lived through it. At the moment, Emmett Hobson couldn't remember the kid's name.

Afterward, the newscaster said that there still was no concrete information about the killer. No leads. No suspects.

"Damn shame," Emmett Hobson muttered, careful not to waste too much energy in speaking. "Hope they get the bastard. Track him down and hang him up by his nuts. Serve the son-of-a-bitch right!"

He could imagine how those kids must have felt, that crazy man bursting on them and hacking away like that.

He really could imagine it, because something just like that had happened to him in 'Nam. And he had survived it, just like what's-is-name, that kid on the news show had survived *this* situation.

But 'Nam had been a close thing—so had this kid's survival, and Emmett Hobson suddenly didn't like remembering either one.

He upped his pace a bit and moved his thoughts onto something new.

Coyotes.

There had been this piece on the news about coyotes. It had come on just after the piece about the funeral. It had been funny almost, when you looked at it in the right way.

A bunch of people over in Agoura Hills had been having trouble with coyotes. Here they spend a bundle on houses up in the canyons so they could have their horses and corrals (and flies, too, but nobody mentioned that on the news) and trails.

And now they couldn't use the trails, because coyotes had started coming down and following the horses.

That was the funny part. It wouldn't be funny if the damned things had attacked kids, like they did a couple of years ago in Westlake, coming down out of the hills to the houses along the edge of the new developments and clawing the hell out of a two year old. Damn near bit the kid's head off, before the mother chased it off with rocks and went back to discover her dead kid lying in his own blood.

That was bad stuff. Emmett Hobson shuddered. But this, this was almost science fiction stuff, horror stuff. The coyotes didn't do anything. They just ran alongside the horses, keeping up with the riders, spooking them but not yelping or biting or anything.

And the rich dudes couldn't ride their horses anymore, for fear of the coyotes.

Emmett Hobson laughed out loud, allowing himself the rare luxury and noting with pride that the laughter was strong and rolled over the weed-choked hills. Not the wheezing pant of an overweight candidate for heart attack and diabetes, but a rich laugh.

Something echoed it.

It was a dog's bark, distant, hauntingly dim and melancholy. Emmett shivered, even though the August night was warm. His T-shirt stuck damply to his back. He could feel his sweat cooling on the nylon trunks, down the back and in his groin.

The dog barked again, slightly closer. He shuddered at the long, lingering bark that slid easily into a howl, the last tenuous note so long that Emmett Hobson realized that he was holding his own breath also.

He exhaled slowly. He checked his watch. The chronometer read 07:45:57—he'd been out for sixty-eight minutes now. At this pace, four miles easily, maybe closer to five.

He turned, standing for a moment in the middle of the trail, his hands on his hips (it felt so good to *feel* hip bones for a change, instead of the shifting, Jell-O-quiver of fat).

If he followed the same trail home, but cut off at Tamarind Avenue and went the long way around the high school, that would give him the eight miles and the new record.

He started walking.

The bark was close this time, off in the darkness to the right.

"Damn dogs," Emmett said, rather too loudly. His voice echoed again, but not as strongly and stridently as he had intended. Even to his own ears, it sounded wrong.

"Damn dogs. Can't people keep the things tied up. Probably shitting all along the trail."

He picked up speed, imagining his thick thighs were pistons, machinery, pumping up and down, up and down without regard for human muscle or tissue or blood.

Up and down. Up and down.

The hypnotic rhythm helped.

The next time he looked up, he could see light reflecting off the baked tile roofs near Whitechapel and Chancery.

Grrrrr.

He stiffened, stopped.

This time the sound came from right behind him.

He turned slowly.

Nothing.

He turned back and resumed his pace.

Up and down. Up and down.

The nearest roof grew a fringe of beige stucco that gave birth to the top of an aluminum window frame. Then the glow of a light inside the second-floor window. Emmett Hobson remembered a joke he had heard on KMDY radio—the comedy station: *I went out looking at curtains the other night and hit it lucky. Most of them were open.*

Emmett Hobson squinted. There just might be a figure in that window. A woman. Undressing. Maybe she didn't know about the trail. Maybe she didn't think anyone would be out here at this hour. Maybe she knew and didn't care.

Maybe....

It screamed beside him, a high-pitched *ky-yi-yi-yi* that threw him back thirty-five years to a night spent on the Nevada desert, huddled against the corner in the back seat of an old Dodge while his folks slept peacefully in the front seat. They were on their way to Chicago to visit Emmett's grandparents and wanted to save money, so instead of sacking out in a motel in Winnemucca or Elko or one of those god-forsaken towns, Emmett's dad had pulled to the side of the road, rolled the window down for some ventilation, and gone to sleep.

Emmett couldn't sleep. He didn't dare kick the back of his Dad's seat and pretend that it was an accident. He had tried that the night before and gotten the strap for his troubles.

So he curled up with a thin blanket over him, even though the night was warm, and listened.

Ky-yi-yi-yi-yi. The coyote's howl had echoed across the desert floor, haunting and eerie and frightening. Emmett had stared in horror, certain that some monstrous beast would stick its foul fangs through the windows and kill them.

He had felt warmth between his legs as his bladder had let go.

Later, with a gentleness that sometimes still amazed Emmett when he remembered that night, his dad had not laughed, but had comforted Emmett and tried to explain away the fear.

He hadn't thought of that night for years. The coyotes on each side of him yelped again. Their duet poured from upraised muzzles and tightened throats that reflected the golden light of the single bedroom window visible above the hill.

Emmett Hobson stared at the humps of darkness circling him, just beyond his vision. He counted five, then six, ten, a dozen. None made a sound now that the first one had announced their presence.

The air was warm, like it had been that night in Nevada. He could hear his father mumbling in his sleep, his mother snoring softly in the front seat. He could see her head thrown back over the headrest, the blood pulsing in her throat

pulsing pouring through the severed flesh.

The old man shuffled toward him, slowly, but cutting away at the distance too quickly for Emmett to react. Even in the darkness, Emmett could see the way the old man's fingers trembled, the way the feet slid forward with stiff, flat-footed, painful urgency. As the old man reached out to him, he smelled something pungently, nauseatingly sweet, like urine mixed with sugar.

The hand almost touched him.

He closed his eyes and screamed.

When he opened them, the Viet Cong swarmed over him, blades raised and bloody.

Warmth flooded between his legs as his bladder released and urine blended with drying sweat in the nylon crotch of his Puma jogging pants.

- 3 -

Madeleine Mueller finished undressing and reached for her nightgown. It was the white lacy one that Dave bought her for Mother's Day to use as a somewhat less than subtle hint. On nights that he felt especially horny (although he would never have used the word in front of her and might honestly have believed that she did not know what it meant), he would lay it out across the overstuffed pillows of their king-sized bed.

He was still downstairs, watching the end of some silly ball game or another, and Madeleine had walked into the bedroom, switched on the light, and seen the nightgown draped over the bird's egg blue of their bedspread.

Tonight, it looked comically like a giant deflated doll slumped up against the pillow. Madeleine nearly laughed out loud but stifled the sound just in time.

She smiled instead.

Now, just as she touched it with one finger, while she was still standing naked in the center of their room, her body bathed by soft light filtering from the single night-stand light, she shuddered.

She glanced up, intending to check whether the window might be open, whether there might be a light draft of cooling night air.

The drapes were open.

The window was closed. Even from that distance she could see that the latch was on.

And someone was looking at her through the window.

"Dave!" she screamed.

Before the sound died, she heard his heavy feet pounding up the stairs.

"Maddy, you okay?"

He was through the door, his face pale, his breathing heavy. Only this time, his breathing had nothing to do with the see-through nightie she held in front of her as she crouched trembling in the corner of the room across from the window.

She pointed with one hand.

"There" she gasped. "A face."

He strode to the window. Beyond their house, there was nothing but fields, mostly covered with knee-high brush that grew vividly green in the spring, then died to brown by July. But now, after dark, none of that was visible. All he could see was his own reflection in the night-blackened glass.

Dave reached over and flicked the dresser light off. His reflection disappeared, as did Madeleine's. After a moment for his eyes to adjust, he began to distinguish shapes and forms outside.

Even though moonlight bathed the series of hills receding into darkness, he could see nothing suspicious. There was no movement visible on the smoothness of their back lawn, or among the low shrubs in the fields beyond. Certainly he could spot no figure racing away after being caught doing a classic Peeping Tom act.

Dave slid the window open. The screen was in place, secured from the inside. And there was nothing below, no ladder, no rope hanging like the serpent in Eden.

He turned back to Madeleine.

"There's no one out there, hon. It's just your imagination."

"No. It wasn't." She didn't try to convince him. She just stated it as a bald fact. "There was someone looking in the window." She was standing now, and held the nightgown tightly in front of her breasts.

"That's impossible." Dave said. "No one can see in from down...."

"Shut the blinds."

Startled by something in her voice, he tugged at the strings, and the powder-blue Levelor blinds dropped into place with a firm, secure *chunk.*

"There. That better."

She reached out for him. She was trembling. Any irritation he might have felt toward her for interrupting the ball game, for screaming and scaring him light that, for letting herself get skittish over a reflection in the window—it all died away. She was terrified of something.

The lacy night gown dropped unnoticed to the floor as he held her, naked and frightened. Only a small part of his mind wondered if there was still a chance for tonight.

- 4 -

By midnight, the ambulance had come and gone. The small, tidy mother-in-law apartment behind George Abendroth's stucco house echoed with silence. Martha had cried for a few minutes, then began calling children and cousins to let them know. Tomorrow she would have to arrange with Whispering Gardens for a service. And transfer most of Mother's remaining assets, the ones not already in her name as well as Fern's.

As far as the Abendroths were concerned, Fern's death was natural, normal, perhaps even an event mildly to be desired. After all, she had lived such a long, full life. And it was so hard for her to get around any more. And she had begun talking to herself, carrying on conversations with people dead for generations. Perhaps it was for the best.

Even later, after they heard of the second death Monday night, and after the subsequent discoveries in that awful little house beyond the hill, just a mile away, they would never had thought of connecting those deaths with Fern's.

In terms of their peace of mind, perhaps that was just as well.

- 5 -

It would be two more days before the body of Emmett Hobson was found. Caryn waited an additional hour beyond the times she expected him, then alerted the police, because she knew how Emmett felt about walking that extra mile. But she couldn't give them any idea as to where he might have been walking. They began the search that night, then, when nothing was found, intensified their efforts the next day. They even brought in the County's helicopter to scan the dry hills from the air.

Tuesday passed. Then Wednesday morning, Wednesday noon.

Wednesday evening, someone called in to report what looked like a body up the arroyo beyond the concrete-capped city water tank. Two deputies were sent out to investigate.

"It couldn't be Emmett," Caryn said when she first heard the report. "He *never* went that direction. Besides that tank is a good ten miles in the opposite direction from where he did go. It must be somebody else."

At first the police agreed with her. There wasn't any immediate evidence that they had in fact found Emmett Hobson. All that was left of the black Puma jogging pants was a blood-reddened, ragged strip hanging from the elastic waist band. There was even less remaining of the white LA Dodgers T-shirt. They never found either of his eighty-dollar jogging shoes.

And most of his face, along with substantial other portions of his anatomy, was missing.

In total, Emmett Hobson had probably lost most of the sixty pounds he intended to lose.

- 6 -

The feasting was growing richer. It was not just children this time, children whose minds had to be bent and forced and twisted.

The old one had whetted his appetite.

Then there had been the man, carrying a life's load of fear waiting to be manipulated and turned against him.

And there had been that moment with the woman as well. But she was not for tonight. She would be there later, waiting, fearing, trembling and naked.

It would come back for her. After it had enjoyed this feast.

Later. In a day or two.

CHAPTER TWELVE

DEATHWATCH

- 1 -

Richard and Bonnie had never heard of Emmett Hobson, either. Although the police knew that Hobson was missing, they had as yet discovered no clues to his whereabouts by Wednesday morning, a week after Emma's death, four days after her funeral back in St. Louis. On that same Wednesday morning, Richard and Bonnie Mann arrived at the house behind the hill.

That morning, they had rented a Ford Escort in dry, neutral beige, the color of the surrounding hillsides. It took them nearly half an hour to make the five mile journey from their Howard Johnson's just off the freeway, to the end of Old Conejo Road. They had followed as best they could the mumbled and vague directions given them by an attendant at the Exxon station at Tamarind Avenue and Janss Road, but still got lost at least three times.

At the end of the Old Conejo Road, Richard was beginning to wonder if they had somehow taken the wrong turn yet again.

"Shit," he muttered under his breath as he strained to read the faded numbers painted on crumbling curbs along the street. He consulted the return address on Donney's last postcard one more time. The card was folded and stained where it had been handled. He murmured the numbers once more and shoved the card into his shirt pocket. Then he surveyed the curbs again. "It's got to be here somewhere."

Bonnie started to say something, then busied herself with the map of Tamarind Valley they had purchased at the Exxon an hour earlier. It was already ripped along one fold, but she struggled to return it to some semblance of its former neatness.

"It's got to be here," Richard repeated. He slammed his open palm against the steering wheel and twisted the key savagely. The engine whined, then caught. He started to pull away from the curb, angling in a wide circle across the end of the street.

"Wait," Bonnie said quietly. "Is that a driveway over there?"

Richard glanced where she was pointing, to a patch of rough ground beneath an arch of branches. It didn't look like a driveway. At best, it might have been an unusually rocky patch of ground in the no-man's-land between two properties.

He pulled the car closer. Even without getting out of his seat, he could see tracks in overlapping parallels where tires had passed over. He cranked the wheel and started up the narrow drive.

"Look," Bonnie said. She pointed to a canted mail box almost hidden by an overgrown stand of weeds and small shrubs. From the road, the battered box was invisible, but apparently the letter carrier knew the route well enough not to need to see the box. Folded papers and circulars lay scattered beneath the box. The top one was barely faded, but the lowest was a dusty, aged yellow. The mail box hung open. Its drop-front lolled like a panting dog's tongue on a hot August afternoon. The box itself was empty, except for a dust of leaf fragments and twigs along one side where evening breezes had entered, swirled, and died.

"He may not live here any more," she said. "It doesn't look as if anyone lives here."

"I know," Richard said. "But it's the last address I have. The only lead. I've got to try."

He drove on. The crunching of gravel beneath the tires provided a constant backdrop to a nagging headache that was developing just behind his eyes. He felt as if he had stared too long against the bright sunlight. The sound of rock rubbing against rock was irritating at first, then hypnotic.

He glanced next to him. Bonnie nodded drowsily in the warm morning air. Their bed at the Howard Johnson's had not been the most comfortable they had ever slept in, and that, coupled with their late arrival in Tamarind the night before and the two-hour time difference, had given her a classic case of jet lag.

The hundred yards from the end of Old Conejo Road to the top of the short rise seemed to stretch interminably as the Ford Escort brushed by fender-tall mustard in the last fading bloom of summer. Beyond, further from the driveway, the blackened stalks of last year's scrub growth angled up like skeletons above a ground cover of desiccated, crumbling brown.

The little Ford Escort went slower and slower, as if unwilling to exert any more energy than necessary to mount the rise.

At the crest, Richard slowed the car. After a moment, he stopped.

"There it is." He pointed down the grade.

"Doesn't look like much," Bonnie said, stifling a yawn. And, to be truthful, the house lying before them didn't.

It was a small, wood-frame house—little more than a shack. In a more affluent neighborhood, a structure like that would nestle in shady pines behind the main house, or lean into the sea winds beyond a row of wind-whipped dunes and bear the more dignified appellation of *cottage*. With dainty blue clapboards and white-painted trim and a postage-stamp lawn of manicured green bordered with zinnias or petunias or nodding pink geraniums, its neat rectangular gardens bounded by white-washed rocks, it might even aspire to becoming a *guest cottage*.

But there was nothing elegant in the squat building at the end of the driveway, with its splintering eaves and weather-stained door and ragged window frame surrounding empty glass that glinted like a cyclopean eye against the morning light.

The only familiar note was the battered VW by the door. Richard nodded toward the car.

"It's the right place. I'd recognize that car anywhere."

"But the place still looks...deserted." Bonnie shivered in spite of the warm air rising from the weed-laden hillside. Richard felt a moment of fear. She looked sluggish. Her speech was difficult to understand; it was as if her tongue were swollen as it rolled inside her mouth. "I don't like it here," she finished slowly.

"Me either," Richard agreed, speaking as much for her as for himself. "But unfortunately it's just what I would have expected from Donney."

He drove slowly down the driveway and stopped a few feet behind the VW's rear bumper. From there he could read the mud-splattered stickers plastered to the rear fenders and hood:

"Fangs for the Memories," in dripping blood-red letters that formed an obscenely rounded heart where the "I" dropped below the line of print.

"I Brake for Werewolves."

"Elvira for President."

And *"Jim Jones Memorial Glee Club,"* with a much smaller line reading *"Kool-Aid, Kool-Aid, Tastes Great"* dancing in purple across the bottom of the white paper.

Richard grimaced. The stickers recalled too vividly the Donney he remembered, the Donney of the last years. Richard had been able to generate a little more enthusiasm for this trip, once everything had been arranged, by imagining how it would be to see Donney grown up and matured by living alone. Now it looked as if nothing had changed.

He got out of the car and shut the door behind him. The *thump* echoed unusually loudly. He jumped and looked back through the window at Bonnie.

"Sorry," he said, unconsciously pitching his voice into a low whisper.

"It's okay." Her voice was still muted, her words difficult to follow.

Stifling his worry over her, he walked over to the VW and studied it closely. The license was caked with so much sun-hardened mud that it was unreadable even from a few feet. The back tires were balding and cracked along the rim. The one on the passenger side sagged low enough to need a few spurts of air. A spider had diligently spun half a dozen webs from the metal rim to a small rock a few inches away. Most of the strands were obviously old, torn and hanging, but a new web—probably finished only a few hours before—still caught a few drops of morning dew. The thin white lines glistened and glittered. A nub of white in the center marked the gravesite of a fly or gnat or some other small flying creature not wary enough to avoid hidden dangers.

"It hasn't been moved for a while," Richard called back to Bonnie. She was still sitting quietly in the car. "Come on," he said, motioning for her to follow.

She rolled down the window and shook her head vigorously.

"I'll wait here," she said.

"Where it's safe," he finished, completing their favorite horrible line from innumerable unmemorable films, uttered by stalwart hero to fainting heroine just before heroine found herself impelled into mortal danger.

"No," she answered.

She seemed more alert. Richard's worry eased.

She continued: "It's cool enough here, and comfortable. I don't feel like going in there. And maybe it would be best if you saw Donney alone. It's still early—not yet noon," she added, referring obliquely but clearly enough to one of Donney's more irritating habits. "He might be asleep."

Donney sleeping naked, the door to his room hanging open, his body twisted on top of the sheets while the shadows the late morning sun cast through tree branches crawled across his sprawled arms and legs like so many thin black spiders on pale white webs.

More than once after Richard's marriage he had wandered through the living room on his way to the kitchen, naked, scratching an armpit or shoulder, his hair wild from sleep.

"Donald Mann!" Emma had huffed the first time, her cheeks and ears turning scarlet. "Bonnie is here!" *As if he couldn't see that for himself!*

"The least you could do is wear shorts or a towel."

The next time, he sauntered through the living room with a pair of wildly patterned red bikini briefs...hanging daintily from his crooked little finger. He had done that half a dozen times, until Bonnie was almost afraid to enter her mother-in-law's house any time before noon. For her part, Emma was frustrated beyond reason trying to figure out some punishment to inflict upon a sixteen-year-old boy already a foot and a half taller than herself and inordinately fractious and independent.

The last time, he came through smiling hugely, scratching at his groin. Emma and Bonnie were hideously embarrassed, and Richard was furious. *Next time,* he vowed, *I'll beat the little shit to a bloody pulp.*

He followed Donney out to the kitchen, stepping through the swinging doors before they had a chance to swish closed.

"Damn you," he hissed through clenched teeth. He pushed Donney up against the pale-yellow enameled wall. He was close enough that their shoulders touched—Richard's encased in a thin linen, Donney's bare and boney.

"Hey, big brother, goin' homo?"

Richard had backed away from Donney's nakedness as if burned but kept his brother's shoulders pinned to the wall with his outstretched hands. He spat out his warning: "That's my wife out there and I won't have you parading around like a male whore in front of her. You may not have any modesty, or care, but she does, and Ma does. You try this again and you'll wish you hadn't."

Donney had grinned—it was a frighteningly tight, taut grin—and mock-saluted. He slapped his naked heels together in a parody of military attention. "Yessir, big brother, sir."

Something about the tone grated on Richard. For a fleeting instant he wanted to slam Donney across the face. He wanted to knee him in the groin and watch him curl in pain. Instead he stepped further back, flushed and breathing heavily. "No next time, you hear?"

There was no next time. Two days after that, Donney walked out. For good. His bedroom door hung open now, his bed flat and smooth, as unlined as a baby's face.

Richard could understand Bonnie's reluctance to enter the ratty house. He walked slowly up to the door and rapped on the splintering wood.

Nothing.

He knocked again.

Still nothing. This was a silence beyond sleep or disregard for visitors. The place *felt* empty, deserted.

He wrinkled his nose.

It also smelled bad, rank and rotten and fetid. Richard cast back in memory for another such smell. For a long moment, he was lost in tumbling years until he suddenly caught an image, held it, and nearly retched.

The place smelled like Grandpa's old three-holer from fifty paces downwind on a hot summer day.

A cold hand prickled the back of his neck.

"Bonnie," he called, his voice urgent and low. "Stay there."

She didn't answer, but she didn't make any motions to get out of the car, either.

Richard reached toward the doorknob. Part of him needed to know what was in that house, but part of him recoiled against the thought of that tarnished metal touching his skin. He felt the bones of Donney's shoulders beneath his hands, pressed against the kitchen wall. He saw that sickly, maddening grin once more, with Donney's face behind it, skull-like and white. He grimaced and wrapped his fingers around the knob. It felt cold and slick, as if it had been dipped in machine oil then stored overnight in a refrigerator.

But it turned smoothly, silently.

He pushed the door open.

- 2 -

Bonnie watched as Richard walked toward the house. She loved watching him, any time, any where...even here in the shadows of this eerie place. She liked the way his pants tugged across his butt. The Levi's he preferred were pulled taut and smooth and round. She never let him carry a wallet in his back pocket.

Because it stretches the material and ruins the lines of the pants, that's why, she explained pragmatically the first time he asked her. But the real reason was that she loved watching the movement of muscle when he walked. She occasionally caught herself thinking that there might have been more than blatant sexism to the old oriental habit of the wife following a few footsteps behind her husband. Bonnie certainly wouldn't have minded, as long as said husband was Richard, and he was wearing tight jeans.

His back was nice, too, Bonnie noted, not for the first time. And so were his shoulders, even beneath the thin shirt he wore. It was white, nearly translucent, with pinkish overtones where it touched his skin.

She felt a flush of emotion that momentarily cast her exhaustion and her discomfort into the background. She sat in the warm car, watching him move toward the front door. He stood there a long time, so long that she began wondering if anything was wrong.

Then he turned and mouthed something. She saw his lips move—those lips that she had kissed and that had kissed hers and that had caressed her breasts and stomach and neck. His lips moved, but no sounds emerged. It was like he was a character in a movie, and the projectionist had turned the sound off. And then flicked the projector to slow motion.

She twisted her wedding band around and around her finger. She dropped her eyes from Richard and watched the small diamond sparkle as it came around each time, glinting like white fire.

Her hands felt swollen and heavy, leaden. They burned where the sunlight steamed through the Ford Escort's front window and focused on her knuckles. She moved her hands and rested them on her swollen belly. She tried to feel the movement of the growing life inside.

Richard stopped making funny motions with his lips and turned—slooowly to the door. He reached for the knob—

Soon. Soon.

—and opened the door—

Swelling, growing, filling her as Richard had swollen and grown and sweetly filled her night after night in the silky darkness of their apartment bedroom

—and walked inside—

Any day now, really. And this time, there had been no problems no

—stickiness on the plastic cover of the rent-a-car seat. Stickiness and warmth and clotted knots of black blood that smelled of death.

Richard!

She stared in horror. Blackness crawled beneath her light blue skirt, crept along the insides of her thighs, hot and sticky blackness that stole her breath away.

Richard!

Before, he had come, running down the hallway to their room in time to see a clot of *deeper blackness, thumb-nail-sized, a bloated watermelon seed pulsed with fading life and caught on her skin. She reached down to flick it off, as if it were an ash-mote floating on the summer air. When she touched it with her nail the pain stabbed through her womb and her stomach, and she retched as the pain twisted around her spine and sliced at nerves. The watermelon seed expanded, walnut-sized, fist-sized, basketball-sized, black and throbbing where it lay on her leg. It sent pinions of fire into her flesh, pulling her life out of her and absorbing it as it siphoned her blood into itself. She pushed at it, screaming frantically. Her hands penetrated its membranous skin and punched through into fiery heat, and the blood cascaded over her knees onto the carpet of the beige Ford Escort that was the floor of the emergency room at St. Louis General and Richard was holding her hand and crying and the Lone Ranger in his white mask held up something and chortled, "Heigh-ho, baby, Awayyyyyy!"*
Richard!
This time she made a sound. It was not the scream that her body desperately wanted, but a tiny moan, a whimper that was barely audible beyond the dashboard of the rented car.

- 3 -

Richard almost stumbled back out of the house. The stench was frightful.
He gagged, felt his stomach heave, and gasped for breath, hoping that his eyes would adjust to the darkness soon.
They did.
The room was a shambles.
From where he stood just beyond the threshold of the front door he could see a broken-down couch that lay like a collapsed coffin in the center of the room. There was a chipped sink along one wall. Along another lay a tangle of twisted wires and battered casings and battered paperback books.
This is a Bad Place, a voice whispered inside his head. He looked around, holding his breath and trying not to cough.
Apparently the toilet had overflowed at some point—whether before or after the wanton destruction of the place he couldn't tell. The walls were water-stained at least six inches up from the floor. Richard noted that there were no baseboards and that there were gaps of several inches between the crumbling drywall and the cracked concrete flooring that underlay the mottled and peeling tiles.

The single rug in the center of the room was twisted and curled back onto itself

He took a step inside.

And barely missed stepping on—in—something that at first looked like a clump of rich dark soil but quickly resolved into a pile of human feces, glistening with flies and white with maggots.

Richard retched, both at the sight and at the smell. There were similar piles here and there on the floor, surrounded by large grey-black spots of dampness where the overflowing water had not yet completely dried. Water-sodden remains of toilet tissue spread across the tiles like smears of snot against a window pane.

"Donney?" Richard called shakily, expelling breath that his nostrils punished him for releasing. His stomach roiled. His lungs burned. His eyes burned.

"Donney?"

- 4 -

Bonnie watched Richard walk toward the house. She loved watching him, any time, any where...even here in the shadows of this hideous place. She liked the way his pants tugged across his ass. The Levi's he preferred were pulled taut and smooth and round and sexy. She never let him carry a wallet in his back pocket.

Because it stretches the material and ruins the lines of the pants, that's why, she explained pragmatically the first time he asked her why. But the real reason was that she loved watching the movement of ass when he walked. She occasionally caught herself thinking that there might have been more than blatant sexism to the old oriental habit of the wife following a few footsteps behind her husband. Bonnie certainly wouldn't have minded, as long as said husband was Richard, and he was wearing tight jeans. She enjoyed imagining him naked, even in the middle of the St. Louis shopping malls.

His back was nice, too, Bonnie noted, not for the first time. And so were his naked shoulders.

She felt a flush of need that momentarily cast her exhaustion and her discomfort into the background. She sat in the stifling car, watching him float toward the front door. He stood there a long time, so long that she began wondering if anything was wrong.

Then he turned and mouthed something. She saw his lips move—those lips that she had kissed and that had kissed hers and that had nibbled her breasts and stomach and neck and groin. His lips moved, but no sounds emerged. It was eerie, like he was a character in a movie, and the projectionist had turned the sound off and flicked the projector to slow motion.

She twisted her wedding band around and around her finger. She dropped her eyes from Richard and watched the small diamond sparkle as it came around each time, glinting like white fire.

Her hands felt swollen and heavy, leaden. They burned where the sunlight steamed through the Ford Escort's front window and focused on her knuckles. She moved her hands and rested them on her swollen belly, feeling the movement, the struggling life inside.

Hurry Richard!

It would be soon. She knew that. She had been wrong before, when they had rushed to St. Louis General and the doctors had examined her and told her that it was false labor, and she hadn't believed them but they were right and she and Richard went home and had an ice cream sundae and laughed over how nervous they had been. But this time it was the real thing *how could I have thought otherwise how could I not have known that the other was false because this hurts so much and there's something wrong I know it help me richard it's not coming right*

The car rumbled over the slick roadway. Richard floored the gas pedal and sped through lights that blinked red to yellow to green to yellow to red so fast that she couldn't see the colors and they all blended into orange like thin blood

like the color on the walls as they followed the arrows down the hallway so nobody could get lost in the hospital just follow the arrows and youll get there okay

Richard!

but the doctor didnt get there on time he was in the john shitting when she came in and the nurse tried to catch but there was nothing she could do

Richard!

was outside pacing because they wouldnt let him into the delivery room without the doctors permission and the doctor was in the john shitting and she was pushing out a dead lump that stank like shit and the nurse screamed and the doctor finally ran in zipping his pants

Richard!

has anyone told the father dont tell him yet he might go apeshit get him out of here dont let him see it get her out of her too ive never seen anything so horribly

Richard!

This time the moan reached further, crept out of the tiny Ford Escort and dropped to the ground and rolled a few feet before it died.

- 5 -

The wrongness increased with each step Richard took into the house.

Obviously there had been plumbing problems here, but Richard knew that there was more wrong than that.

He walked quickly through the living room, holding his breath until his lungs demanded more of the cloying air, then trying not to throw up as the heat-ripened stench percolated through his system.

He barely glanced at the bathroom. The toilet bowl was cracked and stained. Flies were layered so thick on the floor that the light striking them made it look like the chipped tiles were covered with those little silver candy-balls bakers used to put on birthday cakes.

Richard's stomach roiled again.

The other room was the bedroom. It was almost bare. There was just a broken-down bed along one wall, with a sagging mattress half covered with lumps that had once been blankets. A few clothes lay scattered around. A pair of filthy cut-off jeans curled in the middle of the floor like a blue-black puddle. The closet was empty except for a clump of unidentifiable material in one corner that might once have been pants and T-shirts and socks.

There was no Donney.

Richard retraced his steps back to the living room. For some reason, he crossed over to the corner and stared for a moment at the ruins of a television set and VCR scattered like Christmas glitter amidst torn and defaced paperbacks tumbled on the floor. He scuffed at a bit of broken glass with the toe of his shoe.

The pages of one of the books fluttered. Richard leaned over and picked it up, careful not to touch anything but the book.

It. Stephen King. Richard had never read the book. He had watched the movie version on television the fall before, but had neither the time nor the interest to wade through the novel's hundreds of pages.

Donney had read it, though. It had been one of his favorites since the day it was published.

Richard hefted the volume in his hand.

Although the back binding had been badly cracked and a couple of end pages fluttered out when he lifted it up, the book was dry.

The filthy water had not seeped into its pages. Richard flipped through the book.

Here and there, someone had made notations with a red-inked pen.

He read one.

And another.

And another.

His hands shook as he flipped faster through the book, faster and faster, pausing only to read the thin scratching that grew more numerous as he approached the final pages.

The hair on the back of his neck bristled. He no longer smelled the stench of the room, or heard the death-house buzz of enormous, bloated flies.

He picked up another book. *Ghost Story.* And another. *Carrion Comfort.*

Every one was scarred with notations in blood-red ink. In Donney's distinctively angular handwriting.

Richard grabbed half a dozen of the books, each torn and cracked open and losing pages, but each untouched by the overflowing filth.

His hands trembled so much now that one of the books slipped from his grasp and fall on the cold tiles with a sharp *slap.*

- 6 -

Bonnie watched Richard walk. Her lips felt crusted and dry, and she felt a throbbing at her center just watching him, even here in the shadows of this hideous place. His pants raped his ass. The Levi's were pulled taut and smooth and round and lewd. She loved watching his ass, especially like now, when he was suddenly buck naked and she could see the faint line of hair that marched upward in a tight spiral and then spilled onto the spreading muscles of his back and disappeared into the tan just above his belt line.

His back was nice, too, and his naked shoulders.

She felt a heat. She writhed in the stifling car, watching him float toward the front door. He stood there a long time, so long that she began wondering if anything was wrong.

Then he turned and mouthed something. She saw his lips move—those lips that she had kissed and that had crushed hers and that had bitten her breasts and stomach and neck and groin. His lips moved, but no sounds came out. The blood vessels in his neck bulged as if he were screaming. His face flushed, and while he was turned she saw that he was violently aroused.

She felt the heat penetrate deeper and deeper, painful now.

She twisted her wedding band around and around her finger. She dropped her eyes from Richard's nakedness and watched the diamond glint evilly as it came around each time. It burned like white fire.

Her hands felt swollen and heavy, leaden. They burned where the sunlight steamed through the front windows and focused on her knuckles. She moved her hands and rested them on her swollen belly, feeling the movement, the struggling life inside.

Hurry, Richard.

It had to be soon. She knew that. She had been wrong before, when they had rushed to St. Louis General and the doctors had examined her and screamed at her that it was false labor *idiot moron broad* and she hadn't believed them, but they were right and she and Richard went home and got naked and screwed right there on the living room floor in spite of how huge she was and how huge he was and how painful it was. But this time it was the real thing *how could I have thought otherwise how could I not have known that the other was false because this hurts so much and there's something wrong I know it help me richard we shouldn't have done it not this late it's not coming right*

The car rumbled over the roadway. Richard floored the gas pedal and sped through lights that blinked red to yellow to green to yellow to red so fast that she couldn't see the colors and they blended into blood-red that pulsed with the veins in her throat and the blood-red that pulsed between her legs

Hurry!

Her womb was swollen rock-hard and bursting. It hurt hurt hurt *something is wrong its like teeth razing inside me not contractions not amber waves of pain but sharp and cutting and*

Richard!

no no no no no no no its coming nurse get ready breathe deeply now mrs mann its coming just a little more help mr mann hold her shoulders up breathe breathe concentrate on the focal point just a little

no no no no no no no screams

its teeth are clotted with her flesh with the flesh of her womb and it smiles and the smile smells of death and decay and the charnel house

thump thump thump

and the respirator thumps near her head even as the creature gouges with its claws and savages another huge piece of her flesh

the tender flesh where Richard and the blood streams out and her breath is painful painful and then stops and the
   thump thump thump
thrust of her heart stops and she floats quietly above the carnage and sees the monster still ravaging her corpse *and someone screams, vibrating her peace and impelling her back into the pain-riddled body, and screaming screaming screaming at her even as she struggles upward and away from the blood and the body and the pain and the monster screaming screaming "Hey, lady! You all right!"*

Bonnie sat straight up. Her heart was thudding so violently that she felt dizzy and breathless. Hot sweat dripped from her temples.

"Lady!"

Even before she turned her head to looked out the window, she screamed.

- 7 -

Richard felt befouled just holding the books, but the hideously graphic notes they contained were all that he could find in the ruins of the house of Donney—the new Donney, that is; there was no hint of the old one anywhere. Richard salvaged one more, then another and another, stacking them on their sides on the empty shelf until he had nearly a dozen, each stained with the blood-red notes on page after page.

He reached for them, balancing them carefully, knowing that if any of them fell onto the filth-encrusted floor, he would never have the stomach to pick them up.

His nausea increased as he breathed deeply.

Only a few moments more, then he could breathe freshness and life.

He felt dizzy from the stench and the heat...and the fear.

Outside, suddenly, piercingly, Bonnie screamed.

Richard bolted for the door, still carrying the books. He slipped on the tiles but kept his footing long enough to burst through the front door, not listening to the tortured squeal of hinges as they were bent out of shape by the force of his body.

He ran, half-blinded by the light, around the VW and toward Bonnie.

Someone was leaning into the Ford, pawing at Bonnie. She sat stock still, screamed again.

"Get away from her!" Richard bellowed at Donney. For an instant, he saw his brother, naked and skeletal and mocking. Richard screamed.

Then, with a suddenness that left Richard without breath, it wasn't Donney at all, but a kid looking small and scared shitless at the sight of Richard barreling down at him, hair flying, shirt untucked, the stench of sewage preceding him like a harbinger crow.

"She's hurt, mister!" the boy yelled as he backed away from the car and raised his hands. *I didn't do it, whatever's wrong I didn't do it,* the gesture said, more eloquently than mere words. "She's moaning and twisting like she's got a bellyache."

Richard shoved past the boy and yanked the door open. The books fell unnoticed to the gravel. Bonnie looked up at him wanly.

"Richard?" she whispered. She was pale, her hands clutched convulsively at her stomach. She stared at him for a moment, then shook her head as if coming out of a trance.

"Richard." This time the word thrummed with relief. She collapsed against his chest, sobbing. Her breath escaped in great ragged heaves. "I dreamed that...the baby, it was coming again and...and...."

"It's okay," he said. "It's okay."

"I was up there," the boy said suddenly, as if aware that he was no longer in danger of being beaten. "I heard something in the car and came down, and she was panting and crying and acting real funny."

"Are you all right," Richard asked Bonnie sharply as he knelt beside her. The sharp gravel cut through the knees of his jeans.

She didn't answer for a moment, then said, weakly, "Yes, I think so. It was just a dream, a horrible nightmare."

She sat back, but still clutched the cloth of his shirt. Her diamond wedding ring winked in the light.

Richard relaxed a little, leaning away from the car and squatting by the door. He kept his face level with Bonnie's as he studied her.

She tried to reassure him. She smiled and reached out and took his hand. "Did you find...anything?" He knew what she was really asking: *Did you find Donney, or his body?*

"There's something here," he began uncertainly, "something about this house. I felt...odd...while I was inside, and I found some notes"—he picked up one of the books—"that must have been Donney's. They're...scary. I don't like it here."

"Yeah," the boy said softly from behind Richard. Then: "I don't like it either."

Richard looked at over his shoulder at the kid. The boy had regained some of his color, but still looked pale.

"Look, kid," Richard said, still holding on to Bonnie's hand. "I'm sorry. I heard my wife scream, and from inside it looked like...for a second I thought...oh, hell, I made an ass of myself and there's nothing else I can say. Sorry."

"It's okay," the boy muttered. He looked down at his feet, as if embarrassed.

Richard held out his hand.

"Richard Mann," he said.

"Kenny Robinson," the boy answered stiffly. Richard grinned at the boy's attempts to emulate the adult.

"Richard," Bonnie said. "Can we go back to the motel now. I really don't feel too good."

"Yeah," he said. He glanced quickly at the boy. "Look, thanks for trying to help her out, kid. And I really am sorry." He crossed around the front of the Ford and climbed in. "Take care."

Bonnie reached out the window at the last moment and squeezed the boy's hand.

"Yes, thanks," she said.

The boy Kenny looked even more embarrassed.

The gravel crunched as Richard Mann backed into the turn-around, then sped up the hill and disappeared from sight.

- 8 -

Kenny watched the car until he could no longer see it. He stood a few moments longer. Finally, even the sound of its motor had faded away.

He looked long and hard at the house. The broken door hung open like an entrance into night itself.

Even though it was hot and there was no shade that overhung the dusty driveway, the boy watched the house for a long time.

Chapter Thirteen

Divide and Conquer

- 1 -

"But Mom!"

"That's final, young man. No arguments." Anna Robinson set her features into the look both Lawrence Robinson and his son Kenny knew so well. There was no way to change her mind when she was like this, so Kenny immediately switched to Plan B.

"Dad?"

Lawrence Robinson folded the morning issue of the Los Angeles *Times* he had been trying in vain to finish and looked across the breakfast table, first at his son, then at his wife as she stood near the counter. Her back was turned toward the two males at the table—husband and son—and he could see her shoulders working as she sliced leftover ham into thin strips for the evening's casserole.

"Dad?"

This time, Kenny's voice had taken on a whiny, sharp-edged tone. Larry hated that sound, mostly because he remembered using a similar voice himself years ago...and for a similar purpose.

Divide and conquer. The basic strategy of childhood.

It had seemed all right for Larry to manipulate his own parents—Kenny's long-dead grandparents—those long years ago, but he wasn't about to let himself be manipulated the same way by *his* son. Usually when Kenny slipped into that tone of voice, Larry's immediate response was an unthinking and unswerving "no."

This time, however, Larry had to admit that the boy had a valid point.

"Are you done eating?" he said, diverting the momentum of the conversation. Like all adults, when pressed he reverted to an authoritarian stance. His question did not so much express concern over his son's nutritional needs as establish his control over the conversation. It was like when he would suddenly say, from the depths of his easy chair late on a Sunday evening, "Are the garbage cans out?" He knew they weren't; his asking was a parental way of telling Kenny to do the job...without actually having to tell him to do the job. It was an indirect assertion of a father's authority and control.

"Are you done eating?" Translation: *It doesn't make any difference what you want. I recognize the strategy you're using and I'm not going to let you get away with it. I am the father; you are the son. Nothing you say or do can influence me in a direction I don't want to go.*

He sighed. This was all part of the politics of adolescence and adulthood. Still, he noted with more than a little sympathy the dejection in Kenny's glance as the boy stared at his plate. A wad of scrambled eggs hung along one edge, along with a bit of ham too underdone for Kenny's taste and half a biscuit smeared with raspberry jam.

"Yeah, I guess so. Can I go now?"

Larry nodded.

Kenny slid his chair noisily away from the table and left, pouting and sulky and obviously not caring that both of his parents knew.

Larry followed his son with his eyes until the boy disappeared through the door into the hallway.

- 2 -

As soon as it swung closed, Kenny leaned back against the door. He could *feel* the silence and the fear through the thin wooden panels. He could *feel* the defeat.

He knew what he had to do. He also knew that he was helpless without Mom's permission. He couldn't just disappear, couldn't just slip outside and grab his bike and ride over the hill. She would worry herself to death; maybe that was Mother-strategy. Guilt. Fear. Coupled with a love so deep and compelling that the glimpses Kenny had seen of it over the last four days had frightened him more fundamentally than the other images still skulking in his mind.

Maybe he could think of another way.

But there was no other way.

- 3 -

The kitchen remained silent for a long while. Anna Robinson hacked away at the ham slice as if it were an enemy discovered lying in ambush. For such an enemy, there could be no mercy. The knife rose, fell with a sharp *snick*. Then she cut at the meat with long, stroking slices that severed slivers of tissue from the main mass. Again. Again.

Larry Robinson crinkled the newspaper and flipped from page to page, section to section. He didn't notice when one corner dragged through a spot of strawberry jam on his plate and smudged the table-top.

Finally Anna squared her shoulders and turned to face her husband. To confront the issue.

"He can't go. I won't let him."

With those words, she realized that a tenuous compromise had been broached. Battle lines had been drawn. There was no retreat.

Larry dropped the paper.

"You've got to," he said quietly.

Her lower lip trembled.

"I won't. I can't."

"But you can't keep him locked up here for the rest of his life. He's young, he's a boy."

"I know," Anna almost screamed. She turned away and sliced at the ham again. "And so were the others. And now they're *dead!*"

"Shhhhh," Larry said, with such hissing force that Anna spun around to face him. "He'll hear you."

Anna bit her lip so hard that a pearl of blood pooled on it, stained it a deeper crimson than her touch of lipstick.

Larry tried again. "It's been four days since...Saturday—and you've not let him out of your sight for more than ten minutes."

"I *can't.* All I can think of is those boys—Teddy, Chuck, little Timmy, dear God, little Timmy. And it could have been Kenny, too."

She turned away again. Her shoulders trembled, and he saw her touch at her eyes with the edge of a dish towel—something that she would have yelled at Kenny for doing. *Dish towels were for drying dishes, not for wiping people's eyes.*

"It could have been Kenny," Larry agreed somberly. "But it wasn't. And the police haven't found any evidence that the maniac is still in Tamarind Valley. He's probably long gone by now, what with the investigations and all."

"And for someone like Kenny, who's so used to picking up and heading out, four days of house arrest is like a life-time sentence. He's stifling in here. And all he wants is to ride his bike down to the library and read for a while. An hour. Two at the most. Nothing wrong with that."

"I can't."

Larry shoved his chair back and went to her, putting his hands on her shoulders and feeling the deep vibrations of her tears and her fear.

"You've got to."

She turned in his embrace and stepped closer to him. "But what if...?"

"What if you keep up like this? What if you hover over him so long that he begins to believe that everything out there is going to hurt him, that wherever he goes he needs you to be there to protect him?

"That's going to smother him, and he will be as dead as those other boys. Sure, it's tough. On you. On me. On any parent right now. On Kenny, too. Maybe especially on Kenny. But we can't let our fears infect him. He's a good kid. He's level-headed and responsible. A week ago, we didn't think a thing of him riding around all day long, only showing up for a few minutes at a time, then off again.

"*He* hasn't changed."

"I know, but...."

"Anna, you've got to let him go. Just a little. Let him ride to the Library. Give him an hour or two to be alone, to think. Otherwise you run the risk of weakening him."

Her shoulders slumped; he felt the movement and interpreted it immediately. She understood. She hated it, she feared it, but she understood.

"Okay. But you tell him. If I saw him standing there, like he used to wait for Spence, I'd...."

She dabbed at her eyes again.

"Dish towels were made for drying dishes, not for wiping people's eyes," he said, teasingly.

"Oh, you," Anna said, snapping the towel at him. She ventured a shaky smile, but tears still sparkled in her eyes. "Out of my kitchen."

As he reached the door, she said, "Thanks."

He blew her a kiss before entering the hallway.

- 4 -

Kenny sat on his bed, swinging his legs back and forth over the pile of clothing that had grown appreciably over the past few days. To all appearances, he was relaxed, resigned to house arrest.

Inside, he was seething.

It got Spence and the others. It knows that I know about it. And eventually it's going to try to get me. I gotta get outta here and—

"Kenny."

Kenny started, then looked up just as his father pushed the door open, entered, and carefully, quietly, shut the door behind him. He stood there for a long time, looking down at Kenny.

Finally he came over and sat down beside his son. The bed-springs squeaked at the unaccustomed weight.

"Look," Larry began. Kenny heard and identified his father's uncertainty about what to say and how to say it. "Your mother means well. You know that she and I try to agree on things, that when one of us tells you to do something, the other one tries not to contradict it."

Kenny nodded. That had been a problem for a long time. Some of the other kids could get away with murd...with lots more than he could, just by playing mother against father. But his folks were cagey. They usually checked with each other before giving him permission to do most things, and gradually Kenny had discovered that if he respected their wishes in a few things, they gave him even greater freedom in others.

"But this time," Larry continued, "Well, your mom isn't think-ing as clearly as she usually does. She's scared. For you. For the other kids in town. She's afraid that there's someone out there who's just looking for you. You understand?"

Kenny nodded again.

If only Dad knew the truth! Something—not someone—was looking for him.

"And so am I," Larry said. "I'm scared right now, too. I don't want anything to happen to you either. But I don't think it's good for you to sit up here all the time, especially when there are so many things here to remind you of Spence." He looked around the room.

Kenny followed his father's glance, taking in the books he and Spence had read together, the models of dinosaurs and space craft and monsters and cars they had so carefully constructed and dis-played.

Kenny looked up at Larry, hope kindling in his eyes.

"Anyway, the upshot of this all is that you can go to the library."

"Great...."

"But...." Larry held up a hand in warning. "This doesn't mean that you can expect me to back you up against your Mom again. And it doesn't mean that you can stay out all day and scare her to death by not dragging in until after dark."

He held up one finger. "Library only."

Kenny nodded. *I'll ride by it, anyway.*

Larry held up a second finger. "Two hours, on the dot. Not a second more."

Kenny nodded.

Third finger. "Straight there, straight home. No ice creams, no sodas, no stopping for a hamburger."

A nod.

Fourth finger. "Check in with Mom the moment you get back. And I mean the *moment* you come through the door." Larry's expression left no openings for negotiation on any of the points.

"Sure thing, Dad." Kenny nodded, then looked down at his hands.

"Look, Kenny," his father said, putting his arm around Kenny's shoulder. Kenny could feel the warmth of his father's body, smell a lingering hint of shaving cream overlaid with a residue of breakfast. The smells were reassuring in ways Kenny had not expected to feel. His father continued: "I know that you're a pretty responsible kid. You've shown that over the past couple of years. I trust you to do things I wouldn't trust a lot of adults with."

Kenny still looked down. He didn't like the direction the lecture was taking. He could tell that the blood was rushing to his cheeks and ears; his face was hot and he did not dare try to look up at his father.

Because I'm going to disobey you, Dad. I've got to. So don't make it harder by praising me.

Larry reacted almost as if he had hears Kenny's silent plea.

"Just...just help us out with this one, son," he said quietly. "Pretty soon, the fear will pass. Things will get back to normal. They will, I promise. Right now it may seem like the world's a pretty dark place. It may seem like you've lost too much to...well, what I'm saying is, just think before you do anything, and be careful."

He patted Kenny's knee, then stood. The springs squeaked again. Larry looked around the room again. There was something more critical, more typically fatherly in his eyes this time.

"But before you go anywhere, young man, clean up this pig-pen." He pointed at the pile of clothes, then grinned to take any sting out of the words. Business as usual, he seemed to say without saying it—*the kid's job is to mess up the place; the parent's job is to hound him about cleaning it up, even if the room is just getting to the comfortable state.*

Kenny understood the messages—the spoken, and the unspoken.

"Sure, Dad."

Larry left the room before Kenny began whittling away at the pile of clothes. It wasn't really that messy, he knew, and most of the clothes were dirty so he just tossed them into the laundry bin by the door. There were a couple of books to put back on their places on the shelf. A tennis shoe had to be located and set next to the mate that was waiting patiently in the closet. That kind of thing was easy enough.

His camping gear, dumped unceremoniously in the far corner of the room, was more intimidating, however. He swallowed hard as he looked at the shapeless mass that was his sleeping bag—bright red nylon shell, grey nylon lining, bought on sale at Best's six months ago with his own money. It had been inside his tent that night, still rolled up and cinched by a length of rope to his pack frame. The sleeping bag had been unmarked by the night; there were no telltale splatterings of crusting and dried blood to remind him visually of what happened. But its very presence seemed enough of a reminder. He nudged at it with one foot, pushing it farther into the darkness of the closet before he shut the door firmly against the memory. He wondered if he would ever want to use that sleeping bag again.

He sighed and started to work on the pile of laundry.

"Kenny."

Mom's voice sounded faintly from the kitchen.

"Yeah, Mom." He pitched his own to be loud enough to carry. He didn't want an instant replay of yesterday's hysteria if she didn't hear him.

Pause.

He held his breath, waiting for her to call out to him again. His room seemed suddenly hot and close and silent.

"Nothing, dear."

He let his breath out in a long, painful breath.

It hurt. It hurt to see her like this.

If he could find a way to do what he had to do without hurting her any more, he would take it. But if there wasn't....

He'd had time to think about things. He figured that he understood a little more about the attack on the Panther Patrol than anyone else did. He saw Sven the Red-Handed become Spence for a split second before he had fainted; he knew that something had used Spence, then traded Spence's shape for another one and used *that* one to kill the guys. He knew that whatever it was, it was evil and it had fed on the boys' fears that night.

He didn't know what it was, or how it destroyed people, or why if had chosen the Panther Patrol.

But he knew that he would have act on what he knew by himself. Nobody—certainly no adults that he knew—would believe him if he tried to tell them. *My friend went into this old house, see, to sell a newspaper subscription, and while he was in there something took him over, possessed him, like, and then he came out and he was different. Then that night, he slipped away from the campfire and came back as Sven the Red-Handed and chopped everybody up with an axe, and now he's waiting out there to do it again to someone else...to me.*

Knowing that much, of course, didn't mean that Kenny had any clear idea how to fight the Spence-thing.

Nor did it mean that he had any illusions about coming through unscathed, or even alive. Chuck was dead. Teddy was dead. Timmy was dead. Spence—the *real* Spence, not the husk that had moved and breathed and talked and biked all afternoon Friday—was undoubtedly dead.

Kenny could just as easily be dead. Mom was right about that.

But he couldn't just sit here and wait. He was the last of the Panther Patrol—the last who could do anything, at any rate. The last who could fight against the thing that had destroyed the others. And he was about to make his move.

- 5 -

He was still cleaning up his room when he heard the kitchen screen slam shut and, a few minutes later, Dad's car pull out of the garage. Dad had stayed home Monday for the funeral, then again Tuesday because things were still unsettled with Mom. But now it was time to get back to his normal routine. He had to go back to work. Life went on.

The king is dead! Long live the king!

Kenny kept working at his room. He took care to do a better job than usual, even grabbing an old pair of Jockey shorts (hardly dirty at all) and using them to flick away the dust on his window sill and along the book shelves.

Then he sat back on the bed and waited. The clatter from the kitchen gradually diminished, stopped. He waited a little more.

The television started up. Mom was watching a game show. He couldn't tell which one, and anyway he never watched them. Mom liked them sometimes, especially during the school year when she was home alone. They kept her company, she said.

He picked up his bike pack and stuffed a couple of books into it. They were both library books, but neither was due for almost two weeks more. He headed to the door and, just before he went through, took a deep breath, feeling like he was about to dive head-first from thirty feet into a pool of icy water. Or boiling water.

He wasn't sure which.

He entered the living room.

"I'm going now, Mom."

Anna didn't answer him. She stared at the television. A contestant from a city in Minnesota was trying to correctly guess the price of a Mr. Coffee machine. If she got within forty-nine cents, she would win a trip to Bermuda. *For knowing how much a Mr. Coffee costs?*

"Mom?"

"Yes." She didn't look at him.

"I'm going to the library now. I'll be back at noon. And I won't stop anywhere or anything. Dad talked to me."

"Okay."

Her voice was curiously flat. It sounded dull, empty, as if she were anesthetized.

Perhaps she was, Kenny realized. Perhaps her fear was so intense that it deadened her to everything else. He wanted to go over and kiss her, but didn't dare.

Instead he pushed his way out the front door, turning at the last moment to say, "I'll be careful, really I will. I love you, Mom."

She looked at him. She was crying.

He backed out the front door, careful not to let the screen smack against the jamb. Walking slowly, aware that his mother might be watching him from the darkness inside, he brought his bike out from the garage, straddled it, and—scrupulously looking both ways before leaving the driveway—pedaled toward the center of town.

He would keep his promise. Part of it, anyway.

He rode to the library first. By then he was almost flying on his bike. He whipped past the book-return slot, skidded to a stop, and stuffed the two books in.

My alibi. If anyone ever asks, I can have them check the return date on the books.

But that was detective-movie stuff.

What he had to do was real.

He continued past the library, cutting through the shadows of its angular roof as he skirted the dry creek bed and pumped up the path worn by hundreds of kids' feet as they took the short cut from Whitechapel to the library and back.

Up Whitechapel. There were not many kids out today. For whole blocks at a time, it seemed as if Kenny were the only kid left in the universe. A few women stared at Kenny from front windows or screened porches as he pedaled by. More than one started to call out to him, then stopped, biting lips and looking pinched.

He followed Whitechapel to Old Conejo Park. For some reason, he got off his bike and pushed it up Conejo. He passed the first house, the one Spence had taken. Then he passed Mr. and Mrs. Coupon-Clipper's place. His cheeks flushed hotly as he went by.

The house was closed tight. The garage had two new Yale locks on it. There was an air about the place that said "extended vacation, back in a week, a month, maybe never."

He pushed the bike to the end of Old Conejo Road and stopped.

From here on, he would really be on his own. Here was where he took the irrevocable step. Up until now, everything had been free. Even now, he could turn back. He could go home and be a kid and hide and let Mom and Dad take care of him.

Try to take care of him.

But if he crossed from the crazed asphalt onto the white-gravel driveway, he would be crossing an unseen boundary between comfortable reality and a horror that he could barely imagine.

He could be hurt.

He could die.

Or he could help Spence, release his spirit, free his soul...something like that. At the least, he let what was left of Spence (if there was anything left) know that Kenny loved him and would give up anything to help him.

And maybe he could get a little vengeance, for Spence, for Chuck and Teddy and Timmy.

He crossed the line.

His bike tires crunched noisily on the gravel. In the silence, the sound seemed magnified, until the barren hillsides echoed it back doubled and redoubled. The sound unnerved him, so he swerved off the driveway and pushed his bike into the dry growth. A few yards in, where the moisture trapped under the driveway was no longer available to the plants, the groundcover lessened. Mostly, Kenny found himself pushing his bike over heat-hardened soil studded here and there with rounded rocks and clumps of earth. It was easy to push the bike up the hill, scaring lizards and butterflies and even a rabbit or two as he invaded their domains.

At the top of the hill, he stopped and looked behind him. Tamarind Valley lay spread out across the valley. From here, it looked picture-postcard peaceful. Trees swayed in a faint breeze. Houses nestled among patches of green lawn. In the distance, a line of cars followed the gentle curves of the freeway, north into Ventura Country, or south toward Los Angeles. Above the breeze, he could heat the faintest suggestion of the *hummm* that was a combination of engines racing and tires whirling across the concrete surface. From this distance, though, the noise was subdued, almost pleasant.

Sunlight fell across his shoulders. The sky was cloudless. It was a perfect day. At least, it seemed a perfect day as he looked behind him, toward normality and peace.

In front of him, the driveway wound like a silver ribbon over the hill and down to the house. Almost everything about the house was just like it had been Friday afternoon. The dusty VW with a bent antenna didn't seem to have moved. There was no lawn, no trees. A single straggling vine still clung to the side of the house. The door was closed. But now Kenny saw the house with different eyes.

Physically, it seemed the same, but there was something else there, a badness, a wrongness that he could feel in his bones. Beneath the ache and the pain and the emptiness at losing Spence, there was a white-hot anger, and beneath that a darkness that echoed like radar, homing in on the decrepit old house.

He didn't know how long he stood there, just watching. He heard the crunch of tires on the gravel before he actually saw the car when it emerged from beneath the shadow of the two trees by the mailbox.

Startled, he pushed away from his bike and dropped to his knees. A sharp stone cut into his pants leg, but he ignored it. He crouched down until he was mostly screened by knee-high weeds. He tensed as the car approached

The tan car crawled up the driveway, far slower than the condition of the roadbed would have required, especially on a dry, sunlit day. It stopped at the top, dead still, then edged toward the house. It crossed over the ridge, as slowly as if the car itself were unwilling to come any closer to the old house. Kenny could hear the sound the tires made all the way down the hill.

The car slowed, then stopped a ways from the house. A guy Kenny had never seen before got out. He walked over to the old VW and made a big production of looking it over, like he was a prospective buyer and knew that the car salesman was trying to gyp him. He said something to someone in the car, but Kenny couldn't hear.

The man approached the door.

Suddenly, heedless of his fear and of any danger the man might represent, Kenny leaped to his feet. His tensed muscles cramped for a second, then he almost ran down the hill yelling, *Don't go in there, Mister. Bad things happen in there.*

But he didn't. Instead he stopped and knelt again. This time, instead of hiding, he crept down the slope facing the old house. He kept his body shielded by stands of drying weeds, head-high clumps of mustard and prickly tangles of sage. Halfway down the slope, he angled to the left, hoping to avoid a direct line of sight from the one window he could see. He carefully skirted the house, then stopped. He watched for five minutes or so before slipping closer, up to where he could see into the brown car and still not be seen easily from inside the house.

The only person in the car was a girl. She had long hair, and she seemed to be resting. Everything looked normal enough.

But maybe these guys were in cahoots with the Spence-thing. Maybe they were *the thing, disguised as a guy and a girl and driving a dusty tan year-old rented Ford.*

Kenny edged closer. He glanced frequently toward the front door as he moved. He stopped behind a thick clump of chaparral not a dozen feet from the car.

From this perspective, he could see directly into the car. The girl didn't look too old, maybe eighteen or twenty. She had a pretty face, and, from what he could see, a pretty good build, too.

Her eyes were closed. She looked like she was sleeping. The car windows were rolled tightly up, so it must have been hot inside. Kenny could see the glimmer of sweat as it beaded on her face. She rolled her head toward him. Her face contorted and her mouth moved, as if she were speaking...or moaning. He started to his feet, then sank back again. He still didn't know who she was...what she was. And there was the man inside the house. Kenny huddled closer to the scanty shade of the chaparral.

The girl was moving again. Her head rocked back and forth, not gently, like sometimes happened during peaceful dreams, but sharply, as if someone was slapping her face, one side, then the other, then the first again. Abruptly, she stopped. Her head dropped into the back of the seat. She didn't look like she was asleep any more. She looked unconscious. Or dead.

He crept closer, staying as near to the ground as he could.

She was still for a couple of moments, then she started again, rocking her head, twisting her shoulders and making funny sounds that even he could hear. Sweat glistened across her forehead and on her temples. Her dark hair was plastered to her skin.

Kenny couldn't help himself. Maybe she was hurt. She sure wasn't acting like she could hurt him.

He sprinted the remaining few feet to the passenger window and looked in. Up close, she looked even worse. Her eyelids were closed, but beneath them her eyes were flickering so fast that it looked like they were spinning. Her hands were clenched across her stomach and dug into the blue cloth of her skirt, like she was trying to rip her guts out.

He wrenched at the handle. It was hot, and it clicked when he pulled at it, but the door did not open. He glanced down and saw the knob fitting snuggly against the door frame. The door was locked.

He slapped the side of the car door with his open palm, hoping to bring her out of it.

Thump. Thump. Thump

If anything, the sounds made it worse. She moaned, a deep, cutting sound like death personified. Chills raced up his spine, and the skin around his testicles crawled. He backed away and stared at her.

The thrashing began a third time. The convulsions were so strong that the little car shook. In spite of his fear, Kenny slammed his palm against the car door again.

Thump, thump, thump.

She sat straight up, as suddenly as if she had been given an electric shock. Her eyes were wide open, her skin flushed and slick with sweat.

"Lady!" He hammered on the window with his fist, trying to get her to move, to unlock the door, to roll down the window and let some coolness in.

She stared ahead, staring at something the Kenny couldn't see. He almost expected her to grunt a sigh, clutch her heart, and fall over dead.

Instead, she screamed.

Even though she was encased in the locked car, the sound was long and loud and piercing. It echoed off the house.

Reflexively, he screamed as well.

She saw him and started flailing her hands at him, fingers curved as if she were a cat and had just bared her claws. Her hands struck unyielding glass. The flesh pressed whitely against the window as she lashed at him.

She screamed again.

"Get away from her," someone yelled.

Kenny spun around and saw the guy racing from inside the house. The man looked scared to death. His skin was white and his eyes had a wild look that terrified Kenny more than anything he had seen since the campfire in Jenkin's Field. The man's clothes and shoes were filthy, and even as far away as he was, he smelled like the inside of a toilet.

"She's hurt, mister," Kenny yelled, backing away from the car and holding both hands up, keeping them in plain sight. "She's moaning and twisting like she's got a bellyache."

The man pushed past him and yanked on the door handle. He dug in his jeans pocket and pulled out a key chain and slid the key into the lock and pulled the door open. Kenny couldn't see or hear much more for a while. The man was holding the woman and comforting her. Kenny couldn't distinguish any words, but he recognized the sounds one makes to comfort a child, to reassure a loved one, to stave off fear and horror.

He recognized love.

Kenny knew—knew deep inside—that they were not part of the Spence-thing. The woman was hurting too much to be part of that evil, even though there didn't seem to be anything visibly wrong with her.

And the man was hurting for her.

There was no wrongness here, only the consequences of wrongness.

After a couple of minutes, the man glanced up at Kenny. He looked kind of silly and muttered an apology.

"It's okay," Kenny said, thinking of Mom and how he would react if he had seen her in a similar situation—screaming hysterically while some stranger beat on the locked car door.

The man held out his hand and introduced himself. Kenny shook hands and gave them his name as well.

Then the woman said she wanted to go back to the motel. The man disappeared into the car, and before Kenny could say anything more, he had started up the engine.

The woman reached out of the open window and smiled and touched Kenny gently on the hand. Her other hand lay on the man's thigh. For a moment, the three of them were united, a single entity joined by the overlapping of fragile tissue.

And Kenny knew they could help.

He didn't know who they were. He didn't know why they were here. He didn't know what they wanted. But they could help. Would help.

He watched the car as it toiled up the gravel drive. His lips moving with the intensity of his concentration, he memorized the license plate number, memorized each line of the little Ford's rear bumper, as if his life depended on it. After the car disappeared over the rise, he listened, strained to hear the sounds of its tires on the driveway. Finally, they, too, disappeared.

He was alone, standing in front of the house.

He looked at it for a long time. The door hung open. One of the hinges had sprung, so that the darkness inside seemed to seep out, threatening yet, in a scary sort of way, inviting.

When Kenny heard the rustle of movement inside, he ran up the hill and jumped on his bike. He didn't worry about making noise this time. He spun across the weeds to the driveway and, wobbling on the uncertain surface, pumped the pedals as hard as he could.

He didn't look back, but out of the corner of his eye he might, just *might,* have seen a figure emerging from the house.

Chapter Fourteen

Council of War

- 1 -

Bonnie and Richard sat on opposite sides of the king-sized bed at the Tamarind Valley Howard Johnson's. Between them lay a pile of tattered, well-used—if not clearly abused—paperbacks. Bent, torn covers enveloped dog-eared pages that formed an untidy mound against a characterless green-and-brown bedspread.

"I don't understand," Bonnie said after several long moments of silence punctuated only by the sound of fingers flipping through the coarse paper, by the rustle of pages slipping against pages.

"I'm not sure I do, either," Richard said as he tossed one of the books to a smaller pile at the foot of the bed and picked up another. He opened it to a page somewhere near the center, then grimaced as a crude drawing in the margin caught his attention. "I think these are Donney's notes. At least the words seem to be in his handwriting. But...."

But in spite of everything that's happened, I can't believe that my baby brother could ever become the monster that wrote these.

"Ugh," Bonnie said as she threw the book she had been skimming. Disgust was written in harsh lines across her face. The book—a much read, black-covered Signet edition of *Pet Sematary*—slid across the others at the foot of the bed, hung tenuously at the edge of the pile for a moment, then slipped with a plastic *swish* off the pile and onto the thick-pile carpet. It made a dull *thump* when it fell. Neither Bonnie nor Richard noticed.

She watched Richard page through the book he was holding. "What's that one?" she asked.

"The Hunger," he said, barely looking up from the text.

"Who wrote it?" She cocked her head to try to read the lettering on the spine, but the print was so cracked that it was illegible.

He didn't answer her this time; in fact, he acted as if he had barely heard her. Something had caught his attention.

Instead of flipping rapidly through the book, he worked slowly, page by page, stopping often to stare at a notation, at a drawing. Twice he turned the pages sideways so that he could read his brother's writing more clearly.

Finally, as if she could stand the tension no longer, Bonnie shattered his concentration by reaching over and laying her hand over the page he was reading.

"What in Heaven's name are you looking for?"

The words came out almost an accusation, as if Richard were implicated in his brother's madness by association, by the mere fact that he was reading Donney's mad scrawls.

"I don't know." Richard looked across at her. He let the book drop to his lap. "I swear I really don't know. It's just that something...awful, evil...has happened, and somehow Donney is wrapped up in it. Maybe his notes will give us a clue."

"Some of the drawings I can figure out," Bonnie said reluctantly. "Like stick-figures being hung or decapitated or stabbed. Some of the ones I saw were pretty gross, disgusting. Why did he have to use red ink? There were some big splotches that really looked like blood spilled across the pages. But whose are the names? I didn't recognize any of them."

"Most of them were people we knew as kids. Here's one."

He held *The Hunger* out to Bonnie. She scanned the text. A woman was being murdered, brutally and graphically. But much of the print was blurred by the huge red scar that crossed the page in a vicious, jagged line. And the rest was overlaid with compressed, hand-printed letters so angular and twisted that they seemed angry, vicious, cruel.

"I can't read it," Bonnie said.

"It says 'Mrs. Ashburn'," Richard said.

"Where?"

He followed the lines with his finger, identifying crisscrossed letters inscribed so heavily onto the pages that in several places Donney's pen had cut through the rough paper and bled onto the next sheet.

"Oh," Bonnie said after a moment's study. "Yeah, I can read it now. Who is she?"

"*Was* she. She's been dead for, oh, maybe ten years or so. She taught second grade in St. Louis. Both Donney and I were in her classes, a couple of years apart. I don't remember much about her except that she was tall, really tall it seemed, but then we were pretty short back then. So maybe she wasn't much more than average, but she towered over us. And she had a hump. Not enough to be a humpback or anything, nothing grotesque or deforming, just a widow's hump. But to kids, it looked pretty awful.

"She must have been in her fifties or sixties by the time we came through her class. I don't remember much about her, except that when she was out of the class we would call her Mrs. Ass-burn and giggle. Funny, though, it was always Mrs. Ass-burn, like we had to acknowledge at least part of her adult dignity and authority, no matter what we did with her last name.

"I must have gotten along with her okay. I don't remember any problems. But she and Donney didn't travel on the same wave lengths. I'm not sure they even existed in the same universe.

"He hated her, and he took a perverse delight in deviling her. As we walked home each night, he would tell me what he'd done to her that day. They were mostly kids' pranks. Filling her pencil drawer with chalk dust. Hiding all of the erasers while she was out in the hall talking to the principal about something, and swearing the rest of the kids to secrecy. Things like that. I think most of the kids in his class were afraid of him, even then.

"She got back at him whenever she could. Usually in small, perfectly proper ways, but the more I think about it, the more I realize that there must have been a constant state of warfare between the two of them. She'd keep him in after class for problems that she'd overlook in other kids. She'd come down on him hard if he forgot to bring something in for Show-and-Tell, embarrassing him in front of the class."

Richard fell silent. Bonnie waited for a few moments, then prompted him.

"And?"

"And she died. Like I said, about ten years ago. There was a fire in her house, a little three-room place behind one of the new subdivisions in St. Louis. One night it just burst into flame and that was the end. They found her body in what was left of the bed."

He looked up at her, his face stricken and drawn.

"The next day, Donney kept laughing about Mrs. Ash-burn being burned to ashes. Like it was the biggest joke he had ever heard. He hadn't been in her class for a couple of years, but he still hated her. You could tell by the way he talked about her when she died.

"Anyway," he said, holding up the paperback, "I guess he thought that whatever was happening to the characters in this novel should have happened to her in real life."

211

"Most of the rest of the names that I recognize have pretty much the same kind of story. They are all people Donney knew, some of them dead, some still alive. But all of their names are written alongside—on top of—vicious or violent scenes. It's pretty scary."

Richard stared at the pile of books on the bed.

"At least I haven't seen my name anywhere," he said. "Or Mom's."

Bonnie picked up one of the books. The cover on this one had been torn completely off, along with the front pages, including part of the first chapter. There was no way to tell its title or its author. She let it drop open against her palm. The spine was so heavily cracked that the pages lay flat. It was as if this particular set of pages had been read and re-read many times, as if the reader—Donney—wanted to be able to find it at will, whenever he felt like it.

She read one of the paragraphs. Her eyes grew wide.

"Richard," she said in a whisper. "Look at this."

He took the book from her outstretched hand. He didn't recognize the book. Even though he and Donney had both enjoyed science fiction and fantasy and even an occasional dabbling into horror before Donney left, Richard's tastes had later veered back into mainstream fiction. He had read some King, a Ramsey Campbell or two, some of Koontz's latest stuff, one book by Clive Barker that he couldn't finish. But he wasn't an aficionado—*for that read: a fanatic*—the way Donney obviously was.

But in this case, the author's name wasn't really that important, nor was the book's title. The text was what was critical.

Richard read the first few sentences, then looked up at Bonnie. She was watching him closely.

The paragraph was a vivid description of a creature—apparently a werewolf or something like that, but Richard wasn't quite sure from the few lines he had read—that was reveling in killing a man. The author must have believed in letting the punishment fit the crime because it was clear that the victim had been a sadistic, cruel man who had raped a number of girls...and boys. Mostly boys. He had left their bodies mutilated, their minds destroyed

The were-beast in the novel took particular, equally sadistic pleasure in systematically removing the man's external genitalia, layer by layer, accompanied by descriptions of blood and shrieks and agony and a constant current of perverted sexuality flickering in and out as italicized memories. The cumulative effect left Richard stunned and flushed.

The book was simply bad. It was stuffed with the kind of gratuitous violence and sexual exploitation that Richard abhorred in the worst kind of horror novels. What someone had once called "splatter novels."

But bad as it was, perverted as it was, the text wasn't the worst part.

Over the page, again and again, so often and so viciously that Richard had difficulty reading the text, Donney had scribbled the same word. The letters seemed an incantation for revenge that shook Richard even as it suddenly made a world of half-understood implications clear to him.

Hammer Hammer Hammer Hammer Hammer Hammer Hammer

"Do you think...that Hammer...?" Bonnie couldn't finish.

Richard swallowed, his throat suddenly parched and tight.

It had to be. Donney went over there that night. His girl—what was her name?—had teased him about something. He had come slamming through the house just after nine. His ears burned scarlet, his breath was ragged. Richard knew that Donney was upset and furious and, more than ever, unstable. But Donney wouldn't talk, except to repeat Bitch, Bitch, Bitch *over and over until Richard's teeth grated at the explosive hatred Donney infused into that single syllable.*

Richard tried to talk to him.

"What's wrong, Donney? You can tell me."

Donney caught Richard by the throat and pushed him away.

"You're as bad as the rest of them. Poor little Donney. Poor little fucker who can't...."

He slammed out, yelling over his shoulder that he was going over to Hammer's, that Hammer would understand, that Hammer was the only one who really understood him. The only one who loved him.

"The poor kid," Richard said. The book slid from his hands and lay face up on the bed. Even there, propped partially against Richard's leg so that one half was a few inches higher than the other, the pages stayed open. The red scrawl stained the page.

He picked up another book, one that was almost two inches thick, but he didn't look at it.

Donney! What else didn't we know about you! We knew the cruelties, the neighborhood tricks, the thousand small lies and deceptions. But we never knew what really counted, did we. We never knew the real pain and fear.

He glanced down. The thick volume was King's *It.* It had a black cover with scarlet letters dripping down the front. It was pretty much unmarked. He skimmed through it. Not much. He saw a stick figure or two, a drawing of a knife, but no words, no names hatcheted into the text.

He almost threw the book onto the pile when one final page flipped by, and he stopped.

This writing was different. Richard was pretty sure it wasn't Donney's.

It came at the end, after the text, in the blank spaces on the page at the very back. Some of the letters spilled over onto a black-and-white photograph of King strumming his guitar.

Lines of writing marched through the white spaces, different from the rest in every way except in color. The words were red, but a deeper red, tinged with brown; where they covered the photograph, the red ink took on an insidious black undertone. Richard shivered. It was as if the words were not inscribed in red ink, but really in blood, red blood that was transforming to brown as it dried. The visual effect was shattering.

The words were worse.

Each line was neat, almost prissily neat. The writing was so small that there were probably ten or twelve words to a line. And the writing was not angular and sprawling like Donney's, whose teachers had all despaired of him ever mastering a decent hand. This penmanship was small, precise, crabbed and rounded, I-dotted and T-crossed.

Richard began reading.

"My God," he whispered.

Bonnie looked across the bed in amazement. Richard was not particularly religious himself, but Emma was, devoutly so, and Roland had belonged to some fundamentalist sect for years. Neither of them had cursed or used harsh language. And Bonnie knew that she had never heard Richard use the name of God like that.

"What is it?" She strained to see across the expanse of the bed. Richard tipped the book back, hiding the page from her.

He read further. She could see his eyes filling with tears, could hear a ragged catch in his breath.

"What is it, Richard? What's wrong?"

"I...this is...listen." He began reading, stumbling over the words. Each sound ripped from his throat as if through its own volition.

The feast was rich tonight. Three boys, four if I count the one this afternoon. Their terror was exquisitely gratifying. The pleasure of the hunt. The stalk. The kill.

"What does it mean?" Bonnie asked.

"Listen," Richard said, waving his hand in answer. "This is from another part. *Here, I have felt no hunger. There is food every-*

where, everywhere there is fear and hatred, but since the boy killed me and I took my just revenge, using his body and others' bodies, I have eaten my fill. Of their lives. Of their souls."

The book slipped unnoticed from his fingers.

"It goes on like that for two full sides, talking about people being murdered and dying," he said.

"I don't like this, Richard," Bonnie said suddenly. "I'm scared. It's one thing to come out here to find Donney, even if he was weird and hateful and sometimes treated me pretty badly. But this!"

She glanced at the stacks of books, some of the red marking clearly visible. She pulled her legs closer to her body, as if fearing contamination just from the touch of the desecrated paper against her skin.

"And now you have to read me his *diary!* The awful things he imagined doing to people!"

Richard swallowed hard. "That's just it, Bonnie. You don't understand."

"What?"

"It's not *Donney's* diary. It's not in his handwriting. Not in his way of saying things. Nothing on those pages is his.

"Everything in here"—he tapped his finger against the book where it lay next to his knee—"came from...from someone, or something, else."

"That's a pretty lame joke," Bonnie said, trying to laugh and failing.

"No joke. We're into something, bad. We...."

An abrupt clatter at the door startled both of them. Bonnie jerked spasmodically. Her movement communicated to the stacked paperbacks and knocked four or five more onto the floor. The copy of *It* slipped from where it was perched against Richard's knee, but even when it fell flat onto the bedspread, the marked pages stayed open.

The clatter repeated. Someone was knocking, but in the silence, the sound echoed like a threat.

"Who...?" Bonnie looked scared.

"I don't know," Richard said as he stood and walked across the small room. "No one knows we're here. Maybe it's the manager wanting to talk to us about something."

He slid the chain lock open, unlocked the deadbolt, and opened the door.

The kid stood there, looking up at Richard. The kid from that morning, from outside Donney's place.

"Can I come in," the kid said quietly.

"Sure," Richard said. Without thinking, he stood aside and let the kid in. The boy walked through the door and stood for a second scanning the room, as if he wasn't quite sure what a motel room should look like and was checking this for anything that struck him as strange. What he saw must have reassured him because he crossed to the far wall and dropped heavily into the cheap armchair next to the dresser. Richard sat on the foot of the bed. Bonnie had pulled herself up against the pillows. Her shoulders hunched against the wall behind her.

They made a neat triangle as they stared at each other. Richard to Bonnie to the kid, then back again.

Bonnie.

Richard.

The kid.

Kenny, Richard remembered finally, that was his name. *Kenny.*

There was an uncomfortable silence. Richard opened his mouth to ask the kid why he was there, what he wanted, but at that moment the kid looked straight across at Richard and spoke the sentence that Richard probably least expected to hear: "We gotta kill it."

The words stunned Richard. He glanced at Bonnie. The words had apparently had the same effect on her. They had been delivered with no theatrical passion, no childish hysteria. The challenge rang straight, solemn, and quietly assertive.

It was a statement of fact that neither Richard no Bonnie could deny, though they both fervently wished to do so.

"We gotta kill it," the boy said again.

"I know. We do." Richard surprised himself when he spoke. "What do you know about this? How did you find us?"

"It wasn't hard," Kenny said, neither smug nor sneering. Like his first statement, this was a simple statement of fact.

Richard felt himself drawn to the boy, unaccountably warming to a child he had seen only once before, briefly, and that in circumstances that should have distanced him from the boy forever.

"I knew your name, Mr. Mann...," the boy continued.

"Call me Richard." Again, it felt right, but Richard was surprised at saying it.

"Okay, uh, Richard. You told me when we shook hands today. Anyway, she—"

"Bonnie," Bonnie said, smiling a wan but touching smile.

"Okay. Bonnie said that she wanted to go to the motel, and then you left. I didn't get a chance to talk to you about the...*things* that we need to talk about.

"After I got home, after lunch, my Mom laid down for a while, and I got the yellow pages and copied out the names of all the motels in Tamarind Valley, at least those close to the freeway. I figured you'd be most likely to stay in one of them. When Mom got up, I told her I was going over to a friend...to a family we know. They're hurting pretty bad now, and I knew Mom would have to say 'yes.' Instead of going over there, though, I started checking out every motel, looking for your car in the parking lots and asking the managers. A couple of 'em wouldn't tell me anything, so I hoped that if your car wasn't in the lot it meant that you were staying somewhere else. She...Bonnie said that she was tired. She sure looked beat, so I figured that you'd be resting.

"The HoJo was motel number five. I was sure relieved to see that tan Ford in the space outside. I was gettin' tired and hot."

"Hey, let me get you something to drink," Bonnie said "I'm sorry I didn't ask sooner. It's a scorcher out there. We don't have much in the room. Is a glass of water okay?"

Bonnie was already on her feet and moving toward the tiny bathroom.

"Great," Kenny said with a self-conscious grin. "Thanks."

She disappeared into the bathroom. As Kenny started speaking again, Richard heard the rush of water through the tap. Bonnie was letting it run, letting it get as cool as possible. There was probably an ice machine along one of the corridors, but neither of them had thought to bring any ice back to the room when they drove in.

Just thinking about water, Richard felt his own throat constrict. It was suddenly drier and tighter than before. The boy must be parched, if he'd been out riding in the midday heat. Richard hoped that Bonnie would hurry—and think to bring him a glass, too.

"Anyway," Kenny continued. "I got here and saw the car and asked the manager if you were here. He wouldn't say, but just then the phone rang. While he was in the other room, I checked the registration stubs in a pile alongside the desk. I saw *Mann,* and Room 123, and here I am."

"Okay," Richard said when Kenny fell silent, "but why?"

Richard wasn't sure he wanted to know, but he had to ask.

"Look, you were out at that old house today," Kenny said. "You had to have felt what I felt. She...Bonnie sure did. I've seen people having bad dreams, and I've seen people sit too long in the sun and get overheated. What happened to her was nothing like I've ever seen."

Richard nodded.

The boy continued: "Something really weird is going on. Something scary. My friend Spence went into that old house. When he came out, he was...different."

"How?" Richard's question came out sharp, pointed.

"He...I, I can't say for sure. It was just the way he talked and acted. Like it was Spence but not Spence. Does that make any sense?"

Richard thought about the entries in the empty pages of *It*.

"Yes," he said heavily, "it does."

"Then that same night, we were camping out, in a field near here. Spence and me and some guys and...." The boy paled. Richard could see how difficult it was to talk about whatever had happened.

"Hey, Bonnie, hurry with that water, huh?"

"Sure, just a minute." Her voice was oddly distorted by the mirror and tile and the overlay of running water.

The break seemed to help Kenny, though.

"We were camping," he began again, his voice stronger but steady and quiet. "We were telling ghost stories and junk like that, and then someone came out of the trees and...and killed...killed Timmy and Teddy and Chuck...." He recited the names fast, in one rushed explosion of breath, as if they were one word. As if spitting it out would lessen the pain.

The boy looked up at Richard. "At the last minute, I saw who it really was."

"It?"

"The one...the *thing* that killed my friends. It was Spence."

"That's impos...," Richard began.

Bonnie screamed

The sound of glass shattering in the bathroom brought Richard and Kenny to their feet.

Richard ran into the other room.

Bonnie was on the floor. She was leaning against the tile wall between the toilet bowl and the bathtub. The white porcelain surfaces on both sides of her were stained with swatches of red.

The water glass was shattered on the floor.

Water rustled noisily through the faucet.

And poised between Bonnie and Richard, facing Richard, a jagged piece of blood-stained glass held tightly in his fingers, the shard translucently pink with Bonnie's fresh blood, stood Donney.

Mutely, Bonnie held up her wrists. Blood oozed from both of them. It was maybe not enough to kill her, not yet anyway, but Richard could read pain and fear and panic in her eyes.

Richard! Why?

Kenny peered around Richard, taking in the blood and the half-prone body of the woman.

Then something happened, so quickly that neither Kenny nor Richard nor Bonnie would have believed it if the other two had not seen it also.

Donney changed.

For a breath there was someone else. The figure was a boy, smaller than Donney, not as dark of skin or hair. He was smiling innocently.

And then Donney was back again, but this time not quite the same. Harsh lines that had never been there before played around his mouth and eyes. His voice resonated in a way it had never done before.

Richard was reminded unaccountably of Hammer.

The apparition spoke.

"I have tasted them."

The Donney-thing flicked the glass shard away. It landed in Bonnie's lap and caught where her skirt lay tight over her clenched legs. It glinted evilly in the harsh bathroom light.

Bonnie screamed—a thin, high, small scream that a woman might use who has seen a mouse or a snake or some other vermin that startles as much as it frightens. She moved as if to brush the bloody glass away, slapping at it with the back of her wrists. The oozing cuts lay protected beneath the curl of her palms and fingers.

Richard started forward. The Donney-thing held out a hand. Richard stopped. His neck muscles strained with his need to keep going, to kneel beside Bonnie and make sure that she was going to be all right. But he couldn't help but stop.

"I have tasted them," the Donney-thing said slowly, gesturing toward Bonnie, "and the taste is desirable and delicious. There is much to enjoy. Much that I will enjoy, later."

He spoke directly to Bonnie, even though he kept Richard pinioned with his gaze: "You are not seriously harmed, Mrs. Mann." Her name emerged from its throat as a sneer. "A small bandage should take care of most of the blood," it continued coldly.

Then it spoke to Richard, who was still standing as if in a stasis-field, unable to move. "I shall come back later, tonight perhaps, and conclude the feast. Until then, they are yours."

Richard broke from his stasis and lunged toward the figure, his hands outstretched to throttle and crush and destroy. At the moment of impact, his flesh passed through the figure.

And then, in the same instant, the Donney-thing disappeared.

There was no special-effects light show. No sparkles and hums, like on the old *Star Trek* episodes. It was more like coming into a room and seeing a shadow cast from the hall light behind you, and reaching over and switching the other lights on and suddenly there simply was no more shadow.

Suddenly, there was no more Donney.

Bonnie cried out, a moan of fear compounded with pain. Richard rushed over and knelt and sopped up the blood with a hand towel from the counter.

"Hand towels are for washing dirty hands, not for sopping up blood," Kenny said numbly. Richard barely heard the boy's voice in his sudden panic for Bonnie.

He helped her stand and half-carried her to the bed. He and Kenny checked the cuts.

"They're shallow. Not deep enough to sever a vein or anything," Richard said, trying to sound reassuring.

"They bled so much," Bonnie cried.

"It's okay now." Richard cradled her in his arms.

"Uh, Bonnie," Kenny said after a few moments, when her tears had stopped and she was breathing more normally.

"What did he, uh, it mean?"

She looked at the boy as if he were speaking another language.

"That thing in there, it said it had tasted '*them.*'"

She looked up at Richard, then away.

"I couldn't tell you yet, Richard," she said, hiding her face from him as if ashamed. "Not while there was still a chance that...."

"Bonnie?" He sounded stunned.

She nodded.

Richard gently turned her face toward his and embraced her again, holding her even more tightly than before. Kenny stood by, watching without saying anything. Richard finally looked over at the boy.

"We haven't been married very long," he said. "A little over two years. And we want kids. About a year ago, Bonnie got...pregnant. We lost the baby. Early on. It was...messy."

Kenny nodded. He understood what was not being said.

Bonnie's voice filled the silence. "I didn't want to say anything until the first couple of months were safely over. I didn't want to raise your hopes and then...."

She clung to Richard and stared at him as if she were afraid that he would hate her for not telling him sooner.

"Everything's okay, though, now?" he asked.

"So far. There hasn't been any spotting. None of the danger signs. I was going to tell you in a day or two, maybe when we got back home. I wanted to tell you. But somehow that...thing"—she spat the word viciously—"that *thing* in there knew."

"And used it against you," Richard continued. "It terrified you by threatening not only you but the baby only you knew was there."

They sat in silence a few more moments.

"What was it?" Bonnie finally asked.

"I don't know," Richard said wearily. "Maybe a hallucination. An illusion."

"No, it was real." Bonnie touched her bandaged wrist. "I thought it was Donney, but then it...changed. I didn't recognize the boy."

"That was Spence," Kenny said. "My friend. I saw him in there for a second, and then the other guy, the big skinny guy, was back."

"Spence?" Richard said, as if not recognizing the name.

"I told you about him...changing," Kenny said.

"Yeah," Richard said. "And then Spence...killed...." Suddenly he reached across the bed and pulled the book closer. He stared at the open page. "It's impossible. It can't be!"

"What?" Bonnie and Kenny asked at the same moment.

"Look," Richard said, "this will sound crazy, but what we saw in there is crazy. What happened to Kenny and his friends was crazy, insane. And who knows how many other crazy things have happened in this place recently. Listen."

He read several passages from the hand-written entries. He glanced up and saw Kenny stiffen at the mention of three dead boys. Kenny straightened and nodded, as if suddenly a knotty puzzle made perfect if horrible sense.

"This is all about Fear," Richard said, tapping the pages with his nail. "Fear and hatred and death. It's like...like suddenly all the fear and terror and horror that surround us every day built up so much that it reached critical mass."

"What's that?" Kenny asked.

"It's like building a nuclear bomb. You can have all the uranium you want, as long as it's in little pieces that are not close to each other. But when you get a big enough hunk, the radioactivity starts a chain reaction, and if there's enough of the stuff to keep it going, all of a sudden, in a fraction of a second, *boom!,* you've got a nuclear explosion. Critical mass.

"Maybe that's what's happening here. Donney was scared a lot of the time. He hated a lot of people. He spent most of his life terrorizing me. He enjoyed making me squirm."

221

Memories flickered like transparencies in a slide projector as Richard spoke, but he forced himself not to look. There was enough hatred in the room; why dredge up the bones of the past?

"Now, in the world we face, we've got so much more to be afraid of. Nuclear bombs and terrorists and global warfare and muggers and rapists and murderers."

"And freeway shooters," Bonnie said softly.

"Yeah. I remember being a kid," Richard said. "We weren't afraid to walk to the store alone for fear that some pervert would pick us up and molest or murder us. Oh, it happened, sure, but not so often that we worried about it, and not so close that we knew the victims. But now—being a kid must be awful. Everything and everyone is a potential murderer. AIDS, cancer, air pollution. Razor blades in Halloween candy. Child molesters teaching in public schools and slicing up pet turtles and threatening the kids with the same if any of them say anything to their parents. God, how much we fear every day!

"Maybe all the fear we generate just keeps building up, like air pollution against the hills in the summer time. And all of a sudden it's just there, real, tangible. Murderous."

Kenny thought for a moment, then said: "Maybe it's more than that."

"What do you mean?" Bonnie asked.

"I dunno," he said, shrugging his shoulders and putting on that distinct air of diffidence kids can take when they feel like they know more than adults but are afraid to talk about it.

"Come on, Kenny, if you have an idea, let it out," Richard said. "You're as much a part of this as we are."

"Well, I was just thinking...what if it's...if it's real. Not just something made up of fear, but something...I don't know," he said, letting his voice trail off.

"Like the monster in that novel? A space alien that feeds on humans," Richard said. He wasn't intending to ridicule Kenny, far from it. But put that bluntly the idea did seem silly. Here he was, a mature adult, sitting on in a generic motel room on a bright sunny day in Southern California, seriously considering the possibility of aliens from space.

"No," Kenny answered after a moment's consideration. "I don't think so. That doesn't feel right. But maybe something...like maybe an evil creature. My folks believe in God; I think I do, too. And if there's a God, then maybe there are things that fight against him. Maybe they can come where there's fear and hate, and maybe they can look like anyone they want and kill people." Kenny was staring at his hands, as if afraid to raise his eyes and meet Richard's or Bonnie's gaze.

"One of my friends believes in evil spirits." Kenny said. "He says that they can look like anyone. They can look real and solid. Except that when you go to shake hands with them, there's nothing there."

He stopped speaking. For a long moment there was silence in the cramped room.

"And that's what happened that night. It reached out for me, but there was nothing there. It looked like Spence. But it wasn't him."

It was Richard's turn to consider. Kenny looked relieved when neither Richard nor Bonnie laughed at his suggestion. But then, maybe evil spirits were as warranted an assumption as disembodied fear-things, or alien spiders living in sewers.

"Whatever it is," Richard said finally, "It killed Donney and Spence and the others. And it's feeding off their fears—and our fears—and growing stronger and stronger. We have to get rid of it, kill it."

"How?" Bonnie's question was an agonized whisper.

"'We drew a circle and drew him in'," Kenny said softly.

"What?" said Richard.

Kenny looked up and repeated the line. His voice was louder, stronger.

"Wait, I've heard that before. It's from a song, isn't it?" asked Bonnie.

"I don't know," Kenny said. "I heard it last year. One of my teachers read some poetry. I didn't like most of it, but there was this line at the end of one of the poems. Something like, 'But love and I had a will to win, and we drew a circle and drew him in'." Kenny looked from Richard to Bonnie and back. The boy's face wore a mask of surprise, as if he were startled that he had remembered the poem, let alone the line.

"It's from a song," Bonnie said. "They sang it at Mom and Dad's twenty-fifth reception, remember? It was Mom's favorite. The Carpenters? Or maybe The Captain and Teneille. I don't re-member which." Bonnie studied Richard's face eagerly.

"Yeah, but...."

"Why are we here, Richard?" she asked pointedly. "Here in Tamarind, in California?"

"Because...to let Donney know that Mom is dead."

"You could have written."

"I know, but it seemed best to...to try to see him and...."

"And help him. That kid made your life miserable, Richard, but you still want to *help* him."

"Well," Richard began, uncertain of her direction.

"Why are you here?" she continued, turning her attention to Kenny.

Kenny didn't hesitate. He spoke strongly and confidently, as if he had long ago thought the question through. "I want to get Spence out. If he's alive, I want to get him back. If he's dead, I want him to rest in peace. Not be part of that thing and have to hurt his friends."

She reached out excitedly and took Kenny hand in hers. She squeezed it tightly. Then she took Richard's in her other hand. Their fingers scraped against the rough weave of the bandages. Her blood was sticky against their skin.

"That's the difference. Maybe Kenny is right and the thing is evil. We're here because of love. It's here because of hate.

"I know fear. I almost died with the miscarriage. And the little boy who should have been our son but never became more than a tiny bit of tissue—he *did* die. I could die giving birth to the child I'm carrying now. But that doesn't really matter, you see. Because I love Richard and I love our unborn child, and if it takes my life to ensure that my husband has a child, well, that is a risk that mothers have been taking since the beginning of time. Creation requires sacrifice. If this thing is Fear, or even feeds on fear, then we oppose it with the opposite of fear.

"This all sounds silly, I know, but it's got to be the answer."

She looked from Richard to Kenny and back to her husband. Her eyes were pleading, but her face was set in determined lines that even Kenny could recognize.

"It's the only answer we have," she said.

"So what do we do?" Richard asked.

"We go out there, to the house," Kenny said. He let go of Bonnie's hand, stood up, and started toward the door, as if he intended to so there right then, that very moment. "We go out there and we meet it on its own ground."

Bonnie reached out to him and took his hand again.

"And we draw the circle," she added. Kenny grabbed Richard's hand as she repeated the phrase. "We draw the circle and draw them in."

224

CHAPTER FIFTEEN

DRAWING THE CIRCLE

- 1 -

They left the HoJo room less than an hour later. Richard delayed only long enough to bandage Bonnie's wrists properly. He replaced the ripped-up hand towels with lengths of gauze and non-stick tape Kenny bought with a crumpled five-dollar bill and a handful of change he found in his pocket. The boy raced to the All-Nite-Delite across the street from the motel parking lot while Richard and Bonnie bathed her wrists in cooling water and treated the shallow slices with antiseptic. By the time they finished, Kenny had returned, carrying a small brown bag rattling with paper boxes of Johnson & Johnson first aid supplies.

After being bathed, the cuts no longer bled as freely. They were only thin red lines across Bonnie's skin, as fine as spider webs. Much of the terror she had felt when the Donney-thing appeared in the bathroom and slashed at her wrists dissipated as she looked at the lines. They were not serious; perhaps the larger threat was not as serious as she feared, either.

"They don't hurt," Bonnie assured Richard in answer to his worried question. She crossed her wrists and tapped the bandaged areas together lightly. The gauze made a dry, rustling sound in the silence of the HoJo room. "See, nothing. No pain. Really, it's okay. He only wanted to frighten me."

He's saving the worst for later, she thought but carefully refrained from saying anything. Richard could probably handle the idea, but the boy was an unknown quantity in spite of what he knew and how much he had experienced. No use taking chances on having a hysterical kid with them.

She and Richard were crazy enough, anyway, if you looked calmly and rationally at what they were doing. *They were heading out to a filth-ridden hovel to lay to rest the ghost of Richard's dead brother. To kill Fear. Or maybe to exorcise an evil spirit. But at any rate, to put a stop to a Reign of Terror that had more literal meanings than figurative ones.* The thought brought an image of a bloody guillotine blade smashing down, a mad Madame LaFarge cackling away over her knitting. Bonnie shivered, then giggled.

She was not so far from hysteria herself.

A few moments later, they left the room. Out of a habit so long ingrained that she barely noticed it, Bonnie checked to make sure that they had left nothing out of place in the room. She peered beneath the bed, in the drawers, in the bathroom. Its porcelain surfaces were still streaked with rusty brown where her blood had spattered and no one had bothered to clean it up.

There were more important things to do.

"Hurry up," Richard finally said. Kenny was already outside, waiting impatiently, shifting his weight first to one foot, then to the other, as if he were waiting for someone to vacate the bathroom so he could use it.

"Hurry up." Richard repeated. Bonnie recognized from his tone that he was more tense and worried than upset. "It's not as if we aren't coming back. And if we don't"—a frown crossed his lips—"it won't make any difference if the room is messy or not."

Bonnie didn't answer. She ducked past him and half-ran to the Ford Escort. They had parked beneath the shade of an overhanging tree, but now, at midday, the car was in the direct sunlight.

They climbed into the car, immediately stifled by the intense heat that had built up. Kenny settled into the back seat. Richard drove, with Bonnie next to him. She rested her hand lightly on the taut material of his jeans. She felt the heat of his thigh through her hand; it made the cut at the jointure of her hand and her wrist tingle with unaccustomed warmth. Unusual, but not unpleasant.

They backed out of the parking place, and Richard pulled up to the stop sign at the entry onto Tamarind Avenue. He waited for several cars to pass, then angled onto the street.

The act seemed definitive. They were doing it. They were going back to the house and find out what had happened to Donney, Spence, and the others.

They drove in silence.

- 2 -

"Uh, Richard," Kenny said quietly from the back seat a block or two later. "Would you mind...could we go by a couple of places first."

No one asked what *first* meant.

Bonnie glanced at Richard. She understood what the boy must be thinking—there was every chance that he would not be alive in an hour, or two, or three. He might be as dead as his buddies. If he wanted to say good-bye to someone....

But he surprised them.

He gave them directions to his house but did not ask them to stop.

"Just slow down a little," he whispered as the Ford drew abreast of the neat two-story house, its floor plan identical with its neighbors, its exterior distinguishable from them only by the individuality of its rose borders and gardens of annuals blooming in the last flush of summer. A head was outlined against the television through the front-room window. Kenny's mother was sitting with her back to the street, her attention focused on a late-afternoon game show. Outside, the garage door hung open, revealing a garage empty and oddly barren. Lawrence Robinson's car was gone, which meant that he had not yet returned home from work.

"Okay," Kenny said after a second. The little car sped up and left Kenny's mother to her television and her imagination and her fears.

"She'd kill me if she knew what we were doing," he said as Richard angled off Sheffield and left Kenny's neighborhood. "She'd kill me for sure."

Bonnie glanced again at Richard. Richard was barely twenty one; she was a year younger—but the age gap between themselves and the boy wedging himself between their bucket seats seemed increasingly insurmountable.

And yet each was the other's only real hope in the confrontation to come. They might have come out to California to try to rescue Donney, but Kenny obviously had his own crusade, his own vengeance against the monstrosity that opposed them.

Bonnie leaned back and closed her eyes, trying to prepare for what was to come.

The next stop was even more surprising.

"Left here," Kenny said suddenly, then, a block later, "Now turn right. Into this lot."

Richard looked at the sign as they drove past. Community Hospital. Bonnie shrugged. Kenny was leaning forward between the bucket seats, his arms hooked on their headrests. At the angle he was sitting, his face was almost even with Richard's and Bonnie's. He stared at the huge red-brick building as if entranced by its lacy edging of jacarandas, a few still sporting splotches of purple from the summer's bloomings.

"One of the guys, he's in here," Kenny said by way of curt explanation.

They parked and walked across the wide emergency lane and entered the hospital.

At the information booth, Kenny found out the room number for Billy Holmes. 217, second floor, near the burn unit.

They had arrived during visiting hours. They went upstairs. At first, they weren't allowed in the room. Kenny had expected as much. Richard seemed afraid that Kenny would be disappointed. Instead, Kenny stood outside the hospital room, staring at the chart hung on the door, with Bill's name ("William Holmes" looked so stiff and formal, not at all like Billy), and meaningless numbers and code initials penciled randomly (it seemed) in little boxes. Kenny's lips moved, as if he were whispering some deep, dark secret that adults were forever barred from knowing.

The muscles along Kenny's jaw line clenched and his throat grew taut. At last, Kenny touched Billy's name with his finger and turned to leave.

Mr. and Mrs. Holmes were coming down the hall. For a second Kenny looked trapped, as if he were spray painting graffiti on Billy's door and they had caught him at it and would send him to jail.

Instead they smiled at their son's friend, tired smiles with little of welcome, less of joy in them. Their younger son had been buried two days before. Their older son lay inside the room, behind the closed door. He was unconscious most of the time, in agonizing pain during his few moments of wakefulness, and no one knew for certain how long he might have to stay in the hospital.

Richard and Bonnie had backed down the hall to a small niche crowded with a short sofa, an end table laden with three-year-old copies of *National Geographic,* and two armchairs. They sat down, the image of visitors patiently waiting their turn to look in on a stricken father or mother.

Kenny faced the Holmses alone.

"How is he?" Kenny asked.

"He's having a rough time," Mr. Holmes said vaguely.

"Can I see him?"

"Sorry son, but the hospital says relatives only," Mr. Holmes began, but his wife interrupted.

"He's still unconscious, Kenny. He hasn't been awake long enough to say anything to anyone, not since they brought him in. He mostly mumbles—Timmy's name, unrecognizable sounds. We can't even make out most of what he says."

Kenny nodded.

"But maybe you could just peek in, around the curtain," Mrs. Holmes continued, surprising Kenny. Mr. Holmes looked startled and opened his mouth to say something. Mrs. Holmes kept talking, her voice a plea for understanding and help. "Just for a moment, Ed. It means so much to Kenny, and who knows, maybe Billy will know he's here and it will help him, too."

Mr. Holmes nodded mutely.

"Thanks," Kenny said. Mr. Holmes opened the door and ushered Kenny quietly into the darkened room.

The curtains were half open. A light burned on a wood-grain metal shelf opposite the foot of Billy's bed. Outside the windows, Kenny could see vistas of low hills, oak-crowned and brown with drying weeds.

In spite of the light, however, the room seemed dim, dark. Bill's bed was an island of white supporting his still form. He was robed in white, bound in white, his full-arm cast an ashen, ghostly white. The startling darkness of his face—eyes and nose and mouth, pale and drawn but vibrant in contrast to the white bandages—were all Kenny could distinguish.

Bill's eyelids were closed, but his eyes seemed to be flickering wildly underneath. His forehead was damp. As Kenny's eyes adjusted to the change in light, he could see that the white bandages and white pillowcases and white sheets were grey and damp-looking where they came into contact with Bill's body.

"They don't know why he's having such a rough time," Mrs. Holmes whispered. "It's like he's constantly terrified, pulling away from something that scares him. If they touch his cheek, he winces, jerks in his sleep, sometimes even cries out like he's been cut. They think he's reliving...that night, in dreams. Sometimes he moans and tries to reach out, like he was trying to save...."

Mr. Holmes broke off. Kenny heard the sob hidden in the man's voice. He stepped a pace closer to the bed, as much to be close to Bill as to give Mr. Holmes space and the privacy of a darkened corner and Kenny's unseeing back.

Kenny nodded. Part of it might be nightmares, guilt at what happened to Timmy. But part of it, Kenny knew instinctively, was simply that Bill lay midway between being alive and belonging to the Thing that killed Timmy. He was a captive of fear, and no amount of doctoring or medication or isolation in the hospital could change that.

He stepped quietly to the edge of the bed, careful not to entangle his feet in any of the multiple wires and tubes and coils that hung around the bed. He touched the edge of one of Bill's dressings with his finger.

"It's gonna be all right. Panthers all the way. It'll be all right." He spoke so softly that he barely heard his own voice. Bill probably did not even know that he was in the room, but that was okay. He had stopped as much for himself as for Bill, anyway. To build his resolve. To see what the Thing had done and make himself more determined to stop it.

He touched Bill's cheek, lightly, as if afraid that the fragile skin might burst. Then he backed away.

"Thanks for letting me see him," Kenny said to Mr. Holmes as he left the room. "I'll come back later, when he's awake."

A statement of fact, not empty hope.

He walked slowly down the corridor, oblivious to the outsized photographs of Tamarind's hillsides covered with gaily waving fields of blooming mustard, its hilltops crowned with isolated sentry oaks, its ponds awash with the white and grey and brown flurry of ducks pausing in their seasonal migrations.

"Let's get it done," he said as he stood by Richard and Bonnie. "It's the only thing we can do for him."

They walked hand in hand down the corridor and into the bright sunlight outside. It was getting late. There was still a fair amount of daylight left but evening was coming on. Already, by mid-August, nightfall came earlier and earlier, and the nine-thirty afterglow that made summers so pleasant in the valley were replaced by deep night by 8:45 or earlier.

Even though their experiences at the motel demonstrated that their enemy was not restricted in its movements to nighttime, they didn't want to arrive at the house after dark.

There was only one more detour, a quick drive-by, even quicker than Kenny's last glance of his home.

Jenkin's Field was enclosed by thin bands of yellow plastic supported on metal rods sunk deep into the dry ground. The police barricade began well before the first of the oaks that formed the ragged circle out of sight from the road.

"Want to stop?" Richard asked.

Kenny considered it for a moment. He considered getting out, walking as close to the yellow plastic ribbon as possible, and straining as so many other onlookers had done over the past few days to see whatever might be visible. But finally Kenny was content to drive by. There would be nothing in the field that would help them now.

He was a little paler than usual, and his eyes flickered back and forth rapidly as they passed the wide spot in the roadway where cars had so often parked to disgorge loads of scouts heading into the field for overnighters.

"Whitechapel is just down here a couple of miles," Kenny said finally, pointing to a branching street that cut along one side of the field.

Richard turned, and they drove in silence until Richard turned again where the black-on-white letters spelled out "Whitechapel Place."

Kenny had been on this street dozens of times, walking through when the road was nothing more than a graded patch on the hillside, its topsoil stripped away and its rocky substrata lying denuded and vulnerable—

—Hiking through when the houses began to pop up like mushrooms, overnight it seemed, plywood exteriors gradually growing coatings of stucco that faded to half a dozen shades of tan and cream—

—Driving through with his parents when the open houses started, wondering why two people as happy with their home as his Mom and Dad found fun in gawking at garishly decorated rooms in Model Homes—

—And finally biking up and down the extent of the street, challenging the steep up-grade, skimming with the wind on the downgrades, biking with Spence and laughing.

Tonight, the street seemed deserted. More than just a late Wednesday evening, when families were clustered around Formica-topped tables to eat their tuna casseroles or taco salads or tug at crisp-battered legs sticking over the tops of Kentucky Fried Chicken buckets.

Usually, this time of the year, there would be fathers grubbing in borders, mothers sprinkling newly set lawns, kids rattling by on Big Wheels or BMX bikes or Speed-Flyte skateboards.

Tonight, no one moved on the entire length of Whitechapel Place. Many of the houses didn't even have lights on, and the ones that did were lit up with false hopes that made the houses look like

231

Christmas trees, with every window casting a protective gleam into the lengthening shadows, trying to dispel the fear that crept nightly up to the new foundations and oozed into the cracks beneath sliding glass patio doors.

At the turn onto Old Conejo Road, it seemed to get even darker and quieter. Kenny rolled down his window. Though the car drove quietly, its engine barely noticeable beneath the rush of wind against his ears, he heard no sounds except the distant hum of cars criss-crossing Tamarind Valley on the intersecting freeways. Up closer, nothing. No birds, no dogs barking at intruders, no cats screeching, no kids yelling that it wasn't too late to play outside and *can't we stay, just another fifteen minutes, huh, Mom?* Not even a cricket hacking its tune in the brush.

Both the houses on Old Conejo Drive were silent. Mr. and Mrs. Coupon-Clipper had closed up their place tight, with locks on the garage and heavy metal-grillwork security bars in place over every window. Even the light aluminum screen door had been replaced by a sturdy black steel security screen. Arc lights mounted on the corner of the eaves reflected blindingly from the surface of leaves and sidewalks and grass, making the front yard look more like a prison exercise yard than a place to live and roll in the grass and play croquet.

Then they were past the last house and moving in the deeper shadows beneath the two trees guarding the driveway that led to the house beyond the hill.

As they passed beneath the shadows, none of the three looked behind them. None of the three saw the brief movement on the pavement where Old Conejo Road began, or the two figures that came slowly up the grade.

- 3 -

It was almost seven by the time they arrived. Soon it would be night. Darkness would settle like a woven shroud over Tamarind Valley—like the blue-black shroud pulled across the sky in Disney's *Fantasia,* or like the black demon's cloak from *Night on Bald Mountain.*

But for now, and for a few moments more, the final strips of sunlight glowed over the Coast Range to the west, a soft wash of pink and gold blending into cobalt blue.

It should have been beautiful.

On any other night it would have been. But on this evening, nei-ther Kenny nor Richard nor Bonnie noticed the golden aura that tinged the weed-choked hillside, the crystal light that made the distant mountains draw nearer until they loomed like great grey shadows over the ridgeline of the house. The bougainvillea flamed along the side and onto the roof, sunlight emphasizing the natural scarlet of the bracts that surrounded almost invisible flowers—dead, unchanging bracts that hid the tiny, pale yellow mouths that sucked hungrily for life.

None of them noticed.

Their attention was riveted on the open door. It still hung canting from the broken hinge, a black maw opening into darkness like a toothless jaw, gaping and empty.

"It still stinks," Richard said finally, turning his head away as a breeze from the house lifted the reek and pushed it past their nostrils.

"Yeah," Kenny whispered. That morning, he had stood several feet further away and had not been exposed to the ordure that coated the floor.

They stepped closer, until their shoulders and arms touched and they could not move any further without one of them edging in front of the others and becoming the *de facto* leader.

There was utter silence. They did not even hear the faint rustling Kenny had heard earlier, before he pedaled his bike madly away.

And there was utter darkness. Richard almost believed that if he were to light a match and toss it through the open doorway, the match would still burn, would continue to radiate heat until everything combustible in it was consumed—but once it passed beneath the lintel, it would release no light. The light would be absorbed like a sponge absorbs water. Like Evil absorbs Goodness. Like Fear absorbs Life.

"Well," Richard said, squaring his shoulders. "Here goes."

He moved toward the house. He edged forward slowly and deliberately until the toe of his shoe touched the threshold. He turned.

"Are you sure you want to go through with this?" he asked the other two.

Bonnie said nothing. Kenny nodded emphatically. His eyes caught the light of the setting sun and burned dark brown overlaid with deep gold. Richard was startled by the sense of sudden wisdom—*beauty?*—in the boy's eyes and unlined face.

He might be young, but he was a force to be reckoned with.

Bonnie nodded, too, less energetically. Her commitment was no less deep but flowed through different channels than Kenny's or Richard's, Richard knew. Part of Richard's mind whispered that she was jeopardizing not only her own life but the life of her unborn child as well. She had pressed both hands tightly against her abdomen as if straining to feel the fetus within her. She had laced her fingers to make a web to keep all danger out, or a cage to keep the burgeoning life force in.

"Go on," she said, softly. Richard quivered at the strength in her voice.

He stepped into the house.

The darkness inside was cold. It was as if a line had been drawn from lintel to threshold, bisecting the doorjambs. On one side lay golden light and sunset warmth. On the other, there was only coldness and darkness.

Without thinking about what he might be stepping on, holding his breath against the fetid air, Richard stepped across the line. He hurried through the living room to the side window and unlocked it. He shoved the moveable pane upward. Through the coldness and the stench, he could feel a fresh, warming draught blow against his hands. It curled underneath his T-shirt and fingered the tender flesh of his stomach. The air smelled clean and sweet, untainted by the stench behind him. He hated to turn around.

By the time he did turn, his eyes had become accustomed to the half-light in the house, ameliorated by the fragment sunlight spilling through the open window. Kenny and Bonnie were inside as well, waiting at the center of the room. They stood back to back, as if instinctively protecting each other.

"What now?" Kenny asked.

"Turn on the lights," Richard said. Kenny backed away from Bonnie and moved toward the front door. When his heels clicked against the wall, he felt behind him for the light switch. He never took his eyes from the room. His fingers brushed against the wall. He jerked them away; the wall was damp and sticky.

He whirled, his hand slapping at the light switch. In the sudden brightness, the walls were startlingly bare. The paint was peeling in long curling strips. Great patches of it were faded. Slashed remnants of posters hung in tatters opposite the front door.

"Okay," Richard said. "We're here. Let's get ready." He started pushing one end of the sofa that sprawled in the middle of the floor. "Give me a hand, Kenny. Let's give ourselves as much room as we can. We may need it."

Kenny pushed from the back, Richard from the front. Their fingers sank into threadbare nap swollen with dampness. Together they slid the heavy piece of furniture long-wise toward the inner wall, then swiveled it on one stubby, splintered leg. Their feet squelched

234

through unnamable filth as they pushed at the worn and stained up-holstery. Fresh waves of stench rose to greet them as they revealed the accumulations of dirty clothing and cast-off, crumpled papers and crumbling, moldy food that had hidden beneath the sofa for...for who knew how long.

Finally, though, they managed to work it all the way to the empty wall where Donney's posters hung in tatters and shreds.

Richard stood back and looked across the room. Directly opposite, the door hung open, framing the outside world that now seemed a dream of peace and normality. Outside lay a world where the Dead stayed dead, and Fear could be defeated by changing channels from the six o'clock news to reruns of *Mork and Mindy*.

On the right-hand wall, a crumbling fireplace stood blackened and empty. On the left, a worn faucet dripped rusty water into a cracked sink. And along the fourth, directly behind Richard the sofa, the tattered posters framed each side of the doorway into the short hall that led to the bathroom and the bedroom.

"Okay, let it come," Richard said, walking toward the open space in the center of the room.

"Just a minute," Bonnie said. She stepped to the sink and pulled a decrepit broom from a niche beside a cupboard. She had to reach through inches of cobwebs to get it. The broom looked as if it had not been used since the house was first built.

"I'm not going to walk through this stuff any more," she said resolutely and began sweeping the caked-on filth from the tile. She pushed the ever-growing pile toward the fireplace hearth.

Richard and Kenny stared at her as if she were mad. *Here we are, fighting Evil and Terror. Our friends are dead. Our lives are at stake. Who knows what horrors we may have to face tonight? And she sweeps the floor.*

Then something seemed to answer, an unspoken voice that rang through their minds with the clarity of a fire alarm: *What else should she do? She does what must be done. Life goes on. There is more than fear.*

Without speaking, the two—one barely a man, the other barely yet a boy—grabbed at the soiled edges of the rug in the center of the room and folded it over on itself once, twice, like a business letter being readied for its envelope. They lifted it, fetid and sodden and heavy with mildew and worse, and carried it to the fireplace. It made a dull thud when it slapped the stones. Water splattered from the heavy weave, making tiny patterns of wetness against the filth-coated hearthstones. Along the edges, the droplets looked like tiny starbursts against thick dust.

Bonnie followed closely behind the men, shifting her growing pile of rubbish and refuse with each sweep of the broom until it, too, spilled onto the hearthstones.

The floor was not clean—far from it. The room was still heavy with the redolence of human waste and tainted water and rampant decay. The tiles were stained with this deluge and with the tidewater lines of earlier overflows never properly cleaned. Where the damp bristles of the broom had pulled against deep-ground dirt, lighter swatches angled toward the fireplace. The floor would probably never be entirely clean, even if they worked for days with fresh water and stiff-bristled brushes.

"At least we can walk on it now and not worry about what we are stepping in," Bonnie said. She straightened and slowly returned the broom to its rightful place in the niche by the cupboard. Her hand passed through the broken cobwebs again. The webs were as fragile as silk, soft and smooth and slightly sticky. She pulled her hand out and rubbed her palms against the rough seams of her jeans.

She joined the others along the wall, where they were standing beneath the ruins of Dracula and Frankenstein and Wolfman.

The center of the room was empty. The center of the room—for Richard and Bonnie and Kenny it formed the center of an arcane universe, the empty space that seemed at once sacramental and sacrificial as they waited.

"What now?" Kenny asked finally.

Richard shrugged. "I don't know. There's no manual for this. We wait, I guess, and hope that when he...it comes we get an inspiration...."

As he was speaking, Kenny started walking across the room. He paced from where he stood next to Bonnie toward the corner between the fireplace and the wall with the doorway and the window. He looked as if he were counting strides, Jim Hawkins outsmarting Long John Silver and discovering the long-lost treasure.

At the same moment, Bonnie moved away as well, in the other direction, toward the corner between the window and the sink. The faucet dripped slowly, its slick splashing sound abnormally loud.

Midway between Richard and the corners, they stopped, and turned, and waited. Kenny's feet were just beyond the ravaged television and VCR. One heel nudged the sodden cover of a paperback novel.

As soon as they had begun moving, Richard stopped talking. He stayed where he was, but he stood straighter, silent, waiting.

When Bonnie and Kenny stopped as well, he closed his eyes and tried to feel the room.

It didn't feel right.

Not that he knew exactly what they were doing, of course. It was right that they separate, though—that tacit decision resonated deep within him, inside the marrow of his bones. That part felt right.

But there was still something wrong.

They moved again. The triangle they had formed shifted to the left, until Kenny stood with his back to the open doorway.

Outside, the golden light dimmed to dusky grey, with long purple shadows creeping across the hill from mustard plants that had long ago disappeared against the backdrop of night.

Bonnie was almost against the sink. Her buttocks brushed against the cold porcelain. She jerked forward a step or two. Behind her, the faucet dripped, providing the only sound in the house. She turned and wrenched the faucet tight. The water stopped dripping.

Richard was closer to the fireplace now than to the sofa.

They had kept their positions, though. A perfectly equal triangle: father, mother, child. The fundamental unit.

Balanced.

Poised.

Ready.

Behind Kenny, something scuffed against the gravel driveway. He stiffened and started to turn. Fear spread across his face, but Richard made a quick gesture with his right hand and Kenny stopped moving.

"It won't come from out there," Richard said through clenched teeth.

Kenny didn't know how Richard knew, but he felt the rightness of the words. He faced the center of the room again, one apex of an equilateral triangle.

The crunching came closer, grew louder. Kenny's ears burned with the sound. He desperately wanted to turn and look and what was approaching behind him, but Richard held his gaze.

Now the sound was at the door.

The sound stopped.

For a moment—only a minute or two, perhaps, but a year of months for Kenny—there was silence so absolute that Kenny would have sworn he could hears his own heart beat.

Then: "Excuse us."

The sound broke Kenny's stasis. Without glancing at Richard for permission, he whirled on his heel and stared at the two young men that stood shoulder to shoulder just outside the doorway.

"Who are you...?" Richard began, but Kenny interrupted him.

"I've seen you before," he whispered. "That day. The day Spence...."

He fell silent.

One of the young men stepped forward a pace and entered the house. An unmistakable expression of distaste flickered over his face as he crossed the threshold but he kept coming. Behind him, the other man hesitated, swallowed hard, then crossed as well. Both now stood inside the house, blocking the phantom sunlight...and the doorway.

"I'm sorry if we are interrupting anything," the first one said, glancing across the room to take in the tattered walls, the ripped posters, the sodden carpet rolled onto the hearth, and the decrepit sofa canting half on the tile, half on the fireplace stones.

Richard and Bonnie just stared.

So did the other man, still standing a step or two behind the first. Both were wearing dark suits and white shirts, with dark, narrow ties. They looked younger than Richard and Bonnie, but a few years older than Kenny.

"I've seen you before," Kenny repeated. "Spence and I...we passed you." He paused for a moment, then understanding sparked in his eyes and he continued: "You've been here before, haven't you."

It wasn't a question. It was a statement.

And the first man answered with a nod.

"You saw...," Kenny began. "Something...strange happened up here. You saw it."

The first man looked over his shoulder at the second. An unheard communication passed between them. The second man's shoulders suddenly sagged, as if he had just heard news of an unsurpassed tragedy.

"We...we aren't sure what we...experienced. Saw," the first said haltingly.

"But it was evil," the second said. His voice was pitched slightly higher than the first man's, but it rang through the room with a clarity that startled Kenny.

"And we've come to...we came because we...we...." The first man looked back at the second for help, but none was necessary.

"You came because you are part of this, and you were called," Kenny said firmly.

Richard stared at the boy.

"I'm Richard Mann," he said, nodding but not offering to leave his spot in the triangle. "This is my wife. And this is Kenny Robinson. He lives here in Tamarind. We're from...out of town."

The older of the two men nodded in return.

"My name is Thomas Snow," he said.

The second man looked startled for a second, as if he had been expecting Snow to say something else.

"I'm Brian Patterson," he said after a brief hesitation.

Solemnly Snow walked across the living room and held his hand out to Richard. Richard stared at it for a moment. He started to reach for it, stopped, then brushed his fingertips against Snows, as if to check whether they were really there. Smiling, he gripped Snow's hand tightly and pumped it up and down.

Snow broke away and crossed to where Bonnie was standing. While he shook her hand, Patterson approached Richard and repeated the ritual. Then he moved to Bonnie, and Snow stood in front of Kenny.

Again, when he held his hand out, Kenny stared at it, as if afraid to reach out and find that there was nothing there...that the evil he feared had come in a form he had not been prepared for.

"It's okay," Richard said softly from across the room.

Still, Kenny could not force himself to move. He remembered Spence that night—reach out and there not being anything there for him to touch. Tears welled up in his eyes, and for an instant everything in the room disappeared in a salty blur.

"Kenny," Richard said again.

He thrust his hand out and felt the solidity of flesh. Warm fingers circled his hand, curled, and tightened. Suddenly, Kenny reached out with his left hand and grasped the back of Snow's hand, sandwiching it between his own. It was warm and solid and real.

Then Patterson was standing next to Snow. Instead of shaking hands with Kenny, he placed his palm on top of the three hands. It was a gesture rich in confirmation...or in blessing.

They held the position for a long moment, then Kenny dropped his hands.

Snow turned to face Richard. Richard's face was streaked with moisture but his voice was steady.

"Do you know what we have to do here?"

Patterson nodded and Snow spoke: "We think so."

"What should we do?" Snow added.

"I don't know," Richard said. "We thought...a circle."

Patterson and Snow walked across the room until they stood on each side of the passageway leading from the bathroom and bedroom. They kept their backs to the darkness behind them. Bonnie and Richard and Kenny shifted their positions accordingly.

Now, instead of three people standing in a perfect triangle, there were five of them. The figure became a pentagon, with the two young men in dark suits at its base, and Kenny, Richard, and Bonnie arcing above them.

"Now we're ready," Kenny said. No one answered, but no answer was needed.

They waited.

- 4 -

It came through the bedroom door.

First there was a wave of stench, as if the toilet had overflowed again and flooded the bathroom and the hall with raw sewage, then burst into the living room. But there was no sound of water vomited from pipes, no influx of dampness.

Just the smell.

Then the lights flickered, dimmed, and died. Before Bonnie could scream, before Richard could rush to her side and thus inadvertently break the integrity of the pentagon, it began.

He walked through the bedroom door and entered the space enclosed by the five figures.

Donney.

He was tall and skeletally, painfully thin. His shirt hung like cerements from bony shoulders. His worn, filthy Levi's barely covered his protruding hipbones. His eyes lay deep and dark, his face deeply shadowed.

He walked to the center of the room, a living shadow that deepened the night as he touched it. But none of the five had any trouble seeing him.

When he reached the center of the room, the spot beneath the ceiling where the universe opened out into infinity, he stopped and turned on his heels.

He looked solid, palpably real.

He glared at them.

Each of the five, in turn.

Richard saw his brother, the shadow of his brother, the negative, dark overlaying light shadow that he had feared to see. He saw Donney as the boy had become—wild, cruel, untamed in death as in life. The face was a perversion and a parody of all that Emma and Roland had hoped for their last-born. Richard shivered—

and

—Bonnie felt herself naked and exposed and Donney reached a preternaturally long arm and hand down and scratched his suddenly

and obscenely naked groin and grinned broadly, lewdly, at the woman who slept with his brother and who carried his unlittered whelp—
  and
  —Kenny saw a face that he knew only as it reflected generic traits that surfaced in slightly differing forms in Richard. A cruel and cold face, with little in it of human emotion. The body wore only a swirl of darkness that robed it where the slick flesh did not protrude—
  and
  —Snow saw a strange man, tall and skeletally, painfully thin and then she swiveled her hips (suddenly full, inviting) and him and thrust them obscenely at him and she was naked, inviting. And just beneath the gauze that was her naked flesh, barely visible but perversely present, stood the strange man, tall and skeletally, painfully thin, and—
  and
  —Patterson saw the strange man as well, tall and skeletally, painfully thin. And he held his hands out to him and showed him the gouts of blood that marred the wrists and palms. And when Patterson tried to pull away, the strange man smiled, showing broken, blackened teeth, and a tongue a swollen and black as a suicide's—
  It glared at them from the center of the room.
  Then it shifted slightly, and each of the five saw the same thing. The Donney-thing laughed.
  The sound hurt. To Kenny it pained worse than the bone-breaking sound of the dentist's drill biting through tooth and bone, buzzing and vibrating to the center of his brain. He clenched his teeth and tried to keep from screaming. His eyes dimmed with tears.
  Snow and Patterson heard derision, cruelty, and evil bubbling from darkness.
  Bonnie heard the wail of an infant, starving and faint, barely alive, its stomach bulging with the hideously misdirecting illusion of health, its arms and legs stalk thin, thin as the mustard stems outside breaking under the weight of darkness. She strained, but she was bound, unable to go to it, unable to give it the breast, heavy with thick sweet milk, that might save it. She cried out.
  Richard heard Bonnie's moan, rising from so deep inside of her that it was as if she were herself dying.
  But it was laughter he heard, and it did not come from Bonnie.
  "So," the Donney-thing chortled. "You came. Even more than I expected." He turned to glare briefly at the two young men. "Good."

He rubbed his hands together, a singularly unappealing sight, since shreds of flesh separated between his abraded palms and fell to the floor. The fragments seemed lubricated with something dark and glistening and coppery smelling that could only be blood.

Bonnie moaned again.

"Good. Good. A five-course meal."

The Donney-thing swiveled on its heels, away from the two young man. He faced Richard first, then Bonnie, and finally Kenny, who was little more than a silhouette against hazy grey outside.

Suddenly, it was Spence, but a Spence grown tall and hideous and terrifying, his face angular and hollow, the eyes dead.

It lurched toward Kenny.

"No!" Kenny yelled, not at the apparition bearing down on him, but to the others. Richard had started toward Kenny, his hands raised in fists. "No, It's gotta be a circle!"

Kenny thrust his arms out from his sides. He held his palms forward, his fingers extended and curled slightly as if to gather into himself the essence of the four who had come to stand beside him and who were now only a few feet away but too far away to help.

Before any of them could move, the Spence-thing would be right in front of him. It would reach out and touch him, and his flesh would burn and his mind would wither and die.

"It's gotta be a circle," Kenny screamed again. He crunched his eyes closed, wrenching them tight to cut out the sight of the Thing now inches from his face. He concentrated on Spence, the real Spence—*Spence laughing running in the sunlight swimming in the pond at the base of Paradise Falls over at Wildwood (it was supposed to be illegal, but the water was cool and fragrant and enticing) smiling unwrapping a birthday present Kenny had worked a week to earn and saying just the right thing how did you know i wanted a model of a tyrannosaurus spence living living living*

It touched his hand.

Rather, something touched his hand. It brushed the skin along the palm with a fragile breath that startled Kenny more than the biting pain he had anticipated.

He opened his eyes. The Thing was swirling in the center of the room again, straining as if against invisible bonds. It circled without stopping. It urged stiletto-like fingers toward Kenny and Richard and Bonnie and Snow and Patterson.

But something had touched Kenny's fingers. Something had melted into his palm and interlaced with his outstretched fingers and flowed into his blood stream and flooded him with warmth that made his body tingle with what he might identify in later years as a sexual intensity.

He looked first to his right, then his left.

* * * * * * *

Bonnie heard Kenny's cry. She saw the Thing flowing toward him as if it had no legs, as if it were part of an inexorable, hideous current of darkness that would swirl around the boy and surround him and overwhelm him and carry him away. She tried to move, knowing that it was too late, understanding with a freezing zero at the bone that even the five of them were not strong enough.

"It's gotta be a circle," Kenny cried, his eyes closed tightly against the thing that moved toward him. Bonnie cried out to him in empathetic anguish and stretched her hands toward him.

On each side of her, hands touched her shoulders and grasped and pulled her back. Hands skimmed along her arms and down her wrists. The hands were warm where they came into contact with her skin. As the hands passed over her bandaged wrists, the injured tissue tingled and itched as if it were already seven days into healing. Suddenly the gauze hung from her wrists, loose and useless.

Finally, the strange hands flooded into her hands, melted into her palms, and stayed there.

She stared uncomprehendingly at the solid flesh that rested within her hands, then raised her eyes to look.

* * * * * * *

Richard saw them first, as they reached out to clutch at him. He saw them and blinked against the light. In anguish, he shut his eyes and turned his head away from them, devastated at the sight of the power the Thing was marshalling against them. They were only five—too few. They had not understood at all. They had had no idea how strong it would be. And now it would consume them as it had consumed Donney and Kenny's friends and....

They touched him.

Suddenly, the room was...not lighter, no, but everything in it was fully visible, even though the sun had set and outside, darkness was complete. There was light within the darkness, though, a paradox that puzzled one level of his mind but seemed eminently acceptable on other, deeper levels. Through the darkness that was somehow light, Richard saw the clot of deeper darkness seething at the center of the room. It screamed and threatened and cursed. Obsceni-

ties blossomed and died at its lips like rotting buds of some perverted night-blooming monkshood that lived for a moment and then
perished among their own rank redolence.

But Richard didn't care, because he didn't fear it any longer.

He looked around.

The circle was complete. He and Kenny and Bonnie and Snow
and Patterson formed the five anchor points within a circle, dark anchor points that seemed fundamentally solid, gross in a heavy,
physical way that made them stand out from the rest of the smooth
line that enclosed the center of the room. The arcs between the five
were filled...with light, with flowing ripples of power that coalesced
into distinct forms.

At first, Richard did not recognize any of the figures that stood
shoulder to shoulder, hand linked with hand, and filled the intersti-
ces between himself and Bonnie and Kenny and Snow and Patterson
and back again to himself.

He was not even certain—not then, not later—how many there
were. They were fluid, and shifted with each permutation of light.
He had the impossible impression that there were infinities of enti-
ties composing an infinite circumference for the circle, yet when he
looked straight on, they resolved into individuals, unique, with
physical characteristics that grew increasingly, tantalizingly familiar.

For the first instant, he only had a brief impression of individua-
tion, however. For the most part, he had only a sense of many forms,
draped in white robes that glowed without radiating either light or
heat. Or perhaps they were not robes, but malleable, translucent
flesh that swirled and curled around naked wrists and throats and
ankles. He could not tell.

Then individuals emerged from the unidentifiable mass. Across
from Bonnie stood Emma, smiling first at Richard then at Bonnie,
finally looking directly toward the clot of night between her and her
children. Behind her, peering over her shoulder, Richard had a fleeting glimpse of a face half withdrawn and hidden in the shadows of
its own substance. It was there, then gone, then there again, less substantial than a summer mist, but Richard knew at once that it was
Roland, his father.

A boy stood directly across from Richard. He was beautiful and
young. His seemed to be ten, perhaps eleven. But even as the boy
looked through the darkness to Richard, he aged, grew and matured
until he was closer to Richard's own age, trembling on the threshold
of adulthood and manhood and eternity. He spoke no words, but
Richard heard him identify himself, as clearly as if the lips had

moved and the vocal chords had shimmered, vibrating the air between until Richard's ears interpreted the movement as consonants and vowels.

Timmy.

Two other boys stood in the circle as well. From their glances back and forth, it was clear that they knew each other, remembered each other well.

Chuck.

Teddy.

One stood between Emma and Richard, the other between Bonnie and—

* * * * * * *

Kenny's breath balked in his throat. One instant the Thing was almost on him, the next it howled in the naked center of the room, and he was holding hands with a beautiful old woman whose silver-grey hair streamed freely down her back like a springtime shower. Her face was open and smiling.

On the other side, separated from Kenny by several figures he did not know, stood Timmy—*Timmy!*—alive and whole and laughing.

Kenny's head spun.

"What...?" he heard himself begin, then the screams of the Thing in the center of the room drove out all other sounds. The laughter on his right ceased, and the smile faded from the face of the old woman on his left. As one, the figures in the circle—including the five who now seemed little more than dark moments of heaviness and weight—confronted the Thing in the center of the room.

All around the circle, insubstantial figures wove garments of light and stared toward the darkness focused between them.

"Do you think this helps?" the Donney-Thing yelled. Its voice was almost incoherent. It spun on its heels to face each of its accusers, each of its victims, intended or actual. "Do you think that these shadows of nothingness can save you?"

The voice was fevered, rising to a hysterical pitch.

* * * * * * *

Kenny found it difficult to listen to the Thing's mad ravings, almost impossible.

He was watching instead.

Except for Richard, Bonnie, Snow, and Patterson, who were dull and dark and knotted flickerings of shadow—but not as dark as the seething blackness they encircled—the figures in the circle were, well, not light exactly but light-like.

Palely translucent.

Glowing, but subtly and softly, so that you didn't notice at first, couldn't really even call it a glow. It was as if they *were* light, rather than merely reflecting it. They were the essence of light rather than its gross physical manifestation. They were distant suns seen for the instant up close, rather than sixty-watt light bulbs.

He couldn't find words to explain it.

Finally, he fell back on an image from his childhood.

They were like angels.

They were fluid, too, just as the Donney-thing that became the Spence-thing was fluidly ever-changing. But these transformations reassured rather than terrified. At first, Kenny thought Timmy was wearing stained jeans and an old T-shirt, the only clothing Kenny had ever seen him wear, except on hot summer afternoons when he would wear cut-off shorts. Then suddenly Timmy was naked but not naked. Kenny stared at the boy but felt no embarrassment at seeing male-flesh exposed within the circle. It was as if Timmy's flesh were garment and nakedness as well, a swirling robe that was more of Timmy than his old body had been.

Kenny swallowed, struggling to concentrate.

* * * * * * *

Perhaps ten seconds had passed since the figures in the circle had appeared. Surely no more than half a minute.

Richard felt reassured, but in an odd way he also felt even more deeply threatened by the sudden appearance of the others. His mother took her eyes from the Donney-thing in the center of the room and stared into Richard's eyes. In that instant, she penetrated to his soul. He saw trust and love, but something more as well—not fear, but a sorrow so compelling that it wrenched his heart and lungs. *Is he gone completely?* she seemed to say. *Save him!*

Richard knew what she meant.

He focused on the Thing. It was still spinning and spitting invectives, words so foul that Richard's ears burned. He felt childishly embarrassed and deeply offended. *My wife is hearing this. My mother. These young men. These boys. It's indecent.*

He almost laughed at the thought.

Indecent!

246

After what they had seen and heard! After what the Thing had done to each of them!

The Thing heard the half laugh and, as if momentarily released from its confinement, skimmed a few feet closer to Richard. He felt the chill of its proximity and smelled the rankness of the air that passed through it and by it and that was drawn into his nostrils and became part of his body, his every cell, his being. He wanted to expel each atom of tainted air, to cough up any particle that had once been part of the monstrosity before him.

It pointed to him.

* * * * * * *

A young man held Bonnie's hand. He was startlingly handsome, attractive to Bonnie in a way that was intensely sexual and yet ultimately transcended sexuality. He stood tall and strong, vaguely and frighteningly familiar. She knew she had never met him before, in spite of the nagging feeling that she would recognize him at any moment. He was slightly older than she, closer to Richard's age than to hers. Where the folds of his clothing parted at his neck and slipped aside as he reached for her hand, she saw a powerful chest, deeply muscled, intimidatingly yet reassuringly masculine. She knew that he was naked within the robe.

Who? she began.

The Thing surged toward Richard, a filthy tide of blackness washing against him. She tried to run to help him. The young man tightened his grip as she lurched forward. Richard was twisting in agony, his face sheening with sweat as the Thing reached out to touch him.

Let me go, she screamed, unaware that she was making no sound, that no one could hear her but the young man whose pulse throbbed intently against her own and joined hers where their fingers linked. *Let me go. He's dying! Let me die with him!*

"Not yet," the young man whispered without speaking, and his words brought her back to her place in the circle. "Not yet. He may not die. But you cannot help him now. This is his battle. You will have yours...later."

She stared at him, forgetting that across the room her husband was struggling for his life...for his soul, forgetting that her dead mother-in-law stood silently watching Bonnie, forgetting even that the perversion clinging to its illusive life in the center of the room had intended—probably yet intended—to destroy her.

For an eternity that lasted only the duration of a tandem heart-beat, she looked into the young man's eyes and understood what she saw there and felt his palm against hers, flesh against flesh. She wept tears that so far transcended happiness that the agony was exquisite and the joy supernal.

When she looked away, something had changed. Richard stood straight and tall, his face relaxed, glowing softly. A new figure had joined the circle, between the young man who still clasped her hand and Richard, directly across from—

* * * * * * *

Kenny knew at once that the Thing was attacking Richard. He knew that it was showing Richard things, telling him things that no one else in the circle would understand. It was subverting the strength that had led Richard this far and helped him overcome so much already. But Kenny also knew that there was nothing he could to for Richard. At this moment, his new-found friend was fighting his own fight. It was not for Kenny or anyone else to interfere.

He glanced toward Bonnie. Her eyes were riveted on the glowing figure of the man standing beside her. Kenny didn't recognize him, just as he did not recognize the older woman holding his own hand and staring intently across at Bonnie, or many of the other forms that shifted in and out of the living circle.

For an instant, Kenny thought he saw something familiar in both the old woman and the young man, but then his attention spun back to the Thing in the center of the room. Suddenly, with the clarity of revelation, he knew what he had to do.

"Spence!" he cried. He channeled all of his loss and his love and his life into that single word. He had merely remembered Spence while speaking of him to Richard and Bonnie; now he *demanded* him. "You stole him!" he cried to the swirling darkness in the center of the room. "You stole him from us! Give him back!"

In the moment that it would have grasped Richard and drawn him into itself, the Thing whirled. Facing Kenny for an instant, it spun until the features blurred. Part of it was what Kenny had come to know as the Donney-thing. Then it coalesced into Spence's face, grinning evilly. Then it shifted back, spiraling faster and faster, flickering from one to the other as if someone had tinkered with the channel selector on a computerized television. Kenny felt something pull at him, as if he were spinning himself. The centrifugal force was pulling him out of himself and trying to spin him off into oblivion—with Spence.

"No! I won't." He pulled back, setting his heels on the cold tile and clenching his fists, tightening his grip on the old woman on his left, on the unknown figure on his right.

Something slipped.

There was a frantic moment of panic that wasn't fear but triumph, and the hand on his left disappeared, but before he could even register the loss, before he could fear for the break in the circle, the fracture was healed and his fingers curled around a hand that was warm and strong. The fingers were familiar from hundreds of handshakes and thousands of casual touches during football games and basketball games and roughhousing in the backyard *and spence was standing there spence alive and separate and outside again and smiling.*

Timmy stood on Kenny's right. Timmy eleven-years-old again, innocent and fragile, yet enduring.

The Thing in the center howled. It had diminished by its greed to consume both Richard and Kenny at once. Even Kenny could see that. And now the circle was stronger. The glowing non-light surged brighter. Suddenly Kenny wanted to laugh hysterically and weep, to giggle and be silly and jump up and brush his fingers against the ceiling rafters. If he hadn't been gripping Timmy and Spence so tightly that it seemed like he would get dizzy from the effort, he would have jumped and danced and yelled. *Snoopy and the Rites of Spring,* he thought, remembering shared moments of delight when he and Spence first discovered Shultz's cartoons and spent incomparable hours devouring them.

Kenny looked across the circle. He could see through the Thing now. He could see Richard straightening. A smile began to crease his lips. The young man opposite Kenny faced the old woman now standing just beyond Spence. Kenny felt an intensity of emotion that swept across the room and penetrated from eye to eye, ripping the darkness at the center, tattering it even further, scattering motes of it like a whirlwind through the dead and dying ashes of yesterday's fire.

It was coming....

* * * * * * *

The Donney-thing riveted its gaze on Richard. "You hated me," it said in a piercing whine that Richard remembered well and that set his teeth on edge. It was as if he had bit down on a copper penny. It was the taste of aluminum foil against a new silver filling.

Donney's face solidified in the blackness, floating alone and isolated and hungry. "You hated me."

"I...," Richard began, already working out his defense, figuring out how to fend off this attack.

He fell silent and searched inside himself before looking back at the Donney-thing.

For an instant he wanted to deny what the Thing was saying. He wanted to cry out that he had loved his brother, that hatred had had no part of their world.

He opened his mouth to speak.

A flicker in the Thing startled him. It seemed to grow stronger in spite of his resolve to open up and let Donney back into his life.

Then Richard understood the depths of truth demanded to confront evil.

Richard nodded mutely. With that motion, he accepted the charge, with all of its implications. He had hated *Donney breaking the tail stabilizer off Richard's plastic model plane, the last gift Richard had received from their dead father—*

—Donney gleefully and gloatingly tattling on him to Mom every time Richard took a spoonful of cookie dough or ate the last cupcake or snitched the last chocolate morsels and left the crumpled package lying as mute evidence in the cooking pantry—

—Donney hiding behind the couch and jumping out and scaring Richard and Mary on Richard's first date, just when Mary might have kissed Richard—

—Donney thrusting Richard's bedroom door open and standing there nakedly frightened when the lightning struck the Oleson's chicken coop next door and the thunder echoed like living death through the house and Richard unthinkingly impulsively reassuringly held his arms out and Donney ran into the room and huddled by Richard on the bed and they shared a rush of warmth that surprised and stunned them both and that they tried to forget in the bright sunlight and clear skies of the next day

There had been hatred, yes—but there was also love. And the love was fundamentally deeper.

"No!" it screamed. "That's not true! You hated me!"

It reached out, almost touched Richard's heaving chest, then twisted its hands as if it had thrust a twelve-inch Craftsman screwdriver into Richard's gut and wrenched it, burying it deeper and deeper into the tender tissue of stomach and intestines.

"You *hated* me," and Richard remembered *Donney crying silently and touching a picture of Roland that Emma kept hidden be-*

neath lavender-scented lace-edged handkerchiefs in her dresser drawer—

—Donney surreptitiously touching his mother's hair where it glinted in the sunlight as she lay asleep one afternoon on the old sofa, worn out with cooking and sewing and cleaning—

—Donney looking up at Richard with the total awe of a fourteen-year-old for a sixteen-year-old brother driving the family car solo for the first time.

Richard looked directly across the circle and remembered *Emma crying when Donney slammed the door that last night, praying that there was something more she could do for her youngest son, to help him and keep him safe, to let him know that she loved him*

He looked across the circle another way and remembered *Bonnie watching the door all night long, holding Emma's hand and patting it, whispering quiet words that finally brought peace and rest and sleep*

Looked into himself and remembered *himself...loving Donney.*

Pain crescendoed, but he remembered anyway. He clenched his teeth against the pain and remembered with a stolid concentration that amazed him. He accepted the pain the Donney-thing inflicted on him, and embraced it because he knew what the Thing was and what it wanted, and he wasn't going to let it win *this* time. Not after a lifetime of horrible mistakes and stillborn chances.

He straightened and smiled and grasped the pain and pulled it deeper, like a samurai of the highest order fulfilling the time-sanctified rituals and committing *hara-kiri* to ensure the survival of one whose life was dearer than his own. Like an Older Brother laying down his life, willingly suffering death because he knows that the death will ultimately redeem the Younger.

The pain broke off inside as if it intended to lie within him, suppurating and corrupting and rotting until it infected all of his flesh. It twisted of its own life, churned through him, burned through him—

And then it was gone.

The blackness in the center of the room screamed. Donney stood beside Richard, one hand holding his brother's, the other holding the hand of—

* * * * * * *

251

Across the circle, Kenny could see someone who had the face of the Donney-thing but whose eyes glowed with bright light and whose hands gripped Richard's and the young man's.

It was over!

Suddenly, Kenny knew that the horror was past. The Thing in the center winked out—no fuss, no explosion, no special effects.

It was simply gone.

But this disappearance was essentially different from the one in the HoJo bathroom.

The Thing was *gone*—maybe not for good, certainly not for all times and all places. But it was gone for now, from this time and this place, at least.

Kenny scanned the circle. Spence was back, and Richard's brother. And the others.

Without their stolen strength, the blackness could no longer hold its physical form. The demands of physicality were too great, and it dissipated.

Kenny's hand felt cold and damp. He realized with a sudden shock that his hand was empty. He looked left, then right, spinning his head back and forth. The old woman was gone. Then Spence and Timmy and Teddy were gone. He felt an instant of pain, then a soft current of joy.

It was all right. They were gone; death could not be undone. He could not bring them back to life, would not want to now, even if it were possible. Their time here had been measured to the last moment, the last grain. But this time their passing left him warm and comforted.

He glanced at Snow and Patterson—two who had been part of what had happened, but in a deeper sense had stood outside the wrenchings and lent their strength to Kenny and Bonnie and Richard as they had battled. The young men's faces were radiant with joy. Their eyes sparkled with tears.

Kenny nodded mutely at them.

Life would go on.

* * * * * * *

Richard felt the circle break at the same instant Kenny did. First the figure on his right dissipated. Then, after a final, quick tightening of the fingers that became an embrace and a promise and that encompassed more than a lifetime of repentance and forgiveness and love, Donney was gone.

Emma went the same instant, reunited with her child at last. The ghostly Roland followed, his eyes steadily focused on the son he had not yet known.

The young man stayed longer—a second, an hour, an eternity—long enough to move, somehow, between Richard and Bonnie and touch each of them, a single finger brushing against the intersecting lines in their palms. Richard was shaken by what he felt, by the strength that radiated in that single touch.

Then the young man was gone, and the circle was dead.

Only the pentagon remained.

Kenny.

Richard.

Bonnie.

Patterson and Snow.

Without a word, the two young men smile and walked out the door into a darkness that held no fears. They had accomplished that which they had come to do. There was nothing left to say.

Now there was only the triangle.

Father. Mother. Child.

The fundamental unity.

In the house beyond the hill, at last, there was silence and quiet and peace.

CHAPTER SIXTEEN

"MAN IS THAT HE MIGHT HAVE JOY"

- 1 -

In Room 217 at the Los Robles Community Hospital, night dropped slowly, like the great proscenium curtain of some enormous theater under the conscientious guidance of an unseen stagehand adept at pulling just the right cords at just the right moment.

Bill Holmes was dimly aware of the change in light around him. It was just that he could not see it clearly. Not through the veil of flames and ashes and blood and terror.

Even had he been able to see it, he would not have wanted to. He welcomed the darkness. He hoped for oblivion.

Anything would be better than the marginal level of awareness—of memory—he suffered under.

Timmy, he cried wordlessly. His eyes bolted left and right beneath the thin layer of his eyelid.

Light years away, so far that Bill had no conception of their presence, his mother and father leaned across his bed toward him. They were aware that their son was suffering more than they could ever know, yet they were unable to help him in any way.

"Billy," Mrs. Holmes said softly, laying her hand gently on his arm—oh, so gently that she could barely feel the coarse weave of the bandages that separated her son from her mother's touch. "Billy, it's all right. We're here with you."

In Billy's dream world, a quiet breeze blew across his ears, carrying the promises of words and comfort. For a moment, he rested.

Then the flames flared again and the ashes and the blood and the terror and....

Timmy!

"Yes."

254

Bill looked up through closed eyes, and there he was, grinning, standing at the foot of the bed.

Timmy.

Billy felt the sting of tears starting in his eyes, the biting sting as salty tears etched their way down his cheeks. He tried to look up at his brother and discovered that he could not. He could not meet the boy's eyes.

His shame was too intense.

"I didn't mean...I didn't know...." Bill knew no words to communicate the depth of his loss or the extent of his guilt.

"I know. You couldn't have done anything." The voice was quieter than Bill remembered Timmy's being, more resonant. Startled, he looked up in spite of his shame. The Timmy who smiled down at him was not the Timmy he had known for all of his young life. This was a man grown, with the faintest hint of stubble tugging at his ears and lingering along his lips. His eyes flashed with humor. An odd hank of hair curled across his forehead. A Superman-curl, Bill thought, not at all aware of any humor in the comparison—or that the curl was identical to one that would mark his own forehead in a decade or so.

"You loved me, and you tried to save me. That's all you could do. It wasn't your fault," Timmy said simply.

The words were the same ones Bill had heard—subconsciously—for days, as first his mother, then his father took turns sitting at his bedside. In the silent hours of the morning, they would stir, look across at their son and know from the sheen of sweat that he was caught again in his private nightmare. Then they would lean close and whisper, *You loved him, and You tried to save him. That's all you could do. It wasn't your fault.*

This time, though, the words carried new weight.

Timmy was speaking them.

Bill tried to sit up, but Timmy gently pushed him back onto the bed, although Bill could feel only the faintest pressure against his shoulders. Timmy pushed him back against the whiteness of sheet and pillow. He leaned across the length of the bed to do it, and suddenly he was somehow taller than was humanly possible and simultaneously no more than Bill Holmes's hero-worshipping little brother. His body stretched and thinned until it was a blanket between Bill and the terrors of his dreams.

"Rest now. Sleep," Timmy said. "Forget."

"But...."

"Rest." The final consonants were drawn out, like a final breath of fire hissing on a cold night. "Rest."

Billy felt his eyes flickering back and forth beneath his eyelids. But just before dropping into a deep sleep, he spoke through his eyes and bade farewell to his brother, who was now a shining glow that dimmed Bill's sight and made him catch his breath in wonder.

He sighed.

Deeply and audibly.

Both Mr. and Mrs. Holmes were immediately alert. This was a change, and any change was welcome, even if it presaged danger. Anything was better than Billy's continuing coma-like indifference.

He sighed again, more deeply. His eyes blinked open for an instant. It was not long enough for him to focus on anything or anyone, but it sufficed to convince his parents that he would soon surface. It was long enough for them to see the light spilling outward from his eyes.

Then he faded into sleep.

And when Mrs. Holmes laid her hand on his—oh, so gently that she could barely feel the coarse weave of the bandages that separated her son from her mother's touch—she wept to feel his fingers curling gently around hers.

- 2 -

The Bowders had pretty well finished for the night. The younger kids were tucked in bed, saying their prayers with the dying light, then hustling between sheets that crackled crisp and clean and fresh.

Life went on.

The older children sat up longer. They were scattered around the family room, each involved in some activity that ultimately meant nothing but gave them each the illusion of normality. Mrs. Bowder was struggling with a simple counted cross-stitch design of a Christmas tree. She had intended to finish it—and a dozen others like it—and set them aside for small token-presents for friends and neighbors in December. She had absently picked up her sewing basket from its habitual place near her chair, absently started weaving the needle back and forth, not even aware that half the stitches would have to be picked out eventually. The Christmas tree miraculously developed red and blue branches, and the tiny ornaments shimmered in shades of green.

But moving her fingers back and forth helped. There was the illusion of normality. Seeing her errors without really seeing them, she kept sewing.

Just after nine o'clock, at the time Mr. and Mrs. Bowder would usually have begun the raucous process of shooing the older children off to bed—the counteroffensive led with precocious skill by Chuck, who was adept at discovering exceptions and excuses not covered by his parents' all-inclusive fiats—Shawna appeared in the doorway.

She looked vulnerable in her light flannel nightgown, the one with the lace around the scoop neck. Mrs. Bowder had sewn the gown for her last Christmas, and now the hem struck her well above the ankles, but Mrs. Bowder did not notice how small it was on her.

"Mommy."

Mrs. Bowder looked up, panic etched in her face. Mr. Bowder glanced first at the doorway, then at his wife. The three other children sitting or sprawling on chairs and pillows propped against walls stiffened, instantly alert.

For...for whatever might happen.

After what had happened to Chuck, there was no security, no trust any more. Anything might foreshadow a crisis or a tragedy.

"Mommy." Shawna's voice carried that little hint of a whine that meant that she had something to say and couldn't understand why no one would listen to her, just because she was five years old and the youngest.

"Yes, dear," Mrs. Bowder finally managed to say. *Chuck looked like that once, standing in the doorway wearing footie pajamas and wanting a drink of water or a hug or a kiss.*

Shawna ran across the family room, adroitly skirting feet and hands and pets, until she was safely in her mother's lap.

"It's okay now. You don't have to be afraid anymore," she said in her little-girl's voice.

"What?" Mrs. Bowder said.

"He said that it's okay," Shawna said, as if her words would make everything understandable. "Everything is all right now. We can even go back to Idaho if you want to. He thinks it would be a great idea."

She smugly swept the room with her eyes, letting everyone there—all of the *big* people—know that sometimes she knew things that even they didn't.

"Who?" Mrs. Bowder asked. Her voices trembled. "What are you talking about, honey? Did you have a dream?"

"No, Mommy."

"Then...."

"Chuck came to see me just now."

There was a sudden rustle, a sudden uncomfortable shifting of bodies and hearts.

Shawna felt the change, because she looked at each one of them, her brothers and her sisters and her mother and her father, and, in turn, stared each of them right in the eye.

"He came in just now and kissed me good night," she said spiritedly, "And he said it was all right and that we could move if we wanted to. He would be with us there in spirit."

She nodded emphatically, satisfied at having delivered her message.

"Honey," her father began, already concerned about how this new development would effect his wife and his other children.

But he never finished his sentence.

Eight-year-old Mick suddenly stood in the doorway. He looked across the room with an expression of surprise and wordless, wary joy.

"Daddy," he said breathlessly. "Daddy, Chuck was just upstairs. I saw him. He loves me. He loved all of us."

The last was a statement of sheer unwavering conviction.

He ran across the room to bury his face in his father's shoulder.

And then, when ten-year-old Rachel, the last of the younger children to go to bed, appeared at the bottom of the steps with an incredulous look on her young face, Mrs. and Mrs. Bowder simply gathered their children together and wept.

- 3 -

Anna Robinson waited until sunset for Kenny to return. He had promised that he would not be gone more than an hour. He had promised that he just wanted to ride his bike up and down Sheffield *Scout's honor, Mom, just up and down the street* and it had turned eight o'clock, then eight thirty, and now it was nearly nine and he hadn't come back yet. She was pacing up and down the kitchen floor, ostensibly keeping an eye on the stew that would be their evening meal, but actually staring at the hands of the clock as they flew past.

Tires crunched on the driveway. An engine roared in the enclosed space of the garage. Anna Robinson stopped dead in her tracks, one hand half lifted to her throat. She stared at the door to the garage.

When Larry Robinson walked through and laid his jacket and briefcase in their usual spot on the work cabinet, she could barely stand it.

"He's not home!" she cried.

"What?" Larry Robinson stiffened. *Kenny lying dead and the maniac didn't leave town like everybody thought but just waited until he could find my son alone and grab him and—*

"He went out riding," Anna Robinson blurted out, "and I haven't seen him since. It's been hours. He never stays out after dark." She babbled on, mouthing incoherent words that meant nothing except as they became verbal manifestations of a panic, a terror deeper than anything she had ever felt, even worse than when they were awakened that horrible Saturday morning, long before dawn, by the flash of red lights on their bedroom curtains and knew before the police knocked on their door that something terrible had happened.

Larry did not try to stop her. He held her, and only the sense that his arms around her were keeping her from collapsing kept *him* from collapsing. He tried to empty his mind of the horrifying images that drifted up from subconscious levels, things too hideous to put names to.

"Honey," he said.

* * * * * * *

Just then, on the other side of the valley, a darkness died. A seamless circle of light flared, glimmered for its brief moment, then chose to pass on as well.

* * * * * * *

"Honey," he said. His voice was calmer than he would have though possible. "It's all right. He probably just stopped to talk with some friends and lost track of the time."

She looked up at him. Something melted inside her and passed away, and she knew that he was right.

"It's so silly," she said, scurrying around the kitchen. She stirred the stew that was threatening to burn on the bottom of the aluminum pot. "All of a sudden, I was so afraid that something had happened to him. You know? But you're right. He'll probably bust in through the door just as I put the dinner on and complain that I didn't feed him hours ago."

"Probably." Kenny's father kissed her lightly and walked down the hall to wash up.

She was right. Not ten minutes later, Kenny rode up, not on his bicycle, but in a small car driven by someone she had never seen. She smiled and waved as the woman in the car opened her door and

Kenny slipped out of the back seat and ran up the sidewalk waving and yelling.

"Mom! What's for dinner?"

- 4 -

"That was our mistake," Richard said after he and Bonnie and Kenny were outside of the house beyond the hill and standing in the quiet starlight. "We didn't take it seriously enough...or we took it too seriously."

To Kenny, he sounded meditative, not like a man who only minutes before was battling for his life and his sanity, who had just encountered a break in the laws of the universe as he understood them.

"Yes, that was where we went wrong," Richard said.

"What do you mean?" Kenny asked. It was funny to stand here in the shadow of the house and talk like normal people, to feel only the light breeze ruffling your hair rather than the aura of fear that had surrounded the house for days.

"Well, we knew that there was something horrible going on here. That the...the Donney-thing was dangerous. It killed your friends."

Kenny nodded but, oddly, did not feel the infusion of grief that had always accompanied memories of that night.

"It killed Donney. It has probably done more damage around here than we know even yet. Deaths. Disappearances. Maybe just instances of unaccountable fear, parents worried about children, husbands about wives. I don't know what else."

Bonnie nodded, as did Kenny.

"We knew that it was to be feared. But we forgot one thing."

Comprehension lit in Bonnie's eyes.

"I think Emma understood it, at the last moment," she said to Richard. "Remember the expression...the deep peace on her face when we...when we went into her bedroom and she was gone." Richard nodded.

Kenny had no such memory, of course, but he understood Bonnie's point nonetheless. He nodded also, and Bonnie continued. "There is fear, but there is the other thing as well. And the fear is false."

Richard agreed. "Even more than that. We knew we had seen something beyond any human explanation."

"Sven the Red-handed," Kenny added.

"Yeah. We knew that we would have to face it, whatever it was, alone. Just the three of us. Then the five of us. But we forgot.

"Where there is great Evil, there must also be great Good.

"If there are devils, there must also be angels.

"If there was an Incarnation of Fear, there could also be an Incarnation of Love."

"We just didn't know that if we called on them, they would come."

"I think it had to be that way," Kenny said after a long moment of silence. "They came this time. Maybe they will come again. But we're not supposed to count on that. We have to face the fear ourselves, not let it grow so strong that it can take a form like that."

They stood in a small triangle for a little longer. "Do you think we will remember all of this?" Bonnie asked at last.

"I don't know," Richard said. "I want to. I hope we do. But already some things are growing dim. Maybe we should just be happy that we are here, together."

"Maybe," Kenny said.

- 5 -

In their small apartment just off the freeway, Snow and Patterson sat for a long time in silence. Each held a book and passed his eyes over a page, but neither was really reading. Finally, still without speaking, they looked up at each other and smiled. They knelt beside their beds. Patterson spoke words out loud, but each remained kneeling for a few moments longer.

When they slept, there were no dreams.

- 6 -

Early the next morning, two police cars drove up the gravel driveway to the house beyond the hill. Behind them followed the beige Ford Escort. Richard had called the Ventura County Sheriff's department that morning to identify himself and to say that he had driven by his brother's place and had seen evidence of a struggle. Could they come out and check?

They came.

The house was as Richard and Bonnie had left it the night before, with the sofa pushed back against the wall, the filth swept haphazardly out of the center of the room. A thin ring of clean tile circled the center of the room, perhaps a yard in from the wall.

And lying on the bed in the other room, as peacefully as if they were merely sleeping, the bodies of Donald Mann and Spencer Wilcox.

There were no marks, no bruises or contusions. No blood. For a hideous moment, Richard thought that the officers might consider him a suspect; but within an hour, it was clear that the two had died several days before, long before Richard and Bonnie had arrived in Tamarind.

"Funny thing, though, there's not as much tissue decay as you would expect after four or five days," the coroner's representative noted. But after the string of violent deaths over the past couple of days, he was relieved to see these bodies. Even in death, they seemed somehow reassuring. He couldn't understand it.

- 7 -

Almost six months to the day later, early on the morning of February 16, Bonnie shook Richard's shoulder.

"Richard."

When he didn't rouse, she shook him harder, then jabbed him in the ribs with her elbow.

"Richard, wake up!"

He mumbled something sleepily, then suddenly sat bolt upright, as if jolted by an electric cattle prod.

"This it?"

"Yes."

There was a flurry of activity in the old house. The apartment was long gone and almost forgotten, and now Richard and Bonnie were midway through a renovation of the old house. Richard ran from his old room, now graced with an antique oak double bed, and rushed downstairs to pull the car out front. As he ran past the front door, he stopped only long enough to make one telephone call and to grab a small suitcase that had been sitting patiently for almost a week.

Less than ten minutes later he and Bonnie—and the suitcase, in spite of all the myths about forgetful and panicky prospective fathers—were in the car. Ten minutes more brought them to the emergency ward at St. Louis General.

Dr. Maples was already there, waiting for them. He ushered Richard into one room to fill out interminable forms, while an OB nurse plopped Bonnie into a wheelchair and whisked her away.

"Now don't you worry about a thing, my dear, everything will be all right," the nurse cooed. Her voice was soft and quiet.

And she was right.

Intensive labor began a little more than an hour later. Even so, it was sooner than Dr. Maples has expected. For a first full-term delivery, the process was unusually uneventful. And fast.

Less than twenty minutes after that, with Bonnie barely settled onto the delivery table and Dr. Maples and his staff still bustling around getting things ready, and Richard with one green paper hospital slipper on and the other flopping around on the end of his foot, Bonnie pushed once and the baby crowned.

"It's coming," Dr. Maples said, his voice muffled by his surgical mask.

"A boy," he said a moment later, glancing up at the new father and mother.

They didn't seem surprised.

At 1:47 am, on St. Valentine's Day morning, Donald Kenneth Mann was born.

The nurse took the baby, washed it, weighed it, did whatever other arcane things OB nurses do to newborns, then wrapped it in a clean, warm cloth and carried it to the delivery table.

Bonnie looked tired, but not as tired as most first-time mothers. Richard just looked proud, as if he would burst right through his hospital greens.

The nurse laid the baby in the crook of Bonnie's arm and stepped back.

Bonnie curled her arm around the baby, while Richard reached down and held his son's tiny hand in his own.

For the second time, he was deeply, fervently amazed at the beauty he saw and the strength he felt in the spirit who had chosen to become their first-born son.